BLESSED ARE THE PEACEMAKERS

Civil War in the Ozarks

**A HISTORICAL NOVEL BASED
ON TRUE STORIES AND LEGEND**
by
Joe W. Smith

BLESSED ARE THE PEACEMAKERS
CIVIL WAR IN THE OZARKS

Author - Joe W. Smith
Publisher - McCleery & Sons Publishing

International Standard Book Number: 0-9712027-2-9
Printed in the United States of America

ACKNOWLEDGMENTS

Without the generosity and help of several librarians and library researchers this book would never have been finished. Financial and time constraints prevented me from traveling to many of the historical sites as described in the book, so I was dependent on their kindness. I wish to thank:

Trina Smith, Librarian, Viola public Schools, Viola, AR; Melinda Roberts, Librarian, Viola Senior Citizen Library, Viola, AR; Cynthia Hornsby, branch Librarian, Poplarville Public Library, Poplarville, Mississippi. All of the librarians at the Baxter County Library in Mountain Home, Arkansas. They have ordered special material and put up with my overdue books for years.

Charles F. "Bud" Kronsagen, Henderson, AR. His encouragement and editing abilities were vital. Without him there would have been no book.

Jan Kronsagen, Henderson, AR. I originally started this book in 1983, then quit for about ten years. The Kronsagens encouraged me to finish it. Their son Kevin, owner of Ozark Publications, of Henderson, Arkansas, serialized it in a give-away shopper paper called *THE OZARK MOUNTAIN EXCHANGE*. Every Saturday I would get up in the wee hours of the morning and write the chapter that was to be published later the same day. Needless to say, this method of writing caused mistakes. Without Jan's constant incouragement I know I would have opted for sleep instead of finishing the book. For this I will always be grateful.

Val Forgett, President and C.O.E. of Navy Arms Company,

Ridgefield, New Jersey, for lending me a reproduction LeMat pistol for the book cover.

C.D. Kass, Mountain Home, AR gave me lots of encouragement and information about the juncture of the Ohio and Mississippi Rivers.

Roy Reed, Mountain Home, AR gave me encouragement, loaned me books and allowed me to read the story of his great-great uncle Bill Smith, who was a Confederate guerrilla and accused bushwhacker during the war.

Mr. Richard Craker, Monett, MO, Cherokee Medicine Man, helped with Cherokee language, and did an original painting to be submitted for the book cover.

Judge John Crain and Kevin Bodenhammer, both of Mountain Home, AR Civil War reinactors who loaned me books and helped with information about the firing and care of cannons and other details of daily civil war life.

Dr. Wolfgang Lediner, Bakersfield, Mo who spent half a day with me explaining every detail about cannons and their use.

Cleades (Shorty) Smith, Powhatan, AR who invited me into his home and taught me about the old settlement of Powhatan and the Black River.

Dr Steven Vester, Mountain Home, AR. who gave me the history of the Pittman Ferry and Pocahontas, AR.

Bill Gatewood, Curator/Deputy Director, Old State House, Little Rock, AR Mr. Gatewood gave me information about Little Rock and the waterfront as well as information on Confederate battle flags.

Dr. Jimmy Lowe, Mountain Home, AR provided numerous books on the Cherokee Indians.

Charles Sweeney, Iuka, MS. provided detailed information on the history of the area around Iuka, including the battle of Iuka.

Al Gargione, Bakersfield, MO has provided background information, loaned me antique weaponry and provided needed expertise and support.

Sloan H. Lessley, Calico Rock, AR a life long good friend

provided expertise on weaponry, battles and the thousands of tiny details that make any story come alive. Unfortunately, Sloan passed away on May 27,1998.

Sandra Troop, Curator at the Jacksonport, AR courthouse and museum, who took time to give us a short course in the history of Jacksonport.

William W. O'Donnell and Jerry Russell, both of Little Rock, AR who made information about Little Rock available. Mr. O'Donnell's book *THE CIVIL WAR QUADRENNIUM* was especially helpful.

My public school teachers who recognized a bookworm early in life and provided encouragement and quality reading material. They refused to admit that teaching is a lot like trying to stack water and have devoted their lives to the most difficult task of teaching the unwilling to prepare for a future that is, at best, uncertain and unknown. Even with the enduring poverty of the Ozarks region, they accomplished this task with tools and materials that were inadequate and obsolete. I will never forget them.

Mrs. Dana Johnston, West Plains, MO who brought literature to life. Who continued to teach while enduring great personal tragedy.

Mr. Jim Holobaugh, Ava, MO who taught Math and a lot more.

Mrs. Eunice Langston, Caulfield, MO who thought every child was special.

Dr. Glen Cochran, Caulfield, MO one of the smartest people I've ever known, who held all of us to a higher standard.

Mr. Virgil Sheets, Houston, MO who opened up the world outside the Ozarks.

Mr. Floyd Stover, Eminence, MO who taught us that there are absolutes of right and wrong, and on which side he expected us to be.

Michael A. Allard, Military Historian at the Mississippi Department of Archives and History located in Jackson, MS furnished material on the battle and town of Iuka, Mississippi and historic

Tishomingo County.

Alan Turley, of *THE CURRENT*, a newspaper published in Van Buren, MO, gave me information on the Irish Wilderness and surrounding Current River country.

Ralph Moore, Viola, AR did my first proofreading, and through ridicule, embarrassment, and snide remarks, harassed me into improving the story as much as possible.

Cecil and Laura Tilley, Mountain Home, AR. provided information on DeVall's Bluff and the White River area.

Clyde McGinnis, Batesville, AR who provided me with a copy of his book,*A HISTORY OF INDEPENDENCE COUNTY, ARKANSAS.* He also provided much needed information of the White River country.

Bill Sayger, who furnished me a copy of his unpublished book, A HISTORY OF DeVALL'S BLUFF and added information on the Union occupation of DeVall's Bluff.

Bennie Speaks, Norfork, AR, who furnished extensive information on the battles of Gettysburg and Iuka.

Gary Hensley of Mountain Home, AR, who saw to it that I always had a computer to use, and spent endless hours straightening out the messes I created.

Sandy Harber, Viola, AR, who also worked her own magic with stubborn computers.

Junior Ray Hooper, Mountain Home, AR, who furnished information on pocket watches and herbal medicines.

Donnie Sisk, Norfork, AR and Dana Johnston of West Plains, MO along with Dustin and Melanie Bailey of Viola AR, for taking on the thankless job of proofreading.

Dr. Jimmy Neal, Professor of Education, Northwestern Georgia State University, Americus, Georgia. Who undertook the ponderous task of translating the entire novel from MacIntosh to PC language.

Darrel and Margaret Stafford of D&M Photography Bakerfield, MO, for the cover shots.

Merle Campbell, Viola, AR, thank you for letting us use you as a model for the cover photos.

Our daughter, Kim Young, Jonesboro, AR, for drawing the cover art.

My cousin, Bob Smith, West Plains, MO, for his encouragement and help.

John McGahan, for your help in describing St. Louis.

Blessed Are The Peacemakers was nearly finished when my computer crashed, taking my acknowledgement file with it. Therefore I apologize to anyone who helped, but was inadvertently left off of this list.

TO MY READERS

BLESSED ARE THE PEACEMAKERS was originally serialized one chapter per week in a shopper-type paper called the *OZARK MOUNTAIN EXCHANGE.* I wrote the following at the end of the novel and I will include it here.

I cannot begin to tell my readers how much your encouragement has meant to me. Without you I would never have made it through the pre-dawn hours during which most of my writing is done, and it is for you that I write.

I write for those of you who have worked and struggled your entire lives, unthanked and unappreciated, with very little to show for it. I write for those of you who have been pushed into circumstances beyond your control and live in quiet desperation, often wondering if there is a way out. There are those of you who keep on because it is your duty, or because somebody has to do it and you are the only somebody there. There are those of you who are elderly and are struggling to raise grandchildren that you don't understand. There are you who are young and have lost your way and are drowning in a sea of dispair in which the shoreline is not within sight. There are those who wonder if anyone cares. There are those of you who are living in a world which has become so complex that daily existence is a major chore. A world where forgetting to do any of the hundreds of bill paying, tax filing, book-keeping necessities is sure to bring dire consequences. Some of you yearn for a simpler time, a time when the characters in my stories lived, when the struggles of life were clearly defined into black and white, good and bad. A time when men and women seemed to have more control of their destinies. You are my people; you are the people who built this great country of ours by the sweat of your brow and the fabric of your dreams. You and your kind are the salt of the Earth, and I love you for it and as long as you will continue to read I will continue to write. You have just read the conclusion of *Blessed Are The Peacemakers,* which is the beginning of a series on Civil War In The Ozarks. As this series continues, I will attempt to tell the stories of the hard-working people who settled this wild and beautiful land. These people, plunged into a conflict not of their making, suffered as much or more than any people in the United States during the Civil War. Largely ignored by mainstream history books, very little of their story has been told. Theirs is the subject I have chosen, or perhaps it has chosen me. The next novel in this series is called *Sultana!* and deals with a young Ozark Confederate soldier and his voyage aboard that fateful steamer. This novel will be followed by *Paths of Judgment,* which is about two young men, still in their teens, who's fathers have been murdered by bushwhackers and who set out to avenge their deaths.

To my wife, Linda
and the kids, Kim and Joe

They never stopped believing...

PROLOGUE

In the beginning God created the heaven and the earth. And the earth was without form and void; and darkness was upon the face of the deep. And the Spirit of God moved upon the face of the waters. And God said, let there be light; and there was light.

The ones with the white calcium carbonate skeletons were called Foraminifera. The ones with the silica skeletons were called Radiolaria. Microscopic, they swam, or rather drifted, in the vast shallow sea. There they lived, filtering their food from the water. Their food consisted of still smaller organisms. This they did until they died. They died, as all living things do, by the untold millions and numberless billions. Their little skeletons drifted down like snow to the bottom, to where plant-like Crinoids filtered their own food in the slow currents. Meanwhile the Trilobites crawled like cockroaches, leaving crooked trails across the soft sediment. The skeletons of these tiny creatures, the majority of them Foraminifers, covered the sea floor. Strangely, the silica skeletons of the Radiolarians appeared to be attracted to each other. As they drifted down they tended to stick together into clumps. These tiny clumps grew until they were visible. They then grew even larger until they lay on the bottom. More and more of the tiny sharp skeletons joined them until they formed large nodules of the rock that would much later be called flint.

The weight of the calcium carbonate skeletons above pressed down on the ones below and compacted them. Until finally in places the compacted skeletons, later to be called limestone, became several hundred feet thick.

The ever restless mantle and crust of the earth stirred, then turned, stretched and yawned, heaving the layers of limestone containing the flint nodules upward. There the sun started to warm and dry the cold layers of limestone. The top layers started to expand and contract. With the seasons this caused the surface to develop tiny cracks. Many, many seasons passed, and the cracks gradually grew larger. Then tiny lichens started to fasten their little chemotropic hyphae to the surface, and in partaking of the chemicals in the rock left the surface a little rougher. This roughness provided purchase for other tiny bacteria and plants which in turn supported protists and tiny animals.

There were times when the thick crust beneath, unable to contain itself, pushed pipes of molten rock up through cracks in the rock. Sometimes these pipes reached the surface, sometimes they didn't. The great uprushes of magma carried minerals to the surface, there to harden and wait for discovery. Some pipes carried metals only worth a few dollars per ton, but some of them carried the gold and silver so valued by the creature called man. Later on one of the other metals, platinum, considered worthless at first, would be invaluable in building modern civilizations. Sometimes the magma melted its way through living plants and the heat and pressure formed the carbon in the plants into a crystal that the white man would call diamond.

Next came the rains, and the rushing water cut like liquid knives through the buttery limestone. As time passed, the cuts became ditches, then valleys, as the streams and rivers widened themselves and wandered between the hills that were left. Most of the rain drained off into the tiny spring branches which fed what would later be called the Buffalo and Norfork Rivers. They in turn drained into the White River, which flowed out of the Ozarks into the flat flood plain of the greatest of rivers. The White River flowed across and joined it, after first joining itself with the Black River, finally emptying into the Gulf of Mexico by way of the wandering Mississippi. This water carried the dissolved skeletons of the little sea crea-

with it. But all of the water didn't escape, some of it combined with carbon dioxide from the respiration of billions of animals, and filtered into the rock through the cracks. This substance would later be named Carbonic Acid. It was weak enough to be undetectable to the human palate, but it slowly ate away at the bowels of the limestone that was left. This acid left great voids in the rock. Some of these voids finally joined together.

Those voids that opened to the surface were called caverns. Other voids were left in the darkness, slowly growing ever larger until the day that they too, would open to the light of day. Sometimes the caves eroded until the metal-bearing rock of the volcanic pipes were exposed.

Much, much later, in another land far away, there was a restlessness in a creature called man. This restlessness caused these brained bipeds to keep moving, constantly seeking. These seekers were the strongest, the bravest, or perhaps the most foolhardy of their race. They came to this land. Some say they came across the Bering Sea by a land bridge, others say that they came by boat. In any case, they came. Later the white man would mistakenly call them Indians. These Indians, mostly hunter-gatherers, were few in number. They stayed relatively few, their numbers kept in check by disease, starvation and war. The Indians, because of their harsh living conditions, valued courage above all else. The whites called them savages. They did this, not knowing or caring that the Indian's way of life had developed under different conditions than theirs. In the world of the Indian the most courageous survived only until displaced or destroyed by those stronger. Therefore the Indian's way of life revolved totally around war. Through war, an Indian could obtain status, food and goods. War was also a way of obtaining women. Later those whites given to studying such things would say that this women stealing contributed to the diversity of the gene pool and prevented inbreeding, which would have proved disasterous. Of necessity, the Indians settled close to water, both for themselves and the food producing creatures the water attracted. They found that the flint nodules could be chipped into tools. Some of them gradually developed a type of agriculture that kept them alive during the starving time.

Along what came to be known as the White River, small groups of Indians lived in the overhangs of the limestone bluffs and the mouths of caves. Those who were learners would much later call them Ozark Bluff Dwellers. These bluff dwellers hunted, fished and gathered seeds which they stored in dried gourds along with their many colors of corn. They leached the acid from the acorns and hung them in hide pouches. During the starving time these stored goods kept them alive, along with the piles of black walnuts and native pecans piled in the corners to dry.

In the back of one of these caves the soft limestone had been eaten away to leave only the volcanic pipe that would have had a dull shine in the sunlight. With the changing temperature of the seasons, chips of the rock containing veins of the metal known to the whites as silver broke off and fell to the floor of the cave.

The pack rat couldn't know and wouldn't have cared about the value of the metal. She had no concept of latin names or that the name of her particular species was Neotoma floridana. She was young and inexperienced, this was her first litter of young. But her ancestors had raised their offspring in the nest in the back of the cave for hundreds of years. She only knew that by moving very carefully along the passages in the rock she could remove a few of the stored seeds. She would then slip back to her squirming pink babies and crunch the seeds while delicately turning them over in her front paws. She then gave in to her young's frantic attempts to nurse. The rat bore little resemblance to her disease carrying European relatives who had only recently stowed away to this new land. She didn't know that two of these species, the so-called Norway rat, Rattus norvegicus, and the infamous Bubonic plague carrying Rattus Rattus or black rat would eventually crowd out many of her kind. She groomed herself constantly, keeping away the parasites. Her habits more resembled her cousin, the gray squirrel, than those of other rats. Some instinct, some unexplained ingrained habit prompted her to take a tiny piece of the ore with her and leave it as she hurried back to her stick and bark nest carrying the seeds nestled in her cheek pouches. Thus the small chunks of silver-bearing rock built up over a long period of time by successive generations of pack rats. Beyond an occasional flattening of it between two rocks, the bluff-dwellers cared nothing for this metal. Their children were only interested in the sport provided by cornering the occasional unlucky rat as it ventured out at the wrong time. The game ended as they converged on the sqeaking rodent, gleefully clubbing it to death. One of the children invaribly carrying the victim proudly by the tail to the approving adults of the group.

Much later, on another land mass far to the east, those called white men by themselves and accursed by other races, also began to grow restless.

Their land had become crowded, its natural resources were becoming scarce. Their society had become stratified, and had become so rigid that a common man was unable to better himself by his own efforts, or in any way improve his lot in life. Material wealth had become concentrated into the hands of a privileged few. These few inforced the rigid order with rope and sword.

The word came and spread of this new land to the west across the wide water, and they went. The more courageous and foolhardy, as always, went first. Those who had nothing to risk, risked it all. Maybe somewhere in their chromosomes lay a renegade gene. Something deep in their D.N.A. that led, or rather drove them to take such risks.

Later, after the eastern coast of this new land was settled, the Indians were driven out, leaving a relatively safe place for the more timid souls who followed after. There they could complicate their lives and rear children even more timid than themselves. It was then that these courageous ones, their descendants, or those related by spirit moved on. Some moved by choice, others because they were already misfits in the society of the new land. There were external pressures, debts and family problems. A repugnant sign might say,

"No Irish need apply." Then there were those who's skin was a different color, or who had a different concept of life, or who talked funny, or were in some indefinable way, "just different."

There was also internal pressure, the need to own, to possess, especially the need to possess land. To have space, to control one's own destiny, or at least have the illusion of controlling it. More importantly, there was the need to be left alone, to savor triumph, to bear defeat, but to do it in one's own way.

So they moved west, where it was not safe, where the land was still wild. They were the Scots, the Welsh, the Irish, those who talked funny. Those who would escape the ones who had enslaved them. Those who obeyed only their own conscience. They cut the trees, they farmed, they hunted, they lived, multiplied and died, unnoted by history. They fought with, killed and were killed by those who were called Indians. Some of them married into the Indian tribes. These Indians had also been driven to the west. The Indian, who took up too much space, who was an inefficient predator, along with the Buffalo that sustained him, had to go. Their place was taken by the more numerous, more efficient whites, and the remnants of the once proud Indians were herded into small areas. These were areas that were considered useless by the whites. There they languished, beset by alcoholism and those who would in some way or other, exploit them.

Thus it was that this new country was founded by those who could be called too brave, too strong, too foolish, or who were simply misfits. Whose differences caused them to be looked down on by those who stayed behind in the relative safety of established society. These misfits, in turn, looked down on the tamer elements of the human race. Neither group would ever understand the other, and may as well have been of two separate distinct species.

In the century to come the descendents of these misfits would win two world wars, break the sound barrier, walk on the moon and make the path smooth for all of the inhabitants of this great land. But perhaps too smooth? For without adversity to build character, character and its attendants, courage and perserverance, will become as rare as the Indian who once roamed this continent. Those who now possess the land will possess it no longer. They will be driven out by those braver, smarter, or even hungrier.

CHAPTER 1
Little Rock, Arkansas , April 8, 1861

The cold April rain dripping off of his bare head, Rit Gatlin ran his hand down the side of the sorrel gelding in the charcoal darkness and jerked the cinch tight. He turned to his friend Isaac.

"Ready?" He asked.

"Sh- someone's coming." Isaac said, his voice a bare whisper.

They could hear the wail of a train whistle in the distance.

"Let's get out of here, we're going to miss that train," Isaac said.

Jerking the latch open on the lot gate, Gatlin swung into the saddle, as Isaac kicked the gate open with his heel.

"Hold it right there boys." Squinting against the rain, Rit could see the vague outline of the speaker standing in front of them. The pistol in his hand was starting to come up level.

Nerves strung tight, Gatlin almost jumped out of his skin when he heard the long scream of a swamp panther that could only be coming from Isaac's throat.

The effect was instant. The horses all surged together and started for the gate. The gunner jumped to one side as the tide of terrified horseflesh swept past him.

Gatlin hadn't ridden in a long time. He felt vaguely ashamed of his fear as he bent forward and locked on to the saddle leather with both hands. The sorrel was running flat out now as they rounded a corner into the long street, his hooves throwing up a fine spray of muddy water. He heard the sound of the horses' hooves change pitch for a long moment and knew that he was crossing the stone quay reaching up from the Arkansas. The quay had been built to give draft teams good purchase as they pulled wagon loads of goods away from the steamboat landing. Crossing into the mud again, he managed to grab the reins and regain at least the illusion of control. The herd was starting to slow down now as small bunches broke off the main herd to dash into narrow side streets.

"Let's go, Gatlin, I told you we'd miss the cars. They'll be pulling out in a few minutes," Isaac yelled as his faster bay gelding pulled up beside Gatlin, matching his pace. Then he started to pull ahead as he turned away from the river toward the railroad tracks.

Gatlin heard several shots, and turning, he tried to look over his shoulder.

"Come on, I told you that old man couldn't hit a bull in the butt with a bass fiddle," Isaac yelled into the rain.

As he rode, Gatlin tried to shut out the certainty that his horse would stumble, throwing him in the midst of dozens of flying hooves. Unable to do anything about his predicament, Gatlin screwed his eyes tight against the buckshot-sized drops and remembered their conversation with "that old man" as Isaac called him.

"Do I look like some kind of squirrel-toothed-half-wit idiot?" Henry Jones' face had been red as a beet from the effort of yelling. "Well do I?"

Rit Gatlin had been a little taken aback, for he knew that Mr. Jones was one of the biggest horse traders in Little Rock. Gatlin had also heard that Jones was an outspoken advocate of secession. Now that the war was in full swing, Rit and Isaac had foolishly thought the horse broker would sell them a horse apiece on credit so they could join the 2nd Arkansas Mounted Rifles.

Jones had stopped sputtering for a moment, took a deep breath and then with considerable effort jerked a big red bandana out of the pocket of his overalls and wiped his face. He exhaled through his open mouth and looked at the young men.

"Now, you listen here," he said. "I went to Texas and fought alongside old Deaf Smith and the other boys at San Jacinto. With my own two hands I helped tear down the bridge to keep reinforcements from getting to old Santy Anny. I've seen men die by the score. We kilt nearly all of them Mexicans and they kilt jest a few of us. We was mad as hornets after what happened at the Alamo. We caught them asleep and unprepared or they would have slaughtered us like spring pullets. We sure didn't play the Deguello for them like they did for ol' Jim Bowie and the rest of the boys. I'm sure most of them Mexicans were jest pore Indians that had been conscripted and forced to fight, but we shot them down like dogs anyways."

Jones stopped for a moment to catch his breath, and when he spoke again his voice was lower, calmer. "The thing about it is, boys, and I call you boys because there ain't neither one of you much more than boys. Both of you are about the same age I was when I went to Texas. As I was saying, the thing about it is, that you young fellers always think war is such a grand glorious thing where you get to shoot lots of the nameless, faceless enemy. Well, that's not the way it is. War is a dirty, bloody, hateful business. Oftentimes you can see the look on a man's face when you kill him. Then later, when you get time to think, you wonder: did that man have a family somewheres, a mother, father, brothers and sisters? Maybe he even had a sweetheart or wife with a house full of young'uns. Sometimes it don't bother you so bad at the time, because you're so killing mad, but as you get older it all comes back. It finally comes to the point to where all them dead men are with you every night when you go to bed.

"So why would you listen to an old man like me? If you're in such an all-fired hurry to fight yankees, why don't you just enlist in the infantry? There's several units forming up right now. As a matter of fact, if you wait just a little while I'm sure you'll find enough Yankees to fight right here in Little Rock. I want you to know that the calvary has done already took most of my best horses. They set the price and paid for them with paper, paper that may end up being worthless. I feel like I already done my duty and then some. So you go on, join up with all them other panty-waists that think it will all be some kind of Sunday school picnic! Suit yourselves, but I'm not turning over two of my good horses to two Jehus who might just end up dead and then I'd never get paid." With that the short round man turned and stalked on down the street, his back as stiff as a ramrod.

Isaac had turned around and looked at Rit and grinned. "Well, I wisht he would have just went ahead and told us no instead of beating around the bush thataway."

Stung by the horse trader's words, Gatlin smiled in spite of himself. "Isaac, you always manage to make a joke out of everything. I don't see how you do it," he said. Isaac turned and started walking away so fast that Rit had to hurry to catch up with him.

"John Leeper told me that the men of the Mounted Rifles and their horses are riding the steam cars to Devall's Bluff. They're loading up and leaving at daylight in the morning," Isaac said as Gatlin drew even with him.

"Why are they riding the steam cars instead of their horses?" Rit asked.

"John said that there's a big battle shaping up over in Tennessee and Van Dorn wants to get his army crossed over to Memphis on steamboats as quick as possible. We've got to join up now, elsewise the war will be over before we even get to see a Yankee, much less shoot at one."

"It sounds like Mr. Jones believes that the Federals will invade Little Rock. I hear tell that they've done took over Helena up on the Mississippi. Do you think they can take Little Rock, Isaac?" Gatlin asked.

"Rit, you're starting to sound like old man Jones, just blowing smoke," Isaac said.

Gatlin didn't answer, but he was sure that Henry Jones knew a lot more about the war than Isaac McCollum did.

A cold drizzle had been falling when they met in the wee hours of the morning. Gatlin was uneasy. He had never taken anything that wasn't his own. He wondered if they still hung horse thieves.

"Did you tell your mother?" Rit asked.

"Naw, when I went by and got paw's rifle she was sound asleep. Washing clothes for them dirty rivermen keeps her all wore out. Besides she'll just think I took off like my brothers did," Isaac said.

There was a combination wagon shed, stable and office right next to the lot where Henry Jones kept his horses and mules. Isaac had flipped the lock with a short piece of wire and inside of thirty minutes they were at a dead run; the two geldings headed up the street toward the Little Rock and Memphis Railroad.

Just before they left, Gatlin picked up the note he had insisted on leaving for Henry Jones and read it again in the dim light.

WE ARE SORRY WE TUK THEM HORSES AND SADDELS. I WILL PAY YU WHEN THE WAR IS OVER. WE AIN'T HORSE THEVES. Rit Gatlin had signed it for both of them.

As they neared the lit-up station they managed to pull their steaming horses to a halt. They could hear the muffled sounds of men cursing and the rapid tattoo of horses hooves as they were led up the unfamiliar wooden loading chutes into the cars. Within a few minutes John Leeper had taken them to the Sergeant Atkins and they were sworn into the Confederate Army. Their horses were not as hard to load as some of the others. Soaking wet, they followed the other soldiers. As Gatlin glanced down the side of the steam car, he thought he saw a dark shadow slide into the small door alongside the loading chute in the side of the car hauling the horses. He hesitated, trying to get a better look. Isaac shoved him hard in the back.

"Get in there, Rit, I'm ready for a dry warm place."

They moved into a bench-lined car and soon were sitting and munching on the corn dodgers sent up by some of the women of the town. Gatlin was very uneasy because he had heard that the steam cars could travel up to 45 miles per hour. He couldn't conceive of traveling that fast.

He found himself thinking of the man moving into the horse car. He was sure now that it had been a man. Somehow the movements of that shadow had seemed familiar.

The train started with a lurch and as the day dawned, they could see that the rain had gotten heavier. Isaac straightened up and looked out the window.

"Look at that, they've got cables and chains holding them rails in place. What kind of jack-leg railroad is this, anyway?" Isaac asked. Isaac leaned up and asked the man next to him, "How come they've got those rails cabled in place?"

"To keep the whole thing from floating off. This railroad is the only way to get to DeVall's Bluff that's not under water." The soldier leaned back and held out his hand. "I'm Newton Park, and this here's my brother Jim." Just as Jim Park was holding out his hand to Rit and Isaac, he looked around. "Shhhh...listen! Captain Rind is about to say something."

The captain leaned against the end door for support and raised his hand for attention.

"Men, as you've already been told, we're on our way to DeVall's Bluff. We'll have to leave our horses there. There jest ain't enough fodder for them where we're a goin' to. From now on we'll have to fight as dismounted troops." The captain paused, evidently expecting to hear griping and fussing, but the men were too tired and half sick from the swaying train to do much more than mumble. He continued his speech. "The farmers hereabouts will make good use of the horses to make their crop. When we get to DeVall's bluff we'll board steamboats and go down the White River to the Mississippi. We'll then move up the river to Memphis. Traveling east by rail we will probably catch them Yankees somewheres in Tennessee or Kentucky."

When they finally arrived, it was plain that the people of DeVall's Bluff were expecting them. The women of every church in town had put aside their doctrinal differences long enough to prepare a potluck meal the likes of which Gatlin had never seen.

After about an hour of stuffing himself, Isaac looked over at Rit. "We'd better quit afore we bust a gut." Rit groaned, suddenly realizing just how much of the rich food he had consumed. He braced himself against the wooden bench, then managed to get up. They waved and walked out smiling at the women still serving food to the rest of the soldiers who were obviously determined to eat as long as there was a crumb left. Gatlin was so unused to the rich food that he was afraid he would puke up his toenails.

As they neared the train, Gatlin noticed movement along the side of the cars. He could see the flashing shadows from a lantern held high. Gatlin instinctively lengthened his stride, and Isaac noticing, himself hurried to keep up.

8

CHAPTER 2
Richmond, Kentucky

He sat on the hard ground and stared without comprehension at the crimson rimmed shards of bluish white bone already smeared with dirt, protruding from his right shin. He had heard the scream of the fused Parrott shell a split second before the ground opened up in his path. As a solid wall of red clay blotted out his vision, he had felt himself floating free of the earth for a long time. Then he had hit very hard. He lay there on his back, making gagging, sucky noises as he tried to pull precious air into his flattened lungs. Finally succeeding, he pushed himself up. He wiped his nose and mouth with the back of his hand, and it came away bloody. He turned his head forcing himself to look away from his leg. He couldn't see very far. His eyes felt as if they had a film over them. "Isaac?" He couldn't hear his own voice! Where was Isaac? A moment before Isaac had been right there beside him. They had been marching up to the front. Isaac had been talking a blue streak, as usual. At least Gatlin could still remember his words as they echoed in his ringing ears. Isaac had been talking about the battle that had already started up ahead.

"Gatlin, I shore hope they got a bunch of them Federal boys coveyed up for us out there. Us ol' Arkansas boys missed Shiloh but we'll be a smellin' the patchin' before dark, I'll bet!"

Gatlin wiped his eyes with the back of his hand and looked around again. Now he could see better. Not four feet away lay Isaac's hog rifle, and lying against it was what looked like a long bundle of bloody rags. Rit started to crawl toward the rags, digging his fingers into the loosened soil. There was a dirty hand wrapped around the rifle stock. It seemed odd to Gatlin that he noticed the dirt, since soldiers lived in it twenty-four hours a day. Rit Gatlin grabbed the rifle by the buttstock and pulled himself closer. He raised himself up on his elbows as his friend turned his head toward him. Isaac's dark brown eyes appeared to float like islands in the blood that spilled down and filled his eye sockets.

"Mama?" he asked. Isaac sounded like he was a long way off. His voice had the quaver of a small child, a small child hurting.

"Isaac, It's me. Rit, Rit Gatlin."

"Rit, can you get my mama?"

"No, Isaac, but you're going to be all right." Gatlin forced himself to sound confident. "Just hang on, they'll be here in a minute." Looking around, Gatlin saw four more shattered men flung on the ground around them, unmoving.

"Rit, don't let the buzzards get me."

"Buzzards?" Gatlin asked, startled.

Isaac tried to raise up, then fell back. "The buzzards, like at Oak Hills, they say the buzzards was a'circling low, waiting for men to die so's they could peck out their eyeballs. Don't let them get me, Rit, please don't let them."

"I won't Isaac, you're going to be all right."

"My rifle, get my rifle, Rit, don't you let them carry it off."

Gatlin reached down and put his hand over Isaac's on the rifle. Isaac's bony hand was already cold.

Suddenly the sounds around him returned with a rush and the ringing in his ears faded a little.

"You men form up there, fill in that hole in the line. Forward!" It was Lieutenant Glover's voice. "Litter, we need a litter over here!" Two men came at a fast walk carrying a litter made of a blanket wrapped around two poles. They assessed the condition of the four lifeless bodies around Gatlin without breaking stride and headed toward Gatlin and Isaac.

"Take Isaac first! He's bad hurt!" Gatlin yelled, raising his hand.

One of the stretcher-bearers glanced down at Isaac. He bent over and passed the flat of his hand across in front of Isaacs wide eyes. The man glanced at his partner and gave a slight shake of his head. Gatlin started shaking Isaac's body. It was slack.

"No! No! I was just talkin' to him. He'll be all right, just get him back to a doctor!" Gatlin tried to yell but all that came out was a hoarse croak. "I promised him he'd be all right!"

One of the field medics glanced down, not without sympathy.

"He's gone, son. There ain't no use to even haul him over there to the dying tree. We might be able to save you if we hurry. Now you turn loose of that rifle and let us get you to the rear." They plopped Gatlin onto the litter without further ado and took off toward the rear, the sounds of battle fading behind them.

Gatlin, concentrating his total being on maintaining conscienceness, held on to the edges of the make-shift stretcher. Each step they took sent a fresh shock wave of pain to the top of his head. He could feel the back of his head rubbing against the scratchy blanket. He tried to raise up and say something but lacked the strength.

The officers were all shouting orders and out of one watery eye he could see his comrades of the 2nd rushing past. The Mounted Rifles. The name was almost comical, for they were infantry now. Most of his fellow soldiers, their faces pouring sweat and tight with fear, avoided looking down at him. Gatlin knew that none of them wanted to be reminded of their own mortality. It was fundamentally important that a man, especially a soldier, believe with all of his heart that his skill, training and intelligence would carry him through. They had been told, and supposedly prepared, for the fact that some of them would die in the battle ahead. Maybe they accepted this mentally, but with the incurable optimism of the young, none of them believed it would be them. Even Rit Gatlin, a fatalist by experience, did not fully accept his own mortality. Only when a man is old does he come to the conclusion that he is not in complete control of his destiny. Only infrequently did these conclusions come to young men,

men who had stood close and shaken hands with the dark spectre of death.

Gatlin raised his head as the men carried him past the roaring clouds of blow flies. The green and blue-tailed flies alternately feasted, bred and laid their tiny white oblong eggs on the two bloody piles of arms and legs on each side of the tent flap. The flap, even when closed, kept few of the voracious insects out of the surgery tent. Desperately Gatlin raised up and attempted to get off the litter, but one of the stretcher bearers had anticipated the move and easily restrained him. Seconds later Gatlin was lying on the blood soaked ground.

"Medic! Medic! Out here!" one of the men yelled.

Gatlin, feeling himself weakening, nevertheless tried to fight. The four orderlies ignored the feeble blows and carried him inside. They flopped him unceremoniously on the kitchen door, that, complete with white porclain knob, served as an operating table, resting as it was on a platform of two rough sawhorses. Moments later a flap of flesh was laid back to later pad the raw end of the severed bone. Then came the bite of the saw into the living bone. The third full stroke of the short fine-toothed saw started berming up a bloody paste of bone sawdust along the edges of the cut.

Gatlin, with no choice in the matter, lay, his screams muffled down to grunts and groans by a broad leather belt jammed into his mouth by a sweating orderly. The orderly's mumbled curses mingled with those of the three other stout soldiers assisting the surgeon. The surgeon, clad in a blood spattered smock, had a black cigar clamped between his teeth to help dull the stench of blood and putrifying flesh. He did not bother himself to look up at the face of the fellow human being he was mutilating in his attempt to preserve the central core of life. He was long past wondering why he had chosen medicine as a profession, long past sympathy, long past anything but mechanically repeating his training.

The surgeon and his helpers had worked for fourteen hours straight and any attempts at conversation had long since died. Grunts and nods sufficed for communication, since endless repetitions had honed the procedure down to a mindless habit. The only word spoken by the surgeon was "next" to indicate a need to replace the patient with another one.

Private Rit Gatlin could feel the needle tug at his skin as the boiled horsehair sutures were pulled tight. He could distinctly smell the unique odor of his own flesh burning as the blood vessels were cauterized. Each time, the vaporized tissue briefly enveloped the red hot iron in a cloud of blue smoke. As he watched the smoke float up, he wondered if each persons flesh had its own distinct smell.

Morphine, or maybe its relative, the weaker opiated laudanum, would have helped dull the pain, but neither was available. The Confederates had very little of any kind of medicine. Gatlin was given a gulp of raw corn liquor just before they began, but there was no time for it to have worked.

The shot was not much too high. The boy sighting the twenty-pound Parrott gun had, in his excitement, miscounted. This caused him to spin the elevation screw just one extra turn. He was a fresh recruit from New Hampshire and was terrified at the sight of the line of approaching Confederates.

That one extra turn was enough to arc the short-fused case shot out over the skirmish line and into the middle of the line of men moving up. It was also enough to cause his sergeant to have a buck-eyed fit. The result was that the war had both started and ended at the battle of Richmond, Kentucky for Private Rit Gatlin. The body of Isaac McCollum was tossed into an unmarked mass grave along with the other unfortunates of the day.

Next came interminable days and nights, the passing of which were marked only by pain. Pain which came in great crashing waves in which he was drowning. The waves left him heaving and gasping, trying to suck in air and almost failing each time. The pain occupied every nerve cell and forced itself into every corner of his brain. His world was totally contained in his mangled body. The corn whiskey mixed with a gruel of corn meal was often forced into his mouth and he had only a vague awareness of mechanically swallowing it.

Isaac? What had become of Isaac? Isaac McCollins was his only friend in the world. He had dreams of rare moments of fun and laughter, of him and Isaac playing hide and go seek around the docks. He had always been a little jealous of Isaac. Isaac had a mother. Isaac's mother was thin and tired looking but she always kept him fed and clothed with her meager earnings from doing the laundry of the men of the river. It seemed like she had always been able to find a little extra to feed Rit. Her cat-head biscuits covered over with sawmill gravy had put him through many a day of hard work on the boats.

Slowly a vague awareness of his surroundings came back. Still, everything had a fuzzy unreality about it. He paid scant attention to the men in the surrounding beds, eating mechanically and speaking only when spoken to by the indifferent attendants. The women of Richmond came and read to the men. Gatlin heard many of the wounded men ask them to write letters home for them. With no friends or relatives, and painfully shy around women, Gatlin politely declined their offers to write letters for him and after a while they stopped asking. The fuzziness turned into a deep black depression that seemed to float just outside his range of vision, shading everything he saw.

One morning Gatlin came to himself enough to see Sergeant Atkins moving awkwardly between the rows of cots. He was carrying a long rifle along with a possibles bag, with a powder horn hung from a strap above it.

"The stock on your old shotgun was busted. Isaac would have wanted you to have his squirrel rifle. He set a lot of store by this gun," Atkins said as he laid the rifle down beside Gatlin. He stood uncomfortably, shifting his weight from one leg to the other.

Gatlin reached down and picked up the gun, running his hand down the smooth whiskey ash stock. It was worn smooth and weathered to a rich dark brown by many years of handling. He turned it over, making sure there was no priming powder in the pan.

"I cleaned and oiled the rifle up real good. I've got to write to his mother. Maybe the captain will have some sort of an address for her," the sergeant said.

Gatlin shook his head, "It wouldn't do a lick of good. Isaac's mother can't read. Neither could Isaac for that matter. Maybe if you write to her she can find someone to read it to her." It sounded so unnatural to be casually talking about Isaac when he was dead. There it was. Finally the words had formed themselves in his mind. Isaac was dead. Gatlin had known he was dead, but it was so easy to pretend he was still alive. He started talking to the Sergeant. Maybe it would keep his mind off Isaac for a few moments. He looked down at the rifle. "Isaac always said this rifle was the only thing he had left of his father's stuff. Sergeant, did you ever hear of Sloan Lessley, the riflemaker? This was supposed to be one of the first rifles he ever made."

The big sergeant laughed out loud. "You mean the Sloan Lessley that always seemed to have three or four jealous husbands after him? He's a real stem-winder! Last time I saw him he looked like he'd been sortin' wildcats. Seemed that one of them husbands whapped him up the side of the head with a piece of two by four oak. It would have killed an ordinary man. Does he still live up by the Calico Rock?"

"Yep, they say he still does." Gatlin looked down at the rifle. "You know Isaac always gabbed about getting to set the hair on them bluecoats with this rifle. Now he'll never get a chance." Gatlin couldn't stop the tears that were spilling down his cheeks. He did, with effort, manage to keep himself from sniffling.

"Well, I've got to go. I'm, I mean it's...." The sergeant stood for a long moment, as if he was about to say something else. He cleared his throat, then laid his hand down on Gatlin's shoulder. Gatlin didn't look up. Gatlin could hear his footsteps slowly grow fainter as he headed toward the door. He didn't even argue when the orderly came and took the rifle away.

"We've got us plenty of good rifles off of the bluecoats now," he said. "We won't need these little pea shooters any more. I'll take good care of this for you."

16

Gatlin turned over and went to sleep without looking up. He
dreamed of trying to yell out, to warn Isaac, but no sound would
come and he awoke with a start.

He lay there in the early dawn and thought about the river
front and his job loading steamboats. He had been one of the few free
white men working on the docks. He remembered the week before
he left, when he was sitting in the shade of a hogshead eating a piece
of dry corn dodger, and enjoying his first drink of cool buttermilk in
ages. His jaws working, Gatlin idly watched the steady line of river
traffic along the Arkansas. It was obvious that there was less traffic
than in years past. Rumor had it that the new settlements in northern
Arkansas had emptied out as people fled from the fighting along the
Missouri border. Still, Gatlin never tired of watching. Sometimes he
daydreamed of piloting one of the big river steamers. The river was
always full of keelboats along with a few flatboats from upstream.
Some were loaded with furs and livestock, others mostly pigs and
chickens. Some of them were piled high with bark for the tan yards.
When he left it was still too early for the cotton boats, so loaded to
the water line that they appeared to be one long bale of cotton. Several steamers were whistling to pass each other in both directions.

"Dey say you is goin' to fight in the war." Gatlin looked up.
Aaron, one of the slaves who worked beside him every day was standing over him, looking around nervously.

"That's right, Aaron, me and Isaac McCollum is going to
join up."

Aaron glanced around nervously, running his hand through
his short cropped hair. Lowering his voice, he wet his lips and took a
deep breath.

"Take me with you, Mars Rit, please take me with you! Jes'
let me go, I be yo' slave, den' maybe we'll get clost enough to up
nawth for me to 'scape!"

The whole idea was so naive that Gatlin almost laughed out
loud; then he realized Aaron was serious.

"Aaron, I can't take you, it's agin' the law. I could go to jail for even talking to you about it. I'd go to jail and you'd be sold down the river. You belong to mista' Ashley. 'Sides that, we're joining the army. If you went they'd catch you for shore. I don't understand why you would want to leave. You work shorter hours than I do. Mista' Ashley is good to you boys, he feeds you good, he don't beat you, and you get to quit before dark. The way I see it, you slaves are better off than poor whites like me.

The black man squatted down and looked around again, obviously afraid of being overheard. He leaned forward, bringing his face closer to Rit's. "You 'jest don't understand, Mista' Rit. You don' understand because you can't understan'. You don' understan' 'cause pore as you are, you ain't one of us, you's a white man. We ain't nothin. To white folks we ain' even human, we like a horse or an ol' coon dog." Aaron paused for a moment. "Naw," he said, " we ain' even that good. We is like a chair or a gate. We is jes' there, something to be used. Mista' Ashley, he could sell any of us if he took a notion. Don' you see mista' Rit, we is nothin' but proppety, jest plain old proppety."

Gatlin heard Aaron's voice tighten and saw his face twist with emotion. "Sell us, Mista' Rit, he could sell us like we was cattle, an' de' ain' nobody to stop him. You de' only white man who even treated me like I was somebody, and I ain' shore jes' why."

Gatlin had been surprised. "Why, Aaron, you fed me when I first showed up here. I was just a kid, like you, but I was scared to death, hungry and cold, and you shared your own food with me. You took me to mister Ashley and he gave me a job. Course back then I couldn't lift much. The point is, Aaron, I've always liked you, but if we took you along we would all get in trouble. It would be stealing. You would be stealing yourself." Gatlin stopped, embarrassed as he fully realized what he had said.

"See," Aaron said, "We ain' free, like you is, like all white folks is. You may be pore as Job's turkey but you can go where you wants to. You can live where you wants to. Us slaves can' go nowheres without a Pass round our neck on a string like we was a dog. We has

18

to eat what de' massa gives us. Misa' Ashley he treats us good. He gives us niggers a new shirt and new britches ever Christmas. I always thanks him, but what about the man in here?" Aaron pointed to his chest. "He don' never ask us what we think, what it is we feel, cause he don' care, he don' never think about it. He don't think about it any more than he would think about what his horse really feels like. We ain' even 'llowed to learn to read and write. De' white folks de' all say that us coloreds is happy. They hear us sing while we is workin' and de' say we sing 'cause we is happy. De' don' evah stop to think that us darkies sometimes sing just to pass the time, or 'cause we is sad. All white folks thinks we is stupid, so we jes' shuffle our feet, bow our heads and do what we is tole'. Most times it's easier that way."

Gatlin dozed off. His thoughts becoming muddled, he dreamed that he was back on the docks. In his dream he jumped to the dock with a line and jerked awake. Looking around he could tell that he had slept up into the morning.

"Well, back among the living are we?"

Gatlin twisted to the right, straining to keep the weight off his stump. He found himself face to face with a toothy smile that broke up the forest of black beard covering the man's face. The man's bright blue eyes shone with good will. As Gatlin shifted his balance to better see the speaker, his gaze moved down the neighboring wood-framed canvas cot. Gatlin heard himself draw in a sharp breath as he saw that both of the man's legs ended just above mid-thigh. Gatlin, surprised and somehow embarrassed, glanced back up at the speakers face. He knew full well that his reaction hadn't gone unnoticed.

"Thomas Williams is the name. I'm a hillbilly from the Ozarks." The speaker twisted and leaned forward, balancing himself with his left hand splayed on the cot as he extended his right to meet Gatlin's. Gatlin awkwardly shook hands, mumbling his own name. Then he finally found his normal tone of voice.

"Sorry, I didn't mean to stare," he said.

"That's perfectly all right; I lost both of them fighting for the cause I believe in." The mental anguish flared for an instant in Williams' face and his mouth trembled a little before he choked down the emotion brought on by the statement they both knew was a lie. "I just got transferred in here. They shipped a bunch of us in here after Shiloh Church. I was down there under Ol' Fightin' Bob Shaver. The Seventh Arkansas, that was us. I guess they didn't know what else to do with them of us that was too crippled up to move. Have you got any family here abouts, Gatlin?"

Gatlin shook his head. "I got no family anywhere that I know of," he said.

"That's bad," Williams said. "I reckon I've got family most everywhere. Where are you from?"

"I grew up in Little Rock, along the Arkansas River. I've been a orphan most of my life." Gatlin said.

"By George, ain't that somethin'! Two of us old Arkansas boys wind up in a hospital together in Kentucky." Williams said. "My bunch of Williamses is part Indian, but my mama, she shows it more than the rest of us. She still lives up there in the hills above Bennett's Bayou. That's in Fulton County. Last time I heard, John B., he's the only brother I got left, had done took off and joined up with Colonel Jo Shelby's Iron Brigade up in Missouri. I worry about Momma. She's getting old and there won't be anybody there to help her until I get back. By the way, have you got a sweetheart back home?"

Gatlin shook his head and dropped his eyes.

"No, I reckon most of my life I've been pretty busy just tryin' to survive."

Williams smiled proudly. "I reckon I'm engaged to the most beautiful girl in all of Tennessee. I met her in Nashville. As soon as I'm out of here we're getting married," he said.

Gatlin couldn't help but wonder if Williams' sweetheart knew of his injuries. Williams kept talking and Rit felt his depression start to lift just a little. Then he found himself thinking about Isaac again. Gatlin tried not to be rude so he listened politely. By the end of the first day he found himself feeling a certain amount of friendship for this fellow soldier. Williams had an opinion or a comment about everything. He talked about things Rit Gatlin had never had a chance to even think about.

The second day Williams started talking about the federal eagle. "Yessir, Gatlin, that old eagle would fly over his outfit ever' time they fit a battle. We heard that the eagle belonged to some outfit out of Wisconsin. We could see him up there high over the battle at Shiloh Church. He seemed like he was just floating around up there, like a buzzard or something. Somehow or another that old bird knew just how high our rifles would reach and he stayed up there just out of range. Some of the boys say that he rides on a big special perch that them yanks carry along just for him. They call him Old Abe, named him after Abe Lincoln, I reckon. While they're marching he just rides up there and looks around. They say he seems to know exactly when the shooting is about to start and then he takes off again."

Gatlin pretended to believe Williams, but decided that he would always take any future stories with a grain of salt. Who ever heard of an eagle going into battle? Gatlin knew a bird would have better sense. He didn't mention that he had heard that some outfit out of Mississippi had a camel to help carry their gear. He decided that even if that story was true he couldn't expect anyone to believe it. He did notice that several of the men in adjoining beds had paid attention to Williams' story, some who had just been staring off into space before.

Some of Gatlin's comrades from his outfit came by to see him and talk about Isaac a little. They tried in vain to make small talk, but Gatlin could see their eyes stealing down to the flat space beneath his ragged quilt. They tried to make it a point to include Williams in their conversations. Gatlin noticed that although they made a valiant effort, they couldn't help glancing repeatedly over at the vast emptiness beneath the hill boy's blanket. Since Rit and Isaac had joined the Mounted Rifles at Little Rock, they really didn't know the other soldiers that well. Most of the other boys in the outfit had been acquaintances all their lives. Their lack of long time association with Gatlin and Isaac only frustrated real communication. Their visits grew shorter.

As Gatlin fought to drag himself out of the depression, Williams kept up a constant line of cheerful talk. The talk was mostly about the small farm and the time Thomas and his brother spent growing up there. As Williams talked, Gatlin felt more and more of a kinship toward him. Williams' unfailing optimism and sense of humor helped pass the time. For Gatlin it was one of the few times besides his friendship to Isaac that he felt a real connection to another human being. At night he could hear the soldiers softly singing such favorites as "Dixie", "Lorena", and "Barbara Allen" as he had once sung them, but that was another time, another life, it seemed.

After a while the visits from the men in his outfit grew infrequent and finally stopped. He didn't blame them. They might have moved on to the next battle but, in any case, the common bond no longer existed. On one hand he felt abandoned, but on the other he didn't really care. He knew that they felt both guilt and relief. Relief that they weren't crippled or killed and guilt that they had survived the battle unscathed when so many of their friends fell, screaming in agony. These were the very friends that they had shared everything with, that is, everything but their fear. Each of them kept the fear hidden, a tiny monsterous parasite that ate away at their insides. Sometimes the fear manifested itself and some of them ran, but mostly it just lived there, gnawing at their guts.

With his fellow soldiers gone there was adequate compensation in the company of Thomas Williams. The double amputee talked constantly about what he was going to do when he got back to the farm in the hills.

"You can go back with me," he would say. "We'll all three go. Me and Lizzie will help you find you a real hill girl to marry up with. Yes sirree, we'll raise corn and run it in paw's old still. He used to have a contract to sell it to a government distillery over in Missouri. We could start up the business again."

"If real hill girls are so great, how come you had to go to a big

22

city like Nashville to find your Lizzie?" Gatlin asked. It had been so long since he had joked that his attempt of humor felt somehow awkward, not quite fitting.

Thomas laughed. "Oh, she's a hill girl all right, she was raised in the Cumberlands. That's where most of the hill people in Arkansas came from, the hills of Tennessee and Kentucky. Of course, if you're not interested in our women maybe you can look for the Taylor Cave silver mine. Surely you've heard of it, even as far south as Little Rock."

"No, but if I was a betting man, I would bet that some old Spanish conquistidores discovered it. Then the Indians chased them out and they all died or were killed before they could return. There's probably even an old map written in Spanish. That's the usual story. Am I far off?"

Williams laughed. Then using a thick Irish accent he said. "Well, me lad, I've got you this time. There was no old Spaniards and no Indians. Do you want to hear about it or do you want to lay there and make smart alecky remarks?"

"Well, I don't guess I've got any other plans for the day. Tell me all about it," Gatlin said.

Williams pulled himself around in the bed to better face Gatlin who had raised up on his elbow. "According to legend, the Taylor brothers found silver ore in a cave. It was supposed to be almost pure and soft enough so's you could shave it off with a pocket knife. They kept the location a total secret, only coming and going to the cave before daylight and after dark. The two Taylor brothers each had a son. Then when the boys got big enough they took them along each time to help carry out the silver. The thing about it was, they wouldn't even trust their own sons enough to tell them the location. They blindfolded them on the way in and out of the cave each trip."

Gatlin was interested in spite of himself. There was just something about riches, especially fast and unearned riches, that seemed the rawest and most elemental part of a man. Greed had proved the undoing of many an otherwise wise man. Gatlin had never been one to swallow the treasure stories that seemed to make the rounds periodically, yet he was honest enough with himself to admit that he was intrigued.

"Well, Gatlin don't you want to know what happened to the Taylors?"

"O.K. hillbilly, tell me. What happened to the Taylors?"

"They died, that's what. They both died plumb out without ever telling their sons where the cave was located." Williams stopped to see Gatlin's reaction.

"All right, how did they die?" Gatlin asked

"I don't think I heard that part, but anyway the important thing is that Bennett's Bayou is not over 20 miles long and somewhere along it there is a mine of pure silver ore," Williams said.

"Did you ever look for it?" Gatlin asked.

"Never had time. We was always trying to grub a living out of that rocky hillside dirt and trying to keep the bears and panthers from making off with our pigs and calves. But, if you'll go back with me we'll look for it together." Thomas said.

Gatlin spoke before he thought, " How could either one of us get into the cave?"

There was very little conversation the rest of the day, each of them deep in thoughts of what might have been and the difficulties both of them faced in just managing the day-to-day tasks of living.

Over a period of a few weeks the two men developed a bond common among those who have endured great suffering. These two men who would never have met, let alone associated in ordinary times, one a flatlands orphan, the other with a big family from the steep hills far to the north. Thomas never mentioned his legs again after the first day, and Rit found himself slowly rising from the mind numbing depression. Growing up an orphan had taught Gatlin to flex like fine steel and before long he found himself again being thankful for being alive.

Williams' stories quickly made him the comedian of the hospital. He was always teasing and aggravating anyone who would pay attention to him. He particularly liked to bullyrag Moses Pringle, the only black confederate soldier in the hospital.

"Moses," he said one morning, "I'll bet them Yankees was so surprised to see you at Pittsburg landing that they plumb run off. I would have figgered you would have joined the Yankee army anyway, bein' that close and all!"

Moses raised up, favoring the shoulder wound that had put him there.

"Mista Thomas, what fo' did you join the Southern army, anyhow?"

Thomas lay there for a long minute before he answered. "I guess it was partly because everybody else was doing it. I didn't give it a whole lot of thought at the time, but I guess the real reason was to keep the Yankees out. It sure wasn't because of slaves, since we never owned any."

Moses laughed out loud. The laugh sounded bitter. "Well sah, I ain' never owned no slaves neither, and my ol' massa's family freed me when he died. Slavery' gon' be done with no matter who wins this war, so I reckon I is fighting to keep the Yankees from takin' us over, jes' like you an' the res' of these boys." He pointed around the ward with his good arm.

Thomas kept teasing all who were able to stand it, but he never cast dispersions on Moses' loyalty again.

After about six weeks, during which the doctors encouraged Gatlin to walk with a crutch, they brought around a wooden leg with its heavy leather harness for him to try. It required a certain forward flip of the hip in order to walk and keep his balance. Even though it was tiring, he mastered walking on the artificial limb quickly. Within a week he was navigating around the grounds without the aid of a cane. Williams always encouraged him to try harder each time he flopped down on his cot, sweat pouring freely. Good old Thomas, Rit thought, he never lets anything get him down.

Gatlin noticed that the doctors only talked in vague terms about Williams' future. The only thing they told Thomas for certain was that he could go home as soon as he was able to travel. Rit had heard that they could outfit chairs with wheels so that patients could be pushed around. He hadn't seen any in this temporary hospital, so he decided not to mention them to Thomas. This wasn't even a real hospital, temporarily rigged up as it was in a Masonic hall. Gatlin wondered how many other buildings in the small town of Richmond were filled with wounded men.

Gatlin found himself existing in a world restricted to the hospital. He didn't have to deal with being crippled; everyone was crippled in one way or the other, most worse than he. Sometimes he got a unmistakable whiff of the rot of gangrene. He heard two doctors talking about using maggots to clean out the infection. The men he felt sorriest for were the ones they called shell shocked. Some of these men had visible wounds; others had none. Some of them lay moaning softly to themselves; others had outbursts and had to be tied down. A few of them sat silently day after day staring off into the infinite stretches of nothingness. Some of them only came out of these spells when Williams was telling one of his countless tales. Gatlin wondered if he would have turned into one of those if Williams hadn't come along. He still thought about his friend Isaac some every day, but it was getting a little easier to accept the fact that he was gone. Every morning he saw at least one of the patients carried out by the silent orderlies with their board or blanket stretchers. Almost every day at least one of the less wounded would be discharged to make his way in a world not geared for the halt and lame. Most of them came to tell Thomas goodbye before they left. Gatlin had the impression that he and Thomas Williams were sitting in a boat at anchor, while a river rushed around and past them carrying the rest of the world with it.

On Sunday of the seventh week a soldier rushed in, kepi in hand.

"I'm looking for a Lieutenant Thomas J. Williams," he said.

"You've found him, sergeant," Williams said, his friendly smile already in place.

"Sir," the sergeant saluted, "sir there's a young lady named..." He glanced down at the slip of paper in his hand. "Miss Elizabeth Moore, waiting outside to see you sir, she says she's come all the way from Nashville!"

Gatlin saw the color drain from the stricken man's face.

"Let me see that paper, sergeant," Williams ordered.

Unsure of what to make of the lieutenant's unexpected reaction, the sergeant stepped closer, holding out the paper. As Thomas reached for the paper with his right hand, his left deftly plucked the Whitney revolver from the sergeant's holster. With one smooth motion he pulled the revolver, spun it around against the middle of his chest, cocked it and looked over at Gatlin, his eyes had that laughing devilish look Gatlin knew so well. As the sergeant started to move forward, Williams gestured for him to stop, his left palm turned out flat.

"Sorry, old boy, you see, she didn't know. I'd like for you go check on my mama when you get out." With that he pulled the trigger.

Gatlin, seeing too late what was happening, grabbed for him, then rolled to his right and fell off the cot even as he heard the thump of the shot, curiously muffled. The recoil spun the pistol from Thomas' now unresisting hand, and a cloud of white smoke rose toward the ceiling, spreading out as it ascended.

Williams, his shirt instantly soaked with blood, looked down at Gatlin calmly, then with a faint smile he fell back and died. Reaching for him, Gatlin tried to raise himself with a leg that no longer existed. As the end of the stump hit the floor, he felt a surge of pain shoot up through his back and explode inside his head with a white flash. Then everything went black. Rit Gatlin heard yelled orders, and loud footsteps echoed on the plank floor and through it all there was the intermeable moaning. The moaning sounded somewhat familiar and very close.

He must have slept then, because when he woke up the bed next to him was empty. He lay on his side staring at Thomas' cot, tears flowing down across his nose. He could distinctly hear each one as it hit the floor.

"Were you his friend?"

Gatlin looked up found himself looking at the very vision of a southern lady. She was dressed completely in black, Gatlin couldn't help wondering how she had found such clothes in wartime.

He was suddenly very conscious of the fact that he was both unbathed and untrimmed. Gatlin tried to straighten up in the bed, wiping his eyes and nose with the back of his hand. He ran his fingers through his hair, trying to make himself more presentable. Her sad smile lingered for a moment beneath the black bonnet.

"Were you his friend?" she repeated.

"Yes ma'am I was, I considered him my best friend and I hope he felt the same way," Gatlin said.

"Did he ever mention me?" she asked, her eyes searching his face, hopeful.

"You were all he talked about," Gatlin said. "His last words were that you didn't know."

He had said the wrong thing. Her eyes brimmed with tears as she dropped her head. He watched her in silence, afraid that anything he said would make the situation worse. She stood for a long time with her head bowed, her lips moving silently. Finally, she raised her head and turned to go, then stopped. Without looking back, she whispered, "Yes, I knew, Mr. Gatlin, his colonel wrote me just a few days after it happened. I've known all along. You see, I loved him, I've always loved him, I would have married him regardless. It was just his pride, that foolish, stiff-necked hill country pride."

Gatlin could feel his tears start to flow again. He started to speak, but had no idea of what to say, so he sat in silence as she hurried out. Gatlin sat for a while remembering his family, his two friends, Isaac and Thomas, all gone. He didn't speak to anyone else and made no reply when the doctor told him he would be discharged in a week. His mustering out papers would be ready at the same time. Rit Gatlin was no longer of use to the Army of the Confederacy.

Five days later Gatlin walked outside the Masonic hall and looked around. He looked down at the sixty dollars in script and discharge papers, then stuffed them inside his shirt. He started up the street, realizing how weak he had become. Somehow he had to get a horse. Walking in at the wide door with LIVERY painted above it, he stopped for a moment and rested on the rifle. The owner walked out, carrying a wooden water bucket.

"Can I rent you a rig there, soldier?" he said.

"No, but I need to buy a horse." Gatlin said.

"The army done took all the good ones and got most of them killed. I only got one I could sell. He's so pore you'd have to tie a knot in his tail to keep him from slipping plumb through the collar." He paused to spit a stream of amber tobacco juice on the straw covered ground. "I ain't gonna lie to you, son, there ain't a decent horse for sale within a hundred miles of here."

"How much will you take for him?" Gatlin asked.

"I'll take fifty bucks for him, and I'll throw in one of them army McClellan saddles. They're a dime a dozen now that so many horses got killed." The liveryman pulled off his cap and began to absently scratch his head.

Too tired to try to jew him down, Gatlin bought the horse for fifty dollars of his script, drawing a side of bacon and a place to sleep for the night as boot.

The next morning found him slowly riding west away from the scenes of battle. He cut south across Tennessee, surprised at the man-made desolation of the land he crossed. Pushing against the Cumberland mountains, he followed the river by the same name as it meandered south. Gatlin quickly learned to balance Isaac's squirrel rifle across the saddle as he rode.

After crossing the Mississippi River at Cottonwood Point, Gatlin traveled almost due southwest for several weeks. If someone had asked, Gatlin wouldn't have been able to tell them where he was going or what he was going to do when he got there. He was totally wrapped in depression and grief. After crossing the river he rode across the swampy Arkansas delta, and found himself almost unbearably pestered by mosquitoes. Each bite was rewarded by a slap, resulting in a bloody itching smear. Each smear, in turn, attracted more mosquitoes. For variety, there were black horse flies over an inch long, with a bite that felt like a wasp sting. Some nights he found enough punky drift to keep a smoke going. His eyes swelled and he knew they were red as well. At least the smoke provided some relief from the voraciously biting insects. Not wishing to push the old horse beyond the limits of his endurance, he took his time. The only people he saw were at a distance. He found himself with a curious reluctance to approach people, avoiding towns and settlements. He carefully made his camps away from the main trails, doing his little bit of cooking before dark, then putting out the fire. He managed to exist on the side of bacon and some wild greens. Occasionally, he managed to bag a rabbit. As he rode he could see some hills getting closer and closer. Those had to be what the French had called the Aux Arcs or Ozarks. Here the flat land of the delta butted abruptly into the eroded hills. The river in front of him had to be the Black River. On the other side he could see the road snaking its way down through the steep limestone ledges. The ledges were at least twenty feet higher than the muddy river bottom on the east side. He had talked to rivermen who had run keelboats down the Black to the White River and back up to Little Rock on the Arkansas.

As Gatlin rode up on the bank of the river, he stopped to let the old horse blow for a moment. He could see the hulk of a ferry burned against the west bank along with the blackened sandstone foundation of what he supposed had been the ferry operator's house. The drive cable of the current driven craft was lying in the water at one end. Gatlin urged the horse closer to the cut bank, hoping to see a crossing spot.

A man suddenly stood up from underneath a Willow bush in front of him. Gatlin instinctively dropped his other hand down to the squirrel rifle.

"Now, boy, there's no need for that, I'm friendly," the bearded man said.

"Is this the Black River?" Gatlin asked. It had been so long since he had seen another human up close that he didn't exactly know what to say.

"It sure is. I'm afraid you'll just have to swim the river or find a better ford. The bushwhackers done burnt Mr. Ficklin's ferry and his house, too. They used to call this settlement Ficklin's Ferry, but already there are some people wanting to name it Powhatan after some old Indian. Now that the ferry's gone, that's probably what will happen. By the way, my name's Shorty Smith."

"I'm Gatlin, Rit Gatlin."

"You got any news of the war, Gatlin? Do you think it will be over pretty soon? Smith asked.

"No, I don't really know nothin' new. I've been in the hospital. I lost a leg at the Battle of Richmond, Kentucky, a little while after the battle at Shiloh Church. I guess you could say I'm just drifting. I ain't really going nowhere particular," Gatlin said.

"Well, I was on the General Price during the battle for Memphis, but them dang federals shelled us till we had to run her aground and abandon ship. We barely got off of her alive. I hope to get back on another steamer but until then, I came home to see my family," Smith said. He raised up and looked behind Gatlin. "Cleades just signaled me that you are alone."

Gatlin twisted around and looked off to the left and behind him. A gangly boy about thirteen had just raised up from behind Gatlin holding a short heavy rifle.

"That's a wicked looking weapon the boy's got there." Gatlin said. He was a little irritated at having ridden past the boy without seeing him.

" That rifle was given to me by Mr. Sam Hawken up in St. Louis after I helped him out of a bind one time back before the war. It's still a flintlock, but that's good, because caps are so hard to buy now with the war on. It would tear a hole through a man that you could run a steamboat through. You see, Mr. Gatlin, I'm not really fishing. I'm trying to get my corn crop laid by. We've got a thumper mill made out of a sweet gum stump hid back there to grind the corn into meal with. I've also got a few rows of whipoorwill peas and other truck hid back there in that cane brake. We've also got us a good black mule standing back there hitched to a thirteen inch Oliver. Now, if a patrol from either army comes by here, they'll graze my corn down and take my mule. If a band of bushwhackers was to happen by, they would steal my stuff and kill me and the boy, too. So if we see a rider coming, I jest let on like I'm a'fishin' 'til we get a chance to see just exactly who it is we're dealing with. I wasn't sure but what you wasn't some kind of a scout. You see, my family will starve no matter who steals their food. What we raise is all they've got to depend on this winter. It don't take much to get us by, just a little corn, along with some hoppin' john and a little meat. They's plenty of hogs gone wild back there in the slough. I'm also hoping to dry a few fish, too. I'm going to trust you not to tell anybody you ever saw us."

Gatlin heard another noise off to his right and turned. Another boy stood up out of the switch canes and waved at Gatlin, a big smile splitting his face almost in two. He was obviously very pleased with himself for staying concealed for so long. He appeared to be a couple of years younger than Cleades. He was holding what appeared to be a sawed off Brown Bess musket left over from the revolutionary war.

"Don't take many chances do you Mr. Smith?" Gatlin said, embarrassed at having ridden right into what could have been an ambush.

Smith smiled, " Oh, that's just my next to the youngest boy, Tony. He sort of likes to imitate everything Cleades does. 'Course that old musket's loaded down with about a dozen .36 navy pistol balls. I cast 'em myself. My wife's cousin up in the hills brings us down the ore and we melt it down ourselves. I reckon she finds it up there along one of them creeks up there somewheres. She says it crops right out of a limestone ledge. I reckon they just knock it off with a hammer and melt it down. The ore don't look exactly like regular lead. Its a little brighter and heavier. I'll say this for it, it shore does make good rifle balls."

"What will you do if a whole bunch of soldiers show up?"

Smith laughed out loud, "Well, sir, I reckon me and the wife and kids will just sorta fade back into that slough over there." Smith stopped and pointed toward the southeast. Gatlin could see water shining between the trees. "We'd just hide in there amongst the cottonmouths 'til the soldiers left. They'd have to burn the stump and sift the ashes before they'd ever find us back there. I was raised all around that swamp. But, if they get me, that's jest the way she works out. I never figured on dying in no bed with a pink nightshirt wadded up 'round my neck noway!"

Gatlin looked up at the sun. He needed to cross the river before dark. "I'm glad to have got to know you folks. I won't mention that I saw you, and I wish you luck," Gatlin said as he turned the horse upriver.

"They's some people settlin' in up the river three or four miles. They're calling the place Black Rock. We think they ort' to settle down here with us, but they won't. We don't have much truck with them so I don't know what kind of people they are. They been talking about starting a factory to make buttons out of them mussel shells. Well, we'll see you down the creek, Mr. Gatlin." With that Smith turned away and started back down the bank.

Gatlin finally coaxed the old horse into swimming the silt-laden stream. He then headed into the hills, munching on the chunk of corn dodger Smith had handed up to him as he left. He followed a two tracked wagon road that was overgrown with weeds. He passed several burnt cabins, their locations punctuated by tall rock chimneys standing alone in mute testimony to the carnage that the country was visiting upon its own. Often there were fresh graves close by. They were mostly unmarked, although a few of them had rude crosses stuck down in the mounds of dirt. Gatlin had the impression of haste on the part of the grave diggers, as if they couldn't get away fast enough. Some of the graves hadn't even been patted smooth. The dirt had just been thrown on them. The graves didn't look too deep to Gatlin either. Many times he kicked the careless weeds aside and helped himself to vegetables growing in the abandoned gardens. For days on end he rode through the stirrup-high buffalo grass.There were lines of timber along the creeks and rivers, but Gatlin saw only scattered black walnuts and red oaks out in the open areas. Once in a while he caught a glimpse of cattle, obviously gone wild. He even saw a hog run into a cane brake in front of him, its woofing sound of alarm breaking up the rustle of the dry cane stalks.

Stopping near a small creek late one afternoon, he swung down from the tired horse for a drink. He jumped as a startled blue crane launched itself into the air from the water's edge. For a long moment he could hear its squawks echoing down the narrow valley. Gatlin could see two more of the graceful birds in the distance. Their windbeats were perfectly synchronized as they flew one behind the other. He had often watched them along the Arkansas River, returning to their roosts after gorging themselves on the minnows that crowded the shallows. As he bent down to drink, the muscles knotted up in his hip. He grabbed at it and started to knead and massage the twisted muscle, but lost his balance and fell in the water. He didn't bother to look at his reflection. He knew he was a man too thin for his 6 foot 2 inch frame. He knew he still showed traces of the muscles he had built up loading steamboats. But the muscles had wasted away during his hospital stay, as had the flesh padding his face. His cheeks were sunken, making his face come to a point at the chin. His eyes appeared huge and dark, giving him a wolfish appearance. He rubbed his hand over the long stubble of beard already frosted with gray and brushed his dark brown hair out of his face.

Seeing several large crawdads scurry out of sight under the slick moss-covered rocks near the stream's edge, he realized that he was very hungry. His carefully hoarded army hardtack had long since run out. His side of bacon was just a memory and the possum he had roasted over a bed of coals over on the Spring River was gone. Anything that looked that much like a rat didn't really appeal to him, although, if a man was hungry enough its greasy flesh wasn't half bad. That night Rit Gatlin ate boiled crawdads and watercress, using what little bit of salt he had left.

He washed himself in the stream and spread his clothes on a bush to dry. He turned the old horse loose to graze after rubbing him down with the worn saddle blanket. Wrapping himself in the ragged union issue wool blanket, he lay back but sleep did not come soon. He listened to the whippoorwills and screech owls calling. The screech owls with their blood-curdling cries had been a familiar sight as they feasted on the plentiful wharf rats along the Arkansas. Gatlin thought of the past and the future as he watched the curious patterns the lightning bugs formed as they blinked in search of mates. One wind-broken old horse, a ragged blanket, and a long rifle. Not much for a twenty-two year old man to have accumulated. He felt a little sorry for himself as he sat and watched the moonlight dance across the ripples of the small creek. Then he thought of them; the long silent forms wrapped in dirty canvas. He had seen them there, lined up in rows along the road as he was carried to the field hospital. They were the ones who would never go home. They would never again experience another spring night. He thought of them often, especially when he started feeling sorry for himself; sometimes it helped. There were Isaac and Thomas and the others. The ones he had known, now they only lived in his mind.

Gatlin was a man with few illusions about himself. He knew his chances of becoming rich or famous were very slim. So far, his existence on earth had not had any lasting impact on anything or anyone. He told himself he cared for no one and no one cared for him. After seeing Isaac killed and Thomas Williams shoot himself, he resolved that he would never again get close to anyone. To get close to someone meant only hurt. If he were to die that very night, he probably wouldn't be found for months or even years. There would be no one to mourn when his bleached bones were finally kicked out of the dirt by some passer-by. They might not even recognize the bones as human.

People were always talking about being free, he thought. Yet he knew that few of them realized what total freedom really means. Total freedom means no responsibilities, no commitments, but no permanent place to lay your head either; and few people are prepared for that kind of freedom. Maybe that was because it is the nature of man to be a creature of habit. The few people Gatlin knew well had all tended to follow the same patterns of living. They tried to cling to some remnant of a normal existence, even when the war changed everything around them. Even the slaves had kept on working the plantations. They did this even though many of them were well aware that their masters were not only gone off to war, but were most likely dead as well. Gatlin had even seen some of them moving to the battle right up there alongside their masters. They kept on working because the work was familiar and freedom was not. He massaged the stump of his leg.

"Your leg will itch and hurt just like it was still there," the doctor had said. "They call them phantom pains and they are imaginary."

But there was nothing imaginary about the pain that began almost every night, especially when he was tired. Pain that started at the amputation site and slowly crawled its way upward, gnawing at his flesh like a wild beast until it enveloped his thigh and buttock almost to his waist.

Rising just at sunrise, he strapped on the artificial limb with its heavy uncomfortable stiff harness leather straps. He eased his weight into it, warming and settling the leather, and climbed on the old horse. The horse stepped sideways, responding to the change in balance.

"Old pony, you're just about worn out, just like me."

Heading west again, he crossed a small bottomland field which appeared to have been recently under cultivation.

"Wonder where the owners are?" There, he had done it again, talking out loud.

He found himself reflecting on the war, a war between people of the same nation, a war that caused even the members of the same family to fight each other. They fought for the cause. What cause? A man who is dead has no cause. The rights of the states to secede and form their own country? Poor people like himself were in such a perpetual struggle for their very existence that a change in countries wouldn't have much mattered. Slaves? He had owned no slaves, nor was it likely that he would, even if the South won. Glory? In his case that was probably it. He had wanted to belong to someone or something so badly that he had joined up on impulse as the Mounted Rifles passed through Little Rock. Actually he and Isaac had talked each other into joining. Rit had visualized himself riding at the head of a troop of men, waving to the adoring crowds lining the streets. He had imagined smiling at the young girls throwing flowers into the street in front of him. That was it, glory. He had lost his leg for a brief moment of glory that never materialized.

He snapped out of his revery, realizing that he had ridden into what was almost a bluff. Grayish-white weathered limestone ledges jutted out from between the wiry buckbrush.The bluff extended out of sight in both directions. He could discern a faint trail leading dimly upward. Letting the old horse take his time, he pointed him along the trail. He knew he couldn't get off and lead the horse; he was barely able to walk with his peg-leg, let alone climb.

As he topped the ridge he saw a neat log cabin reflecting the early morning sunshine from a clearing still dotted with cedar stumps. "Well, old horse, our luck is improving. Here's an abandoned log cabin, and I'm talking to a horse again," he said as he rode closer to it. "Here's a place to rest up for a few days."

Twin barrels of a shotgun moving slowly out of a window stopped him cold. The tiny gold bead front sight shone like diamond in the morning sunlight! He distinctly heard the double click of the rabbit-ear hammers being drawn back to full cock, first one, then a second later, the other. His heart began to pound, the two parts of the beat separate and distinct from each other! He began to hear the roar of his own rushing blood in his ears. Every nerve in his body screamed at him to turn the horse and run for it. Knowing the impossibility of outrunning a charge of buckshot, he forced himself to calm down and sit quietly. If the gunwielder was a killer, he would have shot first,without bothering to talk. To Gatlin that meant there was still the possibility of talking to him. The gaping maws of the shotgun looked big enough to drive a steam locomotive through. It looked like the shotgun he was carrying when he was wounded. The old horse, glad of a chance to rest, stepped over and began to pick at a blackberry bush.

"I ain't got no whiskey, you border scum stole all the corn! You bushwhacking thieves done took everything I own, now get out!" The voice obviously belonged to someone old, scared, and female.

Rit kept his hands on the rope reins, knowing full well what a shotgun could do to a man at short distance.

"Just back from the war, ma'am. I'm no bushwhacker," he said quietly.

Gatlin started to turn the horse to leave.

"Wait" the voice now held just a hint of friendliness. "Get down and stay a few minutes. I thought you was one of them murderin' border scum. Lay that rifle on the ground, though."

Gatlin slowly swung out of the saddle, half-falling as the still unfamiliar wooden leg hit the ground. He took a couple of limping steps to regain his balance, and when he looked up, he was face to face with the oldest woman he had ever seen. She was tall and thin, and he could see that even as a young woman she hadn't been pretty, but there was strength and character written on her face. Her clear eyes looked like bolts of blue lightning, and they alone told him she wasn't a full-blooded Cherokee Indian. Her skin, wrinkled in a thousand different directions, oaken and suede-like, told not only of her Indian genes but of long years spent at hard labor in all kinds of weather. She wore an old floppy gray hat and a ragged but clean man's Prince Albert coat. Her boots, also men's, were broken down at the heel and curled up at the toe, obviously too large for her.

"What are you staring at, boy?" she brayed. "Ain't you never seen a old woman before? If you're friendly come on in. Are you hungry boy? I've got a pot of turnip soup on. Them bush buzzards have took most everything else. By the way, what's your name, boy?" Gatlin relaxed a little.

"I'm Rit Gatlin and I'd eat almost anything, 'ceptin' possum. I've scarfed down so many possums that I'm liable to dive into a brush pile if I hear a dog bark."

He followed her into the log cabin, built of carefully hewed logs, fastened with wooden pegs. The corners of the logs were sloped smoothly outward so as to shed water. As he looked upward he saw a neatly constructed sleeping loft extending beneath the roof. He also noticed that the furnishings were sparse. There were a few home-made stools and cane-bottomed chairs with a cord bed in the corner. The bed was typical of others he had seen. The frame consisting of two poles fitted into holes bored in the cabin walls and only one bed post where the two poles met. Gatlin stared around the cabin.

"Needless to say, we've pore-hogged around here in these hills since old Heck was a pup." she said. "It ain't much, but it's still home."

"Ma'am, I've never had a real home in my whole life, myself," he said.

"The bushwhackers stole all of the livestock except what has gone wild in the woods. They've stoled all the horses that was worth anything. Once in a while they come by and steal folkses' household goods. 'Course they'll always take any food. Matter of fact, they'll take anything that takes their fancy." The old woman was speaking softly as she ladled the soup out of a black kettle hanging over the fire.

Rit looked up from his seat on one of the cane-bottomed chairs.
"Do you know who these bushwhackers are?" he asked
She handed Gatlin his bowl and sat down with her own.

CHAPTER 3

Willie Johnson raised up slowly from the steep roof, the tar-covered rigging ax hanging loosely from his thick sausage-fingered right hand. He imagined that he could hear his bones creaking as he straightened his spine. Hunching his left shoulder he wiped his sweating face across the place on the sleeve that had once boasted a company name patch. Now there was just a half circle of unfaded cotton. Willie didn't know or care which company. He had bought a half-dozen of them, as he did all his shirts, at a garage sale. This bundle had cost 75 cents apiece. He had jewed the halter-top and stretch shorts-clad lady down from a dollar each by taking all she had. Blinking his stinging eyes, he looked off to the east. It was over there somewhere. He hated to go but she was old, the oldest of his line. Now she was dying of cancer. She had set her jaw and survived everything life had thrown her over the last ninety-five years. She had stubbornly survived three husbands and outlived all of her kids. Now her body was slowly being eroded away by the deadliest killer of them all.

At one time, for a black person to live in the Walnut Park area was the finest thing anyone could imagine. The stately brick homes were built to stand forever. Skilled masons had built them three layers of brick thick and then lathed inside with wooden strips generously covered with plaster. The result was a house that, like the adobe of the Southwest, effectively insulated the occupants from extremes of both heat and cold. But that section of St. Louis had changed greatly even within Willie's lifetime.

Now it was gang turf, and it seemed that murders occurred there almost daily. It may as well have been in a Third World country thousands of miles away from the fancy home he was now roofing. The people who bought this house would probably be rich, or at least well on their way to being so. Even if they were black they wouldn't be able to relate to the world that lay just a little ways across the city. They couldn't relate to Walnut Park any more than they could relate to the cotton fields that their recent ancestors had left. They had headed north, then spread out, trying to escape an almost genetic poverty, or so it seemed. Willie was well acquainted with poverty. He had often told his children laughingly that he had not only lived in poverty, but had been mayor of it at one time.

The few decent people who remained were imprisoned by fear, poverty, building codes and old age. Most of them had lived there all of their lives, and it was home to them. If they sold, the depressed property values would keep them from ever being able to buy again. So they lived there, in a kind of quiet terror and tried to maintain some semblance of normalcy. His aunt Catherine had steadfastly refused to move from the old neighborhood, even when he had offered her a place in his own modest home.

At the end of the day Willie wearily climbed down, carefully collapsed his aluminum ladder he had bought at Wal-Mart, loaded it and piled the tools into the cab of his faded green 1969 Chevy pickup. As he headed into the city, he wished he had brought his gun.

Walking nervously up the steps of the house, he glanced back. He didn't think that the dopeheads would break into his toolbox in broad daylight, but he wouldn't bet on it. He had painstakingly put together those tools from pawn shops and yard sales over the last twenty-five years.

Knocking on the door, he heard a chair scoot somewhere back in the house, and in a moment Mrs. Thomas, the neighbor lady, cautiously opened it.

"You're here," she said. "She's been asking about you, hoping you would be able to come this week. I think she's got something in particular on her mind."

Willie pulled his faded Cardinals cap off and stepped through the door. The smell was a tangible thing, the essence of impending death. Willie knew it well. The smell carried with it other less definable odors. There was the rancid smell that told of years of cooking with hog lard. The greasy smell was well mixed with that of dry rotting wood and various insecticides and roach killers. Wafting through it all was the smell of Prince Albert smoking tobacco, a legacy of Aunt Catherine's last husband. Willie wished he had a drink of cold well water.

CHAPTER 4

She sat down with her own bowl of soup. "Well, some of them are deserters from the armies of both the North and South. A few of them, like Quantrill, have made big names for theirselves. I hear that Bloody Bill Anderson got killed here a while back. Did you know that Anderson rode with Quantrill before Quantrill took off to Kentucky"?

Anxious to continue the conversation, Gatlin tried to remember everything he had heard about Bill Anderson. "Yeah, it seems like I heard about him. Didn't the James boys and the Youngers ride with Quantrill, too?

"They sure did. The James boys have got an aunt up here at Bakersfield, just across the Missouri line, and they've got a whole bunch of kinfolk down at Elizabeth, about twenty mile south of here. Them Jameses at Elizabeth are right fine people. Some people would tell you that the James boys are good boys, too, but I don't believe it. Some people say they only fight the Yankees. Some even say they rob from the Federals to give to pore folks, but it always depends on whose ox is being gored. Now as for the Youngers, there's a bunch of them down on the White River below the Calico Rock, but I don't know nothing about them."

"That squirrel rifle I carry was made by a gunsmith down by the Calico Rock," Gatlin said.

The old lady acted like she didn't hear him. "Yessiree, Bob, they said that 'ol Bloody Bill Anderson was packing six of them Colt's pistols along with two knives and a hatchet when they got him. Word was that he charged right through the federal line and it took two bullets in the back of the head to bring him down."

"Feller in the hospital in Kentucky told me that them bush-whackers always wore big flowerdy shirts with four big front pockets. He claimed they carried the pockets full of extra loaded and capped cylinders for their pistols." Gatlin finally felt like he had contributed something to the conversation.

"Some of them other bushwhackers are like Bill Dark. They was thieves and outlaws before the war, and now they're just preying on the people who are left here, mostly old people and kids, because they make easy pickings. I suppose some of them bushwhackers was decent people at one time, but then turned bushwhacker because they were hungry. Part of these scum that roam the lapland claim to be attached to one army or the other, but they are just common thieving murderers no matter what they call themselves. One of the Sapps said they seen a notice that Jo Shelby had his soldiers nail to a tree. It warned the bushwhackers in the White River Valley to join one army or the other, it didn't matter which. The notice said that any man not in one army or the other would be hung if they was caught by Shelby or his men. But that still didn't get rid of all of them. "

Mrs. Williams acted like everyone knew Bill Dark.

"Who is this Bill Dark feller"? Gatlin asked.

The old lady smiled. "Did I say is? I should've said was. Bill Dark is dead, thank heaven. He tried to ride down a teen-age kid with a horse. Bill Dark didn't know the kid had a gun. Let's see, what was that kid's name? Jim Berry, that's what it was! Berry wasn't but fifteen year old when he done it. Dark chased him around a widow woman's cabin. Berry had gone over to help the widow and her mother butcher a hog. That Berry kid, he hid behind a chimney and shot Dark graveyard dead when he came around the corner of the cabin. That was somewhere across the river at a place they're starting to call Fox, I hear."

Finishing quickly, Gatlin scraped his bowl clean and got up, "Well Ma'am," he said, "I guess I'd better be moving along."

She looked up at him, "Where are you going?"

"Well," he replied, "I'm just drifting, I've never had a proper home. I headed this way because I heard there weren't many people in these hills. Being alone just seems natural to me, I guess." Gatlin started to ask if she had ever heard of Thomas Williams or his family, but the old woman started talking again before he had a chance to continue.

"My husband died before the war," she said with a small quaver that was noticeable even in a voice made hoarse by age. "The two boys, Thomas and John B., they took off and enlisted as soon as the war started. They told me it would be over in a few days. Well, that was back in '61, and here it is 1863, and they're not home yet. I haven't heard from either of them in over four months. They could be prisoners or even dead, for all I know. One of them's with Colonel Jo Shelby up in Missouri. The other'n, Thomas, he took off and joined up with the Seventh Arkansas over here at Pocahontas. He wrote and said he was in Shaver's outfit."

Gatlin almost choked! This had to be her! This was Thomas' mother! Of all the places he could wind up, he had stopped right here at their cabin! He dropped his eyes down to the soup bowl trying to figure out what to say. He didn't trust himself to speak. He had known that he was drifting west for a reason, but he had been so deeply depressed that he wasn't really conscious of where he was going. He hadn't been headed somewhere as much as he was running away, away from the hurt and pain, but mostly away from himself. Now that Gatlin thought about it, he might have been unconsciously following Thomas' directions since he had left Kentucky.

Tears started to run down her cheeks. They followed the deep ravines that were the wrinkles in her face. "I'm all alone, and I'm a tough old woman. I've lived in these hills all of my life. I've seen flood, drought, snow 20 inches deep on the level, and I remember the awful earthquakes of 1811 and 1812. They lasted nearly the whole summer. We lived in the open fields, we was so a'feared that the cabin would fall slap-dab on top of us. I well remember how in

November of '33 we had so many falling stars. The show went on every night for nearly a month. Everbody we knowed, which was mighty few, they all started praying day and night. Most of them thought it was the end of the world, but I knowed the signs wasn't right according to the good book. My mother was a full-blooded Cherokee Indian and my father was a Scotchman. I was married at the age of 15. My man was Irish, and had worked his way to this country aboard ship. He just sort of wandered in, just like you, I guess. We had fifty years of happiness together. Two boys are not all we had, there's two boys and a girl buried beside their daddy in that walnut grove down the road. One of the boys tried to swim this bayou when it was spread clean across that bottom over there during the spring floods. The othern', Isaac, he was such a fine young man. He got kicked in the head by a mule. Isaac died that night; he never come to. The little girl died with me holding her and praying that she wouldn't be took, but I guess the Lord knows bettern' me. She wasn't but three, it was the pneumonia that took her."

She looked up at Gatlin, "I'm not asking for your pity, you understand, I've lived through the best and the worst of times, but there's nothing worse than being old, poor and alone. The eatin' ain't real good around here since the armies and the bushwhackers done butchered every hog and cow brute we owned, unless there's still a wild hog or two in the woods."

Gatlin turned to stare into the fire. He couldn't tell her now, she didn't need to know that Thomas had killed himself. He would put it off for a little while.

"Well, maybe I could stay a few days and help you out some. After all, not many people would offer a hungry stranger a bowl of soup."

She smiled and once again those ageless eyes took on a sparkle that didn't come entirely from the tears. "You won't have to stay long. Surely my boys will come home, surely this war will be over soon."

The days passed quickly, late summer matured into fall and

the fall lingered on. Gatlin often stood in the early morning sun, admiring the leaves as the greens faded into yellows. Then the yellow shades became mingled with the many hues of red that made the rolling hills flame. There were four apple trees behind the house. Gatlin eagerly gathered the apples and spaced them apart in the loft so they wouldn't rot. The old woman always bragged on the Winesaps, but Gatlin loved the Lady apples for their spicy flavor and the audible snap when he bit into one of them.

For the first time since he could remember, Gatlin found some semblance of happiness. He kept trying to find the right time to tell her about Thomas. It got so that he hated to tell her simply because he had waited so long. He tried to imagine how she would react. He was afraid that she would turn on him in her grief. He couldn't stand the thought of seeing her hurt. He had found the mother he had never known. She seemed to require so little to get by, it would be a shame to destroy what little hope she had left.

Sometimes they fished in Bennett's Bayou, eating freshly caught fish. Gatlin was amused to find that although the old woman would have charged Hell with a bucket of water, she was deathly afraid of snakes. He enjoyed scaring her at every opportunity.

"Now young'un, you watch that path up ahead. They's apt to be a big old cottonmouth laying acrost it. They like these trails down clost to the creek. They know the rats run down these paths. Ain't nothing an old cottonmouth moccasin likes better after filling his gut with fish than a fat rat for dessert. If you was to get bit, I'd have to put the madstone on you."

Gatlin looked back, a little surprised. "Now, Mrs. Williams, don't tell me you believe in those things."

"You ain't jest a bird trackin'. I've seen this one work; its been in our family as long as anybody on the Indian side can remember. My momma said it come from the stomach of a white deer. That's the strongest medicine there is. And don't you be making fun of it."

Gatlin could tell that she was getting upset, so he didn't mention it again. When they got back to the cabin, she lifted up one of the hearth stones and pulled out an ancient doeskin pouch. She slipped a large mussel shell out of the pouch and unwrapped the thong that held it closed. Gatlin moved closer. He had heard tell of madstones but had never seen one up close. It was flattened, whitish-gray, and porous. "I thought it was supposed to only cure madness. Are you trying to tell me it'll cure snakebite, too?"

She slid it carefully out into her palm. "But, of course, it'll cure the bite of a mad dog, or any kind of snakebite and it'll kill the poison from catfish fins, too." She said.

"How does it work?" Gatlin asked, "Do you have to say magic words along with it?"

"They ain't nothing worse than a smart aleck who's dumb as a box of dirt besides. Now you shut up and listen here. You just stick it on the wound and leave it until it falls off. Iffn' it won't stick, that just means that the bite wasn't from a mad or poison critter to start with. Now after its used you have to put it in sweet milk for a day or so to make it work again." The old lady looked over at him, as if daring him to laugh, so he got busy scraping down a groundhog hide.

Gradually becoming more skilled at hunting, Gatlin managed to find enough wild game along the ridgetop to get them through, even though there were times when he had to block the exact species from his mind as he ate. Squirrels, skunks, and an occasional groundhog, as well as many other small animals fell prey to the old rifle or to traps he had learned to construct through trial and error. They had few visitors, but Mrs. Williams talked about the neighbors constantly. They occasionally heard horses go by in the night. Gatlin was relieved each time he heard the hoofbeats fade away to dark silence.

Then one morning, he eased down into the switch canes along the creek, hoping to scare up a deer. The thick frost crunched like new snow under his feet as he walked past the tall weeds with the sap pouring from their ruptured stems. The sap had frozen into the beautiful complex floral arrangements that the old woman called rabbit ice. He walked as he imagined a experienced woodsman would, know-

ing that it was impossible
to keep the canes from rattling as he moved carefully through them.

He stepped into a small clearing and looked around. The canes had been smashed down and the ground looked like it had been plowed up in an area about thirty feet across. Gatlin moved forward curiously, wondering what manner of creature could have done so much damage. Hearing a grunt, he turned, cocking the old rifle. The wild boar stood, slobbers dripping off of the two inches of honed ivory sticking out of both sides of his snout. He slung his head, chomping, the tusks making a rapid clicking noise as he tried to focus on this intruder. The bristles stood up along his back as Gatlin drew a bead between the little brownish-red eyes. As powder flashed toward the touchhole of the rifle, the hog charged with a grunt. Gatlin, his vision obscured by the resulting smoke, felt himself being hurled to the ground. He rolled over, grabbing the butcher knife stuck in his belt. The hog was lying about six feet behind him, its nose plowed into the ground. He glanced down at the long, deep cut in his artificial leg. He ran his thumb across it, it felt as if it had been done with a spokeshave. He pulled himself over to the boar. Running his thumb along the tusk edge, he realized that they were as precisely sharpened as a surgeon's scalpel. He got up, and felt a cold clammy sweat. He had heard that hog cuts often got infected and set up blood poisoning.

He gutted the boar and managed to drag it back to the cabin. Mrs. Williams looked at it with approval. "Probably went wild, or it may have descended from some of ourn' that we lost track of. Anyways, you're lucky he didn't have off with your good leg. Before the war we always had community hog killings. We scalded them, then scraped the hair off, you see. You've got to be mighty careful; if you get the water too hot you'll set the hair, then they're nearly impossible to scrape clean. Then we'd chunk the hide and the fat under it into squares. We'd always render the lard out in that big black kettle leaning agin' the cabin over there. Then we'd make cracklin' cornbread with the leavings. But I suppose you'd better just skin it.

It's faster."

There was no salt to cure the meat, and Gatlin knew it would spoil in spite of the cool weather. Carrying the meat into the small smokehouse, he glanced down and noticed the deposits of dried salty drippings from years of meat curing. Quickly shoveling up the dirt floor he poured it into the cook pot and skimmed the dirt off as the water boiled away. In just a little while he had plenty of salt, although it was a dirty brown in color. After rubbing the meat down with the salt, he let it lay for a few days to drain.

After that he kept a low hickory chip fire going for several days to finish the curing process. Mrs. Williams, looking on, made sure that he rubbed the ends of the bone with dried chili pepper to keep the skippers out. He looked at the hams hanging from the ceiling by their Yucca bindings with some satisfaction. The pork would be their final bastion against starvation if the winter happened to be really bad. There were a few vegetables left in the garden hidden behind the cabin. Sometimes when Rit walked to the garden he had the distinct feeling that he was being watched. A few times he could have sworn that he caught a glimpse of movement out of the corner of his eye. This bothered him greatly, although he didn't mention it to Mrs. Williams. Gatlin had seen insane people before, and although most people made fun of them, he didn't think it was something they could really help. He wondered if perhaps he was going crazy, too. Almost every evening the old woman sat and threaded green beans crossways to dry, using a needle and thread. Dried onions hung from the rafters in bunches. Gatlin saw more of the V-shaped tracks of wild hogs in the cane brakes along the banks of the small creek called Bennett's Bayou. Gatlin wondered who this Bennett was. Was he an early settler or perhaps a trader? There was probably no one left in the hills who really remembered.

Mrs. Williams' husband had secured a contract to produce whiskey for the government licensed distillery over in the edge of Missouri.

"We didn't make any of that so-called Indian whiskey. Ours

was the simon pure stuff. I've heerd that some of them traders put in chewing tobacco for color and add a little strychnine to make the customers a little crazy. What we made was the pure quill. I swear to my time, when you put your nose to it, you could nearly smell the bare feet of my boys that plowed the corn."

She had managed to plant a corn crop by herself, but it had been gathered in the dark of night by person or persons unknown. Therefore, there had been no whiskey produced in the copper still by the spring this year. Gatlin found it curious that the old lady could talk with such enthusiasm about whiskey production while preaching the virtues of totally abstaining from drinking the stuff.

Gatlin gradually grew used to the inconvenience of the artificial leg, and with time it was becoming just that, an inconvenience. He also noticed the phantom pains becoming more infrequent and stoically endured the pain, knowing it would pass in a few hours. He steadfastly refused the bitter willow bark tea that Mrs. Williams used to treat her rheumatism.

The fall of 1863 had been pleasant. It was as if summer, knowing what was to come, hated to give up its gentle hold on the land. There were a few cool nights in September. Several killing frosts came in November. Gatlin loved to get out just after sunup. As the sun rose it melted away all the frost except the part shadowed by the huge Oak trees that grew along the ridge. Gatlin felt a sense of simple pleasure at the perfect image of the tree left in frost, but soon that, too was gone, only to reappear the next morning. After Gatlin killed the wild boar the weather stayed warm until just after Christmas. Gatlin was a little worried about the meat spoiling, but the salt did its work well. During this time Rit and the old woman dried and stored away as many provisions as they could. Periodically, some of the neighbors stopped by to check on Mrs. Williams. From what he had seen, Gatlin gathered that they were all having a hard time, also.

"Why haven't any of these bushwhackers come by since I've been here?" he asked one day.

The old lady looked up from the few wild persimmons she

was mashing into a paste, "I suppose they think we have nothing left that's worth stealing, and they're right. They don't see us as a threat. After all, what can an old woman and a cripple do? So they simply leave us alone because we are not worth bothering with."

Gatlin began to see sundogs almost every afternoon in the western sky. They appeared as pieces of rainbow out to the sides of the sun. He knew that they could only mean bad weather to come. On January 3, 1864, winter belatedly made its presence felt across the Ozark hills. First, as always, there was the wind. The wind that was like a cold knife, cutting through clothes as if they didn't exist. It tore the leaves from their little sockets, put their usefulness and beauty to an end, and piled them up agains the tree trunks. There, tiny little creatures would digest them until they were returned to the soil, only to be made into leaves again. Gatlin spent a great deal of time thinking about such things. Would his body rot away only to be reborn as a leaf, or perhaps someday, another man? Then one night came the fine bits of snow, the snow that tore into the exposed skin like thousands of tiny needles. He and the old lady only went out for necessities and to gather wood for the ever-hungry fireplace. The snow filled their ears, numbing them. Their eyes became sore at the corners from the constant wiping of instantly frozen tears. Then on the second day of the blizzard, the wind died and there was only the silence. The snow continued, at times cutting visibility to nearly nothing. For three more days it fell slowly, the giant flakes reminding Rit Gatlin of the many bales of cotton he had helped load on the steamships in the life he had led before. The old lady talked constantly of the effect the heavy snow would have on the few wild creatures left by the foraging human predators. Gatlin said very little. He was enjoying being warm and his stomach being filled at least part of the time. You never get over it, he thought. Once a person has starved, the thought of having enough food is never far from their mind. The urge to eat past one's capacity was almost impossible to resist. The taste or quality of the food was unimportant, lost in the overwhelming urge to experience once again the stretched tight feeling of the entire digestive system. When the snow stopped, Gatlin ventured out to shoot some small game. He was also able to pick up birds that were too weakened by the storm to resist, and they made tasty additions to the sparse diet of dried vegetables.

For the rest of January and February the snow would start to melt, only to be replenished by a new supply. The sky stayed the same unvarying gunmetal hue. The bare hills had taken on a bluish color. There was no sign of the sun from its low angle just above the horizon. It was as if he and this old woman were the only people on earth, Rit reflected. "I wonder if she could have survived this winter if I hadn't happened along? But then there's no way I could have lived through this without her either." She now seldom mentioned her sons and he wondered if she had accepted the possibility that one or both of them could be dead.

According to the old Lady's almanac, it was the first of March that bad weather broke, the snow started to melt, and the temperature rose rapidly. It was almost as if nature was sorry for the bad winter and was trying to make amends. On March third, Gatlin was up a little before sunrise. He carefully shook out his old broken calvary boot before pulling it on; fiddleback spiders were active even during cooler weather, especially indoors. He left the old woman sleeping. Gathering up a pick and shovel he started out to the little field behind the cabin. He stopped and stood for a moment watching the sun's rays spreading like a giant fan across the rounded humps that were the Ozark hills. The high places reflected the sun's rays as a brilliant gold, while the hollows remained in deep shadow. He could see little wisps of fog rising like columns of campfire smoke as the remaining snow started to melt.

54

CHAPTER 5

"Why can't life always be this quiet and peaceful?" he wondered, as he stood and watched the new day gradually emerge from the darkness. He had managed to learn to keep his balance while swinging the pick and enjoyed the solid sound it made as it bit into the moisture saturated soil. He began to smell the richness of the ground as he worked it, he loved the earthy heaviness of that smell. It was so quiet he could hear the echoes as each swing of the pick shook the still air. He became so engrossed in this task of ground preparation that he failed to hear the sound of horses moving up behind him. Stopping at last to catch his breath, and perceiving movement out of the corner of his eye, Rit whirled to find himself almost face to face with a complete platoon of Union Calvary. The only thing he could think of was that he was still wearing his the butternut clothes that more often than not passed as a Confederate uniform!

"Well, gentlemen I do believe that we captured ourselves a genuine Confederate rebel soldier!" Gatlin must have moved slightly, because the tone of the voice changed. "Stand still there boy!" He looked at Gatlin, "No one's going to shoot you unless you try to run, that is."

Gatlin laid down his pick and looked up at the speaker with a calm face. He recognized the double gold bars of a Union captain. His eyes were drawn to the man's face. A tilted back black hat framed the weathered face of a man who had obviously spent more time staring down the spine of a plow mule than the sights of a rifle. There were deep laugh lines radiating out like points of a star from his snappy brown eyes. But his mouth was drawn into a thin line which indicated that he was a force to be reckoned with. Gatlin could smell the metallic odor of his own blood rushing to his nose as his heart raced. The dryness of his throat made it difficult to speak.

"I couldn't run if I wanted to," he said, his voice sounding small and tight. He looked up knowing that his naked fear was obvious to everyone watching.

The captain looked at Gatlin coldly, "I am prepared to treat you as legitimate prisoner of war if you can prove you are a soldier in the army of the Confederacy and not a deserter or bushwhacker." He paused and took a deep breath. "If you have no such proof, we will hang you from that walnut tree over there." He gestured with the brass-framed Colt Navy pistol in his hand. "I heard about Shelby's warning posters up and down the White and I agree with him."

Pointing to the cabin, Gatlin said, "If you'll let me get my bag, I'll show you my discharge papers."

"Why were you discharged?" asked the Union officer.

Rit leaned down and pulled up his faded pants. "Wood instead of flesh and bone," he said. The captain's impassive visage softened."Where were you wounded?" he asked.

"In the Battle of Richmond, Kentucky," Gatlin replied.

The patrol followed Gatlin as he walked awkwardly across the small field to the cabin. No one spoke. The only sound was the dull clump of the horses hooves on the wet, thawing ground. As he walked toward the front door, he almost smiled as he noticed the twin barrels of Mrs. Williams shotgun move slowly out of the window. The union captain was no fool. He raised his hand and the troop halted. He nodded toward the cabin, his eyes never leaving Gatlin's face, "Tell your friend in there to relax. We've had enough killing for one day."

Moments later Gatlin walked back out the front door with his discharge papers in hand. Behind him eyeing the soldiers suspiciously was the shotgun-toting Mrs. Williams. Looking the papers over carefully the officer read as if to himself, "Rit Gatlin, Company G, 2nd Arkansas Mounted Rifles, Discharged August 14, 1863, James W.

Caughran, Commanding Officer."

"Well, Mr. Gatlin, we're sorry to have troubled you. I'm Captain Eli Hughes of the Sixth Missouri State Militia, headquartered in Springfield, Missouri. Now, maybe you can help us." He turned toward the silent group of soldiers behind him, "Bugler, sound assembly."

No sooner had the clear notes of the bugle sliced the still air that another troop of calvary topped the rise and started toward them. Gatlin counted 16 horses being led, some with supplies and weapons tied to them. But he could see that four of the mounts carried more somber burdens. They were unmistakably human forms, even tied as they were across the saddles. Two of them were wrapped in white canvas, while the dull colored, ragged homespun clothes of the other two made it evident that they weren't soldiers, more closely resembling bundles of dirty rags than human beings, Rit thought, as he watched them ride closer. Just behind the bodies was another man whose hands were tied behind his back. This was made obvious by the stiff manner in which he sat his horse.

Captain Hughes interrupted the silence. "We have engaged no less than three bands of guerrillas and bushwhackers in as many days. We had no casualties until this morning when we encountered a band of bushwhackers led by a man named Cain."

"Where did this happen?" asked Mrs. Williams.

"Just where Bennett's Bayou and Bennett's River flow into the Norfork River, along what my scouts call Moon Ridge," answered the Captain. "They got away, but not before killing two of my troopers."

As the horses with their cargo of death stopped, Hughes started walking toward them. "Follow me, Gatlin." Captain Hughes stepped to one of the horses, ignoring the small pool of viscous blood. It dripped from a body wound and was slowly collecting on the ground. He grabbed one of the dead men by the hair and turned his face up, "Do you know this man?"

Gatlin looked at the greasy black beard covering most of the slack face, the eyes an opaque blue as they stared sightlessly up at him. "No, sir," he replied.

"How about this one?" Hughes asked.

Gatlin soundlessly shook his head. The body was that of a young man about his own age, with light brown hair and a fine, downy beard and mustache.

"Let me look at them." Mrs. Williams was walking toward them, still toting the shotgun. She looked at the first man, "This one's named Frank Russell. He was as sorry a man as ever drawed a breath. Them Russells is all sorry. My husband always said that hell would be so full of Russells that their feet would be sticking out of the winders. He's the one that killed that traveler named Anderson and his slave, too, matter of fact. He's stole from everyone up and down this valley. I think this particular Russell came down from Missouri." The old woman looked at the younger man, "This here is one of them Howard boys from over in the edge of Fulton county. I thought he was in the Union army, though. I can't imagine why he would be riding with these murderers. He came from a good family," she concluded.

Captain Hughes nodded, "He's the one that told us the leader's name before he died. He said he would have liked to have seen his mama one more time. We'll try to get word to her." The Federal captain's voice had a sad note. He had, no doubt, been faced with the same task numerous times.

Hughes touched his hat brim, "Much obliged, Ma'am," he said. Then he turned to Gatlin, "raise your right hand and repeat after me."

Rit raised his hand and repeated, "I Rit Gatlin, do solemnly swear to uphold the laws of the United States of America and promise not to take up arms against it as long as I shall live."

Captain Hughes looked him in the eyes, his expression stern. "You realize that if you violate this parole that you can be hung without trial don't you?"

"Yes, sir," Rit answered.

Hughes turned to Mrs. Williams, "You wouldn't happen to know this prisoner would you ma'am?"

Mrs. Williams looked at the man on the horse for a long moment, her old blue eyes seemed to flare with hatred. "Name's Johnny Monroe, and he's as bad as the rest of them. They've carried off everything that's loose in this part of the country. They've raped women and shot little children and old men. I say hanging's too good for any of them." Her voice had gotten loud and shrill at the end of her outburst. The prisoner, who sat impassively, eyes straight ahead, suddenly turned and spat, missing the old woman by a fraction. The big, red-faced, obviously Irish sergeant next to Monroe raised the carbine in his hand and swatted the bushwhacker in the side of the head as casually as if he were killing a mosquito.

As Monroe hit the ground with a grunt, the sergeant touched his cap, "No manners, ma'am, but the good Lord willing we'll teach him some afore we hang him." He smiled, showing tobacco stained teeth.

The captain swung into his saddle and looked down at the old woman and the young man. "Be careful. This country is still full of bushwhackers, and they will be moving around now that warm weather is here. We know that a good part of them spent the winter in Texas, so they'll be coming back through, headed north."

They stood together silently and watched until the Federal troops were out of sight.

Now that the bad weather had broken, spring seemed to come quickly. The grass turned green almost overnight. Ducks could be heard as they came and fed along the stream and left again the next morning, traveling to their nesting grounds far to the north. The honking of the long ragged lines of geese could be heard at dusk every night. The land seemed to be jumping with the excitement of new life, both plant and animal.

The old woman began to talk of planting a corn crop to make whiskey to fill the contract. She hunted up a few garden seeds to plant the plot Gatlin had broken up with the pick. If they could just plant a small patch of corn and keep it hidden from the guerrillas, they could not only have corn, but could grind precious corn meal as well.

The whiskey still sat on a small flat ledge about halfway down the bluff below the cabin. It was small, and three huge cedar trees growing over the ledge effectively shielded the dull shine of the copper from view. Otherwise, it would have been carried off by the metal hungry Confederates. A broken off section of limestone made a smooth wall on the west side and a small spring provided adequate fresh cold water. It is said that good whiskey requires good water and the coil must be immersed in cold water to insure an even condensation of the alcohol. Gatlin knew little about whiskey (he had never been able to afford it, and even if he could have, he had watched too many men on the waterfront consume cheap whiskey until at last it consumed them). However, Mrs. Williams was an expert.

One night she sat and explained the distillation process to him so thoroughly that he became enthusiastic in spite of himself.

"I sure wish Thomas could have been here, we could've done....." Gatlin said. He caught himself, then tried to think of how to continue. He looked through the open window at the moon slowly climbing up through the oak trees. But it was too late, the old lady had lived too long around men.

"You knew him didn't you, Rit?" She asked quietly. "You knew him well."

Gatlin turned to face her, he felt his mouth tremble. He fought to control the shaking in his voice "Yes I knew him, he was like the brother I never had." That wasn't the right thing to say either and he stopped talking.

"He's dead, ain't he? I've had a bad feeling about Thomas for quite a while. He was the youngest, you know. I always figured John B. would manage to get by somehow, but Thomas, he always had to be in the thick of things. Us old women is hard to fool. I always thought it was a curious thing that you just happened to show up here just when I needed help so bad. I should have knowed it weren't no accident. Did he send you or did you come on your own?" Her eyes started to get big and Gatlin couldn't look her in the face.

"Well, ma'am, he sorta told me to check in on you."

"Then he didn't die in battle?"

Gatlin stood up and looked down at the puncheon floor for a long time. He had intended to pretend that Thomas had been killed instantly, but it was too late now. He didn't know what to say, he had never lost anyone to suicide, but it seemed to him that such a death would be ten times harder on the family. She had been so obviously proud of her boys, how could she stand it?

"Young man you look me in the eye and tell me what happened to my boy, you tell me right now. A mother has got the right to know the truth."

Gatlin looked at her weathered face with those startling blue eyes then glanced away, "No ma'am, he didn't, he died in a field hospital." Gatlin's throat tightened, tears started to come to his eyes. He turned away as he saw her start to lose the rigid self control he had gotten so used to. He forced his jaw muscles to relax and continued. "He died of the wounds he got at Shiloh Church." It wasn't a lie, not really. If Thomas hadn't lost his legs he wouldn't have killed himself. Now that he had embarked on this course there would be no turning back. He didn't think anyone at the field hospital would write a letter. People who killed themselves were somehow regarded as cowardly by most people. Gatlin knew how bad officers dreaded to write the death letters to the families of the men killed in battle. Williams had told him that his outfit, the Seventh, had moved on, so Gatlin was sure that his fellow soldiers thought he was still alive somewhere. If that was the case, then there would have been no letter. He would deal with such a letter when and if it arrived. She had sat down on her bed and was weeping silently.. Gatlin turned around and climbed the ladder to the sleeping loft. By the time he lay down the tears were pouring down his face as well. He tossed and turned for a long time before he fell into an exhausted sleep.

So the next morning he set about to clear a little spot of bottom land in the middle of the bamboo-like switch canes which grew along the creek. The canes grow up to twelve feet tall and would afford concealment for the growing corn. He walked to the plot before daylight every morning, having several alternate routes and never using the same one twice in a row.

Food had become a precious thing in this war-torn area. The large numbers of men moving through the Ozarks required a constant supply of victuals for themselves and their horses. They acquired these goods by foraging. Both armies were supposed to pay for everything taken from civilians, but most of the time they did not bother. Especially if they suspected the people owning the seized property had sympathies for the other side. The bushwhackers who claimed to have Southern sympathies, and the jayhawkers, or Union supporters did not pay for anything. Any show of resistance by their victims resulted in instant violence. Often whole families were killed for hoarding food or livestock, especially horses. Times such as these had never been known before in this land of abundance, this young United States of America.

The last frost came and went, and the first week in April Gatlin began laboriously planting the corn by hand. He made the holes by jabbing a sharp stick in the ground, dropped in the seed then closed the hole by jabbing next to it and leaning the stick over. He was so awkward and unskilled that the first rows were already coming up by the time he had finished planting He had just finished and had straightened up to rub his sore back when he heard the shots from the direction of the cabin. He started hobbling up the bluff as fast as he could, remembering that on this particular morning he had left the old squirrel rifle standing in the corner of the cabin.

"She's got her old shotgun," he thought, "She's a tough old lady, she can take care of herself." Then he realized that he hadn't heard the dull boom of the muzzle-loading shotgun. It had been the sharp "pop" of a pistol. He started to run, taking long strides with his good leg, and slamming the wooden leg into the ground to get purchase for the next step. The tender flesh at the end of his stump started tearing; his breath started to feel like lances of fire piercing his lungs. Yet he kept on, and ran around to the front of the cabin, making no attempt to avoid noise. This total lack of caution put him directly under the guns of the three bushwhackers before the idea to do otherwise even occurred to him.

Gatlin saw the three men, then the body of the old woman lying in a heap between them and the cabin door. He half fell to his knees beside her. There was nothing he could do. She was lying in an odd twisted position, unmoving. Gatlin had to do something. He made an involuntary gesture as if to reach for the shotgun on the ground.

For the first time one of the killers spoke, "You try to use that gun and you'll end up like the old hag, boy. Now just pick it up slow by the barrels with your left hand and pass it up here." The speaker was a fat, greasy looking man wearing a pair of bib overalls, the suspenders partially covering the flowered guerrilla shirt.

The overalls, like their owner, obviously lacked both tailoring and laundering. The heavy Remington Zouave rifle in his hands looked well cared for, as did the pair of Colt's revolvers holstered on his belt. Numbly, as if in a trance, Gatlin slowly stood up and painfully limped over and handed up the relic of a weapon.

The man in the middle looked down at Rit, "Boy, we heard that these folks made whiskey, so we stopped by to get us some, and that old fool tried to kill us. Self defense, that's what it were, self defense." He reached into a pocket in the bib of the overalls, and pulled out a gold pocket watch and glanced down at it. "Now we're going for a little ride and in about two hours, we'll be back, and if we don't get what we want, you'll be laying on the ground beside that ugly old squaw woman there." As they started to ride off, the leader stopped his horse and yelled back at Gatlin, "That whiskey better be good and not some of that sink-tallow stuff."

They left him there kneeling beside her. She was the only friend he had. Thoughts ran through his mind in whirl that left him dizzy. There was a sense of unreality, of being on the outside watching himself. Something inside refused to accept the events of the last hour. Time ceased to mean anything. He had no idea of how long he had been there. Scenes, mostly disjointed and not coherent, flooded into his mind. A mother he could only remember by her smell and warmth. A father who was a giant to him. His only memories of him were his size and great friendly booming voice. These memories were replaced by others, less pleasant. Gatlin had been raised by relatives who were only concerned with how much work he could do. There were fleeting images of taunts and fights with his foster brothers and sisters. The merciless beatings that came because he was always blamed. There were the arguments about letting him stay. The hateful voices in the night, until he started to think of himself as "that orphan kid." At last he ran away to try it on his own. Since no one came to look for him, he guessed that they were relieved he was gone.

He had drifted around Little Rock, mostly working for room and board, although one kindly old wainwright had taken him in for a time. The old man taught him from a tattered Bible he kept wrapped in wagon canvas. At night Gatlin used pieces of coal to write on tattered pieces of wagon covering. Then one day the old man grabbed his head and fell down while pounding a wagon rim. After that the old man couldn't move his arm and could only make jabbering noises. His children came and got him. The house was sold and Gatlin stood by and watched a slick looking man auction off the shop and all the equipment. Nobody paid any attention to him, and he was homeless again. Yet in spite of it all, he had remained a gentle person, never wanting trouble with anyone, fighting only when pushed. When he joined the Mounted Rifles, he was living in an old packing crate on the waterfront. He had been treated kindly by the slave, Aaron. The shame of not being able to rescue Aaron was still with him. Mister Ashley had hired him to help unload the steamers that chugged their way up the Arkansas River. Yet he managed to keep himself clean and, except for his ragged manner of dress, would have appeared a gentleman. Most of the mounted riflemen were gentlemen. They were of the land-owning class that had rapidly grown in central Arkansas.

The pain in his leg slowly dispelled the mists of memory, and he, hearing voices, stood up and turned to see two armed men slowly trudging up the road toward him. He recognized the Sapps, father and son, Thomas and William. They had occasionally stopped by for a few minutes at a time to visit.

They walked up and stood silently beside Gatlin, Finally, Thomas Sapp spoke quietly, "She's dead, lad, there's nothing you can do."

As he stood beside the body of the old woman who had taken him in, a change began to take place in this man, Rit Gatlin. There was a exquisite searing feeling that started at the base of his brain and seeming to tighten every muscle in his body, moving upward until it threatened to blow the top of his head off. His head and neck felt as if they were swelling, and he could feel his molars move with the force of his clenched jaws. Men have killed, and the act of killing does not always make a man into a killer. Yet, at that moment, Rit Gatlin became a killer. He wanted to lash out at anything and everything around him. He wanted those men to hurt as he hurt, to be killed as they had so casually killed. Yet he knew that their deaths would not be enough. Killing them and a thousand more like them could not even the score. Oddly, Rit thought of being stung by a red wasp as a young boy. As the sting started to swell, he got a cup of coal oil and found a nearby wasp nest. He didn't know or care whether the wasp that stung him was there or not. One dash of the coal oil and the wasps fell, all dead instantly. But it still wasn't enough, it would never be enough. His need for vengence was not satisfied even after he had distroyed three more nests. One of the books he had read talked about a thirst for vengence. He understood that now. He suddenly remembered the Sapps, standing by, their heads bowed, both of them obviously at a loss for words.

He picked Mrs. Williams up gently. She was surprisingly light. "I guess I'd forgotten how old she really was," he said. He carried her into the cabin and laid her on her old rough hewn bed, hearing the cornshuck mattress rustle as he did so. He turned and walked back outside.

CHAPTER 6

"They're going to come back to get whiskey in two hours, and when they do I'm going to kill them," he said, his voice shaking with rage.

"We saw them when they rode by, and we could tell by looking that they're professional killers. Anybody with one eye and half sense knows you ain't got no chance against all three of them," Thomas Sapp said.

"I've got to give it a try. I can't let them get away with this." Rit replied.

The men both stood, silently looking off up the valley, for several long minutes.

Then William Sapp broke in, "We've both got families. Even if we killed these murdering devils, their comrades would just make it worse on us. They might even murder our whole families, but, on the other hand, we thought a lot of Phanta Williams, she helped birth our young'uns. She was always there when folks needed help."

Thomas Sapp interrupted, "She was a fine old woman all right. She's stayed up many a night tending folks who were sick or hurt."

"We don't have much time. Let's see to our guns. They could be back any minute," said William Sapp.

Gatlin felt relief wash across his skin. With all three of them, maybe there was some hope.

The elder Sapp spoke again, "However, you know we ain't got no chance in a fair fight don't you? We've always been farmers, we use guns to hunt and kill varmints with. But we ain't never shot at a man before."

Gatlin looked at him. When he spoke his voice was flat, with no emotion. "I don't plan a fair fight. Three men shooting an old lady ain't hardly no fair fight is it?"

Gatlin placed William Sapp at the window that had been Mrs. Williams favorite observation spot, and since the bushwhackers would be approaching from the north, he positioned Thomas Sapp around the west corner of the cabin. He planned to meet them at the front door himself. The two hours dragged by on turtle's legs, and the waiting began to work on the men's nerves. Gatlin tried to think of something else, but found himself looking up the the road every few moments. His mouth was getting drier and he had difficulty keeping his tongue from sticking to the roof of his mouth. His mind ran through every possible way the fight could happen. He knew that it was likely that he would be killed, but he no longer cared. In fact, he would welcome death if he could just take those three with him.

Thomas Sapp whistled tunelessly to himself, and William was muttering what Gatlin knew was a prayer. He could feel his breath catch as he watched them. After all, he thought, the Sapps are just farmers and I'm not even a well-trained soldier, let alone professional, as the enemy certainly is. He was standing in the open door when they came. They were calmly walking their horses back down the road. One was still leading his old horse, but one of the others was leading a big sorrel. The sorrel ran nearly sideways part of the time, always pulling back on the reins. As they drew closer, Gatlin could see the McClellan saddle had big saddlebags fore and aft.

The day had gotten uncomfortably warm as Rufus Beasley and the Harper twins made their way down the Bayou road earlier that day. The body of the former rider of the big sorrel gelding, a Union army courier, was now lying in a ditch just up beyond. He had been stripped of his boots, uniform and valuables, having ridden into the arms of the three bushwhackers. Beasley was known as "Weasel" to his acquaintances, (it could not be said that he had friends) because of a certain facial resemblance. He was short and fat, which was unusual in these times of famine, with strands of greasy red hair pasted across a bald scalp. If asked, he wouldn't have been able to remember the last time he had bathed and shaved. His scraggly beard had the appearance of a half plucked bird. Beasley had been a petty thief and burglar before the war. Like many people of weak character, he found the confusion of warfare an ideal environment in which to develop into what he fancied was a full-blown outlaw. He had no loyalties to either the North or the South, having enlisted in the Union Army once and the Army of the Confederacy twice. He enlisted when broke and hungry, then deserted when he saw a chance to get away with money, equipment or horses. He never stopped to ponder the right or wrong of his actions. He only considered whether or not they benefited him directly.

That other people were human beings with feelings never entered his mind. He was able to kill without a vestige of mercy, but there was no malice in him either. He was simply indifferent. The twins did not register on his consciousness as friends or even comrades at arms, they were merely a momentary convenience.

The three of them had banded together as stray starving dogs would, without loyalty or trust. In fact, as they came to know each other better, distrust had developed as each became aware of the others' true character traits. Then just by luck they had taken up with the Colonel. Beasley was pleased when the Colonel called them his best scouts, but he didn't have the intelligence to realize that the Colonel was endulging himself in a bit of facetiousness. Beasley had shot the old woman as she raised the shotgun, but even if she had been unarmed, he would probably have killed her anyway. He and the twins simply found it more convenient to kill most of their victims than to worry about possible identification and vengeance later. Now the Colonel would surely be pleased that they had the courier's horse.

The Colonel was smart and he would know exactly what to do with the papers in the saddlebags. If they just stuck with the Colonel they would all soon be rich.

Andrew and Simon Harper, named after two apostles of Jesus

by their circuit rider father, rode on either side and slightly behind Beasley, their undesignated leader. "I wonder why we had to take this old crowbait of a horse," Simon thought. "That crippled feller's not going anywhere." He was irritated at Beasley. It just wasn't right to shoot women and kids. He had been raised better than that. He glared at Beasley. "Look at that! He just took that odd new pistol off that bluecoat messenger and didn't even ask me or Andrew if we wanted it. Next thing you know, he'll be trying to keep that fancy horse for himself instead of selling it". Simon couldn't count money, or read either, for that matter, and he and his brother had often wondered if they were getting their fair share of the loot.

Unaware of the glares of animosity directed at his back, Weasel Beasley was getting thirsty. "I hope that crippled kid has some good whiskey made," he thought. "I might even let him live." It never entered his mind that Gatlin might try to get away or resist. After all, they had taken his horse and the old woman's shotgun.

Andrew Harper's back ached and his left arm was starting to go numb as the high strung sorrel kept pulling back on the bridle. He, too, was glaring at Beasley's back. Unlike his brother, Andrew hadn't given much thought to that fancy pistol. But the sight of the gold Waltham watch in Beasley's greasy hand was almost more than he could stand.

The old lady wasn't the first woman Beasley had shot. Andrew could still see the whole thing in his mind's eye. Two weeks earlier the three of them had overtaken an old couple, heading south, their horse so old and worn that it could barely pull the light wagon on the level. Andrew had glanced across their goods and rightly decided they had nothing worth stealing. He nodded and touched the brim of his hat at the old woman, anticipating that Beasley would ride on past.

"Where you headin'?" he heard Beasley ask.

The old man looked over from his walking position beside the wagon. "We're a' headin' to Batesville to get away from the Yankees and bushwhackers. If you've got any sense, you'll go, too."

"Are you sayin' I ain't got no sense?" Beasley asked, the challenge in his voice unmistakable. He turned his head toward the twins. "Boys this old man is sayin' we ain't got no sense. I'd call them fightin' words."

A little more perceptive than her husband, the old woman started to reach back in the wagon. Puzzled by the sudden turn of events, Andrew had barely had time to turn his attention to them before he saw Beasley reach for his gun.

"No!" He heard Simon yell just as the old woman tried in vain to drag the unwieldy old musket from the wagon.

Beasley shot her and as she dropped the musket, and started to fall, her husband, frozen in place by surprise, started to move toward her, only to be shot in the back. He fell by the wagon without making a sound other than a dull slap as his body hit the ground.

In an instant Beasley was on the ground, flipping his reins around a wheel. He climbed into the wagon and started throwing out their meager belongings. Muttering to himself, he didn't notice the looks of shock directed at him by the twins.

Finally the bushwhacker climbed down. "Nothin' worth taking," he said as he walked over and rolled the old man's body over with the toe of his brogan. Bending down, he jerked something from his victim's pocket. "Well, finally I hit the jackpot. This here's a genuine Waltham." Beasley raised it to his mouth and bit down on the case. "Pretty near pure gold, too. These must have been rich folks at one time."

Greed overriding the remnants of their common decency, the twins helped tear the wagon apart searching for hidden compartments. Finally they rode off, leaving the bodies and the remains of the wagon standing on the trail, and leading the miserable horse. Beasley stuck the watch in his pocket without any discussion on the matter. Beasley told Colonel Cain about getting the horse, claiming they had found it wandering near a creek. He made no mention of the watch to Cain.

Andrew thought about calling Beasley's hand on it. He was sure that Beasley had seen the watch and decided on the spot to murder the old folks for it. But deep down inside, he knew he would never work up the courage to say anything. He could never face up to a man who killed so casually. He brushed off the thought to brood about another thing that rankled him. Andrew's sympathies lay more with the South. " So why do we keep killing Confederate soldiers?" he wondered. "Old Weasel is always making big plans, always telling us how rich we are going to be." Yet they went hungry most of the time, and almost never had a warm, dry place to sleep. If either army ever found out about all the scouts and couriers they had so ruthlessly murdered, there would be the devil to pay. He wondered about the Colonel, him and his men. The twins had joined up with him just because of Tom Howard. Now Tom had managed to get himself killed by that Union patrol. And not only Tom, the Federals had killed Russell and it looked like they had captured Johnny Monroe as well; at least Monroe was missing. After that, Andrew began to seriously question Colonel Cain's leadership ability. "Maybe me and Simon ought to sneak off from the Colonel, leave Beasley and the rest. Then me and Simon could drift west over into the Indian territory," he found himself thinking.

As they approached the cabin, Beasley could see the one-legged man standing just inside the half opened door, watching their approach. "Hell", thought Beasley, "I'm probably going to kill this man and I don't even know his name." Beasley wrestled with that thought for a moment, his first and only attempt at introspection.

Stopping his horse about thirty feet in front of the cabin door, Beasley leaned forward in his stirrups and started to ask about the whiskey, but as soon as he opened his mouth, he saw Gatlin's right shoulder drop. The crippled man, his face contorted with hatred, seemed to expand to fill Beasley's entire field of vision as the slender barrel of the flintlock came from behind the door jamb and started to rise. Beasley tried to yell a warning, but no sound came! Instinctively he grabbed for the courier's pistol, but the unfamiliar button-down holster thwarted him. As he dug frantically at it, he heard two dull booms. They sounded distant, like summer thunder. Everything seemed to be moving in slow motion and he suddenly became aware of the bright colors of the spring day, a beautiful day. Funny that he hadn't noticed it before. Still tearing at the flap, his eyes focused on the old rifle as it came level. The shiny ring of wear around the muzzle of the octagon barrel looked like a tiny halo as it reflected the sunlight. The light was perfect, he could even see the hammer fall as the sparks ignited the priming powder. Weasel's hearing was acute, and he heard the whoosh of the priming powder as it blew out sideways, the fist-sized puff of smoke obscuring Gatlin's face. Beasley heard the main charge ignite and watched the orange rose of death spring from the end of the barrel and reach out to engulf him. The grains of unburned powder stung his face, and he felt a dull burning sensation at the base of his throat. Even as he realized the pistol was useless, he heaved sideways on the reins. The horse, trying to respond, almost fell as he was pulled around, but then quickly recovered and was in a dead run within thirty steps. He was getting away! Somehow Beasley knew that the twins were dead, but he was escaping! He would come back, he would find other men to join him. Simon and Andrew had been useless anyway. The most important thing was that his luck, his good luck that he had come to depend on, the luck that had carried him through for so long, was still with him! He would make it! He took a deep breath, for in a minute he would be out of rifle range. Rufus Beasley exhaled through his mouth. Something hot was running down the front of his shirt! There was a time of floating. Then the floating suddenly stopped. He knew he was no longer on his horse. He reached out to each side to try to sit up. His hands caught the straight smooth sides of the rectangular limestone ledge. "It's shaped just like a kitchen table top," he thought. He could feel his heels hanging off the end. He ran his hands down the sides again, then started to turn over and look. He couldn't turn over. Why was he suddenly so weak? He was looking directly up at the bright blue morning sky, and then it started slowly turning dark. The darkness was working its way up toward the center of his vision. Strange, he hadn't noticed that it was coming up a storm. Strange to be lying

on a rock table top. So strange. Rit Gatlin stopped reloading the squirrel rifle.

CHAPTER 7

To Gatlin, totally enveloped by fear, those few seconds seemed to expand exponentially. Dozens of deeply vivid, sharply detailed images were burned into his mind's eye, each distinctly piled upon one another in sequence. The cumulus clouds of black powder smoke pierced by lightening bolts of orange flame. The twins swept backward off their horses, the wide eyed shocked looks that stayed fixed as they were flung, dead almost instantly, backward into the yard. The horses rearing, their eyes showing wide expanses of white as they ran backward on their haunches, both of them almost losing their balance. The bushwhacker leader whirling his horse to get away. Gatlin watched as the man bounced higher with each bound of the horse until he slid off and rolled along the ground. His arms and legs were outflung loosely as his bounced, rolling over and over. A faint cloud of dust rose and hung in the still morning air. When the bushwhacker stopped rolling, he didn't move again. Relieved of his rider, Beasley's horse stopped running, then walked over and smelled of his fallen rider. Then, as an animal used to shooting and the violence of men, he started cropping grass beside the body.

With a rush, Gatlin's other senses kicked in. The rotten egg smell of black powder still hung in the air and his ears rang. He shook all over, he was suddenly cold, and his teeth started to chatter. He could hear the quiet sniffling of the Sapp boy as the enormity of the deed sank in. Gatlin stepped off the porch and picked up the twins' weapons. He could still hear the roar of his own blood in his ears, and his heart thumped like dull hoofbeats.

"Young man," he said to William Sapp, "Could you ride up there and bring that man's body back?"

The quiet request had the desired effect. William Sapp stopped sniffling, climbed on one of the now calm horses and trotted off as Gatlin busied himself gathering the reins of the other mounts. In a few minutes Sapp returned with Beasley's body draped over his saddle. Sapp looked down at Gatlin. He was rubbing his eyes and his face was smeared with burnt gunpowder.

"You know them bushwhackers will come lookin' for their men, and they'll kill us and all our families when they find out what we done, don't you?" he asked. The boy's voice shook as he tried to regain control.

"I've involved you too much already. Both of you go home and tell no one of this," Gatlin replied.

The older Sapp now spoke, "We hep't kill 'em and we'll see the varmints buried, though they don't deserve it. Iff'n we don't, the buzzards will gather and every bushwhacker in the country will come a running."

"I'll tend to it," Gatlin said as he stooped down awkwardly to check the dead men's pockets. "If they had kinfolks, they should at least be wrote to."

But there was no identification on any of the bodies. Gatlin quickly went through the fat man's saddle bags. There was only a faded set of enlistment papers with his name on them. The bags also contained four more Colt brass-framed revolvers and their accompanying gear.

"We'll help, anyway," Thomas Sapp said. Soon the other two bodies were loaded and the little caravan started down the winding trail to the corn patch. No one spoke as they dug one large grave, unceremoniously dumped the three bushwhackers in, covered them, then smoothed the ground and replanted the young corn over it.

"I'll he'p bury them, but I'll be danged if I' say words over 'em," muttered the elder Sapp. "The devil probably don't even want them."

The three men stood for a moment staring at the apparently undisturbed corn.

"What are you going to do with their horses and gear, Mr. Gatlin?" William Sapp asked.

"I think that we should try to see that the Union Army gelding gets to the Confederates. He's a courier's horse. This passel of scum undoubtedly killed his rider. You men take what you want of the other stuff."

Thomas Sapp spoke, "We'd better hide the other horses in that little valley south of here for awhile."

Gatlin finally forced himself to say what had been on his mind since the shooting stopped. "We'll bury Mrs. Williams in the morning. She deserves to be put away nice."

Thomas Sapp stood looking at the ground. "We'll help you dig the grave."

"No," Rit replied, "I want to do it by myself, if you fellows don't mind, but tell any of the neighbors you see."

William Sapp spoke. "They's mighty few of us left. Anybody that had any place to go has done left the country. But we'll be there!" He bent over and picked up the two colt 1860 army style pistols belonging to the twins "We'll take these two. You'd better keep that new fancy-looking one there. You'll probably need it."

Gatlin stood and watched as they led the horses away to the hidden valley. He left his old horse standing, head drooped, sides still moving from the excitement and old age. He picked up the courier's saddle and walked into the cabin. Mrs. Williams, lying on the bed, appeared to be asleep. There was barely a spot of blood where the fatal bullets had struck her chest. Gatlin stood there and gazed down at her. He guessed she just didn't have much blood to lose."Why didn't you just hide?" he asked her out loud, as if she could somehow hear him. Then the tears came. His thin shoulders shook as he sank down, his head rustling the corn shuck mattress.

He had been happy for the first time in his life. There had been someone like family. He expected that he would feel better after avenging her death, but he felt nothing. He was numb but for a deep aching emptiness that made the sides of his neck and his chest hurt. Why? Why couldn't they have been left alone? Why couldn't her last years have been peaceful? Why had her whole life been such a struggle? He knelt there, steeped in his misery, but when he looked up, it had gotten dark and the full moon was rising.

Now, he moved, and moved with a purpose. He built up a fire in the fireplace and getting his digging tools, headed down the two track road to the huge walnut tree. The tops of the trees lining each side of the road almost met. They created deep pools of darkness where the moonlight failed to penetrate, and with his nervous system still on full alert, he could hear insects and tiny tree frogs as they went about their business. Farther away, there was the whippoorwill and the echo of the owl's hoot. Next to her husband's well-tended grave, he started to dig. He dug like a man fighting fire. He pushed his tired body until the backs of his leg started to hurt. The hurt spread up into his buttocks until every fiber of his body ached. He often stopped to wipe tears until his eyes got gritty at the corners and his stump became sore. Blisters appeared and then broke, their fluid lubricating the handles of the pick and his shovel, but converting mental anguish into physical pain seemed to help somehow.

He carefully kept the sides straight, shaving the red clay downward with the spade. He threw out shovel full after shovel full of the sticky earth with the full moon providing plenty of light, As the eastern sky turned pink in anticipation of the coming day, he started back to the cabin. To a casual observer, he would have appeared elderly as he limped along. The ache in his chest had somewhat dissipated, but he still felt as if he were a character in one of his own dreams.

What could she be buried in? There were no boards to build a coffin. Now his mind seemed to get it's second wind, and in spite of his fatigue, he was thinking clearly again. He remembered the old wagon. Gatlin walked behind the cabin and ran his thumb down the gray weathered Oak sides, relieved that they were still solid. Grabbing the hand tools, he had a servicable burial box built by midmorning despite the deep soreness in his hands.

Walking back inside, he picked Mrs. Williams up, hurriedly wrapped the old Prince Albert coat around her, carried her outside and laid her into the make-shift coffin with a blanket folded underneath. He turned and went inside, washing his face in the wooden piggin. Hearing voices, he looked down the road. The Sapps and their families had arrived as well as a few other neighbors.

CHAPTER 8

Everyone stood in a small group, their faces betraying their despair. They instinctively tried to form a protective formation. Phanta Williams was dearly loved by the community. Death had been no stranger in the Ozarks for the last three years. The spectre of death was usually accompanied by its first cousins, disease and deprivation. As Gatlin opened the door, several people moved in and picked up the makeshift coffin. As they walked out, he picked up the family Bible lying in the corner by her bed. He was not unfamiliar with the Bible, for it had been the only book available when he was taught to read. As the group walked quietly he leafed through it; someone needed to read or say something. As they drew near the grave, he opened the leatherbound volume.

It seemed he was expected to take charge, so he opened the Bible as two green oak stakes were driven in near the grave and frayed ropes tied to them. Gatlin thumbed through the Bible to Ecclesiastes, Chapter 3 and began to read:

"To everything there is a season, and a time to every purpose under the heaven; a time to be born, and a time to die; a time to plant, and a time to pluck up that which is planted; a time to kill, and a time to heal; a time to break down; and a time to build up; a time to weep, and a time to laugh; a time to mourn and a time to dance; a time to cast away stones, and a time to gather stones together, a time to embrace, and a time to refrain from embracing; a time to get, and a time to lose; a time to keep, and a time to cast away; a time to rend and a time to sew; a time to keep silence and a time to speak; a time to love, and a time to hate; a time of war, and a time of peace." He paused, then went on. "She was the nearest thing to family I had."

The rest of the morning was a blur. People shaking hands, the ropes lowering the coffin into the ground, the rattling of the rocky soil as it hit the lid. Even with the neighbors there, he had never felt so alone. It seemed that he had always been alone.

Finally, Gatlin stood at the graveside, everyone gone except the two Sapps. "I ain't part of the Confederate Army no more, but they might need the papers that's in them saddlebags. I wonder where the nearest Secesh army post is?" he said.

Thomas Sapp rubbed his beard with his rough calloused hand. "They's a camp over at Yellville, about 35 or 40 miles west of here. I think they're calling it Camp Adams. There used to be an Indian village there years ago, but the Indians are all gone now."

"What kind of Indians?" Gatlin asked, grateful for the chance to think of something besides death and dying, at least for a little while.

"Shawnees, actually. I think they say they was three Shawnee villages up an down Crooked Creek. Shawnee Town was what they called the one at Yellville. They claim them Indians lived in split Cedar cabins, just like white folks do. Anyway, we'll see you, Gatlin. We've got to go. Now, you listen here, Gatlin." The old man's voice was slow and stern, "That country over around Rapp's Barren is alive with bushwhackers. If you go, you'd better travel at night." With that, the Sapps slowly started down the road.

Late that afternoon, Gatlin walked down into the hidden valley, the soreness in his leg stump and hands causing his walk to be even more jerky than usual. He easily caught the big sorrel gelding and one of the bushwhacker's horses, leaving his old horse to graze out its time in peace. Leading both horses, he eased back up to the cabin.

Any movement requiring a swinging motion of the body was still difficult, but Gatlin had both horses saddled by the time the rich orange colors of the sun had started to fade. He strapped on two of the bushwhackers pistols and picked up his old squirrel rifle, setting it against the cabin, he mounted, holding on to the reins of the sorrel with some difficulty. Then leaning down, he grabbed the squirrel rifle by the barrel and balanced it across the saddle.

It was not difficult to follow the twin tracks of pale dust winding through the hills, and soon the moon started to rise, making vision much easier.

According to the neighbors, he would have to cross both the Norfork and White Rivers as well as numerous small streams along the way. It was difficult balancing the old rifle and controlling the high strung sorrel at the same time, and soon he was having to switch arms to relieve muscle cramps. Evidently the horse had never been led for any distance. Before long he began to catch a glimpse of the silver ribbon of the Norfork as it meandered along, bluffs on one side, and rich bottom land on the other. At this time of year, the river was bank full, but the water was not still dingy from the spring rains. He could make out the flashes of reflected light as large schools of minnows swarmed out of the way as the horses splashed across. He was glad it was still shallow enough for the horses to wade. He had heard of people being drowned by trying to swim a horse that was afraid of water. The water dripping from their sides left dark trails in the sandy gravel as they climbed out on the other side.

Soon he started to pass darkened cabins along the road, and an occasional dog barked, but none of them approached him. Gatlin supposed they had seen much night traffic along this road. He neared the tiny village that had to be Rapps Barren from Mrs. Williams' description. He remembered well the cold winter night she had discribed the surrounding area to him.

"Ever hear of Colonel Orin Dodd?" She had asked.
Gatlin had looked up from his boots he was rubbing with grease, trying to get them to shed snow a little better. "No, can't say that I have."

Mrs. Williams laughed out loud, "You know, I guess us hill people somehow get the idea that all of you flatlanders know each other. Anyways, Colonel Dodd is a rich planter from down by Augusta on the lower White River. A few people here in the hills have got a slave or two, but most hill people have a hard enough time just feeding themselves. But Colonel Dodd , he's got him a whole gob of darkies. He brings them up here to work on a place he bought out by Rapp's Barrens. The slaves love to come up the river on a steamboat to work in their 'mountain home' since the summers were much cooler, and there weren't no skeeters. Now, most of the newcomers have started calling it Mountain Home. You know, I've often wondered what's happened to all those slaves since the war started?

"Well," Gatlin said, "they say a bunch of them ran off and joined the Yankee army. Another bunch joined the Southern army. There was one in the hospital where I was at. He had fought at Pittsburg Landing with the 7th Tennessee, that's Nathan Bedford Forrest's outfit. They asked him why he joined up, and he said same as everybody else - trying to keep the Yankees out of our country. The boys in the hospital said there's thousands of them fighting for the South. Later on, I seen a bunch of them just standing around close to the army camp. They acted like they was lost, didn't know what to do. It was kinda sad."

They spent the rest of the night discussing slavery and whether the system was economical. Gatlin was very interested in Mrs. Williams views on states rights and many other issues, and found that this old lady who had never traveled beyond her beloved hills was surprisingly well-informed.

Gatlin suddenly became aware of an irregular vibration. The stillness of the night amplified it until the ground fairly shook. Without hesitation he jerked the horses off the road into an old orchard, and moved back away from the road. Gatlin dismounted and turned the horses heads away so that the reflection from their eyes couldn't be seen. He had no sooner finished this task and was petting the horses when a dark lump of horses and men thundered by, headed east. Counting on their passage to distract any observers, Gatlin swung into the saddle and rode through the settlement. About a mile out of town he crossed a small stream and turned off into a stand of tall trees. By the time the sun was rising, Gatlin was well concealed, horses unsaddled and grazing, and he himself already deep into an exhausted sleep, pistol in hand. Physically and emotionally drained by the events of the past few days, he slumbered away the hours. Only occasionally did he turn over in the thick green grass, getting up once to relieve himself and drink from the cold waters of the tiny branch. He was glad he had thought to rub himself down with Pennyroyal; otherwise, the ticks and chiggers would have eaten him up.

He awoke with a start. The pistol came up, even as his eyes popped open. There was the sound of slight movement and the hammer came back as he rolled to a sitting position in the strong morning sunlight.

"Sure jumpy, ain't you, Mister?" The boy who spoke sat on a rock about ten feet away, chewing on a weed stem. "Are you in the army? That sure is a big gun."

Gatlin sank down again, his head aching from the sudden awakening. He was weak with relief. The red-haired boy smiled and freckles appeared to move across his face.

"Betch'er hungry. I'm supposed to be watching our cow so them bushwhackers won't steal and eat her. Wanna piece of corn dodger bread, Mister?"

Gatlin gratefully took the hunk of cornbread and wolfed it down. He pulled himself together enough to speak. "What are you going to do if they try to steal your cow, son?"

"Sling rocks at 'em I guess. Mama just said to watch her." The boy's face fairly glowed with the excitement his imagination was creating. He continued," I ain't got no gun. Paw took our'n when he went off to war, but I bet I could shoot yours. I can shoot real good, but I'm also a pretty good rock slinger. I sure am! Do you want me to show you?" He reached around his neck and pulled out a sling.

Gatlin smiled wearily, "No, I don't think so, but I had one of those when I was a kid."

"I kill rabbits for us to eat with this here sling." He talked so fast his words ran together. Gatlin felt himself liking the kid. After all, the boy had handed over what was probably his only meal of the day to a complete stranger without a moment's hesitation. Getting up stiffly and pushing down on his wooden leg, Gatlin started to move toward the saddle. "Why, Mister, you're crippled!" the boy said. "Did you get shot?"

"In a manner of speaking," Gatlin replied as he started to dig through the saddle bags. He came up with one of the pistols, a brass framed .36 calibre Navy, shoved deep into a well worn holster. "Boy, if I give you a gun will you be careful and only use it to protect your family and shoot rabbits?"

The boy's face went from pink to bright red with excitement. "Sure, Mister, I'll be real careful," he said gratefully as Gatlin handed him the pistol,with a flask of FFg powder and a handful of lead balls. "Paw, he showed me how to load one of them new Colt's pistols like this 'un. I even know how to put hog lard over the ends of the balls and everything."

"Now don't you tell anyone I'm here. I'll be gone as soon as it gets dark."

"Sure, Mister, sure," the boy said as he backed away, the weapon and holster held against his chest with both hands. He looked wistfully at Gatlin for a moment, started to speak, then wheeled and ran. In a moment he was out of sight. Gatlin stood there for a long time, wanting to yell at the kid to bring the gun back, knowing he would probably shoot himself with it. Gatlin felt irritated and disgusted with himself. He tightened his jaw muscles, knowing that impulse had caused him to act so foolishly. Normally he wouldn't have even considered turning an untrained kid loose with such a weapon.

It was starting to get dark as Gatlin saddled up and rode out onto the road again. Another moonlit night ride and a river crossing put him into the Confederate encampment at Yellville the next morning, a little after sun-up.

CHAPTER 9

The steam cars rattled along the railroad, the rails swaying back and forth, almost floating in the delta mud. The livestock cars hadn't been cleaned, only slueced out with buckets of water. The sheriff had unlocked and jerked the chain off of him at the last minute, muttering "I'll be danged if I'll let 'em have a good chain at no more reward than I'm gettin' out of the deal." Instead, the deputy had found a piece of heavy sea- grass rope lying outside the jail.

Aaron felt himself being lifted high over the two deputies' heads, both his ankles and legs tied together and his hands secured behind his back. They had to heave to get him through the high door. He had no chance to break his fall as he hit the rough oak floor on his right shoulder and face. He vaguely heard a door clang shut. After a while he came out of a semiconscious state and managed to scoot over where he could brace himself in one corner of the car. He didn't look around at the gray sky. He knew it was there, for he could feel the rain as it hit the slats and was turned into a fine spray that soaked him. There was no way to keep his head up out of the slime with its attendant earthy smell, so he didn't bother to try. The dull ache in his shoulder and the splinter in his cheek slowly brought him fully awake again. All he could do was lie there and wonder. What would happen to him now?

He tried to remember what he had heard about slaves who had tried to escape. He knew that most of the ones who had tried to run had been recaptured. He had seen them a few times passing by on the street. Almost all were chained and thrown into the back of a wagon. Once he had seen one staggering at the end of a rope, the other end held by a man on a horse. He had heard that most of them were sold down the river. They said it was hotter there, unbearably hot. There were sugar cane fields that went on for miles, and the unfortunates who ended up there were starved and worked to death and rarely lived five years. Why had he tried to run? Why couldn't he have just been happy that his life wasn't more miserable than what it was? He wondered briefly about Rit Gatlin and Isaac McCollums. "It don't look like it would've hurt mista' Gatlin to have claimed me as his servant," Aaron thought. "No, it wouldn't have worked, as bad as he hated to admit it, it wouldn't have worked. Gatlin lacked the bearing of anyone wealthy enough to own a slave.

Later, Aaron stood with his head down, trying to let his eyes adjust to the bright daylight. His right eye was almost swollen shut. Ashley had locked him in a little shed by the docks overnight. That was a bad sign. If he had been beaten, he could have returned to his quarters. No, something else was afoot, something worse, much worse. He was hungry and he had to have water. He thought that he would ever crave water again after being soaked to the skin during the long trip back to Little Rock.

"Aaron!"

He looked up, and almost looked Ashley in the eye, then his training took hold and he dropped his gaze.

"Aaron, you know I'll never understand why you wanted to run. I've been good to you boys. I've never beat you, I fed you good, and I just don't understand."

"I jes' wanted to be free, Mista' Ashley, thas' all I wanted, jes' to be free." Almost instantly, Aaron regretted that he had spoken up. He stood, fully expecting Ashley to hit him.

The old man stood for a long moment, "You wouldn't be any freer in the North, Aaron. Most of them Yankees up there work men, women and kids daylight to dark, seven days a week. They all just barely get enough to starve through. Heck! They're worse off than you. At least you know you've got food coming every day and a place to lay your head at night. Them factory workers up north struggle to make it through every day of their lives. What do you think about that, Aaron?"

"But they is free, Mista' Ashley. They gots a choice, I got no choice."

"Choice, my foot!" Obviously irritated at himself for even taking the time to explain himself to a mere slave, the old man tapped his knee with his cane. "Very well, Aaron, I can't keep you here. You might run again. You've been too good of a hand to sell down the river. They's some slave-breakers around here who take runaways like you. In one year they guarantee to break a sassy slave of running or kill him, one or the other, but I'm not going to do that either."

Aaron stood staring at the ground. He said nothing, for there was nothing to say. He was somewhat relieved. At least he wasn't going to the sugar cane fields or or taken to one of the hated slave breakers.

"What I am going to do is, I'm going to sell you to a friend of mine named Dickenson down in Mississippi, in Coahoma County . That's far enough south that you can't never run again. Do you understand me?"

"Ya'sa"

CHAPTER 10

The muddy road that passed through Yellville consisted of two deep ruts. There were several two story clapboard houses on each side of the street, their faded whitewash a testimony to the town's past prosperity. As Gatlin neared the Confederate encampment that sprawled without design on both sides of a small creek, the quality of the buildings deteriorated. There were several hastily thrown up log cabins and rough- sawn board buildings. These housed the whiskey sellers, card sharks and camp followers that always seemed to congregate around army encampments. The characteristic stench of uncovered latrines, greasy wood smoke, rancid grease, and aging horse manure caused Gatlin's nose to twitch as he rode in. The crowded camp itself consisted mainly of lean-to shelters and ragged tents. Several of the tents were stamped U.S., proving once again that the resourceful Confederates were capable of equipping themselves at the expense of the government from which they had removed themselves. Gaunt soldiers carried wood toward cooking fires that were being rekindled from glowing coals, tendrils of smoke already starting to curl skyward. Gatlin rode up to a soldier whom he correctly supposed was a sentry. The soldier was sitting slumped over against an oak stump. He was dressed in butternut-colored lindsey-woolsey. The only presentable thing about him was the well-oiled long rifle resting across his drawn up knees. The guard's bullets were undoubtedly contained in the possum hide bag, tanned with the hair outside, hanging from his belt. Blubbery snores rumbled up from deep in his chest making little whistling noises as they exited his slack mouth.

Gatlin sat and watched for a moment massaging his tired leg, a rare smile lighting up his face. "Atten-hut," he shouted. The sentry jerked awake, jumped up and stood at attention, his rifle properly at his side. Anger, then embarrassment crossed the soldier's long face, he stood there, not knowing what to do. He relaxed when Gatlin asked, "Could I see the Commander of this camp?"

The soldier pointed at a large two-story hewed log building across the creek. "That'd be Colonel Shaler. He stays in Isaac Wilson's hotel."

The slight smile still on his face, Gatlin turned the tired horses and rode the fifty yards or so to the imposing structure. He dismounted, noticing the big sorrel seemed more at ease than Gatlin had ever seen him. Tying both horses to the knotty pine hitching rail, he pulled the McClellan saddle with its heavy saddle bags off the sorrel gelding and threw it over his left shoulder. Leaning to counterbalance the weight, Rit then walked the three stone steps to the door and rapped on it with the muzzle of the squirrel rifle. Instantly, the door was ripped open almost tearing it from it's heavy iron hinges.

A red haired soldier with Sergeant's stripes on the sleeves of his homespun shirt jumped out and yelled, "Didn't I tell"... His voice trailed off as he realized that he was staring face to face with a rank stranger.

"Could I see Colonel Shaler?" Gatlin asked.

The Sergeant stepped aside and motioned him inside. Without another word, he led Gatlin up the narrow stairs and down a long hall to a corner room. He knocked and opened the door, "Someone to see you, sir," he said.

Rit Gatlin lowered the saddle and rifle to the hall floor, then stepped inside. The man at the desk stood up, with a momentary tightening of the lips that sufficed for a smile.

"I'm Colonel Shaler, commander of Camp Adams," he said. "And you are?"

"Rit Gatlin, of company G, 2nd Arkansas Mounted Rifles."

Gatlin reached inside his shirt, pulled out his papers and

handed them over. The colonel sank back in his chair and studied the papers as Gatlin studied him. He saw a tall thin man, gone prematurely gray, whose once elegant uniform had been inexpertly patched and incompletely laundered. The Colonel was obviously tired, with worry lines crossing the corners of his eyes.

After a moment he looked up. "What do you need, Rit Gatlin? Are you wanting to re-enlist?" Again, the almost smile.

"No, sir, we had us a run-in with some bushwhackers."

The Colonel raised one ragged sleeve and motioned to the bunk along one wall. "Have a seat there, Gatlin." Gatlin sank into the bunk gratefully.

Gatlin told Colonel Shaler the details of everything that had happened since his arrival on Bennett's Bayou. The Colonel sat at rapt attention, his eyes never once leaving Gatlin's face.

"You say you brought the horse and saddle?" he asked.

Gatlin nodded.

"Well, bring the saddle in here and let's take a gander at it," the Colonel said.

Gatlin stood up and walked to the door. He caught the jamb with his right hand for balance, swung the saddle inside and laid it on Colonel Shaler's desk. The commander carefully removed the bush-whackers' pistols from the saddle bags and laid them aside. Then he turned the saddle bags upside down and dumped the oilcloth wrapped papers on his desk. He started to pick them up, then stopped and looked up. "Have you eaten, Mr. Gatlin?" he asked.

"No sir," Gatlin replied.

"We don't have much." The Colonel raised his voice. "Sergeant get this man something to eat! Sit down, Mr. Gatlin." The Sergeant appeared with a bowl of stew and coffee.

"Not a great meal. The stew is made from an old milch cow and the coffee was brewed from roasted acorns, but it'll fill you up," the Colonel said as he looked quickly through the papers.

He glanced up at Gatlin. "Have you looked through these?" he asked.

"No sir," Gatlin replied as he ate the hot tasteless stew and sipped at the bitter brew.

"You have done the South a service, Gatlin," the Colonel said. "But it won't make any difference in the final outcome, you know. We've lost the war. From now on we're just prolonging the inevitable. We may have stood a chance before Gettysburg. If we had won there, either France or Prussia might have sided with us. But now that chance is gone. Everyone knows that the South is mostly agricultural. We simply don't have the factories to produce war materiel. Some thought that Britain would help us, but they're wrong, wrong as can be. Them redcoats got no stomach for another fight so soon, they still remember what we gave 'em at New Orleans." His voice dropped, "I've often wondered why Arkansas got into this war anyway. So many men, so many good men gone, their wives and little ones left, so much destruction. It'll take a hundred years to get over it." Shaler stared at the stained puncheon floor; he seemed to have forgotten Gatlin was there.

"There's not enough food, never enough food, not enough horses and guns. When men are fighting they can't work the land, can't grow anything, and it's always too cold or raining, and I'm so tired, so very tired." He pulled himself out of his train of thought and looked back across at Gatlin, "I'm sorry, young man. I drift off at times."

Obviously embarrassed by letting Gatlin see his softer side, he started examining the pistols. "Good guns," he murmured. Shaler then pulled out the new pistol Gatlin had taken from the bushwhacker leader. It seemed so long ago. Had it really only been four days?

"Mr. Gatlin, are you a firearms expert?" Colonel Shaler asked as he pointed the pistol toward the floor and, pulling the hammer back slightly, giving the cylinder a spin with his fingertips. The revolver responded with a smooth whirl of finely fitted parts.

"No, sir, I really don't know a lot about weaponry other than the training I had in the Army."

"Let's go outside, I could do with a breath of fresh air." The

Colonel stood up, pistol in hand, and started down the hall without a backward glance. Gatlin, setting his bowl and cup down on the floor, followed him down the stairs, arriving at the front door just in time to see the Colonel step off the porch. Following him around the corner of the building, Gatlin could see a slab of limestone leaning against a black jack sapling about twenty yards away. The slashes of white on the weathered stone showed its frequent use as a target.

"Observe closely, Mr. Gatlin," the Colonel said as he raised the pistol and started firing. The fresh white chips forming an irregular circle no larger than his hand. He looked down, fiddled with the gun for a moment, and then raised it again. A single dull boom echoed across the little parade ground.

He turned around. "Quite a weapon, Mr. Gatlin, quite a weapon. It's called a LeMat, named after its inventor. It's .42 calibre and fires nine shots, then you swivel the striker on the hammer and it fires a .63 calibre shotgun barrel loaded with buckshot located in the center where the cylinder pin usually is. As I said, it was invented by a doctor by the name of LeMat from New Orleans, but he had them made in Paris, France.(Shaler pronounced Orleans as OR-leens, as Gatlin had heard other hill people do). I've only seen one of these before. General Stewart carries one, as do most of the other generals Those bushwhackers must have taken it from that courier or picked it up on a battlefield. Although I don't know how a yankee could have ended up with such a rare southern weapon."

Shaler turned and walked back toward the building. "I might also mention that General Beauregard also assisted in the development of the LeMat pistol." Gatlin was surprised to find that the brilliant general had also been an inventor. Back inside, Colonel Shaler picked up a bullet mold and cleaning kit, along with a sack of round balls and a powder flask from his desk. He shoved the kit and holstered pistol across the table. "Here, Mr. Gatlin, since the Confederacy can't replace your leg or offer you Army protection, you'd better take this pistol. We will keep the other pistols. The South desperately needs weapons, especially revolvers. There are no standard weapons. Most of my men are armed with guns they brought from home. I'm sure you noticed that most of them are dressed in civilian clothing and parts of Federal uniforms. Some of them showed up without any weapons except home-made bowie knives. At Oak Hills we had to arm them with weapons from our own casualties." The Colonel continued. "You know, Gatlin, they say that the Northern newspapers are already starting to call it The Battle Of Wilson's Creek."

Gatlin picked up the LeMat and he noticed that it was very heavy and seemed to be just a little bit awkward to handle, somewhat out of balance. Holding the hammer back, he pulled the trigger, catching the hammer with his thumb to keep from damaging a nipple. As little as he knew about pistols, he could tell that the pull was hard and the release wasn't crisp enough. However, the fact that it shot ten times without reloading would overshadow any other minor faults.

CHAPTER 11

"Mr. Gatlin, I have been totally honest with you. It is just a matter of time until we are forced out of this post. The Federals have raided the saltpetre caves east of here, twice. Once they capture those caves, the South is liable to have to scrape the bottoms of cow piles to get enough saltpetre to make gunpowder. Them Federals keep sending large patrols deeper and deeper into Arkansas. Many of my men have given up and deserted to go back to their families. Desertion is punishable by death, but I can't bring myself to have a man shot for just wanting to put in a corn crop to keep his family from starvation. When we have to pull out, the Bushwhackers will be worse than they already are, if that is possible. Gatlin, you strike me as a man who is a basically gentle man. I don't know that you have it in you to be a killer. You won against those bushwhackers once, but luck and surprise was on your side. Remember this young man, luck is like a pendulum and it can't be depended on at all. It will always swing the other way. It always seemed to me like it swung more to the bad side than to the good. My advice to you would be to drift, go west, heck, go all the way to Oregon or even California. They say that out there you wouldn't even know there's a war going on. You've got no ties to this country. There's nothing to keep you here. Those bushwhackers you killed will have friends. They'll come back, and if you're lucky, they'll just kill you. They are as expert as Apaches at torture. Face it, Gatlin, you're crippled. You'd be no match for a well prepared enemy."

The Colonel's harsh words cut into Gatlin like a knife. He

hadn't heard it said by someone else out loud before. A cripple. Although he had thought the word many times. Somehow it sounded different when someone else said it. Gatlin felt the familiar dark cloud of depression creep into the recesses of his gut.

He stood up, his face stiff. "Thank you for the advice, sir," he said, his lips a thin line as he picked up the LeMat and buckled it on. Picking up the accompanying gear, he started for the door. He did not look back or say goodbye, and neither did the colonel. This time the red-faced sergeant didn't look up as he walked out. He leaned the long rifle against his horse and swung into the saddle.

Starting east, Gatlin left the camp, turning the Colonel's words over and over in his mind. What should he do? Should he go back to what he already thought of as home or head west into the unknown? There was really nothing to go back to on Bennett's Bayou. The only person he had cared about there was gone forever. Yet he felt pulled back, back to the place where he had known some measure of peace and happiness. "I'm like the former slaves," he thought. "I'm afraid of the unknown, and prefer the familiar things."

As he rode by the rough cabins that surrounded the camp, head down and deep in thought, he saw movement out of the corner of his left eye. As a red-faced, sandy-bearded man staggered out of one of the doors into the street, he grabbed for Gatlin's horse's bridle for balance. Gatlin, stopping his nervous shying horse, looked down at the dull alcohol-induced shine in the man's small piggish eyes. Then in those eyes he saw the dawning realization that here was a stranger, someone to bully, to push around. Then the blue eyes started to gleam in anticipation.

"Watch out where you're a goin' stranger," the man grunted.

Gatlin didn't reply. Pulling the horse aside, he started on. The hatchet-faced drunk grabbed for the horse's bridle again. "What's the matter, are you deef? Looks like ol' Dave Tutt's going to have to teach you a lesson." His right hand started for the large bowie knife set in a crossdraw scabbard on his left side.

Gatlin's mind shifted from deep study to survival. With no

forethought, he changed his grip on the squirrel rifle lying across the saddle, jerking the buttback hard against his thigh. The long barrel swiveled in a short arc contacting Tutt's head just in front of and above his right ear, the impact making no more sound than the snap of a man's fingers. Tutt's mouth flew open as a wad of brown chewing tobacco was launched from between his yellowing tusks. His eyes fluttered and he dropped straight down on his knees, stayed there just a moment, looking for all the world like a man praying, then fell soundlessly sideways into the mud. Gatlin, looking down, was amazed, as always, that violence could erupt so quickly. Suddenly he sensed movement and swung the rifle back to the left, thumbing the hammer back to full cock. Two men who had started to rush out into the street stood frozen in half-running position.

After a few seconds of silence one of them spoke. "We ain't armed, but you done knocked ol' Dave colder'n a wedge and he'll kill you for it when he comes to. Iff'n I was you I'd light a shuck out of here. He's done killed two men already. He's the toughest man in town."

Gatlin glanced up and down the street. "Looks to me like a mighty small town. A one-eyed yellow tomcat looks mighty big 'til a bulldog shows up. Your friend Dave had better lick his flint before he makes another razzia at a rank stranger." Now that the danger was past, nervous reaction was setting in. Gatlin's voice sounded tight to his own ears. "Now you tell ol' Dave that if he comes after me again, I'll whup him 'til he runs rabbits. Now get back inside before I salivate the both of you."

The men scrambled over each other, trying to get back through the door. As Gatlin rode away, he glanced back over his shoulder. Colonel Shaler, standing on the hotel's second floor balcony, raised his hand in a slow salute. Gatlin pushed the horse into a fast walk to put as many miles between himself and trouble as possible.

The sun set over his shoulder as he rode on toward home. Glancing down he noticed that the impact of the rifle barrel had jarred the front sight out of it's dovetail. Without a doubt it lay back in the street, ready to be stomped down into the mud.

Author's Notes:

Saltpetre is potassium nitrate. Along with sulfur and charcoal it is used to make black powder.

Dave Tutt was shot and killed in a gunfight on the town square of Springfield, Mo., July 20, 1865 by James Butler (Wild Bill) Hickok.

CHAPTER 12

Dave Tutt sat on a split log bench, eyes closed, his injured head cradled in both palms, his elbows resting on the rough split-oak table. A chipped cup half full of whiskey sat in front of him. Tutt was aware that the circle of admirers that usually surrounded him had mysteriously disappeared. For the past year, they had watched him bully his way around the town of Yellville and the army camp. Most people presumed that he was tough because he talked a good game. They hadn't noticed that he carefully chose his fights, and that the two men he had killed were both drunk and unaware they were in a real fight until it was too late. He had always hinted about other fights and other men killed in other places. As soon as his head quit hurting he was going to track that stranger down and kill him, he told himself. Nobody crossed Dave Tutt and lived. Yessir, he'd teach him not to mess with ol' Dave Tutt. He was totally engrossed in his pain and his plans to get even. Then Tutt became aware that someone sat down across the table from him. He slowly raised his head and found himself staring into the pale blue eyes of a stranger dressed completely in home-spun clothes. "Who was that man that warped you, and where was he from?" The voice was low, yet there was an underlying note of menace.

"Get lost! I don't know what you're talking about," Tutt growled.

"Very well. Never argue with a man who knows his own mind. That was one of my mama's favorite sayings," the stranger said coldly as he walked out the door without looking back.

After several hours of soaking down the rotgut, Dave Tutt stood up and the bartender met his eye, hoping for payment. Instead Tutt's flat glare told him that the subject was better left to another time. "Oh, well, he'll be back and I'll collect then," thought the bartender. He busied himself wiping the few glass whiskey bottles behind the bar, trying to keep the shake out of his hand. He was afraid of Tutt and he didn't like the feeling.

It was fully dark as Tutt stumbled drunkenly along the board sidewalk toward his shack. The few passers-by moved away, having heard of his encounter with the stranger, rightly expecting that his mood would be murderous. Suddenly, he was slammed against a rough board wall. Tutt made a grab for his knife and felt it lightly plucked from his hand. As he was spun around, the hand at his throat effectively shutting off his wind, he felt something cold move up his right nostril.

"One move and you'll split your nose plumb through to the eyeball." The voice was low and casual. "You know you really need to be taught some proper manners. My mama always said that good manners could hide poor breeding."

Tutt felt a queer looseness in his gut. He had no doubt as to who the shadowy figure was. The cheap whiskey went cold in his stomach. He was sure he going to throw up. Why hadn't he just answered the man's questions?

"Now, had you ever seen that man who gunwhipped you, that is, before today?" Tutt started to shake his head and even that slight movement caused a trickle of blood to roll out of his nose and start down his lip. He could taste the metallic saltiness of his own blood, and now cold sober, realized that he was a dead man.

"No, sir," he said. "One of my friends told me that that feller was part of that bunch that settled over east of here on the other side of the North Fork River."

The man in homespun lifted up the corners of his mouth at the "sir" coming out of the mouth of the same man who a few hours earlier had dismissed him with contempt. "I think I'd better cut your throat, Mr. Tutt. I don't want to have to watch my back from now on. You pretty much look like a backshooter to me."

Tutt blubbered protests as the stranger stepped back, put his hands across his face. Then the stranger gestured down the street with the blade and Tutt ran. He ran expecting a bullet in the back, as he had never run before, and he didn't stop running until he jerked open the plank door and stumbled into the shack. He stood for a moment, then fell to his knees on the filthy dirt floor, the whiskey and what little food he had consumed splattering down his shirt, the sour rancid smell filling the room. He reached up on a shelf and grabbed the bottle. Taking a long drink, he sank down on the rope cot. Every day for the rest of his life he would remember the slight pressure, so deadly, inside his nose.

The stranger in homespuns rode out the other side of town headed east. His head was held high, eyes straight ahead, missing nothing.

Gatlin tried to dismiss the incident with Tutt from his mind as he rode. The colors slowly faded into black and white as the darkness started to crawl up out of the steep hollows and rise toward the hilltops. As Gatlin rode, carefully watching the darker places, a three quarter moon started to rise in front of him. Long wisps of cloud periodically cut it into slices as they sailed past. Gatlin was grateful for the moonlight, but he knew full well that nightriders of all kinds would be out. It was with a certain amount of relief that he eased into the woods near Rapp's Barren again to rest away the daylight hours. As the sun set again, he awoke and drank deeply from the small spring in the edge of his hideaway.

He then filled the army canteen with the ragged canvas cover. He wondered about the boy to whom he had given the pistol. It was an impulsive act and he deeply regretted it. But, on the other hand, a woman and a boy unarmed would have no chance against even one armed bushwhacker. At least the boy had appeared competent and maybe the pistol would increase their odds of surviving the war. There was no sense wasting effort thinking about it, for he would never know how it turned out anyway.

Gatlin considered himself to be, above all things, a realist. He knew that the behavior of a certain percentage of mankind was only kept in check by the physical presence of the law. As soon as the fear of punishment or reprisal was removed by war or some type of disaster, people quickly turned against their fellow man. It then became the law of the jungle, the strong and ruthless preying on the weak, helpless or unprotected. Dave Tutt and others like him percieved manners or attempts to be polite as weakness. In times like these the thin veneer of civilized behavior peeled off as if it had never existed, and the human predators became so calloused to the sights and smells of violence that they became even more cruel and ruthless. Gatlin recognized in himself this tendency. He spent no time thinking about the men he had killed. They had given no mercy and therefore received none. Then he whacked Dave Tutt as casually as swatting a fly. But Gatlin also realized that a certain amount of this ruthlessness increased his chances of survival, and survive he would. He felt determination flow into him. He would live on the bayou and take care of Mrs. Williams' place until her other boy returned, if he ever did. John B. needed to know what had happened to his family. Gatlin also realized one important difference between himself and Tutt. He had been forced into violence; Tutt had chosen the path of violence, and liked being feared. Gatlin was sure that he carefully cultivated his reputation for being a tough. He would continue to push people until one pushed back, and only then he would be forced to change or perish. Gatlin was sure how Tutt would choose, since change was not part of Tutt's makeup.

The tired horse didn't want to walk fast. Gatlin was tired and hungry himself, so he didn't push him. After riding all night, it was well after sun up when he started up the trail toward the little cabin. He came alert with a jerk. He had dozed off and started to slide out of the saddle. Raising his red rimmed eyes, he could see what appeared to be smoke. As he topped a rise he could see two thin columns of black smoke rising straight up in the calm heavy air of carly morning. Was it his cabin? No, it was too far off to the left. Without hesitation he headed toward it. He hurried the horse and raising the frizzen with his thumb, glanced down to make sure the priming of the old squirrel rifle was still in place. He unsnapped the holster flap of the LeMat, lifted it, then slid it back.

He felt his muscles start to tighten, and a vein began to throb in his temple as he rode. Now he could smell wood smoke with enough other smells mixed to remind him of the trash fires around the waterfront in Little Rock. As he rode around a bend in the trail, he could see the wreck of what had been a homestead.

Gatlin rode cautiously closer. Debris was scattered everywhere. The bushwhackers, and he didn't doubt for a moment that it was bushwhackers, had totally emptied the cabin, searching for valuables before they fired it. He stopped the horse, keeping his eyes on the surrounding fields and woods to avoid ambush.

Hearing what sounded like a groan, he started forward again. He drew the LeMat pistol, transferring it to his left hand and letting the forearm of the squirrel rifle rest on his left wrist. There was no other sound. His imagination must have been working too well, perhaps a sign of the mental deterioration he feared. He had heard of men who spent all their time alone finally going stark raving mad. He slid the LeMat back into the button-down holster, then dismounted. The muscles in his thigh started to cramp and he stood kneading them with his right hand. He felt the cold fury rise within him again. He started to shake, reacting physically to his anger. For here a whole family's dreams and hopes lay shattered. Everything they had worked, sweated, scrimped and saved for, was burned, scattered or stolen by these human predators. No, they were not predators, they were buzzards, scavengers gathered to feed on what honest folks had earned by their sweat and blood. The now familiar urge to kill grew within him. He could shoot them all without blinking an eye. But what about the people who lived here? Had they been killed or carried off? As Gatlin started to walk toward the smoldering fire, he heard the faint sound again, almost obscured by the popping sounds of smoldering wood. Moving quickly toward it, he saw a man lying behind an overturned bed, half hidden by the torn feather mattresses. Gatlin limped toward him, laying the squirrel rifle down as he awkwardly bent over the wounded man. Gatlin remembered him from Mrs. Williams' burial. Everyone called him Levi, Levi Casey. The young man's whole shirt front was soaked with fresh blood, one coating of viscious liquid over another layer, starting to dry and turn black. The fear and anger heightened his perception, flooded his brain with sounds and smells. He could hear the dull buzz of dozens of blow flies as they almost covered Casey. The metallic smell of blood and powder smoke crawled up his nostrils, blending with the overwhelming odor of wood burning.

Casey's face was waxy looking. He wasn't moving. His eyes were closed. Maybe he was dead after all. As Gatlin started to straighten up, he heard another groan, then Casey said, "Woman, kid, got to get up."

Gatlin remembered Casey's having a wife and young son. "It's all right, Casey, I'll get water," he said.

Trying to run, Gatlin almost fell in his haste to jerk the canteen from his saddle. As he lowered himself beside Casey again he heard a slow exhalation of breath. He grabbed Casey and started to yell, "No, you'll be all right. I'll help you." He felt a sinking feeling in his gut.

Levi Casey, the young man with an open contented expression, was dead. Gatlin slowly straightened up. Was anything going to survive this senseless war? Yes, evil would survive, evil and the perpetrators of it always seemed to survive, as the innocent were slaughtered.

CHAPTER 13

Gatlin was positive that there was no hope of finding Casey's wife and kid alive. He had a vague impression of Casey's wife, a tall, slim young woman with the high cheekbones characteristic of Indian heritage. Her long auburn hair matched that of their son who appeared to be about four or five years old. Now there seemed no doubt that they had been murdered, or worse, by the bushwhackers. The only consolation was that Casey would not suffer the mental anguish of wondering. But Gatlin was already starting to learn to wall off his emotions, to put his feelings on hold in order to get on with the business at hand. The most pressing business right now was to give Casey a decent burial. Gatlin thought about hauling him to the family cemetery where he had buried Phanta Williams. He finally decided that Casey would rather be buried near his own home.

Now he had to find digging tools that hadn't been carried off. It was either that or go to the cabin to bring back the tools he had hidden. He hoped that he hadn't been burnt out in the few days he had been gone.

Gatlin led his horse close to Casey's body and bent over to try to hoist him across the horse's back. Out of the corner of his eye he saw a blur of movement. Throwing up his arm he tried to turn and his instinctive action saved him from being brained with a piece of split oak. As it was, he lost his balance and went to his knees, his arm numb from the blow. Recovering his balance, his hand going to the pistol, he both heard and saw his fleeing assailant at the same time. The little boy was running toward the field, his wail of anguish and fear undulating in the still air behind him. Gatlin's pain and surprise were forgotten in a rush of compassion. He yelled, "It's all right," starting to run awkwardly after him.

The boy ran about 30 yards then dropped from view in the tall grass. Gatlin followed cautiously. The kid might have other defensive surprises in store. But as he drew closer he could hear the unmistakable sounds of a child crying for its mother.

A horse was lying still, it's bare belly turned toward him, legs stretched out as if still trying to run.

The little boy's head was visible above the horse's side as Gatlin moved closer. Gatlin walked around the horse, and stood looking down at the boy and his mother. He could imagine what had happened. Levi Casey had tried to make a stand, to defend his family, no doubt against overwhelming odds. His wife, seeing her husband shot, had grabbed the plow horse and tried to get away. The large calibre bullet hole in the side of the horse's head told the rest of the story. The killers had wanted the woman bad enough to shoot a good horse to keep her from escaping. The boy was probably thrown clear as the horse fell, but the woman had not been so lucky.

Gatlin reached down and pulled the now unresisting, wiry little fellow to him. The boy responded as if he now realized that he was a friend. His eyes closed as Gatlin knelt down and gathered him into his arms, making reassuring sounds. He sagged against Gatlin's body like a limp dishrag, all the fight gone out of him. The boy had probably been here all night alone. Gatlin could imagine the terror and sheer isolation he felt, because he had often felt something similar when he was a kid. He had often wanted to be held, to feel shelter and safety and love, if only for a little while. But after his own parents were gone there had been no such comfort. As he knelt there, all the memories came back, a few pleasant, many not so pleasant. Gatlin felt the child grow more relaxed and realized that the little boy had fallen into an exhausted sleep.

Gatlin carefully braced his good knee into the dead horses side and slowly stood up, laying the worn out boy across his shoulder. He could feel the muscles in his lower back pull and knot as they tried to compensate for the non-existent lower leg muscles. He would lay him in the shade while he attended to the buryings, hoping that he wouldn't wake up and run away.

Gatlin laid the small form down on to the thick dark green carpet of moss under a large oak tree and returned to his horse. He would try to pull the dead horse off the woman's leg, freeing her body. His eyes kept returning to the long view, searching the tree line for any sign of enemies. He reached down and gripped the handle of the pistol, gaining some small amount of solace from the fact that he could, at least, still defend himself and the child. He led his horse through the debris. The bushwhackers hadn't left much of value, and what they hadn't carried off, they had destroyed.

As he led his horse past the oak tree, he found the boy still sound asleep, curled up into a tight ball. His own mount started dancing sideways as he led him closer to the dead horse, but calmed down as he jerked down hard on the bridle and started talking quietly to him. The rope halter appeared to be stout enough to stand the dead weight of the dead horse as he pulled it off the woman's body. Hooking up the rope, Gatlin moved around the dead horse. As he moved, he happened to glance down at her, something he had avoided doing up to this point. It just didn't seem decent somehow, staring at a dead woman. He had never been around women much. The few that lived around the waterfront were ragged pathetic creatures, mostly prostitutes and petty thieves, and except for Isaac's mother, he had managed to avoid much contact with them. Phanta Williams had seemed more like a mother to him, and their conversation had centered mostly around the things they had to do to survive.

Now that Gatlin looked down at her he couldn't seem to look away. Casey's wife had been a beautiful young woman, no doubt about it. He forced himself back to the business at hand. Before he lost his leg he had dreamed of a woman like this and kids, but now, now it would never be. At least Levi Casey had lived the dream for a little while. Having only met Casey once, Gatlin didn't know if he had appreciated his family or not. For all Gatlin knew, he might have

been a lazy, good for nothing wife-beater. But Gatlin didn't think so. The place showed signs of being neat and well kept, and Gatlin had the impression that here had lived a happy
hard working family.

As he bent over to finish securing the rope, he noticed that the bluish swelling in her right temple was the only obvious mark on her body, although she was dirty from the fall that had left her leg pinned beneath the dead horse. Gatlin suddenly stopped his knot tying; there, there in her neck was a movement!

CHAPTER 14

As Gatlin looked away for a moment, a cold chill shot across his skin surface as if he had been drenched with cold rain. Yet he could have sworn there was movement there. His heart racing, he slowly bent over, forming a V of his forefingers and thumb. He slid his hand beneath her chin and touched her neck. Yes, it was there all right, a faint slow heartbeat. Her skin was hot and dry to the touch. He straightened up and started jerking frantically on the bridle to reposition his horse.

He had to tighten the rope in such a way that the weight of the dead horse was pulled up and away from the injured woman. As he nudged his horse forward, the dead horse's head doubled back, lifting it. If the rope broke or the carcass slid, she would surely be crushed! Gatlin moved as quickly as he could, grabbing the limp woman under the arms and jerking her backward. She came loose much easier that he had expected, causing him to fall backward. Embarrassed at himself, he quickly got up and loosened his horse, then turned his attention back to Mrs. Casey.

After long hesitation, Gatlin gingerly felt her leg. It didn't seem to be broken, but was badly swollen and bruised black. He wondered if gangrene had already set in. He again felt her throat. It was still there, the slow regular movement. Gatlin then felt the hard knot in her right temple. He had no medical training at all, but had seen plenty of men get hurt on the docks. Being a keen interested observer, he had learned quite a bit. Most people were forced to do their own doctoring because doctors were scarce even in a city such as Little Rock. The few doctors who practiced there weren't too crazy about venturing into the rough river dock area. Gatlin knew that a mushy feeling knot often was the sign of a cracked skull, which usually meant a slow lingering death. Even those who lived were often affected mentally by their injury. He was relieved that she had no deep cuts. He didn't know a lot about blood poisoning, just that a wound had to be kept clean, otherwise the crawling red streaks would start to move out from the wound. If the limb wasn't amputated immediately, as it had been in his case, a miserable death was sure to follow.

Gatlin straightened up, remembering the sleeping boy. He walked over to the spreading red oak tree and stood looking down. He exhaled a breath of relief since the boy was still in a deep exhausted sleep. The thick moss beneath the tree acted as a cool mattress. He looked up. The sun was already past its zenith. He had already decided that they were going to stay here for a while. He felt uneasy; he had no idea how he would defend them if the bushwhackers returned. Here he was, caught in the open with a badly injured woman and a helpless kid. He felt of his sore arm. Well, maybe the little boy wasn't so helpless, but he would require care, nevertheless.

He started back toward the woman but he was unable to resist bending over to pick up a big black leather-bound family Bible which had been lying open, its pages making a soft fluttering sound as they slowly turned in the breeze. He glanced inside the front cover. There were their names, Levi and Sarah Casey, Married July 24, 1857, in Crossville, Tennessee. Just below was listed the son, Samuel Timothy, born June 3, 1858. So that was her name. Sarah. He said it over to himself several times. He closed the heavy book and started back to Mrs. Casey. No, he would think of her as Sarah from now on. As he walked, he found a feather bed wadded into a dirty lumpy heap near one corner of the ruined cabin. He was thankful that they had thrown everything outside before they fired it.

He tried not to think of the bushwhackers who had done this. They had come unwanted and uninvited into the lives of honest hard working people who were minding their own business and had totally devastated their lives. But, once again he felt the return of the hatred, felt the strength from it flow into his arms. He clenched his fists. They would pay, they would pay a thousand times over.

Gatlin wadded the feather bed into his arms and trying to keep from falling, walked back to Sarah Casey. Spreading it out, he managed to drag her onto it and tie the rope to one corner. Soon, he had her lying beside her son beneath the Oaks. Now he had to take stock of the situation. These people had to have food and water. He wondered how he would get anything down the unconscious woman without choking her. Walking around, Gatlin managed to find two large spoons, scorched, but still useable and a cast iron dutch oven that still had its lid. He was surprised that the bushwhackers hadn't carried it off. He took the battered canteen off the saddle and started to walk in a big circle. He needed to hurry. His stump was starting to ache, and he was beginning to tire. There had to be water near. He soon found it, below a well-used trail running down hill from the cabin. He lifted the LeMat from its' holster again. It made him feel more secure hearing the sound of smooth metal against well-oiled leather. There might be someone at the spring, only about 75 yards from the house. Casey had built his house far enough away from the spring so that wild animals could still come and use it. He had also built a rock wall around the spring forming a pool from which Gatlin filled the canteen and Dutch oven. Back near the cabin, and slightly off the trail, Gatlin could see the flat top of what most people called a root cellar. It was well made of dry-laid limestone rock, and covered over with a thin piece of ledge rock. In the cool, certain vegetables stored this way would keep well until the next year's crop came in. Gatlin leaned over and pushed the lid back. He smiled to himself. Here were potatoes, turnips and a few sweet potatoes. They were wrinkled and the potatoes had started growing white sprouts and turning green, but they looked beautiful to him.

He quickly filled his shirt tail with vegetables. Then, carrying his canteen and Dutch oven in his left hand, he hurried back to the oak tree. There he found both of his patients still quiet.

He had entertained the hope that the woman would wake up while he was at the spring. Trying not to think of just how bad she might be, he set about digging a small hole down through the moss to the solid bedrock below. With his knife he enlarged it until it would hold the pot. As he worked, he considered cutting some meat from the Casey's dead horse, but not knowing how long it had been dead, he decided against it.

Filling the hole with dead wood, he lit it with a smoldering chunk from the burned cabin. He quickly pared the vegetables into the Dutch oven. As the fire died down to glowing coals, he set the Dutch oven down into the hole and using a flat board scooped more coals onto the lid, which had a raised rim around it for just such a purpose.

After he finished, Gatlin walked back and forth through the debris. Finally he found a worn shovel with the handle nearly burned off, and a long piece of steel that appeared to have been part of a buggy axle at one time. He alternately pulled on Levi Casey's body and rested. His stump started to get sore. He was soon soaking wet with sweat from head to toe. Finally he managed to get the body into a flat area where the soil was sure to be deeper and less rocky. He had it to do, so he started to dig, first tearing the soil loose with the buggy axle then shoveling it out. The sun was starting to set by the time he got Casey buried. In spite of his exhaustion, Gatlin found a piece of hand riven shingle and burned Casey's name and the year into the wood with the tip of the heated shovel.

He wished he could think of something else to write, but couldn't. He split a piece of paling part of the way down, inserted the shingle, then used the shovel to drive it into the soft ground of the grave. "That'll have to do. I'm not even real sure of the date," he said out loud. He stood and looked down at the grave a moment. "I'll do the best I can," he said. "If I only knew what to do." He started back up toward the big red oak.

CHAPTER 15

Rit Gatlin walked back to the tree. Wearily he sat down, leaned back against the tree trunk, and unstrapped his wooden leg. As he sat massaging the sore stump, he realized just how tired he was. He had no idea what to do next, so he sat there watching Sarah Casey and her son, one unconscious, the other peacefully sleeping. He picked up the family Bible and opened it again. He looked to make sure and beneath the marriage record it was listed: Samuel Timothy Casey, born June 3, 1858. He idly started to turn the pages of the Bible. His eye caught a verse in the left hand column, "... and God saw that the wickedness of man was great in the earth, and that every imagination of the thoughts of his heart was only evil continually." It seemed that that was so, even today, Gatlin thought. He lay back in the cool moss. He would stretch out for a few minutes while the soup cooked. Soon there were three sleepers beneath the oak. The sun kept moving and the natural light started to dim. Soon the numerous tiny night creatures that live on the fringes of man's existence, some, in fact, dependent on him, returned to their nightly routines. They were all unmindful of the fading echoes of violence that so often followed this fellow creature, man.

Gatlin's mind snapped to full alertness. His sharp survival instincts had risen closer to the surface and been honed to a razor's edge by the events of the past few weeks. He had become much more aware of his surroundings. Colors were much more vivid. There was a higher contrast between objects and their surroundings, and his hearing seemed more acute. His hand had already pulled the

LeMat pistol from the holster as he stiffly sat up. Already his left hand was strapping the wooden leg back on. He guessed he had slept several hours. That worried him. What if someone had walked in on them while he was asleep? He felt vaguely ashamed and resolved not to allow it to happen again. He moved to the small fire, and threw a few more sticks on the coals, sure the soup would be done by now.

As the fire started to catch on, he saw Sarah Casey with her son lying asleep beside her. Suddenly goose bumps rippled across his body. There was something moving just beyond the firelight. Not quite a shadow, more a form, no, a mere suggestion of a form, but it was there, all right. He had the feeling it was circling. Gatlin jerked on the wooden leg, wincing as it slid across his sore skin. Then he stood up, pistol in hand, and kept turning, trying to draw a bead on whatever it was. It could be a wolf, or a mountain lion, but both of those generally fought shy of man. He thought he could barely hear a low rumbling growl. Maybe a few more sticks on the fire would help. He holstered the pistol leaving the flap open, then bent over to pick up the sticks. Gatlin knew better, but he looked into the fire as he fed it, losing his night vision.

As the realization of this fatal error hit him, Gatlin stepped back, the pistol coming easily into his hand. Hearing a rustle behind him, he whirled, thumbing the LeMat to full cock. Snatching a brand from the fire in his left hand, he held it up high. A boy could be seen in the gloom, both arms wrapped around the big brindle dog, his face buried in its coarse hair. It was a huge, ugly beast, showing evidence of both Pit Bull dog and Shepherd ancestry. Its heavy jaw muscles made twin bulges that met as a deep crease on top of his head. The scars on his face and neck gave evidence of previous encounters. Slowly lowering the gun, Gatlin took a step toward them. As the dog turned and faced him, its eyes glowing red in the firelight, the black lips slid back to reveal two perfect rows of gleaming ivory. A low rumble reached Gatlin's ears. The boy moved, and as the dog turned and licked the boy's face, Gatlin could clearly see both the entrance and exit wounds in the loose skin beneath his neck. So, another member of the family had survived the attack, he thought.

Gatlin reached down and pulled the Dutch oven from the fire. Both boy and dog watched him, missing nothing. He set the pot down and carefully lifted the lid. "You hungry, boy?" He quickly corrected himself, "You hungry, Sam?"

Gatlin could tell by the boy's reaction that he had used the right name. He had guessed that the Caseys wouldn't have called him Timothy. He handed the boy the big spoon, the dog's glowing eyes following his every move with suspicion. Here was a dog that had been betrayed, shot by members of a species he trusted. He would not soon forget it. The boy started to eat, quickly and noisily, his fist wrapped around the spoon handle. Gatlin sat and watched him. The boy had doubtless seen everything that happened during the bushwhacker raid. If he hadn't seen his dad shot, he had seen him soon afterward. He had watched his home burn down, along with anything that might have been his. Gatlin could sense puzzlement and suffering in the boy's eyes. He knew the child was acquainted with death. Death was no stranger to the children of the frontier, especially during this time of war.

"Sam," he said quietly, "Sam, you know your pa's gone." He couldn't bring himself to say the word dead. Dead sounded so short, such a brutal word, so final. He continued, "Your pa's gone and your mama's bad hurt. I'll try to help her, but you'll have to help out. Will you do that?" The boy continued to eat, his eyes fixed on Gatlin. The eyes had a flat look. Gatlin could only imagine the confused pain that must dwell behind them. "Will you help me Sam? Those bad men may come back."

The boy ate another three bites then slowly nodded his head. Gatlin slowly sat down and watched the black of the night creep toward gray. Then came the various pinks that lightened until they became the reds of the coming day.

When he looked around again both boy and dog were asleep, but the dog's eyes flew open as he shifted position.

Gatlin heard a low moan and twisted further to his left. Sarah

Casey was lying on her back, eyes open, her head thrashing violently from side to side. He grabbed the canteen and moved quickly to her side. The moan came from between her clenched teeth. He sat down and raised her up, supporting her back with his good knee. He knew she had been without water for at least eighteen hours. She stopped thrashing as he gently tipped the canteen into her mouth. At first the water ran out of her slack mouth, then she started to drink eagerly, pushing at the canteen.

"Easy, easy, now."

Gatlin hoped to keep her calm as he continued to give her tiny sips of the water. Her eyes stared straight ahead, a curious faraway blank look in them. When Gatlin judged she had drunk enough, he lowered her carefully to the ground again. As he raised up, he became aware of the boy and dog standing very close behind him.

"It's okay," he said, "Your mama is hurt real bad, but we need to try and get her to eat."

He got the Dutch oven and the other spoon. Resuming his position, he started to feed Mrs. Casey. As with the water, at first the soup spilled out of her mouth and dribbled down her chin. Gatlin was careful to only feed her the broth, so as not to choke her. Then he tried a few small bits of potato and she started to chew. But still there was no change of expression. He fed her about a cup of soup, lowered her and set the pot back near the fire. Her eyes closed and she appeared to be unconscious again. At least she had come to. Some people died from head injuries without ever waking up. He had seen it happen on the docks. Now for shelter before the next summer thunderstorm.

CHAPTER 16

Gatlin knew he had to make a move. Their position was too exposed to both the extremely changeable weather of the Ozarks and the unpredictable raids of the bushwhackers. He was sure there were several bands of them still in the area. Now that Sarah Casey was, he hoped, able to sit a horse, he would move back to the Williams' cabin. He was anxious to know if the cabin had been burnt. The garden he had planted needed tending. The Casey's dead horse was beginning to smell, and he knew that over the next few days it would worsen until it fairly saturated the air around the ruined homestead.

Gatlin turned to the boy. "Sam," he said, "we've got to leave here, we've got to go to my place. Do you understand?"

The little boy looked up at him, still not speaking, but Gatlin was sure that he understood. His mind made up, he started to look for anything that would be useful to them. There wasn't much that wasn't burnt, but he found another feather bed and some homespun clothes for both the woman and boy. He thought about trying to drag the feather bed with Sarah Casey behind the horse, but soon decided it was too risky. The horse might spook. He led the animal over to where she lay. Bending over, he braced himself and lifted her up, finding that she was surprisingly light as he set her astraddle of the horse. Her eyes were open again, but she didn't react at all.

Wadding up the feather bed he laid it across the saddle in front of her. Motioning to the boy, he swung him up behind his mother. The big bulldog seemed to be getting used to him, and had stopped growling, now only watching Gatlin suspiciously. "Hold on to your mother, Sam," he cautioned, "And don't let her fall."

Gatlin fed them all from the last of the soup and filled the Dutch oven with vegetables from the root cellar. He carried it along with the squirrel rifle in his left hand as he urged the horse along, leaning his right hand on it's neck. The four miles were slow, the only sound being the rhythmic squeaking sounds of the saddle and the regular steps of the horse broken by the harsh sounds of his own labored breathing. The woman sat the horse loose-jointed but still able to keep her balance. Gatlin had to stop and rest. He stood for a few moments watching a red-tailed hawk cruising low to the ground. The raptor's tail twisted, controlling his turns as he expertly skimmed the buffalo grass, his head turning from side to side. As Gatlin shaded his eyes with his hand to get a better look, the hawk dropped into the foliage. There was a brief flurry of movement. The bird dropped his head, and then raised it, his hooked beak covered with rabbit fur.

The little boy rode with his arms around his mother's waist, his cheek resting against her back. His eyes looked large in his soot-smeared face. The dog walked behind and off to the side, watching, missing nothing.

* * *

The next afternoon, the man in homespuns stood and read the grave marker out loud. "So, you're dead, are you?" He walked over to the horse and pulled out a heavy Bible. Opening it to Joshua 7:21, he read about Achan's family being distroyed because of his sin: "As the avenger of blood I am obliged to kill them all." He realized that he was starting to talk out loud to himself more and more. It had been nearly six years since he had trailed the Caseys to Memphis. He had stood well back and watched the KATE KIRKWOOD as it pulled away from the dock and chuffed it's way downstream, twin stacks billowing white smoke. He then decided to catch the next boat out and be right behind them when they arrived in the White River country. There he would do what he had been sent to do, then head back into the Clinch mountains. He was positive that the thief from the waterfront would be too scared to tell anyone of their encounter. He had considered cutting the scummy rascal's throat, but ridding the Memphis waterfront of human trash was not his mission. He was sure that his family would frown on such actions if they ever found out.

Leaving the docks he had walked casually into a waterfront tavern, his plan was to listen for gossip of the White River. He noticed the barmaid eyeing him curiously as he moved up to the bar.

"What'll it be, stranger?" she said, her painted mouth stretching into some semblance of a smile, her eyes studying him coldly. Ordering a beer, he took a sip of it, while the bar maid lingered. "Not from around here are you?" she asked.

The man in homespuns was somewhat flattered by her interest. He had never considered himself an attractive man. In fact it was very unusual for a woman to pay him any mind at all. "I'm from the Clinch mountains, Ma'am," he replied. He half-wished she would leave, but found himself hoping she would stay. She chattered on as he sipped his beer. Not a drinker of store- boughten beer, he nevertheless thought the brew tasted uncommonly bitter. He found himself answering her questions as briefly as possible. Besides, he wasn't feeling well. He started to sweat. He felt dizzy and a little sick at his stomach. He hadn't realized he was all that tired. He started to feel an overwhelming urge to sleep, and although he fought hard to stay conscious, his head started to nod. His eyes closed, then bounced open as he noticed that the bar maid's smile had disappeared and she was watching him intently. The last thing he remembered was her mocking laugh as he felt himself falling from the chair.

She quickly bent down beside him, the concerned expression firmly in place for all to see. The bartender walked down to the end of the bar, wiping his hands on a dingy towel. A few patrons had looked up, vaguely interested in the proceedings. The bartender reached down and got the man under the arms and started dragging him toward the back door.

The barmaid reached over beside the bar and picked up his trappings. The whole operation was neatly and quickly done.

"Just had one too many, folks. We'll just put him in the back room to sleep it off. You all know how these back country men are. They got grit in their gizzards when it comes to fightin', but one whiff of anything but corn likker and they're out like a light." A few customers chuckled as the clink of glasses and the slap of cards resumed.

When the the man in homespuns awoke, he noticed a peculiar rocking motion to the bunk on which he was lying. As he had started to raise up, the movement of his right arm was abruptly halted. Looking down, he saw a short length of chain fastened from his wrist to an eyebolt in a timber attached to the wooden wall. Turning he could see that the wall curved inward at the bottom. He spent the next five years in enforced labor aboard the freighter JOHN D. PHELPS.

When the time finally came, the lights of New Orleans were shining across the harbor as he slipped over the side, hung for a moment then dropped into the stinking water. He left behind the leaky ship, the surly crew who, to a man, hated him, even the others who had been shanghied, and the body of the first mate lying in the shadows, a cargo hook buried to the handle in his skull. The man set out for home, stopping only to beg or steal food on the way. He furnished himself with clean clothing from clotheslines beside the road.

Reaching Memphis one night, a little after dark, he stopped by the back door of the saloon. It hadn't changed much in five years, except that the paint had peeled a little more and the rancid smell of the garbage in the alley behind was a little stronger than he had remembered it, even though he had smelled his share of odors while on the ship. He paused only long enough to light a rag and stuff it into the bunghole of the barrel that stood in the storeroom next to the unlocked back door. It was the barrel that held the coal oil for the lamps. As he headed east, he stopped and stood for a moment savoring the sight of the orange flames showing their black edges as they hungrily ate their way out the roof of the two story building. In a few minutes they would light up the waterfront. The residents would be lucky if they could contain the fire to just the one building. Feeling no concern for them, he didn't look back again.

Now, as he stood staring at the grave, he thought about the man who had killed his cousin. What he felt couldn't be described as hatred. Not having known Levi Casey personally, he couldn't feel personal hatred for him. What he felt was more a sense of duty. That sense of duty was the only thing that kept him alive aboard ship. He had often thought that he would enjoy taking vengence on his family's behalf, but now he knew better. He would finish the job, but he wouldn't enjoy it.

His dead cousin had hardly been a credit to the Clebourne family, or to the human race for that matter. But according to the law of the Old Testament, he had a bounten duty, and that duty he must perform.

Once back home, in the hollows of the Clinch Mountains, his kin had resupplied him without question and he had once again started on his quest for vengence. He neither asked for, nor received more help than necessary from them. His family knew he had a job to do and that he would either do it or die trying.

The Mark Of Cain

Bennett's Bayou, tributary of the Norfork of the White River, State of Arkansas

In uneasy silence the twelve men rode up the wagon track toward Missouri. Even a casual observer would have noticed that their horses were deep bodied, and long legged, much better quality that even those ridden by regular calvary units further east. Each man carried at least two Colt percussion revolvers. The men's pockets bulged with extra cylinders, capped and loaded, allowing them to remove the barrel wedges and slip on another cylinder and be firing again in less that ten seconds. They carried well cared for Calvary model Sharps .54 caliber carbines formerly in the hands of the Union calvary. They rode carefully and only occasionally glanced at one another, wary of the same kind of ambush that they had often initiated. Their uniforms were faded Union blue, as befitted men who had seen a lot of action. A more astute observer might have noticed that some of the tears in their uniforms were fraying out in a somewhat circular pattern. The rhythmic oiled squeaking of their gear filled in the brief silences left by the regular sounds of the horses' hooves against the limestone ledges that made up most of the road surface.

The men knew that the Colonel was in one of his deep smoldering, silent rages, rages that a each of them had seen firsthand, rages that bordered on the insane. The rages could turn murderous in an instant. Colonel Charles Morgan Cain rode a few steps ahead, scarcely aware of the men behind him. He had wanted that woman, wanted her bad. Now she was gone, dead, pinned beneath her horse. He had to have a grudging respect for her husband, who, caught by surprise, still managed to give her a chance to escape, sacrificing his own life in the process. Cain was not concerned about the kid, except as a witness, and he never left witnesses. He was sure that by the time they returned the boy would be dead or at least easy to catch. The kid had hit the ground running as his mother's horse fell, and in a moment he was into the trees. Cain didn't want to waste time hunting him. Practiced as they were at killing, some of Cain's men still shrunk from the cold-blooded murder of women and kids, except for the Zulu.

The Zulu had been slightly behind and to Cain's right when the woman's horse had burst from the log barn.

His rifle was already up and swinging when Cain spoke' quietly, "Don't kill her."

The Zulu didn't reply, but his muzzle moved down slightly and as the shot rang out, the woman's horse dropped dead.

As Cain rode he thought about the Zulu, a natural woodsman, expert with any type of weapon, and devoid of any emotion.

Cain knew himself and his ambitions well, but although he had thought about it often, he couldn't fathom just what motivated the Zulu. The black man didn't appear to categorically hate the race that had enslaved him. No doubt it had been Arab slavers who had snatched him from his people in Africa, while he was yet a youth. Cain knew from the clipped accent that the Zulu had not been born in America.

Cain liked to think of himself as a man totally without fear, but yet, as he looked into those impenetrable black eyes, he had felt a chill creep deep into his soul. It was as if he himself were standing naked, with every thought and motive exposed. Yet the Zulu accepted and followed his orders without question or complaint. In fact, he was by far the most reliable of the men of his command. His command, he smiled at the thought. His command.

Cain was not a colonel, but it was important that his men believe that he was. It had been surprisingly easy to exchange his Confederate Lieutenant's uniform with that of the dead Union Colonel.

After the confusion of the first day at Gettysburg, in the dark of the night, he stole a horse and headed west. He had been sure he would never be missed in the confusion.

CHAPTER 17
Gettysburg, Pennsylvania July 3, 1863

Rumors flew. Some said that General Hill was pushing to-ward Gettysburg because he had heard there was a large stock of shoes there, shoes that were badly needed by the ragged Confeder-ates. Historians would later say that the two titanic armies had blun-dered into each other, each unaware of the other's proximity. But blunder or not, the result was a three-day battle which broke the point of the South's spearlike thrust into the North. The battle of Gettysburg, as it would be called, dashed General Lee's last desperate hopes of taking Washington and Baltimore, thus relieving the relentless pres-sure of the siege that was strangling Vicksburg.

The fog-like black powder smoke, with its rotten egg smell, started as almost indefinable wisps that followed the air currents. Then as the battle progressed, it gradually filled the gaps until it hung like a low cloud over the battlefield. The participants then took on a ghost-like quality as it became increasingly difficult to tell friend from foe as the uniforms of both sides turned the same spotty color. The bright summer sun was dimmed to twilight. Since most Union infantrymen used paper cartridges in their rifled muskets, tearing the powder-filled cartridges open with their teeth caused the lower parts of their faces to turn black with powder stains. Although most of the southern troops were armed with captured Union arms, they were short of the prepared cartridges. Most of the time they had to mea-sure and pour loose powder down the muzzle before ramming down each Minie ball. After the battle, several weapons found were loaded nearly to the muzzle with alternating loads of powder and Minie balls. The noise and confusion were so great that those soldiers had not known their weapons were not firing.

The musket fire, like gigantic plumes of popcorn, washed across the battle field with irregular waves of sound, At regular intervals the cannons roared, shaking the ground as they bounced with recoil, sending out their screaming loads of canister. The steel balls in each canister load acted like giant shotguns, mowing down men like wheat stalks before some great invisible scythe. The rare pauses in the firing were filled with screams of the wounded and dying, as the troops regrouped to attack again and again.

Cain's platoon had walked into this withering fire, as they met the 6th Wisconsin which had been sent to reinforce the 147th New York. The New Yorkers, who had failed to get the order to withdraw to Seminary Ridge, nevertheless had inflicted a terrible toll on the advancing Confederates. The Federals were forced back rapidly until they were steadied by fresh infantry under the command of General John Reynolds.

As his men surged forward, sensing victory, they had run past Cain and disappeared rapidly into the mist.

Cain, who was afraid of being seen as cowardly, hurried to catch up, weaving among the ragged bodies of the dead Secesh, interspersed with the blue-clad Union dead. He almost fell over a Union Calvary Colonel. Barely catching his balance, Cain gaped at the man at his feet. The Colonel looked up with a weak sad smile and pointed to the deep bullet cut running just above his ear, the white of his skull plainly visible beneath the blood oozing from the wound.

"Looks like I'm your prisoner, Reb. Now if you'd be kind enough to get me some water."

A plan which had long been simmering in Cain's mind burst full bloom into his consciousness. Cain glanced around quickly. He was alone for the moment among the wounded and dead. "Yes, you may consider yourself my prisoner," he said politely as his eyes fell upon the blanket roll draped across the shoulders of a dead infantry sergeant. He stepped up the hill and pulled a full canteen and the threadbare woolen blanket loose. Holding out the canteen, he moved close.

The Colonel's eyes opened wide as he realized what was about to happen and he tried to yell, but only a croak of "No, please" escaped the enveloping blanket. Ignoring the weak struggles of the dying man, Cain dispatched him very quickly. Then he proceeded to change clothes with the corpse, watching all the time for any activity that might give him away. If he could just get the uniforms changed he could disappear. The change took but a few moments, and, even with his pistol at hand, Cain's heart beat drumrolls of fear. His own men would hang him without preamble if he was discovered. Cain had never been a believer in the Southern cause and he had been sure for a long while that the South must inevitably lose. The South was agricultural, the North industrial. It was that simple. The South could feed armies, but could never muster the war materiel for an extended campaign.

Cain's father had been an overseer on the great Millwood Plantation in western Virginia. Overseers, who were often hired from the ranks of what was often referred to as "poor white trash" by the landed gentry, were nevertheless paid well. Cain, as a young boy, was afforded some, but not all of the privileges of the planter's children. There was a line of distinction there between them, a thin line to be sure, but a line, a very distinct unbreakable line. Young Cain was very aware that he could never be one of them, even if he should become rich. The elder Cain had been hated by his charges and because of his needless cruelty and drunken rages, barely tolerated by his employers. After beating a young black man to death with a singletree over a misunderstood order, he was discharged and was thereafter only able to find menial work.

Young Cain's mother died early in his life, leaving him solely under his father's twisted influence. After his father's discharge from the only work he knew, they moved to Roanoke.

The older Cain spent the rest of his short drunken life ranting and raving against the plantation owners in the taverns when he had money, and at home when he didn't. Everyone in the town dismissed him as a drunken fool and paid him scant attention. That is, he was ignored by everyone except his son. Young Cain greatly admired his father, and maybe because he had nothing else to cling to, the boy was convinced that his father was the wisest of men. He hung on every word his father uttered, committing his ideas and attitudes to memory and adopting them as his own. Thus, the older Cain thoroughly implanted his hatred and mistrust of his fellow man into his young son. The younger Cain learned his lessons well, for even as a young child, the boy seemed to enjoy being unusually cruel to other children and animals. Most of the people of the town were too well mannered to say anything. But they nevertheless endeavored to keep their children away from the one they referred to as "that Cain boy." There were often repeated whispers that, "The boy wasn't quite right in the head." There were veiled hints and rumors about hanged cats and dogs skinned alive, but there was no real evidence, so the local law did nothing. Somehow, Cain managed to become friends or more precisely, associates, of the sons of the wealthy landowners and shopkeepers, although none of them actually liked him. Perhaps they sensed in some indefinable way his well hidden contempt for them. He was able to defy convention, doing many things for which they, because of their more conventional upbringing, lacked the nerve. Thus young Cain provided a diversion for youngsters who were largely idle, with plenty of time on their hands and a coin or two in their pockets. It seemed that there was always a certain group around who admired him because he defied the restraints of society. None of his teachers trusted him, but they had to admit "that Cain boy is smart as a whip."

When the war started, Cain enlisted along with most of the other young men, not through any sense of loyalty or duty but with the idea of further ingratiating himself with those in power. Although his reckless bravery and love of killing won a commission, he was cordially hated by those in his command because of his disregard for his men.

Cain knew that, at Gettysburg, as in the past, the dead would probably be interred in hastily dug mass graves. Especially after such a hot day, the men of the burial details would be very anxious to finish their grisly work. They would check for papers, with only a cursory glance at the bodies. Cain did, however, leave his Spiller and Burr revolver in the dead Colonel's hand after the uniform swap. Before he laid it down he turned it over in his hand. The revolver was the Confederate version of the Whitney Navy Colt, made in Atlanta, Georgia. Leaving it would further divert the attention of the burial detail. After belting on the Black leather belt with the U.S. on the buckle, he pulled the officer's 1860 Colt Army from the backward holster on his right side and found it completely empty.

Suddenly he swung the pistol at a slight sound behind him. One of his platoon, a man by the name of Pearson, was holding his stomach wound with one hand and struggling to reach across to his rifle with the other. He had evidently observed the murder. Pearson gave up on trying to get the rifle and decided to yell for help.
Seeing Pearson open his mouth to scream, Cain took two steps and rammed the Union colonel's saber into the base of his throat. Wiping it quickly on the man's homespun shirt, Cain glanced around, then headed west, planning to swing around the flanks of both armies in the premature dusk.

Cain had heard that after the Battle of Elkhorn Tavern, also known as Pea Ridge, both the main armies of the North and South moved eastward to concentrate on what they considered to be the more strategic areas. This left the Ozarks of Arkansas and Missouri mostly under the control of various bands of deserters, bushwhackers and renegades, most notable the so-called guerillas. Some were led by such men as Quantrill and Bloody Bill Anderson, and Anderson's associates, the two James' brothers, and their cousins, the Younger boys.

After he walked far enough that he was clear of both armies, he turned southwest. As he started to move carefully out of the battle area, the noise, smoke and screams faded behind him. Wading through the green grass, he came upon a small group of five calvary horses. Two wore new Union saddles and the other three had belonged to the South, judging from their trail worn condition. They were all peacefully grazing together. They associated because they were all of the same kind. They were completely oblivious to the fact that their owners had were probably lying dead just over the hill, their differences dead along with them. Cain gathered the two Union mounts, one of them with a newly issued .54 calibre Sharps calvary model carbine slung across the saddle. He stopped for a moment and examined it. He had heard of them but had never seen one. The half lever dropped a block which opened up the chamber for insertion of the paper cartridge. As the lever was closed, the block moved back into place shearing off the end of the paper. With a percussion cap on the nipple, the hammer on the side then cocked the weapon for firing. They were so new that he had heard that only a few Union calvary units had them. Mounting one horse and leading the other, he headed out across western Pennsylvania. As he rode, he was amazed, at the contrast between the quiet of the night and the carnage he had left behind. Despite the ringing in his ears, he began to hear the sounds of the night creatures as they moved aside from his path. He rode all night, to get as far from the battle as possible.

Daylight found Cain near a small clear stream, so he washed, allowing himself and the horses some rest before moving on. He decided to ride openly in daylight, since he was sure that as a calvary colonel he would not be stopped or questioned by any roving patrols that he couldn't avoid. Evidently all of the troops were concentrated in the area around Gettysburg. He rode completely through western Pennsylvania without seeing a single soldier. Cain crossed rivers at fording places on the back country roads and avoided towns and settlements altogether. He stopped at isolated farmhouses, and the people, eager for news of any kind, always offered a hot meal and a place to sleep. He hinted that he was on a special mission of some sort, and they didn't press further.

He crossed into the flat farm lands of Ohio, then Indiana and into Illinois, switching horses daily. He became more and more at ease in his new identity. Cain listened carefully to the farmers' gossip and often spent the night with relatives of the people he had visited on the previous night.

Colonel Cain, as he now began to think of himself, rode, after about four weeks of fairly leisurely travel, into the cane brakes that separated the mouth of the Ohio River. Cain gazed in wonder at the rich flat farmland in the V created by the junction of the Ohio and the wide muddy Mississippi. It was a little past sundown and Cain had not seen a farmhouse for several miles. As he rode closer to the river, he saw a thin ribbon of smoke trailing up through the bamboo-like switch canes. Partly from curiosity and partly from tiredness and hunger, he started toward it. There seemed to be a narrow well-defined trail through the canes and he followed it to a little clearing. Suddenly, he came upon two men. One stood by a small fire, the other, a very black man, was bound hand and foot, lying on his side on the ground. Cain had blundered into the camp of a slaver, a man who hunted down runaway slaves and returned them to their masters for the reward offered by their owners.

134

CHAPTER 18

The slave hunter, reacting instantly as he saw the flash of the blue uniform through the cane, dove behind the fire, making a desperate grab for the double-barrelled muzzle-loading shotgun resting upside down on a rock, both hammers at half-cock. As he rolled and started to bring the gun to bear, he froze, then dropped it as he found himself staring down the muzzle of the Colt army revolver in Cain's hand. The slaver straightened up and a sly, ingratiating, fawning sort of grin crept across his face, showing a mouthful of broken yellow teeth edged in various shades of brown and black.

"Sorry, Sir," he said, "for a minute there I thought you was a robber. A body can't be too careful these days. I was just about to fix me and this escaped nigra slave here some grub. I got us a side of bacon and I'll make some corn pone. You're welcome to stay."

Cain, still sitting on his horse, nodded, but made no comment. The cleared area in the switch canes had obviously been used many times for camps. Someone had even carried in some rough chunk rocks for a fireplace, a wise move on their part because the smooth stones along the river often contained trapped water which would turn to steam and explode rock heated by fire, creating a shower of sharp fragments. Cain sat and studied the scene for a few minutes, while the slaver, emboldened by his lack of comment, busied himself slicing bacon into a large cast iron skillet with a hickory handled butcher knife which he pulled from the pack. He was tall and almost cadaverously thin, his eyes with their yellowish cast set in a splotchy, unshaven face shaded by a black flop hat. He wore store-bought bibless overalls that were shiny in front with ground-in grease and dirt. His red striped shirt showed prints from numerous hand wipings across the front. Cain watched closely for any sign of another man hidden in the canes, waiting for a chance to ambush him. Appearing to take no notice of Cain's lack of friendliness, the slaver kept up nonstop chatter as he made up cornbread dough and dropped it into the sputtering grease left by the bacon in the skillet.

"Yes, Sir, what I'm doing is legal, you know. This here boy's an escapee out of North Mississippi. Got himself up into Ohio and was living up there free as a bird, had himself a real job, milking cows. Beats all I ever seen. Us decent white folks can't hardly find work, and here these slaves just waltz in and get theirselves a job right off. Yes, sir, it keeps me busy trackin' them down and returning them back to their rightful owners."

Cain spoke for the first time, his pistol muzzle still following the slaver's every movement. "Looks to me like you've been awfully rough on that man. What happens if you let him die?"

The slaver stopped his task long enough to look over at the slave who lay on his side, his bonds obviously painfully tight. "Now," he said with the aire of explaining something to a child, "he won't die. Most of them's got it too easy anyways, if this'n had been beat enough, he wouldn't have run off in the first place. I've got a paper on him." He reached in his hip pocket and pulled out a stack of much folded grimy papers and pulled one off the top. Unfolding and smoothing it out, walked toward Cain, who followed his movement with the pistol. Turning the flyer toward Cain he held it up with both hands.

Cain read: **Reward $100.00 for return of Jonas to Sunflower Plantation, Iuka, Mississippi. Hershel Johnson, Owner.** Below was a fair drawing of the black man and a further note. **Jonas was taught to use firearms and other weapons by a previous owner. He has escaped before and I will not be responsible for any injury done by him.**

"Now," the slave catcher said, "You can see why I've got him hog-tied. This'n's a bad one. Iffn' I didn't need the money, I'd just shoot him for the trouble he's caused me." Cain carefully reholstered his Colt, but was still wary of the slaver.

Cain was hungry and the day was nearly gone, so he swung off and unsaddled both mounts, tying them so that they could graze on the blue-stem grass growing up in the canes. He was careful to keep an eye on the slaver, leaving his calvary holster unbuttoned. As he worked he happened to glance over at the escaped slave. The black man was lying very still. He gave no sign of the discomfort the ropes must have been causing him, but his dark eyes followed every move the white men made.   The slave catcher talked nonstop as he finished cooking. Cain listened closely, trying to find out about the lay of the land and the people of the area he had to pass through.

He had heard talk around the campfires that after the Battle of Elkhorn Tavern, also known as Pea Ridge, the defeated Southern Army of General Van Dorn had moved across the Mississippi to the east to fight. They were transferred to what the government in Richmond considered to be the more important theatre of the war. Cain had also heard that the Union Army had moved west and north, and that the hills of the Ozarks were mostly devoid of sizeable forces of either side. Both armies tended to avoid the hills and hollows of the eastern Ozarks if possible. The steep rugged area had too many possible ambush sites and did not lend itself well to large pitched battles. Supply wagons only moved across the area with difficulty.

Cain reluctantly took the offered food, consoling himself with the knowledge that the heat would have neutralized any residual filth from its handler. After they had eaten, the slaver moved over and loosened the slave's arms enough to enable him to eat. As the black man ate silently, murderous looks of pure hatred poured out of his dark eyes.

"You're free,"Cain said, addressing the slave directly for the first time, "Go ahead and untie your legs."

The slave catcher whirled around. His anger and disbelief quickly turned to fear as he heard the double clicks as the barrel tilted up and the hammer came back on the Colt, ready in Cain's hand. Cain was a bit surprised at himself. He certainly felt no pity for the human chattel before him. It was simply not part of his makeup to have real feelings for anyone but himself. The only feelings for his fellow human beings concerned their usefulness, or lack of it, to himself and his own well being. It could have been simple boredom, or it could have been a desire for conflict, but Cain didn't pause to reflect on his own motives. In an instant he knew he had made the right decision, because he so enjoyed the fear on the slaver's face.

Cain looked at the slave. "Now you tie *him* up," he said, indicating the slave catcher with a wave of the pistol. The slave moved quickly, as he pulled the very same rough manila ropes around the arms and legs of his former captor, jerking the knots down tight. The slaver, finally realizing that he was wasting his breath, at last fell silent. The slave, his task done, turned expectantly toward Cain.

"You can go," Cain said "I'll take care of him." He noted with satisfaction the stark fear that tightened the dirty face of the slave catcher.

Cain had acted on impulse, but now a plan was taking shape in the back of his mind. He would give the slave a head start, then turn the slaver loose. The thought amused him; his only regret was that he would never know the outcome of the game. He had the feeling that given even footing, the black man might come out as the winner. The escaped slave sat down and started eating, giving no indication of a desire to leave. Most men would have taken off running, Cain thought, with grudging respect. The slave catcher complained and whined constantly. His voice, belligerent at first, was now starting to get a quaver of fear about it. Then he started to beg. The slave, his meal finished, sat on the ground. Still not a word came from his lips. He's probably not able to speak, Cain thought. After a while the slave, Jonas, lay down and slept. The slaver stopped whining and had begged for water for a while, then that, too, stopped. Cain sat back from the fire, determined to stay awake. He knew he should leave, but he was curious about both the slave and his former captor. The cruelty that was so much a part of his nature was fueled by the situation. He was intrigued by the cat and mouse game. It brought back memories of some of the games he had played with animals when he was a boy.

Cain woke with a start, his hand bringing the Colt army pistol up as he stirred. Something was wrong. It was too quiet. Dawn was just breaking and a foggy mist from the rivers had dampened their clothes. Cain waited. He could see the dark form of the slave squatting by the embers of the dying fire. He turned to look at the slaver who was now turned on his back, and as the mist cleared for a moment, he saw the hickory handle of the butcher knife protruding from the left side of his chest.

CHAPTER 19

The slave catcher was dead. Cain knew he was dead. Even without the knife there was no doubt. The death angel had passed over and the body seemed to shrink, to become less defined somehow. Cain had been an interested observer of this phenomenon since his first battle. He glanced quickly over at the escaped slave, but he was gone! Cain always liked to think of himself as fearless, but next to the dark river, shrouded in drifting eddies of mist, he was afraid. It was the same lost, helplessness he had felt as a little boy waiting for his drunken father to come home, often wetting himself in anticipation of the beating he knew was coming. It was a helpless dread, knowing what was going to happen, yet being unable to do anything. Then feeling the familiar ache after the sharp pains had subsided, loving and hating his father at the same time. He remembered standing over his drunken father as he slept, butcher knife in hand, unwilling and unable to put an end to it. He was ashamed of this fear. The fear that he denied, the fear that had been with him for so long. The fear that had hardened into a hatred and mistrust of his fellow man. He could feel the muscles along his neck and spine tighten. Why had he stayed? Why hadn't he ridden on as his own good sense had told him? The fog muffled sound as well as sight, and he felt as if he and everything around him were wrapped in cotton. Pistol in hand, he started to stand up, to run, to cry out, to scream! Every muscle in his body locked, and for a second he found himself incapable of movement. He took a deep breath and settled back. This was nonsense. He was being a fool. Cain was sure that the escaped slave was, even

142

now, running for his life, headed back north away from the two rivers.

He heard the scrape of something moving across the collar of his uniform. Almost before this message reached his brain, the cold metal of the shotgun barrel came to rest at the back of his head. Cain heard the soft double click as one of the hammers came back to full cock.

"Lay it down," a soft deep voice commanded, and Cain carefully laid the Colt on the ground. The pressure on his neck eased as the black man moved around in front of him and, squatting, picked up the pistol. "Who are you, and why did you turn me loose, white man?"

Cain relaxed. The man had something in mind. "I'm an officer in Mr. Lincoln's army," he replied, trying to make his voice sound authoritative. Cain believed that only the curiosity of the black man and the color of his uniform had kept him from sharing the slaver's fate. Squatting there, the black man asked questions. Cain answered each one carefully, hoping he was convincing. This man, Jonas, must have been at large for a good while.

"I am a Zulu, and I will ride with you to the border states," he finally said. Cain had no plans except to get away from a sure defeat. Now he had a thought: if he could manage to capture the Zulu, he could sell him in the South. But then he remembered the look in those dark eyes.

In time, the body of the slave catcher, minus his butcher knife, slid along the soft muddy bottom of the broad Mississippi. It would be days before the accumulating gases of decomposition brought the body to the surface many miles downstream, and, in this time of war, one more body in the river wouldn't provoke more than a passing comment among its discoverers.

The old man operating the ferry across the Mississippi at Pottsville was curious about the Union officer and the black man as they led their horses on the boat with its split log sides. They stood silently holding the reins on the trip across the light-brown, fishy-smelling river. The young often squander their lives, the old who survive learn not to take risks, so the old man merely nodded, set them across and went back to his shady spot and his fishing poles.

Cain soon learned that the Zulu was an expert woodsman, able to secure small game for food easily and Cain found grudging admiration for this man, who rarely spoke, and who gave no indications of his thoughts.

They rode along the swamp trails, the stagnant water pushing up against the sides of the high ground, south along the west side of the mighty Mississippi river. No longer did they stop at houses or towns. Cain knew from army gossip that the people of this region were of uncertain loyalties, and he was afraid that a Union officer and a black man traveling together might draw unwelcome attention.

A bend in the trail concealed a group of men until it was too late to avoid them. Cain's hand dropped to the Sharps, then relaxed. These men, in various bits and pieces of uniforms, mostly Federal, were obviously deserters.

They were gathered around a man lying on his back near the fire. Perceiving no threat, Cain and the Zulu rode boldly into the camp. Cain hoped that at least some of these men retained vestiges of their military training.

"What's happened here, men?" he asked briskly as he dismounted and walked over to them. He noted that the Zulu, still mounted, had remained far enough back to cover the whole bunch with the shotgun.

The men, so intent, were surprised. They all straightened up in acknowledgement of a superior officer; however none bothered to salute. "It's the Sarge, he's snakebit, sir, and he's mighty poorly," one of the men said. He pointed to a muddy brown cottonmouth moccasin lying off to one side, its head smashed with a black chunk of cypress root. Its thick stubby body still moved slowly, its tail rhymically whipping against the ground among the dead leaves that had fallen from the ever-present switch canes. In reptiles, death throes sometimes lasted for hours, or until the coolness of the night lowered the body temperature.

Cain moved closer, and the men moved back in deference to his rank. The man lying on the ground was dressed in a ragged Union militia sergeant's uniform. He was huge, with round folds of fat lapping down over his belt and spreading out along the ground. He was moaning softly, his lumpy face sweating profusely, the color of dough. The raspy rise and fall of his chest was loud in the silence. As Cain leaned over, he could see the two tiny blue-ringed black holes still oozing thick, syrupy-looking blood. The large neck artery pulsated rapidly, carrying its lethal load deeper and deeper into the stricken man.

One of the men spoke. "The Sarge was bending over to start a fire in that pile of drift over there." Cain knew that cottonmouths did not usually bite unprovoked, but the heat from the fire would have registered as pain in its miniscule brain. Being a pit viper it would have naturally struck at the nearest warm flesh.

Cain straightened up. He could tell that these, enlisted men all, were watching him, waiting for orders. The Sergeant had obviously been in charge. "Men, " he said, "your Sergeant has taken a bite in the worst possible spot." He paused for a moment, "He will likely die."

There were no murmurs of sympathy, no visible reaction from the men. They just waited. They were used to taking orders. They had recieved months of training in taking orders. They had done as the Sergeant told them and now that he was not giving orders, they didn't know what to do. Even though they had turned their backs on the army, they had been conditioned to follow orders, no more and no less.

No one questioned Cain's authority or asked about the Zulu still sitting on his horse with the shotgun resting on the inside of his left elbow. Cain decided to carry his presumed authority a step further. "We'll go ahead and camp here for the night while we see if he survives or not." he said.

CHAPTER 20

After a meal of roast swamp rabbit, the men checked the ground for snakes, then bedded down around the dying fire. As they settled down, Cain sat for a while and studied them. He trusted none of them, not even the Zulu, especially not the Zulu. They were the dregs of humanity, and he was sure that they could be molded into his own private army. If the Sergeant didn't recover, Cain knew that they would follow him. He got up and walked over to the kid sitting on the ground next to their fallen leader. The young man, dressed in his ragged union uniform, jumped up, saluted, then unsure of himself, sat back down.

"You and the Sergeant here, close were you?" Cain asked.

The private looked up, "Hated his guts," he replied with a bitter note in his low voice. "But he knew the country and we were all afraid of him except John Monroe and Tater Poag over there." He pointed at a man with black hair and a neatly trimmed beard lying beside a gaunt sandy-haired man with parts of a Confederate uniform on. "I figger one or the other would have killed the Sergeant sooner or later, although it would have taken some doin'. I've seen him permanently cripple a man with his bare fists and he's an expert shot with any type of weapon."

"What's your name, private?" Cain asked.

"Thomas Howard, Sir." he replied. "I'm from Fulton County, over west of here. I ran off to join the Union army, mostly to spite my Mama, I guess. She's a widder woman, and I was the onliest help she had around the place. Anyways, I took off and enlisted. I fought at

146

Wilson's Creek, and them Rebs whupped us good. There for a while I wondered if any of us would get out of it alive. Then after it was over, we took off for Rolla. I got so homesick I could have died, so I watched my chance and snuck off. Thought I'd go see my Mama. But I ran into Sergeant Massey there." He indicated the snake bitten man. "And I went along with him because I was too scared to leave. The rest of these men just kinda joined up with us along the way, one or two at a time. Massey, he's bad, they're all bad, the whole bunch. Most of them are deserters, partly Union, partly Confederate. The rest are just plain outlaws. Tater Poag there, he claims to have killed a man in Texas in a knife fight." Howard pointed at the sandy-haired man now lying on his back, snoring loudly. "I shore wish't I'd jest stayed in the army and never took up with this bunch, myself. Last week we robbed a little old store outside of Sikeston, Missouri, north of here. We took canned stuff, hams, everything we could sack up. They didn't have much cash money, but we took what they had. Then when we started out, Johnny, he turned around and shot the owner. Shot him jest like you'd kill a bug. He was jest an old man, who wouldn't have done nobody no harm, and Monroe shot him right there in front of his wife, and her'a crying and takin' on somethin' pitiful the whole time.Then him and Tater laughed jest like it was nothin'. Them two, they're the worst. The Sergeant always had him big plans. He said we would rob us a payroll or supply wagon and we'd all be rich, but here we are hiding in this nasty swamp, up to our armpits in snakes and being eaten alive by 'skeeters. I jest wish't I was back home. I'd be finishing the milking about now, and I'd be getting ready to go in and eat warm corn pone and some side meat and gravy. I'd be warshing it down with some cold buttermilk from the spring house."

"Do you know Fulton County well?" Cain asked.

"Almost ever foot of it," Howard replied. "Lived there all my life. Purty country, clear water, good land, not like this stinking mudhole of a place. The onliest snakes up there in the hills are copperheads and a few rattlers and they're mostly afeered of people.

There's a few cottonmouths along the creeks and rivers, but they're babies compared to that'n," he pointed to the dead snake stretched on the ground.

Cain reached over and poked at the fire with a stick.

Howard stared into the fire, "We'd have about as much luck finding the Taylor Cave as we would robbing a payroll wagon."

Cain looked up, "What is the Taylor Cave?" he asked, idly.

Howard smiled. "Colonel," he said, "every kid who was raised in northern Fulton County grew up listening to the legend of the Taylor Cave. I'd hate to say how many old caves I've gone into and how many holes I dug looking for that silver mine. That was back when I was jest a kid of a boy. "

The Colonel was intrigued by the silver mine, but he also knew human nature. If he showed too much interest the Howard boy was almost sure to clam up, so he tried to keep his tone casual. He asked a few more questions about Fulton County, then bored in on the subject of the silver mine again. "Just who were these Taylors anyway?"

"Well, sir, the Taylors were supposed to have been two brothers who discovered a cave containing pure silver. They covered the entrance with a big flat ledge rock and only went in to work the mine before daylight and left after dark. Each of them had a son and when the boys got big enough to work, they took them to the cave. Only trouble was, they blindfolded the boys until they got to the cave. Then after they got done working they blindfolded them again to take them home at night. Then as the story goes, the two brothers were killed by outlaws. The two Taylor boys searched under every ledge rock for miles around. After several years of searching, they gave it up and went out west. Some say they were both killed in California during the gold rush of '49. Others say they'll be back after this war is over to hunt for their silver mine."

"Do you believe that the cave really exists, Howard?" the Colonel asked.

Howard looked at him across the fire, "Well, I've never actual seen none of the silver, but I've heard them that say they have, so I 'spect the cave's really there all right. Some say the cave has to be along Bennett's River or Bennett's Bayou, one or the other. I heard one feller say that it has to be along Little Creek somewhere. Little Creek flows right into the Bayou. In any case, there's a lot of rough country up there." Howard stopped talking as if he realized he had talked too much, and suddenly stood up.

"I'm going to sleep now, Sir." Howard then laid down by the fire.

Still thinking about the silver mine, Cain walked over and squatted down beside the snakebit Sergeant. Unbelievably, the fat man was getting better. He was still unconscious but his breathing was easier. Cain laid his hand flat on the sergeant's chest. The rattle was gone. The Colonel slid his hand up and felt of his neck, the heartbeat was slow and regular. It was starting to look like he might recover in a couple of weeks. Massey's huge body had absorbed and diluted the poison that would have killed a smaller man in short order. Cain stood up. He didn't have the time or the inclination to wait for the recovery of a man he was sure would only mess up his rapidly forming plans. He glanced around carefully in the light of the dying fire. Since they had received no orders, the men hadn't even bothered to set a watch. He walked over to the calvary saddle on the ground and pulled out the accessory pack for the Sharp's slant breech calvary carbine. Taking out the cleaning rod and holding it against his leg, he walked back and squatted down again. Cain looked around; all the men appeared to be asleep. From his angle of vision, he didn't see the Zulu lying on his side watching. Cain placed the end of the thin steel in the Sergeant's ear, held it steady, then whacked it with a fist sized rock. There was a clink and a quiet crunch as the tempered rod penetrated the thin barricade of bone and slid easily into the soft mush of brain tissue that was the essence of Sergeant Massey. The remainder of the night passed quietly.

The next morning, the men were riding behind Colonel Cain, headed west toward Fulton County. Since the high ground restricted their lateral movements, Cain took the precaution of sending out one scout and rotating the duty among the men. Cain felt very satisfied with himself. He had gained the beginnings of a small army with a minimum of effort. They moved swiftly, stealing available horses along the way. On the second day, they crossed the Pittman ferry across the Black River. Like the Mississippi River ferryman before him, Pittman had learned that the price for survival was keeping his mouth shut. From there they waded the icy swiftness of the Spring River, their horses lunging against the stinging cold. After that the streams were smaller and easily fordable.

Meanwhile, an Indian carefully studied the fat. bloated dead man and the ground around him before bending down for a closer look. His nose told him almost as much as his eyes. Millions of unseen saprophytic bacteria were already beginning the insidious work for which they were so uniquely adapted. The sun was already well up in the east. The condition of the body told him that it hadn't been more than twelve hours since the fat man lying before them had been killed, given the speed of decomposition in the summer heat. The buzzards cast their fleeting shadows on the scene. They were in no hurry. They circled, craning their red wrinkled necks, their confidence absolute. For them there was no losing. Sooner or later, their turn would come. It always did. So they rode the upsdrafts, wings unmoving, patiently waiting for the Confederate troops to leave.

General Jeff Thompson, the swamp fox of the Confederacy, leaned far to the right and then to the left, taking the opportunity to stretch his tired, sore muscles while still in the saddle. Behind him, his men sat quietly, a few of them looking over their shoulders. They were worried that the appearance of their rear guard would signal that the blue coats pursuing them were getting too close. Thompson totally trusted the judgment and ability of the Mohawk and knew that in a few minutes he would have the full story of what had happened here in the last few hours.

Finally the Indian turned and walked over to stand beside the general's horse.

"What happened to him, Ajax?" the general asked.

"Snake bit." The Indian pointed at the dead snake. "But that not what kill him." He pointed at his ear with his forefinger.

"Shot in the ear?" The general was fully aware that the Mohawk could speak perfect English when it suited him. Today he had elected to play the inscrutable red man.

"No, something else, but quiet, real quiet. All other men think snake what killed him."

"Who were they, a Union patrol?" The general was clearly puzzled.

"No, they ran away, maybe ten men, two come later from different direction."

"Deserters? Well, the country's full of 'em. Let's get moving before the bluecoats catch up with us." With that General Thompson turned his horse and started south, the scout once again moving out ahead.

Two days later, on the South Fork, the band of deserters ran into Rufus Beasley and the twins. Since they were cousins of Thomas Howard, Cain quickly recruited them as scouts. Trusting no one, Cain had not tried to gather any more men. As a matter of fact, his force had shrunk with the loss of Monroe, Russell and Howard in a running battle with the Sixth Missouri. He was fairly sure that all three of his men had been killed in the battle. Monroe might have been left alive, but Cain had repeatedly drilled into the men that they must not let themselves be captured alive.

He also knew that the Union captain couldn't have gotten a good look at his face. The thing he regretted most about the battle was the loss of Howard. Howard was the only one of the deserters that had both keen mind and an extensive knowledge of the countryside. He needed a man with both of these qualities, so sadly lacking in most of these men.

The Irish Wilderness, Shannon County Missouri

A bright canvas cover popped in the breeze as the supply wagon hurried to make up for lost time. Lieutenant Brixey wiped his sweating face across the bright blue sleeve of his uniform blouse. He glanced across, but none of the men in his squad would meet his gaze. They hated him. He knew that, and perhaps he could have stood their hatred. But it was worse than that, they not only hated him but held him in total contempt. Contempt because these combat veterans knew him to be both inexperienced and inept. Contempt because he had gotten them lost and then refused to listen to them. Contempt because this was his first field command. In their eyes he wouldn't have been fit to even shine the boots of Lieutenant Sweeney. Sweeney had drowned trying to swim a "green broke" horse across the Jack's Fork River. Lieutenant Charles Sweeney. How he hated even the sound of the name. He could just imagine them talking, "Sweeney wouldn't have done that, Sweeney had good sense. Sweeney wouldn't have gotten us lost." He had been compared to the former lieutenant every day since he had taken over. He had tried to measure up, to please them. But he knew all the time that he was just a clerk, had clerked in a store, joined the army, been a company clerk. He knew he even looked like a clerk. He felt small and inadequate. He knew that no matter what he did, he would just make their dead commander look more like the hero he had been. He looked over at the men again. They rode loose in their saddles, their eyes straight ahead, their attention strictly on their horses and the winding path that passed for a road. Each of them frequently glanced over at the supply wagon. It was unusual that the Union headquarters in St. Louis would send any of the new Sharps carbines to any Army post west of the Mississippi. Yet these new weapons had been on their way to Colonel Monks at West Plains when Brixey took a wrong turn that took him east and south toward the Arkansas border. Now he was trying to find his way back with as much haste as was possible with the worn out team of mules, eight tired resentful men and two cranky teamsters.

Brixey glanced about uneasily. He knew Bloody Bill Anderson was dead. Anderson had been killed in an ambush similar to the very ones he had used so successfully against Union troops. Yet Brixey was uneasy. He knew the woods were full of bushwhackers that would drool at the sight of the new carbines. His own men still carried the old 1842 model smoothbore muskets that the government had recalled, taking them back to Harper's Ferry. There the smoothbore barrels were rifled and rear sights installed. The old muskets slung a .69 calibre ball with such questionable accuracy that the sights were all but useless. Lieutenant Brixey knew that if his command was attacked, there would be no way to unpack the new weapons from their sticky grease in time to influence the outcome of a battle. Brixey glanced around nervously, something just didn't seem right. He looked at his men, started to mention his feelings, then decided against it. He didn't want to be thought even more of a fool. Besides, they were more experienced soldiers than he was anyway.

The large dead oak log lay across the road, still attached to its stump. Brixey's squad stopped and all stared straight ahead, their faces showing their resentment for the order they all knew would come.

Brixey tried to make his voice sound authoritative. "You men there, dismount and move that log. You teamsters just stay on the wagon; they'll be able to handle it." The men all reined in their horses and dismounted. In doing so they all managed to turn their horses so that the lieutenant had no choice but to notice their glares of pure hatred.

"Sir!"

Lieutenant Brixey jerked his head toward the teamster who had gotten his attention with a loud hoarse whisper. There was none of the usual tone of contempt or disrespect in his voice. The one word only conveyed one thing-cold naked fear!

"Sir, that tree's been cut!"

The lieutenant looked back toward the tree, his gaze sliding across the astonished troopers. Their weapons were still attached to their saddles! He opened his mouth to yell an order, already knowing it was too late. The rifles crashed in one short volley. Brixey froze in disbelief as his men were knocked sprawling, most of them dead when they hit the ground. The teamsters both rolled off the box a second later, falling directly behind the rearing mules as the hybrid beasts ran sideways, their breeching straps slipping. Brixey was already turning his horse to run! The fear started closing off his throat! In his panic he had completely forgotten about the new Colt pistol in the button down holster on his belt. His total being was occupied with his own survival as the horse lunged into a full gallop. Coming to himself he reined in the horse, causing him to slide as the steel shoes tried to get a bite in the grassy road. NO! He would not run, Austin Brixey might have been a clerk, but he was no coward! He'd show them! They would never snicker behind HIS back again! Behind him the killers frantically reloaded.

Cain raised his pistol, irritated that his men had completely ignored the obvious target the Lieutenant presented. Cain's irritation turned to surprise as the federal officer let out a long scream of pure anguish and rage and turned his horse around toward them. Brixey rammed his spurs into the gelding's sides. He leaned forward. He could feel the muscles of the gelding's neck working against his cheek. His horse, unused to such cruel treatment broke into a dead run, clods of dirt filling the air behind him. The only thought in his primitive brain was to get away from the pain being inflicted on him by his rider.

Brixey, his face wet with salty horse sweat, raised up and started firing. He came on, completely oblivious to the fact that he was firing too fast and that the recoil was causing his shots to go high.

He was almost on the bushwhackers as the return fire swept him backward off his horse. He fired his fifth shot as he hit the ground. Lieutenant Austin Brixey sat for a moment in the dust, then fell over as his pistol slid from his fingers. He wished he could somehow tell his men that he was sorry, sorry he was just a clerk.

154

"Fool," Cain said, his voice without emotion as he looked down at the body. He turned to his men, "Catch those loose horses and gather everything up. We're moving out," he said.

* * *

Bennett's Bayou, Fulton County*, Arkansas

As his little procession rode up over the hill, Gatlin felt the tension leave his mind and body in a warm rush. His muscles felt heavy from the sudden release of the tension. The simple cabin was still there. He was home. It felt like home, the first real home he had known in years. There was no evidence of human activity in the few days he had been gone. He had topped the hill halfway expecting to find the whole thing burned to the ground.

He looked up at the boy, "Sam, we'll stay here for a while and see if your mama gets better."

At the mention of his and his mother's names, the boy looked down and Gatlin thought he saw a slight nod, but maybe not.

Sarah Casey allowed herself to be lifted from the horse and walked after her son into the cabin. Gatlin chopped the remaining vegetables up for more soup. This time he added seasonings and while the boy ate with more enthusiasm than before, Sarah Casey still ate slowly. She chewed almost bovinely, as if it was taking all her concentration, without any sign of conscious thought. Gatlin got up and went outside to check his garden. The dog lay by the front door, head on his paws, his eyes following every move.

As Gatlin started around the cabin, he saw it next to his boot track. Different from the woman's shoe print and the boy's bare foot, he had never seen one before, but he knew exactly what it was! It was unmistakably, a moccasin print! He studied it, then followed the prints as they headed for his garden spot. There in the garden, he stood and remembered the morning Captain Hughes had ridden up on him. It seemed like years ago, instead of a few weeks. He took

---

* Now part of Baxter County, AR.

time to think about Mrs. Williams. He wished she was here, for she'd know what to do with the injured woman. Suddenly his mind snapped into focus and his hand instinctively grabbed for his pistol, then froze, thinking how foolish he must look. Someone had worked his garden! The weeds had been pulled and dirt pulled up to the plants. There were lots of moccasin prints. It could be an Indian! Mrs. Williams had told him the Indians were all gone, moved west by the government, moved to what was now called the Indian Territory.

Back in the cabin, the boy sat and intently watched every move his mother made. Gatlin sat down and ate, then took the horse out back and turned him loose. Rit felt edgy and somehow vaguely uneasy. He felt as if he ought to be doing something, but he didn't know what. He walked out to the road and back. He wondered if the Sapps had moved? He didn't dare go see about them. He would have to take care of Sarah and the boy now. He wondered about the men who had so ruthlessly murdered Levi Casey. Would they return? Had they also killed the Sapps? He hoped not. He felt so alone, but then he had always felt alone. It had seemed sometimes that he was the only inhabitant of this beautiful wild land. Now it wasn't much different, except there were the three of them. The next few days found Gatlin working daylight to dark on the cabin and in his garden, only taking out time to prepare food. Maybe it was his imagination, but it seemed that Sarah Casey was moving a little faster as she ate and moved around. The boy Sam, with the ever watchful dog, followed every step he made. He found himself keeping up a nonstop one-way conversation with the boy, who listened with apparent interest but had not, as yet, uttered a word. The woman Sarah was able to care for her personal needs, but still spent hours staring off into nothingness. Periodically, Gatlin bent over and stared into her eyes. Actually, they were quite beautiful eyes, he thought, but he got no reaction, not a flicker of expression. He talked to her often as he worked, but got no response.

Gatlin kept finding fresh moccasin tracks and made sure he kept a gun at hand. Each night he checked the caps and loads in his pistol. He intensely disliked having to reverse his hand to draw the pistol from the calvary holster which placed it butt forward on his right side. One night he cut two parallel slits in the opposite side of the holster, and threaded it onto the broad belt that had been Phanta Williams' husband's. This set the pistol butt forward on his left side so that he could easily reach across to draw it. The LeMat itself didn't have a natural balance. It just didn't come to hand easily. This bothered him, but he figured the increased firepower more than made up for its other shortcomings. He sat and turned the holster over in his hands, studying it. He picked up the knife and cut the flap off the calvary holster, then added a leather loop to slip over the hammer of the LeMat to keep it from falling out. The pistol was still somewhat awkward, but the new arrangement allowed the gun to be drawn much faster than before. Gatlin tried it a few times. It was much better.

His horse grazed around the cabin but every few days Gatlin went down into the valley to check on the other horses. They had plenty of grass and the creek provided fresh water, so they never seemed to wander more than a few hundred yards.

CHAPTER 21

"Stop, Aaron." He pronounced it Arn. "Aaron, you gots to stop, I can' run no mo'. We gots to go back. We can be back by daybreak. The fiel' boss or Mista' Dickenson, they ain' even gon' know we been gone."

The other man stopped in the darkness, his chest heaving. "No, Burrill, you go on back, I ain' never gon' go back. They'll have to kill me first. I heard dem yankee so'jers done took the town of Helena. I's gon' make it. "

"But we can' make it, they'll get them hound dogs after us, and they'll run us down fo' we gets to the river. Skeeters done et us up and when we gets to de river they'll be them cottonmouths and 'gators. They'll eat us up. Les' go back befo' it's too late." The man called Burrill stood hesitantly. He had absolutely no faith in his ability to lie. He was sure that if he went back the Massa would find some way to blame him for Aaron's disappearance. After all, they had shared the same shack. If he kept on running, they would both get caught. "I should'a knowed better, I 'orta knowed better than to have anything to do with anybody from up river. Where was it? Some place he called Little Rock. He said sumptin' 'bout runnin' away befo'. Dat's why dey sold 'im down de' river."

"Come on, Burrill, les' get movin,' we gots to find a place to hide by daylight. We got's to stay hid 'til dark. They say they's a place up the river called Friar's Point. Then a little island in de river, then we gots to swim de' river to de lights. That be Helena. Then we find de blue soj'ers. Then we be free. Free, Burrill! den we decides what we do, not some boss man." Aaron, stood, hoping Burrill wouldn't go back. The biggest reason he'd brought him was to keep him from telling. He hoped the Massa would think they had just gone off fishin', and that would help slow down the search. If they could just make it to Helena, everything would be all right.

CHAPTER 22

A week passed, with no sign of the bushwhackers. Gatlin found himself wanting to hope, desperately wanting to hope, to deceive himself into believing that they wouldn't return. He knew that he could very easily convince himself that they were gone for good, but no, he had to be prepared. To fall into a mindless routine, to let down his guard even for an instant, meant death. At one time he had convinced himself that the painless oblivion of death was what he wanted, but now everything had changed, now he had to survive at all costs, because of the woman and the boy.

He kept the shotgun and the old squirrel rifle leaned against the hand-split door casing. He had worn the LeMat for so long that he felt totally naked without it. The boy Sam, with his big brindle dog, seemed to follow Gatlin every step. He showed the boy how to set snares, and let him and the dog check them each afternoon. He was almost afraid to let them out of his sight, but the boy seemed to be coming out of the emotional blockhouse he had built around himself since the shooting. Each evening just before dark he brought in a rabbit, a squirrel, or, sometimes, a groundhog. Sometimes, when Gatlin skinned them, there were unmistakable teeth marks that told him that the dog and not his own poorly designed snares had been successful. He almost always had a pot of stew hanging from the forged iron claw in the fireplace, although he knew that soon the hot weather would force the cooking outside into a rude rock fireplace built beside the cabin for that purpose. Gatlin knew they couldn't exist on stew alone so each morning he fried a squirrel or rabbit, along with wild onions. By trial and error he managed to cook hot cakes made of dried cattail root. When dried and pounded, the cat tail root made an ideal flour substitute. Growing up on the Arkansas River had taught him more than he would have thought possible. He and Mrs. Williams had run out of cornmeal and there was no hope of more until his corn crop was ready. There was still an abundance of wild strawberries and mulberries, although the latter had to be soaked in water to remove the countless tiny bugs. Gatlin supposed the bugs weren't harmful, since Sam came in every day with the juice liberally smeared around his mouth.

On what he judged was a Monday of the second week, Gatlin returned from working in the garden and seeing about the horses. As he walked toward the cabin, he enjoyed the fresh feeling of the morning . He stood for a moment and savored the sight of the sun's rays as they were scattered by the columns of silvery mist rising from the oak covered slopes to the east. This was truly a beautiful country, a country to grow with, a country to raise strong young sons in. He started, almost ashamed of himself for daring to dream of the future, something that he had not done in a long time. If only he had met the right woman before... Suddenly, he looked down, and there again were the twin trails where someone had walked through the dew.

Who was this Indian? Gatlin wasn't sure that their strange visitor was an Indian. For some reason Gatlin thought of the visitor as a he, but now he wasn't so sure. He had seen some of the homespun clad settlers from the hills, wearing moccasins when they brought their furs into Little Rock to trade. The Indian, if he was an Indian, must not mean him, Sarah or the boy any harm; otherwise the visitor would have tried to do something to them in the past week. Nevertheless, the unknown presence made Gatlin very uneasy.

As Gatlin drew near the cabin, he saw that the trail through the dew had passed near the front porch. Moving closer, he saw a half grown wild turkey lying on the porch. He picked it up and walked in the front door. Sarah Casey was fixing breakfast! He stood for an instant admiring the practiced ease with which she worked, before the full import of what he was seeing sunk in on him. Shocked by her rapid improvement, he lost his balance, and stumbled against one of the cane-bottomed chairs. As it crashed to the floor, he managed to regain his balance. Embarrassed, he looked over at her; she hadn't even turned around at the noise! He stood still for a moment, then feeling a little foolish, Gatlin clapped his hands together. There was no reaction from Sarah Casey! He sat down abruptly in the chair as the full impact of what he had just seen hit him with an almost physical force. Her mind had gotten much better, but she was totally deaf! He had been so concerned with survival that he hadn't given her senses a thought.

Sensing that she was being watched, Sarah turned around and smiled, but it was the somewhat vague smile one gives a stranger or chance acquaintance. She seemed to be struggling, trying to remember him.

Gatlin got up and walked outside. He sank down on the massive slab of limestone that served as a front step. The boy Sam, walked outside and sat down watching him expectantly. The brindle dog lay down next to the boy, watching him with adoring eyes.

Gatlin started talking to the boy as he had since the first day. "Sam," he said quietly, "Your mother can't hear."

He glanced at the boy, whose mouth moved soundlessly for an instant. When his voice came, it sounded hoarse. "Will she get better?" he asked.

Gatlin, startled at the response, relaxed a little. At least the kid could both hear and speak. Up until now, he hadn't been sure about either Sam's speech or mental condition. He suddenly felt a senseless happiness, as a sense of elation swept over him. He felt like yelling out loud but was afraid he would shock the boy back into silence. "I don't know, son. I really don't know," he replied quietly, hoping Sam wouldn't raise the wall of silence again. Gatlin hesitantly reached over and put his arm around the boy's shoulders, Sam stiffened for a moment, then relaxed, and they sat that way for a long time.

162

CHAPTER 23

Once Sam had broken his silence, he seemed more than willing to talk. His willingness quickly became typical boyish eagerness as he warmed up to Gatlin. The boy followed Gatlin, keeping up a constant barrage of questions as Gatlin went down to see about the horses. He asked about Gatlin's leg and the war. He asked where the horses came from, and Gatlin found himself telling the kid his entire life story.

Sam listened intently, then sat very still for a long time before he spoke. "I'm awful lucky to have," the boy's voice quavered as he hesitated, "I'm awful lucky to have had a mommy and a daddy, Mr. Gatlin. I miss my daddy so much, and he ain't never comin' back, is he.?"

"No, son, he's not." Gatlin could hear the trembling in his own voice. He stood silently for a moment, looking out across the hills. Clamping a lock on his own emotions, he tried to find words to somehow ease the boy's hurt. He remembered so clearly his own pain when he finally realized that his parents were gone and would never return. Parents were the nearest thing to God that a child could know, and his were gone. He had spent many a night curled up in his rags after yet another beating, hoping and dreaming that somehow, someday they would return. Somehow they would come back and everything in his world would be all right. Gatlin knew from his own experience that the concept of death was almost totally foreign to children, who are by nature optimists. Gatlin had thought about this quite a bit. It was good that this was so, because the bright outlook, the energy of children is what has kept the species going. Each generation suffered, enduring, each in turn hoping things would be better for their children, hoping against hope that their children wouldn't make the same mistakes. Yet somehow, they knew, deep in their marrow that all must blindly find their own way. Maybe it was this same optimism that acted as a two-edged sword, sustaining the human race, yet carrying with it the seeds of failure. Gatlin wished there was some way to convey his feelings to the boy. Gatlin knew that this would be difficult, if not impossible, because his long years of practice at hiding his emotions had made reticence part of his nature. At a loss for words, he reached down and pulled the boy to him, feeling the shaking of Sam's thin little body as they clung to each other.

Suddenly a thought struck him. "Sam," he said, "there's been someone coming around here, yet ol' Tige there never barks or has a fit about it." At the mention of his name, the brindle dog looked up and cocked his head sideways. A slight smile moved across the little boy's face. "I think he's an Indian," Gatlin continued.

"Beartrack is my friend." With this statement, the boy, with the dog hot on his heels, bounded away and bent down to lift a rotten log. He exclaimed at the bugs and worms he found there. Sam seemed to have forgotten his sadness of a few moments before, leaving Gatlin to stand and wonder. But at least he wasn't going crazy. There really was someone out there. He had been sure, but the affirmation of his sanity gave him quiet a bit of satisfaction.

The next day Gatlin worked in the hidden corn patch most of the day. Sam and Tige ran back and forth from the cabin to the corn patch. Gatlin was uneasy but hated to spoil their mood. He was afraid their tracks would lead someone to the corn patch and another crop would be lost. In the late afternoon sun he started up the bluff toward the cabin, but on impulse turned toward Mrs. Williams' grave. Pulling off the slouch hat she had worn, he stood and ran his fingers through his hair, looking down at the mound of red clay, already starting to flatten out. He knew that in time the soil would settle back in place. The grass would again cover it as if there was nothing beneath it. Is this all we have to look forward to? Gatlin thought, Do we work and struggle all our lives only to end up here? The soft nicker of a horse caused him to turn, and his hand automatically moving to the pistol.

"Easy there, I mean a man no harm who would take time to visit a grave."

Gatlin found himself facing a tall fairly thin man with a ready smile that lifted the corners of his handlebar mustache. Gatlin couldn't help but notice that the smile didn't quite reach the pale blue eyes. They were wide spaced and looked very sad, haunted even. His hair was cut the same length across the back and hung about three inches below his ear lobes, exaggerating the thin prominent nose. The haircut tended to give his whole face a square appearance. The man wore a round crowned hat, almost like the derbys worn further east, but with a flat brim. The hat was pulled low, so that his eyes seemed to glow from the shadow, cat-like.

Here, Gatlin knew instinctively, was a dangerous man. His belt held a brass-framed Colt Navy pistol in an open holster, similar to the way Gatlin had rigged the LeMat. In spite of the heat, the man wore a buckskin jacket that, unless Gatlin was mistaken, concealed at least one more pistol. He could tell by the way the jacket hung almost straight down from the man's left shoulder. There was a D-handled Bowie knife hanging on his right side in a deer skin scabbard tanned with the hair left on.

The man spoke again. "There was an old lady just up the road that used to feed me occasionally and give me a place to sleep a few times. If I was a gambling man, I'd bet that right there is her grave." With Gatlin's nod, he said, "I'm sorry, she was a fine old woman."

Gatlin swung his hoe onto his shoulder. "You'd just as well come on up to the cabin and eat a bit of supper. Mrs. Williams would have wanted it that way."

"Much obliged, I'll be glad to. What happened to her, if I might ask?" the man said.

Gatlin found the man an attentive listener. By the time they had walked back to the cabin he had started to tell the whole story. As they walked to the front door, the daylight was starting to dim. Sam and Tige came running around the corner of the cabin, and the man smiled and stuck his hand out to Sam, who eagerly shook it.

The boy turned toward Gatlin, "Mr. Hickok always comes by. Him and my dad always visit..." The boy hesitated, and his face started to draw up. It was as if he had somehow buried the pain for a little while and now it had forced its way back to the front of his thoughts again. Wiping the tears with the back of his hand, he turned toward Gatlin. His eyes pleaded for Gatlin to speak for him, to say the hateful words.

Then Gatlin spoke. "Levi Casey was murdered by bushwhackers. Mrs. Casey was badly hurt and seems to be deaf. She's got some kind of a lick on the head. She don't seem to remember anything." Gatlin forced himself to speak matter-of-factly. Putting it so might lessen the hurt for the boy. "I am Rit Gatlin, lately back from the war. I was staying here with Mrs. Williams. Now I'm taking care of the boy and his mother."

"I am Jim Hickok," the stranger said, by way of introduction, "but most people have taken to calling me Bill for some reason."

As they walked into the cabin, Sarah turned and smiled at them with that friendly yet somehow empty smile that Gatlin had come to know. Hickok spoke to her, removing his hat and sat down in one of the cane-bottomed chairs. Sarah had another big pot of rabbit stew hanging on the claw, and Gatlin dished up stew for each of them. Sarah set a dutch oven filled with cat-tail flour bread down in front of them, then sat down and started to eat shyly, glancing up frequently. Gatlin believed she knew she should remember Hickok, but somehow just couldn't make the connection.

Gatlin became engaged in one of the longest conversations he had enjoyed in years. Hickok was full of news about the war. He reported that the Federals were now firmly entrenched in parts of the South and the endless war might soon be over. "But if I know ol' Pap

Price, he'll try to invade Missouri at least one more time. Him and Shelby both think that if they can just get up there, they can raise another big army from among them Missouri boys."

"Didn't Shelby post notices on trees all up and down the White River that he would hang any man he found who hadn't joined one army or the other?" Gatlin asked. "At least that's what Mrs. Williams said."

"Yep," Hickok said. "He's getting tired of fooling with them murderin' bushwhackers, although I've heard that Price is all for letting some of Quantrell's crowd join the Southern Army. I'll bet ol' Shelby's having a fit about that one."

As Gatlin listened to Hickok, he wondered who's side he was on. Just what would such a man be doing riding alone in such country? As Gatlin discribed the attack on the Caseys, Hickok seemed very interested. He asked many pointed questions, listening intently.

After their supper was over, Hickok spoke up. "Mr. Gatlin," he said, "after supper every night, I always see to my weapons. It has been my observation that a poorly maintained weapon isn't much more than an expensive club. I hope you don't mind me doing it in here." Looking down at the boy, Hickok continued, "Sam, you've heard of old Jim Bowie, haven't you?" The boy looked up and nodded, hero worship plainly on his face. "Well," Hickok continued, "old Jim would have been dead back in '26 if Norris Wright had've been more careful about cleaning his pistol. Then Bowie wouldn't have been around to make himself famous at the Alamo, would he?" As he finished speaking, Hickok reached down and tousled the boy's hair, getting an embarrassed smile in return.

As he listened, Gatlin glanced over at Sarah, who was busy putting up the few eating utensils. He hesitated, hoping she wouldn't be alarmed by the open display of guns. "No, I think it'll be all right," he said.

With that, Hickok went outside and in a little while walked back inside carrying a rifle. Gatlin watched Sarah for signs of fear, but saw none. Evidently she had been raised around guns and regarded them as most people did, as just another necessary tool. Gatlin lit a tallow lamp and sat down, glad of the chance for some more conversation. Hickok brought out a small tool kit and went to work. He removed the wedge that secured the Colt Navy's barrel and ran a rag through the full length of it. He then held it up to the light, inspecting the rifling closely. He pulled the caps off the nipples, then apparently satisfied with their condition, stuck them back on again.

Sam sat and watched the cleaning with total fascination. After a while he asked eagerly "Mr. Hickok, could I learn how to shoot it? I want to kill them bushwhackers, the ones that shot my pa. Mr. Rit there, he won't let me learn how. He says that the bushwhackers might hear the shots and come a runnin'."

Hickok looked down at him with a sad smile. "Son, it takes a whole lot more learning to know when not to shoot than it takes to shoot. You see, my old pappy used to say that the first bullet is chisled in stone, anything after that is just insurance."

Sam moved closer, "What does that mean, Mr. Hickok?"

"What it means, son, is that once the gun is fired and a man is dead, you can't undo it, no matter how bad you want to. That man's face is in front of you every night when you go to sleep." His eyes turned opaque. He was obviously far away, alone with some demon that tormented his soul, something that worked on him down deep where the real Bill Hickok lived. His eyes came into focus and he turned to Gatlin, "I unload them every third day unless it's wet weather or they've been fired. That means one of them gets a fresh load every day." Hickok looked down at Sam and held the cylinder out toward him.

"That one's empty, Mr. Hickok," the boy said, closing one eye to look down the empty chamber.

"Yep," Hickok said, "you never want to rest the hammer on a cap. If you happened to drop the gun it would go off for sure. A man could blow his own fool head off that way." Hickok smiled at the boy. Gatlin watched as he reassembled the weapon, then pulled a second pistol out and gave it the same treatment. The second Colt had the end of the barrel sawed off even with the shortened loading lever. Hickok held it up for Gatlin's inspection. "You can see that I've enlarged the trigger guard and shortened the barrel. It speeds up the process. Not much, but sometimes it doesn't take much to make all the difference in the world."

Gatlin noticed that he only disassembled one weapon at a time, keeping the others ready at hand. He wondered just exactly what type of character this Hickok was.

Last of all Hickok reached for the rifle. "Colt revolving rifle," Hickok said, tapping the worn walnut stock. "There's a lot of people say they're unreliable. They call them thumb busters and worse. I've found them to be an excellent weapon. They're the same as any other rifle. The secret is to keep them clean and dry. The rifle uses the same size ball as the pistols, .36 calibre, which makes it a lot handier for a man who has to travel light. Of course you've got to watch and not put your hand around the front of the cylinder. There is always a powder flash around it that can give you a nasty burn." With that, Hickok thoroughly dissembled the rifle, pulled the loads and put in fresh powder, ball and caps. Gatlin couldn't help but admire the speed and precision with which he accomplished the task.

Sam finally went off to sleep, the big dog padding along behind him. Gatlin hated the thought of having the dog in the house, but maybe it would help the boy. With the dog, he obviously felt safer.

Hickok, finished with his own weapons, walked over and at Gatlin's nod picked up the squirrel rifle. "Looks like you've lost the front sight," he commented.

Gatlin felt a little foolish. "Yeah, I had to warp a feller up side of the head with the rifle when I was over at Camp Adams. They said his name was Dave Tutt."

Hickok looked up from his examination of the gun, obviously surprised.

"You've heard of him?" Gatlin asked.

Hickok tightened his mouth in what passed for a smile. "Mr.

Tutt and I have had our differences. I expect I'll probably have to put a quietus on him one of these days, that is, if somebody else don't beat me to it. If you've got a piece of bone, I can make you a new sight in a few minutes."

Gatlin reached down into his ammunition bag and pulled out one of the boar's tusks, which he had kept, not really knowing why. "That'll do real fine," Hickok said, already pulling out a small three-cornered file from his tool kit.

As he watched Hickok file out a flawless bead and blade front sight, Gatlin wanted very badly to ask Hickok what had brought him into this devastated area. The distinct smell of ivory dust hung in the air as Gatlin tried to figure out how to broach the subject. Somehow Gatlin knew it would be insulting, so they sat and talked some more about politics and the war. Gatlin soon realized that here was a man who really knew what was going on. He talked on about the fall of Little Rock and the fighting along the Mississippi. But Gatlin noticed that he never talked specifically about his own business. As the tallow burned down, both men finally went to sleep.

* * *

Hickok came awake suddenly, aware that he was in the Williams cabin, his instinct telling him something was wrong. His mind always seemed to start functioning a split second before his hearing and sight. Hickok didn't move, and got his bearings, aware of the Colt in his hand. He didn't know what had awakened him. He knew that the Allen and Thurber was still in its holster in his right boot top. Hickok was a very private man by nature and hadn't mentioned his other weapons to Gatlin. There was the pepper box pistol and the coffin-handled rifleman's knife, in its scabbard, the handle just even with the top of the waist band of his britches. He might have rolled over on the knife and awakened himself, but he didn't think so. He set a lot of store by that knife. It had been made for him by Dave LeMoine, the Cajun from over at Rapp's Barrens. It had helped him out of more than one fix. Hickok listened to the night, his senses honed to a razor's edge by years of outdoor living even before he had started scouting for the Union Army. He thought about this man Gatlin. He seemed to be exactly as he appeared on the surface, but Hickok had long ago learned that people are not all too often what they seemed. Gatlin could be a Confederate spy. If he was a spy he could have recognized Hickok from some description. Hickok's activities, after all, were not unknown to both sides.

Forcing his facial muscles to relax, Hickok listened. He could distinctly hear the slow breathing of Gatlin, the soft sounds of the woman and boy and the loud snoring of the dog. He gradually isolated out the squeaks and noises typical of any house. He didn't move an inch until he had identified every little sound. Only then did he slowly raise up, gripping the Colt. Glimmers from the half moon allowed him enough light to move silently to the front door. He stood there for a moment in his sock feet, listening. He could see the fog lying like a soft wool blanket filling the steep valleys and rolling out over the hills, as he eased the door open on its thick bullhide hinges and stepped out on the small covered porch. He noticed immediately that the usual night sounds were missing. "You could hear a cricket clear its throat out here," he thought. The leather thong was jerked tight around his throat before he had time to react! Hickok started to struggle even as he felt himself pulled backward against one of the cedar pole post supports. The pistol in his hand was jerked away and, with the post against his back, there was no way to lunge backward. Tensing his neck muscles only made the searing pain worse. His scout's vision started to dim, and he would have fallen if not for the post. Hickok must have passed out for a few seconds, because he was next conscious that the pressure had let up enough to let him breath.

Hickok could feel the rancid breath as it blew across his cheek. "How many are in the cabin?" The voice was quiet, raspy, and barely audible. "Is there just the woman and boy?"

It took a major effort, but Hickok raised his left hand and pointed to the string that was still almost choking him. The pressure lessened, and he sucked his lungs full of the sweet precious night air.

Hickok knew it was now or never. He slid to the right, firmly bracing himself against the pole with his legs still shaking. Continuing the same movement, he reached back over his shoulder with his left hand and whopped his assailant on the burr of the left ear. He felt the satisfying smack of the blow as it rattled his assailant's eardrum. In spite of the fact that he had a firm grip on the leather, the raider's head snapped to the right from the blow!

Hickok, now with fresh oxygen flowing to his brain, grabbed the slim knife from behind his belt with the first three fingers of his right hand and swung it backward in an arc, putting all of his ebbing strength into one desperate underhanded blow. He felt the blade scrape on bone then slide over to the left and up. The knife was torn from his grip and the pressure on his neck was gone! Hickok was unable to keep himself from sliding down the post. He rolled over on his all-fours, gagging and retching, aware that he was wide-open for another attack. He desperately ran his hands back and forth flat across the porch, filling them with splinters before finally locating the Colt. His thumb roostered the hammer back to half-cock as he balanced himself on his trembling left hand. His head swiveled back and forth in the darkness. He tried to see movement, a reflection, anything that would help anticipate the attack he knew was coming. He knew the knife blow had connected, wounding his assailant, but probably not seriously. If stalker was smart, he would start shooting any second, Hickok thought he would not risk another close-in attack. He knew better than to yell for Gatlin. The one-legged man might very well shoot him by mistake.

"Who are you?" The voice, deep and low, came out of the darkness. Hickok swung the Colt in the direction of the sound. He eased the hammer on back until it slid soundlessly into the full cock notch. His trigger finger moved a fraction to take the slack out of the trigger. Bill, as he now was known, waited, saying nothing. He knew that the muzzle flash of one shot would be enough to outline him, a perfect target. Hickok knew his opponent was hesitating for the same reason.

"Smart one ain't you? O.K. I wouldn't talk neither. You've killed me and I'm ready to holler calf-rope."

Hickok listened closely, the voice was getting thicker with something, possibly pain, or bait for a fatal trap.

"That pig-sticker of yourn done split me wide open just below the short ribs. You ripped up my liver and gizzard. I'm a-bleeding to death, and by mornin' I'll be dead as a hammer. I hope you'll give me a decent burial, whoever you are. They say the hogs got out and eat on them corpses after the Battle of Prairie Grove. Mister, I'm asking you to do the Christian thing here and bury me deep."

Hickok listened for the sound of any movement. His muscles were starting to cramp, yet he didn't dare to move. He desperately needed a drink of water to take the metallic taste out of his mouth. Any creaking of the puncheons beneath him might bring a hail of gunfire. It sounded like the man was starting to talk through clenched teeth. Pain? Maybe.

"I've got a letter in my pocket, with an address in Tennessee writ on it. I'd be obliged if you could write or somehow get word to them, tell them I done my job best I could."

The tone of the voice was changing, getting friendlier, a little whiney, and more at ease. Now Hickok knew the whole thing was bait, something to suck him into a trap. He listened carefully, knowing that here was a man who was capable of outsmarting him, and one tiny mistake meant death.

The man went on. "There ain't no need in that woman and kid sufferin' no more. Just who is that man in there with that woman? Where did he come from? Are you him? Or is there two of you? I found Casey's grave. Won't you at least tell me your name? I'll bet you're one of them pukes out of Missouri. I at least got a right to know who it was that killed me."

Hickok wanted to answer, but without him the ones inside would't have a snowball's chance in Hell. If Hickok hadn't woke up, they'd probably all be dead now.

Hickok heard a slight sound. He knew it for what it was, the sound of a pistol cylinder turning! He panicked, reacting instantly, throwing himself flat and rolling off the porch. A split-second later the silence of the night was torn apart with five shots that blended together into one rolling sound. All the bullets slammed into the same area of logs about five feet to Hickok's left, exactly where he had been lying seconds before. It could have been the sound of his own breathing or maybe the man was operating on instinct alone. Hickok was now lying prone. He knew he was well protected by the corner of the porch. The gun flashes had outlined the shooter and he instinctively pointed his Colt, then hesitated. Something made him stay under cover rather than return fire, exposing himself.

Hickok heard raised voices in the cabin, but he still didn't shoot. He turned his head and yelled, "Stay put, Gatlin!" There was instant quiet in the cabin.

"Now you can't blame a man for making one last try, now can you, boy? Now I'm out of loads, so I guess you won after all. I just had to try that newfangled Colt Revolver I got a few days ago. Now I can't see to reload it in the dark."

Hickok figured that if the revolver was really empty or even had the last chamber loaded, the man still had to have another pistol. A man that smart wouldn't gamble his life with a weapon that hadn't proven its worth. He flattened his left hand, easing it across the ground. Finding a fist-sized rock he threw it against the cabin wall. It struck and rattled across the porch.

"Just how dumb do you think old Clebourne is, anyway, son?" The voice was strained, but still deep and menacing. "Just because I got careless once, you must figure I'm green as a gourd. I was just trying to be careful, too careful. I ort'n to have been plundering around here. I shoulda just finished you off, instead of asking fool questions."

Hickok didn't move. His whole body was strung as tight as a fiddle string. He didn't know Gatlin. For all he knew the crippled man might come out the door at any moment, only to get a bullet for his trouble.

Inside, hearing the shots and the warning shout, Gatlin pulled himself up the wall, jerking the LeMat from the holster beside him on the floor. There was no need to worry about Sarah, she wouldn't have heard them. He slipped the wooden leg on, leaving the straps loose. As he moved to Sam's sleeping loft, he heard a soft growl. "Sam," he whispered, "be still and don't let the dog move. O.K.?" He could hear the boy's teeth chattering with fear in the darkness, but he kept quiet. Hickok must have gone outside while they were asleep and either shot someone or had been shot. In any case, Gatlin knew that if he opened the door he would just get himself shot, either deliberately by the intruder or accidently by Hickok. He crawled up beside the boy, staying by the edge of the sleeping loft, and hoping no shots came through the cabin. He knew he had no choice but to wait for the morning. He felt the boy move over closer to him, and he put his arm around him and pulled him close. In a few minutes Sam's breathing became deep and regular again. Gripping his pistol, Gatlin and Ol' Tige settled themselves in for a long sleepless night.

Hickok lay very still, trying to stop shaking all over. He was no stranger to violent death, but he had never ceased to be amazed by its sudden appearances. How long had it been since he had awakened? It couldn't have been more than fifteen minutes by his big watch, probably less. Yet in that length of time he had been locked into a fight for his life, why he had no idea, and probably never would. The damp coolness started to seep into his bones, but to be the first to move was to be the first to die. He was tired. It had been a long day in the saddle, but to sleep would be fatal as well. He turned his head and noted the position of the stars, the moon would set long before daylight. He wondered how many other men were lying out under the stars. He knew that in the battlefields to the east men would be preparing for battle. Some would be writing letters home, and some would be lying on their backs, looking at the stars and thinking of family and loved ones. Hickok himself had no loved ones to think about. There was not one living soul who cared whether he lived or died, but he couldn't complain, he chose this life, for better or worse.

He wondered about Gatlin. He had seen the way Gatlin looked at Sarah. He'll take care of her and the boy, he thought. If they survived they would become Gatlin's family.

Hickok almost jerked as another thought struck him. What if the man out there wasn't alone? He didn't think so, but there could be more of them out there, lying in ambush. Hickok quickly pushed that thought out of his mind. During the three long years of war, he had trained himself to concentrate on only one crisis at a time. He had learned not to waste his energy fretting about things over which he had no control.

The stars moved ever so slowly in an overhead arc toward the west. Hickok thought several times that he heard slight movements somewhere out in front of him, but he wasn't about to shoot at noises now. He had made that mistake once back in Nebraska at Rock Creek Station. Each night when he closed his eyes, he saw again the look on the face of young Monroe McCanles as he fell down beside his father lying dead on the ground, a round ball from Hickok's old plains rifle buried in his chest. If Hickok had only known that Dave McCanles was just trying to collect a debt from the stage company! If he had only known that the man had a son. Hickok had let himself be deceived by slick talk and his own need for money. It had looked like a simple job; just throw them out and be done with it. He should have known better. Now, he had to live with it every day of his life. He knew he would never forget or forgive himself. The image of that little boy would be with him every night for the rest of his days.

Finally, Hickok began to see a faint redness in the eastern sky. The urge to sleep was overwhelming as it always is at dawn after a sleepless night. It shouldn't be long now, in less than an hour one or both of the men in the yard would be dead. He concentrated on the area in front of him, wanting to be the first to see, the first to shoot. He waited. The sky turned redder and he waited. He could make out the tree tops now. He waited, not a muscle moving, forcing himself to breathe very slowly. He was careful to blink only one eye at a time. He began to make out the bulk of something lying about twenty feet out in front of him.

He waited some more, and could finally confirm that it was a man. Hickok was tempted to fire into him, to try to get a reaction. But no. He slowly stood up, and could feel the lumps that were his muscles slide over one another, sore as boils from stretching out on the cold ground. His eyes never strayed for an instant as he kept his pistol trained on the intruder. He took one tenative step, then another, circling so that the man would have to raise up and fire across his own body in order to get in an accurate shot. As Hickok moved along, his nerves were so tight that he felt like one of the puppets he had seen one time up north.

The man was dead all right. One hand held a heavy mountain pistol; the other was clutched up against his right side. The wound had bled heavily, staining the butternut colored homespuns and dry-ing black on the ground. Hickok stood for a moment before reaching down and closing the wide staring eyes with the tips of his fingers. He tucked his own pistol behind his belt and picked up the mountain pistol, at the same time removing the new 1860 Army Model Colt from its holster. Hearing a slight noise, he whirled as Gatlin moved out through the door.

"Gatlin," Hickok said, "do you know this man?"

Gatlin shook his head, "Never laid eyes on him before in my life. Are you all right?"

"Oh, I'm a little dauncey, but I guess it's mostly nerves." Hickok replied as he let out a deep breath.

Before Gatlin could make a move to stop them, Sam and the dog were out the door and standing beside them.

"Sam, this man tried to kill Mr. Hickok. He may have been trying to kill us too, do you know him?" The boy shook his head, his eyes never leaving the dead man. "We'd better get him buried. There's no need for your mother to see him, it would only make her worse." The boy nodded his head mechanically, the familar blank look on his face again.

Midmorning found Gatlin walking beside Hickok's horse as

the two men headed down the road. About fifty yards from the cabin, Hickok stopped. "Gatlin, my business takes me to the West and I'm in a considerable hurry or I would offer you some assistance, but, since I can't, I'll offer some advice. You need to get that woman and kid out of here. I think the bushwhackers will get a lot worse before they get better. Unfortunately, it's about a hundred miles to any kind of safe place in either direction."

Gatlin shook his head, "I can't take a chance on moving the woman right now. I guess we'll just stick it out."

Hickok stuck out his hand, "Well, I'll wish you luck then, but don't you let your guard down, even for a minute. The good book says there's 'the quick and the dead;' but in this war it's the smart and the dead, or maybe the lucky and unlucky." With that Hickok rode down the hill and out of sight.

Chapter 24
The Missouri Border

Riding a few yards in front of what he now thought of as his army, Colonel Morgan Cain was in rare good humor. He had ridden into West Plains, Missouri, and made contact with Colonel William Monks, the local Union militia leader. Monks had seemed willing, even eager to accept him as an equal on some unnamed secret mission for the Union. Monks seemed to be a man so blinded by his hatred of the Confederacy that he had little energy for anything else. This suited Cain just fine, for he would use Monks to his advantage.

Over the last few days, a plan that had been vague and nebulous in Cain's mind had begun to take shape. Here was a land, almost empty of the people who had settled and cleared it. Some of them were dead, no doubt. Most of the rest wouldn't return until the war--which the South was sure to lose--was over. Cain had seen enough to know that this war had almost drained to resources of the nation. The people living in the cramped cities of the North would need food. No longer would the hungry hordes of people be able to depend on wild game as a principle source of meat. Most of the game in the East had been decimated by constant slaughter and habitat destruction. The nation had spent the last three years fighting, not producing food. The great foraging armies had not only consumed the country's food supply, but each army had by turn also destroyed the people's will and ability to produce it. Several times he had spotted large groups of wild cattle in the cane brakes along the streams. There were hog tracks everywhere. Evidently when the civilians had

been driven out, they hadn't had time to gather their livestock. After food, the next
consideration would be rebuilding the railroads. The timber was here for the cross ties, sixty and seventy-foot red oaks grew in abundance along the ridge tops. It only had to be cut and floated down the river. The iron ore was here. He had seen its outcroppings in several places, and besides, somewhere out there was a cave full of silver. What Cain saw was an empire waiting to be claimed. All he had to do was remove the rest of the settlers, make sure none returned, and then just wait for the war to end. As a Union officer, it wouldn't be difficult to obtain title to the land he could claim was abandoned. Cain, believing he knew the dark side of human nature, was sure that the defeated South would suffer greatly at the hands of the vengeful North. Historically, the victors in any given war were not overly concerned with the rights of the vanquished. "To the victor belong the spoils" was not written in vain.

As he rode, Cain began to think of politics. With such a vast stretch of prime land under his control, he would be wealthy enough to run for public office, maybe even the U.S. Senate. His appearance had changed in the last two years. None of his boyhood acquaintances would remember him, especially with his new name and rank. He would proclaim himself a war hero, the liberator of the Ozarks. There would be no one left alive to dispute his claims. Of course, there remained the problem of his men. They knew too much of the murderous nature well concealed behind his smooth manner and handsome exterior. They knew of the men left dead in their burned out cabins, of the women and children carried off and killed, of the horses stolen. He had confided in none of his men, not the Zulu, not Howard, none of them. He knew that most of them were brutes, interested only in whiskey, women, a full belly and what little loose money could be had by petty thievery. Cain was sure that some of them would be killed in the next few months. When he was sure the war was over, he would arrange something to insure their silence, perhaps an accident in one of the numerous caves. It would be easy to lure them into one with the tale of the lost silver mine.

Cain frowned. He didn't know why, but suddenly he was bothered by the thought of the kid that had run into the woods. The boy had to be dead by now. There was no way he could have survived on his own for two weeks, not a boy that young. He regretted that they hadn't taken the time to hunt him down while they were at it. He had let himself be distracted, he had wanted that woman. They had stopped to water at the spring, and he would never forget her standing there, her water bucket in hand, holding the boy's hand, unafraid. In fact, she had looked at him as if she could read his lustful thoughts and held him in utter contempt. Cain had wanted her alive, at least for a while. Now, he remembered that there had been another cabin not too far from the one they had burned. There had been no sign of habitation, yet the place was too well kept to have been empty for long. There was even a garden. They would have to make another sweep through the valley to make sure. He couldn't afford the risk of leaving even one witness.

Cain's eyes came into sharp focus, narrowed, and he looked over his shoulder. "Men," he said, "we're going back to the Bayou." He heard them muttering behind him. Only the Zulu said nothing.

CHAPTER 25

"Is that you Willie? Come on in here."

Willie moved into the room and sat down in one of her old high backed kitchen chairs by the bedside. "How are you doing Aunt Catherine?

"You know dang good and well how I am, I'm dying, but after all what can a body expect? I've outlived all of my friends and enemies both, and I miss them all."

Willie smiled in spite of himself. The old woman was still full of piss and vinegar. Somehow she always managed to make him laugh. "You'll probably outlive all of the rest of us, they'll probably have to knock you in the head on judgment day."

"Now Willie, you know that I'm the last of my line. Both of my young'uns died of the fever when they was young, rest their souls. Now it's up to you and your kids to carry on the family name." She leaned back and undid a safety pin at the end of her pillow. She reached out and grasped his hand and put something in it. "Here," she said.

"What is it?" He asked. Holding it up in the dim light he ran his calloused thumb across its surface.

"Its elephant ivory, from Africa, it belonged to your great grandpa, Ulysses Johnson. Go on now, take it in yonder to the light and look at it, then come back and I'll tell you about it."

Willie walked into the front room and held it under the lamp. He fumbled around in the bib of his overalls and dragged out a pair of reading glasses he had picked up at Wal-Mart. He turned the carving over and over in the light. It was beautifully done, just about the size of a silver dollar. it was, judging by the grain, made from a cross section of an elephant tusk. It was about three-eighths of an inch thick, with a hole drilled in the upper edge. The raised part of the disk was carved into an elephant. Its foot was resting on the body of a lion. It warmed to his touch and seemed to glow with a light of its own. It had a curious pattern of marks that reached about three-quarters of the way around the perimeter. The marks had to be part of the design, but Willie noticed that there seemed to be no real pattern to them.

Willie walked back into the darkened bedroom. "It's awful pretty, Aunt Cat." He said, as he sat back down in the chair.

"Well, like I said, it belonged to your great-grandfather. He said it belonged to a man he called the Zulu. When I asked what a Zulu was, he said, "we was Ibo, but he was Zulu." I was just a little girl then and didn't know enough to ask more questions. The only other thing I remember him saying was that Johnson was not our name. Grandpa said that when the bluecoat soldiers asked his name, he told them Ulysses. When they asked his last name, he told them Johnson, 'cause he didn't want them to think he just had one name."

Willie walked down the sidewalk. The grass growing through a crack was nearly six inches high. He reminded himself to get back over here and at least trim the grass. He looked down at the carving one last time and shoved it into his pocket.

Jerking the truck door open, he slid across the piece of poly tarp that served as a yellow and blue seat cover.

CHAPTER 26

She shifted uncomfortably , the backs of her sweaty legs sticking to the slick vinyl seats. She had been heavy even as a child, and now after trying innumerable crash diets, she had given it up. She looked at her reflection in the side mirror with distaste. She had to get in next week and get the roots retouched. She briefly considered letting it go back to brunette, but she had dyed it blond for so long she couldn't conceive of anything else.

Why did he insist on driving that silly four-wheel-drive pickup truck? She hated it. It rode too rough and made all kinds of weird noises. She had tried to get him to drive her minivan, but no, he had insisted. She ought to just drive off and leave him, but the pickup had a four-speed transmission, and she couldn't drive it even if she had the nerve to try. Besides that how would she find her way out of these steep hills?

What made him this way? Why couldn't he be like the boys she grew up with?   Maybe it all went back to the fact that he had been so poor when she met him. At that time he was desperately working his way through college on a work-study program. He was the first of his family to attend college. In fact, his fresh honesty and enthusiasm for life was what had first attracted her attention. She couldn't honestly have said she had been attracted to him. Her mind just didn't work that way. The folkways and mores of the society she was raised in required that she have a husband, and she had pursued him so relentlessly that he finally gave up and married her.

She wasn't extremely intelligent and never would be, but she knew that she could take the right man and make him successful. After all, wasn't she the only child of a very wealthy man? Her father was so adept at buying cloth overseas, having it made into shirts, then importing the garments into the U.S. to have one collar button sewn on each shirt. They could then sport the beautiful red, white, and blue "MADE IN USA" label and be bought by Americans who thought they were helping keep their countrymen employed by paying a few dollars more for them than the ones labeled "MADE IN SRI LANKA," wherever that was.

She had finally come to realize that he would never be the sophisticated man of the world she had hoped to marry. His people had been raised here, right here in this wretched piece of country with its ticks and chiggers. Why couldn't he have just gone back to New York with her? Why did he insist on getting not only a Master's in history but going back and getting a doctorate in the boring subject as well. He had gone on to become a teacher, and, furthermore, insisted on taking a teaching position in an Arkansas university. A position where money and prestige were as rare as hen's teeth.

She would divorce him if it weren't for the boys. It was not that she was concerned about their growing up without a father. She would never have admitted it, but she simply didn't want the responsibility of raising them herself. He always took them with him, even on these silly trips of his, these "expeditions," as he called them, to search for Indian artifacts and evidence of the early settlers. In between expeditions he was always either teaching or reading some obscure publication. He kept dragging home personal papers written by some of the early characters of Arkansas. He had become so enthused about Arkansas and especially Ozark history that it had become embarrassing. He insisted on talking about the early settlers of the Ozarks to anyone who would listen, even to the women of her garden club when he happened to wander in during one of their meetings. He didn't know they were rolling their eyes at each other when he wasn't looking. She looked up the creek to where he and the boys had disappeared. How long was this going to take? After all, he had promised to take them to Silver Dollar City after he got through. She looked dejectedly at the selector on the dash that said AIR CONDI-TIONER. She knew it didn't work.

CHAPTER 27

The one known to the whites as Dan Beartrack, but who, even after all these years, still thought of himself as the Cherokee Yo'Nuh Uta' Sinuh-Yi, stood and looked down at the hoof prints in the dusty twin tracks of the wagon road. They were now grown up in weeds. He could still hear the soft sound hoofbeats as the band of bluecoats rode around the curve and out of sight. He glanced down the road again, making sure there was no rear guard, shifting the Bois D'Arc bow to his left hand as he did so. He looked down again, eyes narrowed. It was the same horses all right. Each track was now as fixed in his mind as the face of an old friend. It was the same band of men who had so ruthlessly pulled the raid on the Caseys, who had been the only real friends he had in the world. He felt every muscle in his body pull taut, although to a casual observer he would have only appeared to straighten up slightly. It was if the man the whites called Beartrack had never existed. He was now indistinquishable from his forefathers who had fought in battles never to be recorded in the white man's history. Beartrack now would follow the paths of war, as had his father and generations of fathers before him. There would be no quarter asked or given. He forced himself to relax. He had to work out the trail, had to know where they were going and why.

His grandfather had taught him that although tracking is done with the eyes, the most important part of it takes place in the mind. In order to be successful, the tracker must learn to put himself in the place of his prey, thus Beartrack had learned to think like the Wolf, the Deer, the Bear and later, other humans.

Beartrack remembered how his grandfather had taught him about the Nunnehi, the little people; but he had never learned how to track the little people. He had often begged his grandfather, "Tell me about the little people."

The stern old man known as Warclub would sometimes almost smile. "They have long gray beards, down to their toes and long gray hair, much like old white men, the U-Ne-Ga, but they are Tsa-ragi', like us. But they are shorter than you, my son. The women are beautiful and their names can be heard in the sound of the water. The men's names can be heard in the sound of the thunder."

Beartrack, nine years old at the time, asked eagerly, "When will I get to see them, Grandfather?"

The reply was long in coming. "They are always with us. You can almost see them living behind waterfalls, in patches of sage, under ledges, on the sides of steep mountains. You can almost see them, and then they are gone. They are here to help, most of the time, but if you see them, you must not tell for seven days. When you die, they will come and lead you to the spirit world." After that, Beartrack could get no more discussion on the matter from the old warrior.

Beartrack stood for a moment, remembering how the old man had insisted that he learn the old ways of his people, as well as the ways of the whites. The old man made him learn to make the flint knives and arrowheads of his people. Although at the time he could not understand why, since the metal tools and trade tomahawks obtained from the white men were much better. He learned about the useful plants. He knew that to rub himself with the Pennyroyal that flowered white on the wide limestone glades would drive away the ticks and mosquitoes. He learned to brew the willow bark tea to cure headaches. He learned that the brain of an animal could be used to tan its hide. He learned to build many different kinds of shelters. He learned how lashings could be made of grapevine bark. He learned to cure jerky and to pound it with berries and fat to make what the whites called pemmican. When he wanted to ask the old man why all of this was important, the scowl on the old man's face made him hold his tongue.

His grandfather had scouted for the British-led Tories during the Revolutionary War. The British, like the French traders before them, had promiséd to keep settlers from the Cherokee lands. This was before his people learned not to trust the word of any white man. The old man had often taken him to the forests and cane brakes along the river when Beartrack would much rather have been playing or fishing with the other boys his own age. His grandfather had made a game of it, laying out a trail through the hills and river bottoms that often took Beartrack two days to figure out.

His father had been killed in the great battle at Horseshoe Bend. He and many other Cherokees had joined the settler army under Andrew Jackson to make war against their ancient enemies, the Creeks, reasoning that they had hated the Creeks much longer than they had the whites. One of Jackson's men, Sam Houston, fought so well that the Cherokee accepted him as one of their own. Even as a youngster, Beartrack could see that his people had adopted the white man's ways of farming. They ran flocks of sheep and herds of cattle and became more and more indistinguishable from the white settlers to the east of them. The only exception was Beartrack's band that lived on Chickamauga Creek. They and they alone still retained the old ways. The Cherokee had been forced into peace after losing numerous battles with the armies of settlers. Armies that invaded and destroyed their towns in retaliation of Indian raids on the whites' homesteads.

Beartrack's grandfather made sure he learned that tracks do not exist merely as footprints; often a trail is only pressed down grass or leaves, and even when a footprint is found, it is often blurred or indistinct. He gradually came to realize that tracking requires that the tracker put himself into the mind of the animal or the person being tracked, and this Beartrack was able to do instinctively. Even as the memories filled his mind with images, the Indian started an easy lope down the road that cut across the lapland. He had to get ahead of the bushwhackers before they reached the cabin. Any white man would have guessed Beartrack to be in his early forties, but in reality, he was fifty-five.

As nearly as he could tell, it had been twenty-five years, or thereabouts, since the long ragged lines of Indians had trudged silently past him as he kneeled beside his wife, Tranquilla, his arms wrapped around her, urging her to try and stand.

The calvary officer had been kind compared to most of the soldiers. He stopped his horse beside Beartrack. "When she gets better you can catch up with us," he said, his voice sympathetic.

They both knew she wasn't going to get better. Beartrack looked up at him for a long moment. "We would be in our cabin now with a warm fire if you whites had left us alone." His bitter voice was so low that the calvaryman had to strain to hear him above the roar of the winter wind and the chatter of the sleet against their clothing. He spoke English well, but nevertheless the Indian's voice carried accents and inflections that were solely Cherokee. There was no further conversation. The soldier turned away, and the sound of his horse was lost in the storm. Beartrack reached down and brushed the frozen white grains from Tranquilla's hair. He waited with his head bowed until the noise of the soldiers, the rhythmic squeaks of their saddles and the sounds of his people shuffling along, had passed, absorbed by the fury of the storm.

His people, were proud, maybe too proud. They were the Tsa' ragi. They had once had beautiful farms along the Tennessee river. Now they were no more. The cabins, the goods, all burned. Once they had been mighty. Once they had fought great battles with the Creeks. His great-grandfather had been killed by one of their thick arrows with its finely-chipped flint tip. Beartrack didn't hate the Creeks; he had never hated them, but he had often wondered what had happened to what few of them that were left. The Creeks had been fierce fighters. They had tested his people since the time of the old ones. Strong enemies were good and they kept a people strong, but the U-Ne-Ga, the whites, were different. Their thoughts were not the thoughts of the Indian. They fought in winter and made war on

women and children. They distroyed the food supply of their enemies, and they did not respect courage. Many of them had no sense
of honor, and they even spoke of owning land. Beartrack's people
lived on the land, but how could people own land? The land belonged to the Buffalo, the Deer, the Eagle, even to the Quail. The
Indian, as the whites called him, knew that he was only one of the
creatures that shared the land.

The whites came and they kept coming. At first his people
had. fought, but the whites weren't good enemies. They used their
guns to kill at a distance, and there was no chance for the Tsa'-ragi to
prove courage. Soon the Cherokee recognized that these white men
could not all be destroyed; there were too many of them, so the Cherokee tried to live peaceably with them. The French were easy to live
with. They came and traded and lived much like the Indian, adopting
Indian ways, marrying Indian women. Then came the English, with
their red coats, the English, who managed to involve the Indians in
the white man's war, thus turning the hatred of the colonists toward
the Indians. Alhough there were many battles with the early settlers,
they still lived somewhat like the Indian, and over the years there had
been many marriages between the two peoples. Then came the greedy
whites, the lazy ones. They gave or traded Beartrack's people the
firewater, the white man's whiskey. To many Indians, whiskey spelled
disaster. The Indian was unused, both genetically and culturally, to
alcohol.

These greedy white ones coveted the fine lands of Beartrack's
people, the bottom lands that lay cleared along the Tennessee river,
the wooded limestone hills above them. They didn't want to work
the land, they were too lazy for that. They wanted to sell the land.
They started to complain, these greedy ones, that the Indians had the
best lands. They started to complain to others like themselves, those
who did not remember how it was in the very beginning, when the
Indians had taught the whites to raise the Indian corn, as they called
it. Along with the corn they planted the squash, the pumpkins and all
the other foods that kept the whites from starving through those first

bad winters. Beartrack's grandfather had told him these stories, as his father had told them to him, but now all that was forgotten.

There was a new white father in Wa-Shing-Ton, he was the Indian fighter who had won the war against the Creeks. He was the man the Cherokee had regarded as their friend among the whites. This man who now seemed to burn with hatred toward all Indians, was Andrew Jackson. Now the white government said the Cherokee must all move, and they must not fight. They had gone to the white man's court, and they had won, but it did no good. Jackson had challenged the court to enforce their decision. The Cherokee must give up their beautiful river bottoms with the hundreds of ducks feeding in the shallows. They must give up the cane brakes with the deer. They must give up the clear waters and move far to the west, far west to another land that the whites promised would be even better. Beartrack wondered why, if the new land was so good, the whites did not move there themselves. Since most of the Tsa' ragi,' or Richahickan, as they now called themselves, had become farmers, they had lost the will to fight.

The young men had not been taught to be warriors in many years. The government sent soldiers, many soldiers. As the soldiers started to surround the Indian cabins one by one, there was not time to organize resistance. Most of them had not resisted. With the optimism borne of self-delusion, they had wanted so desperately to believe that the lands to the west really were better. They reasoned that anything would be better than the constant harassment from the whites around them. Beartrack and Tranquilla, with their two small children, had sat in their small cabin, frozen with the enormity of the unbelievable. They waited for the soldiers to come and take them, as others had been taken, being allowed to remove only what personal property they could carry. They knew what was happening, but they found themselves able to accept the inevitable, unable to resist. The greedy ones would be right behind the soldiers, and they wouldn't wait until the Indians and their escorts were out of sight before they started to loot and destroy the possessions it had taken lifetimes to accumulate.

At first Beartrack had been determined to fight them, but his grandfather and his wife had convinced him resistance would be futile. As the soldiers approached, his grandfather had stood up from his bed. Beartrack had noticed that the old man had been failing more and more of late, but after all, he was eighty summers old. The old man moved to the back of the cabin and came back with his red cedar bow and arrows.

"What are you doing Eni' si'?" he asked, using the respectful Cherokee term for grandfather.

The old man stood up straight and proud, his watery black eyes showing anger and pride. "Son of my son, the one known to the whites as War-Club, to the Cherokee as Atasu' will not go, he will stay and fight."

"Then I will also stay," Beartrack replied.

The old man turned and looked at Beartrack, their eyes meeting for a long moment. "No," the grandfather said emphatically, "You must think of your little ones. You must learn to live in the world of the white man, you must learn more of his ways, you must survive, and you must survive for them." He pointed to Beartrack's little family. "You go now, for the white soldiers come."

Beartrack reluctantly gathered the red trade blanket and opened the door just as a squad of soldiers stepped up. Behind them stood a crowd, some of whom Beartrack recognized as men who had been chased off Indian land, some of whom were suspected of stealing Indian cattle and horses.

196

CHAPTER 28

Beartrack knew the ringleader of the band of whites well. His name was Billy Luttmann, but both whites and Indians called him "Bully." A known cattle thief, Luttmann had been suspected of burning several Indian cabins and barns as well. Then there was the matter of the Indian girl out berry picking who disappeared without a trace after he had been seen in the area. Luttmann stood just behind the soldiers, a jeering expression on his face; and from what Beartrack had seen of the white man's whiskey, he knew Luttmann and his two brothers, Curley and Slim, who stood with him, were drunk on it. Beartrack stepped outside the cabin, holding his little ones close and gripping Tranquilla's hand. He stood by the soldiers and looked at the hated whites. He saw their eyes burning with lust, and it was not only lust for his woman. He had seen those thoughts in men's eyes before, but this was a different lust, a lust he couldn't understand, but he knew it for what it was, a lust to destroy, to tear down, to kill.

The Indians were supposed to take no weapons with them, but under his loose-fitting calico shirt was a the Green River skinning knife, its curved blade honed to a razor's edge, and the head of the Hudson's Bay trade tomahawk that had belonged to his father. He reached down and felt their reassuring outlines, but the weapons would not help him against such odds. The soldiers were supposed to be there to protect the Indians as they left their beloved land. Beartrack knew that the squad of soldiers, even if well intentioned, would be powerless against a mob of the lawless white men. As he hesitated outside the door, he saw his grandfather shuffle forward, his ragged sleeping blanket wrapped around his thin shoulders. The old man's coarse white hair was pulled into braids under a tattered derby hat. That hat had been thrown away by some white man, and found by old Warclub, and decorated with an eagle feather. It was his most prized possession. The burly commanding sergeant, not wishing to appear sympathetic to the Indian's plight, roughly pushed Beartrack away from the tiny, clay-chinked cabin that had been his home for so many years. Beartrack, his smoldering anger ignited, pushed back. As the sergeant hit the ground on his back, the rest of the soldiers rushed forward. Old Warclub, his muscles protesting at the speed at which they were being moved, jerked his bow from beneath the blanket and with the precision of a lifetime of practice, and nocked an arrow. Its flight, a moment later, made an almost audible hiss as it split the air. The arrowhead, with its rippling jagged flutes, had been painstakingly knapped from a nodule of flint as big as a man's head. Bully Luttmann, his attention riveted to the commotion, did not see the arrow that tore into the base of his throat and imbedded itself fully a half inch into the fifth cervical vertebrae. He hit the ground writhing and pulling at it with both hands. Even as Bully Luttmann's nervous system failed, Warclub's second missile was entering the center of Slim's chest. The bow coming back to full draw again, when the Sergeant, alerted by the twang of the bowstring, turned and grabbed for the heavy flintlock pistol hanging from his broad leather belt by a hook. The hook, designed to secure the pistol, slowed down his move. In the second it took him to react, the third arrow had been launched on its fatal trajectory. Curly, reacting to his brother's grunt of pain, turned toward him, and the third arrow, likewise intended for his chest, transfixed his lower rib cage. The arrow's bloody tip extended itself almost four inches from under his right arm. The turkey feather vanes contrasted with his filthy cotton shirt as the arrow pinned the garment against his body. Warclub, the old Chickamauga warrior, was smiling. He was happy for the first time in years. He smiled even as the flint finally ignited the pistol's main powder charge and he was driven back against the cabin wall by the impact of a half-ounce round soft lead ball. The old Indian died instantly. His fall was punctuated by the flare of orange and a cloud of black powder smoke. The soldiers, the other ruffians, even Beartrack himself, were frozen in time and space. Probably a full second passed before the crowd of ruffians surged forward. The squad of soldiers, following their training, whirled to face this new threat. The click of the hammers on their Harper's Ferry muskets made a long ragged sound in the sudden stillness.

The Sergeant, quickly charging his pistol, turned to the crowd of thugs, "You men move up to that hill side there and start digging a grave with whatever you can find." Anticipating their protests, he turned to his own men, "If any one of them refuse, shoot them," he commanded in a loud clear voice. He turned to Beartrack, "If you injuns have any kind of service, you have until the grave is dug, if you try anything you'll be in that hole with the old man."

Beartrack, his mind overwhelmed by the events of the last few moments, pulled the clutching hands of his woman and children away then walked over and knelt by his grandfather's body. It was plain from his last expression that the old one had died completely at peace with himself. He had also taken three of the Cherokee's enemies with him, this is what he wanted. He hadn't wanted to leave his beloved land, and now he wouldn't have to. His body could stay here forever, to become part of the land again. His spirit had already winged away to the land where the Great Spirit dwelt.

Beartrack stood up and turned to face the Sergeant. "The Tsa' ragi will bury his own dead," he said slowly. The Sergeant nodded, respect in his eyes, as Beartrack walked over and picked up the trade ax that had been left outside the cabin. He turned and walked in the opposite direction from where the crowd was dragging the bodies of the Luttmann's. He walked to the top of a small knoll overlooking the cabin.

After he had hacked a crude grave into the red clay, Beartrack walked back down and picked up his grandfather's slight body. Wrapping him in the blanket, he laid his grandfather gently in the grave, then with the musket of one of the soldiers trained on him, he carefully placed the bow and crossed the two arrows on top of the body. After filling the grave, he noticed that the associates of the Barger brothers had finished filling their mass grave. Beartrack straightened up, "We are ready," he said, as he walked back to stand with his little family.

CHAPTER 29

She walked, or rather stalked, through the swinging doors past the receptionists and secretaries. They all looked the other way, their lips pursed in disapproval. There weren't any of them who didn't feel as if they could do her job and do it twice as well. She walked down the hall, her stiletto heels echoing on the tiles and turned into the studio door. Sliding into the chair, she glanced at the teleprompter and then at the clock. She ignored the glares of the technicians and shifted her weight, wetting her lips and working her facial muscles to loosen them.

Her makeup, hastily applied at home, failed to hide the effects of too many margaritas and two failed marriages, not to mention an only son serving hard time in Mexico for narcotics smuggling. At one time she had been considered a rising star slated for the prime time shows out of New York, but it was too late for that now. She was destined to spend the rest of her working life moving from one small television station to another, becoming increasingly bitter and always blaming others for her failures.

She started to read, her voice slightly rough from too many late nights and unfiltered cigarettes. She still knew exactly how to put in intonations of sorrow while discussing the arson that burned a whole family; righteous indignation when telling a bit about child abuse; or a neutral tone when reading the fillers on a slow news night. Tonight she used the neutral tone.

"The forensic report on the skeleton unearthed near Chickamauga Lake last month has archaeologists and anthropologists buzzing with excitement. You may remember that authorities at first believed that the skeleton belonged to the victim of a recent murder. However extensive testing by the state crime lab has revealed that while it is true that the skeleton is in all probability that of a murder victim, the there is a surprising twist. This particular murder appears to have happened at least 130 years ago. The skeleton now appears to be that of a native American, and anthropologistst noted the bone structure is consistent with Indians of the Cherokee nation. Because of the complete preservation of the skeleton, pathologists were able to establish the cause of death. It appears that the victim, an elderly male at least 70 years old, met his death at the hands of an assailant wielding a large calibre muzzle-loading pistol. The round lead ball passed directly through the victim's breastbone and was found flattened and lodged in the seventh thoracic vertebrae. Authorities say death must have been instantaneous. On a related note, representatives of the Chickamauga reinterred the skeleton in the same area it was found. If you will recall, it has been just a little over five years since eight skeletons, mostly women and children, were discovered outside Chattanooga at Ross' Landing. Historians say Ross' Landing was used as a gathering point for the Cherokee Indians before they were forced by the U.S. Government to embark on a journey that later came to be called the Trail of Tears. This journey ultimately led to the deaths of over 14,000 Indians as they were being moved to what is now the state of Oklahoma."

"Could your dish cloth be harboring disease-causing germs? We'll continue with the second part of our five-part series ARE THE GERMS WINNING? when we return." As the camera light went out she put down the papers she was holding and let out a long ragged sigh.

CHAPTER 30

As Beartrack, the soldiers and his family topped the ridge above the cabin, he stopped and looked back. There in the bend of Chickamauga Creek, the tiny cabin was already in flames, and he could see the small figures of the white men starting to gather his cattle. He stood for a long moment as if to burn the image into his mind. Tranquilla leaned against him, both arms wrapped around his ridged forearm. The two little boys, not fully understanding, looked up at their parents for some sign, some indication, however subtle, that everything was going to be all right. Finally Beartrack, by sheer willpower, tore his gaze away from the beautiful valley, this valley where he and his people had lived since the time of the old ones. He looked down at his wife and boys. When he spoke, the words came slowly, his voice hoarse with feeling. "My grandfather told me that when the Tsa'ragi` first came to this land, there were strange white people here, people who's seeing was not good in daylight. My people called them the Moon-eyes. They had settlements all along the Tennessee River. They were not mighty warriors, their medicine was weak so they were driven away. What happened to them we do not know. Now Beartrack understands in his heart how they must have felt, these strange whites of the old time whose ghosts wander here still." He swept his arm across, pointing at the horizon, then continued, "As a warrior, I know that it has always been so, that a people only held a land until another tribe came, those with better bows, stronger medicine or more warriors. The Moon-eyes got no mercy, and the White-eyes will likewise give no mercy to the Tsa-ragi`."

Tranquilla listened, tears flowing down her cheeks, her eyes fixed on her husband's face. Beartrack stood, his face expressionless, taking a long look at his people's land for one last time, then silently turned, and not waiting for his family or the soldiers, started to pick his way down the backbone of the ridge that was strewn with broken ledge rocks.

They were assembled with hundreds of their people at a place called Ross's Landing. Although Beartrack knew a good many of them, there was very little visiting, and no joy in the occasion. Each family was caught up in their own loss and misfortune, not paying much attention to the troubles of others. Many of the older ones were sitting, staring off into space, taking no notice of the goings-on around them. Beartrack was afraid they couldn't adjust to the change, a new life. He had watched such things before. Maybe a leave-taking from this world was necessary before entering the spirit world. Beartrack had noticed and wondered about this. Even as a young-ster, he had noticed that the old progressively lost interest in this world, to focus on another, a new world that now held their interest. As their relatives fed them, they chewed instinctively, mechanically, without relish. Even the little ones didn't run and play, but were uncharacteristically quiet, sitting and watching their elders, their eyes wide, trying to fathom what was happening and wondering how they would be affected.

Tranquilla watched the old ones for a long time, then turned to Beartrack, "Will we ever be like them?' she asked, wondering.

Beartrack shook his head, "Maybe we'll all be like them," he said, deep sadness in his voice, "My grandfather chose his own way, and Beartrack is glad in his heart that he did."

They were loaded, along with their meager possessions, onto four flatboats, together with a streamboat, and started down the Tennessee River. Beartrack and Tranquilla stood uncomfortably and watched their beloved land slide past. By the second day some of the Cherokee started to sicken from the unaccustomed motion of the boats and the strange food. Soon the boats would be pulling to the shore each evening to bury the day's dead. The soldiers tried to take care of their charges as best they could, but very few of them had any medical training. Even if they had been trained doctors, their ability would have been useless, because these people weren't dying of sickness of the body, but something far more serious, a sickness that had no cure, the sickness of the heart. On the evening of the fourth day they came to a series of rapids, which the soldiers called the Suck, the Boiling Pot, the Skillet and the Frying Pan. Beartrack listened to their fearful talk and wondered. His family had never traveled to this area, and he had no idea of what to expect. First there was a rumbling, a vibration that was more felt than heard. It was felt in the thick puncheons that made up the hull of the flatboat, it was felt in the bones and the teeth, it permeated every pore of one's being. Then the rumble steadily increased until it became a roar, a roar that drowned out all conversation, all other sound. Beartrack looked down at the boys, but they were gone! While his attention had been diverted by the approaching rapids, the boys Tas'a nuwa, Hawk, and the little one Tsay'ku', Jay, had slipped away to the other side of the boat to get a better view. Beartrack, his heart in his throat, started to push his way across the crowded deck toward them. He started to shout, but couldn't hear his own voice. Suddenly Tranquilla rushed past him, her mouth open in an unheard soundless cry. She was the primitive mother, operating solely on instinct, fighting to save her young, as all creatures do. Beartrack himself fought for balance, finding it impossible to move, as the flatboat entered the Suck. The steering oar hit a huge underwater boulder, splintering the great wooden pin that allowed it to swivel. The steersman tried unsuccessfully to keep his balance, failed and was flung through the air, arms and legs akimbo, then disappeared into the foaming waters. Its steering gone, the flatboat could only whirl and spin helplessly like a wood chip as it, along with its unfortunate cargo, was carried along by the relentless river. This, the second flatboat in the flotilla, started to slow with the increased drag and the third flatboat began to gain on it. Something, some premonition of danger, made Beartrack glance up from his futile attempt to reach his sons.

He could see the drawn white face of the other flatboat's steersman as he tried without success to avoid a collision. At this point the runaway flatboat slid in front of the first one, turning sideways across its bow, long streamers of water drenching the occupants. There was no overcoming the irresistible grip of the current. As it smashed the two boats together, the shuddering impact could be heard over the background roar of the rapids. As is the manner of such things, time seemed to slow down, giving an observer a unique perspective. Beartrack could distinctly see the wood grain in the heavy oaken timbers of the other flatboat as it was pushed ever closer. He realized that it was going to ride up and over theirs. He could see the Cherokee clinging to the other boat. Every face, wide eyed, turned toward them! Finally, he caught sight of his boys, frozen with terror as the sides of the smitten boat started to bend inward, then to splinter. His boys, finally realizing what was happening, turned toward the only salvation they knew -- their parents, their parents who were always able to fix everything. Forever burned into Beartrack's mind was the stark terror in their young faces. Even at a distance he could read the beseeching look in their eyes. Escape was impossible. Some of the Indians were ground under the heavy hull; others were flung into the air, seeming to sail slowly, gracefully, only to be sucked down instantly by the foaming white water. Beartrack and Tranquilla were both flung to the deck, their fall cushioned by squirming Indians.

That evening, they buried sixteen of Beartrack's people and three soldiers, along with his sons. They were buried on a little knoll overlooking the treacherous rapids. There were several older graves there, marked only with little piles of rock. The life went out of Tranquilla's eyes then, although her tears were silent.

The rest of the journey down the seemingly endless Tennessee seemed a continuous blur. The river ran south, then turned north to finally join the dirty-brown Mississippi. The convoy of misery started its float down the broad river. Any one of the buckskin-clad frontiersmen who had fought the proud Cherokee would have been hard pressed to recognize the savage grandeur of his former enemies in any of these ragged bundles of humanity.

Beartrack's immediate concern was Tranquilla. The loss of his sons had wounded him deeply, but he knew that somehow he would survive. Now Tranquilla seemed to lose the will to live. She stopped eating even the meager amount of food they were given. She sat on the boat, staring at the floor boards, her eyes flat and black in her slack face. He tried to talk, but all he got in return was a blank stare. As he looked into her eyes, it seemed that she had retreated to some private grieving place deep inside her soul, a place she wouldn't allow him to enter. He tried to talk of the new lands, tried to pretend that everything would be better there; but it did no good. When she stepped off the flatboat into what the soldiers called Arkansas territory, she was so weak that he had to support her, and he thought that she felt unusually warm. Still, with him helping her along they made it until they came to the hills and the blizzard hit.

After the convoy had moved on and left them, Beartrack stood up with Tranquilla in his arms and started to walk. The walking became slower. The walk gradually turned to stumbling. It was sometime in that long night, with sleet crunching under his thin moccasins and the wind gnawing away at his exposed skin like some incredibly vicious animal, that his beloved Tranquilla's spirit left her. He squeezed her tightly to him. She couldn't die, she couldn't. But he knew, he had seen it happen too many times on this journey. But he knew, he knew when he felt her body go slack. He didn't know how long he walked. When he finally sank to his knees, he was far beyond exhaustion and his lightweight shirt crackled with the ice. The gray dawn came and he felt an irresistible urge to sleep. Blessed sleep, blessed oblivion, no more hunger, no more hurt, finally there would be rest for his aching body. But deep within him there was a reservoir of strength, a primal urge to survive that would not be denied. After remaining motionless for a while, he came into focus again. Sometime, he didn't know when, the storm blew itself out. He raised his head and wiped the ice from his eye lashes. The Tsa'ragi looked to the east and watched a pale winter sun crawl over the hills and spread its milky light across the ice covered hills.

He laid his wife's body aside and stood up, discovering that he was on top of a long ridge. There were huge red oaks laced with small groves of cedars that had afforded them some small protection from the sleet storm. He pulled the long knife from inside his cheap cotton pants. He was thankful now that the soldiers hadn't searched them. Moving quickly now that he had a purpose, Beartrack stripped the silky dead outer bark from the surrounding cedars until he had a double handful. Picking up a loose piece of flint, he knelt painfully in the shelter of a projecting limestone ledge, and struck sparks from the back of the knife into the dry bark. The pile of tinder soon started to send up a thin whisper of smoke. Then when a wisp of flame sprang up, he fed it carefully with tiny twigs and limbs he had broken off the surrounding cedars.

CHAPTER 31

Crouched over his tiny fire, Beartrack started rubbing his arms and legs. His blood started to stir, to respond to the warmth, to push down its tiny pathways again. It felt like thousands of tiny needles being jabbed into his flesh and twisted. Finally that part was over and he felt his blood start to circulate near the skin, taking advantage of the few calories of heat the fire afforded. It seemed that once the primitive flame of life residing deep within his soul decided to fight for survival, his whole body marshalled its forces in that direction. As he squatted there, the ice on his light cotton clothing melted, soaking him even more. Since he was afraid to remove even this scant protection, he stayed close by the fire watching the steam drift off his wet clothes until at last they were reasonably dry. Once he had warmed himself, he realized he was going to have to leave the blessed lifegiving warmth of his fire in order to find food. There was no need of putting it off, so he started off down the east side of the long ridge. He curled his toes under in the thin wet moccasins to better get a grip on the steep frozen surface. He was surprised to find water so near, a clear creek, rimmed with ice. It made a curve into the almost bluff that comprised that particular part of the ridge. A small spring, filled with watercress, ran its warmer waters into the creek, cutting a small pathway through the pane of ice. It was here that Beartrack knelt, making a cup of his left hand, carefully supporting himself with his right and drinking deeply.

Moving upstream, he came to what the whites called a slough. It was a cut-off loop of the stream as evidenced by the driftwood thrown up along its banks. As he walked along the edge, he almost stepped on an unfortunate Mallard drake, its feet frozen on top of the ice. Quickly dispatching it, Beartrack soon had it coated in the abundant blue clay from the stream bed and roasting in the coals of his fire. While he waited for the duck to cook, he popped the tails off of small green winter crawdads and hurriedly peeling them, ate them raw. He had gathered several large creek mussels after noticing their trails in the sand beneath the ice. They weren't the warty-backed mussels he was used to back home, but he put them close to the fire to steam open for later. As he chewed, his hands were busy carving a seasoned oak handle for the trade tomahawk from the limb one of the huge trees had shed during a not too recent storm.

Later he peeled away the baked clay, removing the feathers and down with it. He forced himself to eat slowly, allowing the juices to run down his sore throat, savoring each bite. He was afraid the rich duck meat would make him sick. After eating part of it, he laid it beside the fire and began to dig a grave in the frozen ground. While walking back to the fire to warm himself, he found the crevice. Eons of time had flaked away layers of the limestone until it had formed a perfect burying place. Beartrack cut small Cedar limbs and carefully lined the crevice. Laying Tranquilla's body gently into it, he straightened her ragged Calico flour sack dress and looked down at her, at the thin face etched with trouble, even in death. The hunger, cold, loss of the little ones and being uprooted from her native land had served to sap her will to live. He used a seasoned cedar pole to laborously slide another piece of limestone over the crypt.

Beartrack sat down by the fire, and for the first time, allowed himself to grieve for her. He remembered their marriage, done in the old way because of his Grandfather's insistence. There had been the birth of the two boys only one short year apart; he thought of them, with their seemingly boundless energy, how he had loved them, planning to see them grow someday into strong men when the trouble was past. Now the trouble would never be past, at least for him. He remembered Tranquilla's easy gracefulness. More than anything he had loved to watch her work. The way her hands moved swiftly with no wasted motion as she went about her daily chores. He thought of the calm studied way she had faced want and trouble. But everyone, no matter how strong or brave has their breaking point. The loss of their sons had pushed her past her ability to bear it. About himself, Beartrack was not sure, maybe he had reached his breaking point in a different way. What would become of him now that he had no reason to live? Would he become one of those the whites called crazy? He tried not to think of that part of it.

Tranquilla had been raised by a white doctor and his wife after her own mother had died giving her life. Thus she was given a name meaning calm and quiet, but, with a definite Cherokee sound. The name had suited her so well. The doctor and his wife made sure that she kept in touch with her people, and she had returned to them when she was grown. Yet somehow she never quite fit into the tribe again. She was always respected, but always regarded as a little apart from her people. She had always seemed grateful to Beartrack for taking her to wife, as if she had been afraid she would remain unclaimed among her people.

Staring off into nothing, Beartrack sat there all day and all night, coming to himself only to feed the fire. He had already decided to stay here in this almost empty land. He now hated the whites. He wanted to make constant war on them, to exact vengeance for all the wrongs he had suffered. He wanted to fight on until he was killed, dying as a Tsa''ragi should die, in battle. But soon he found that just providing food and clothing for himself took most of his time. He found a large cave in the side of the ridge, not far from Tranquilla's grave, and moved in. Sometimes he lay in the light of a dying fire and studied the dull shine of the particles tracing a line that led farther back into the cave. He felt that he was not alone. The spirits of the little people must dwell here. Often he thought he saw them out of the corner of his eye.

A rat moved forward nervously, her whiskers twitching. She was the latest of a line that had lived in the cave for hundreds of years. Her fur was ragged, and her paps hung nearly devoid of milk-producing tissue. Her latest litter of young were almost starving in the back of the cave. The light was not like the light that shone into the cave and warmed it on cool mornings. Somehow she knew that this creature would provide food, but with the food would come danger.

CHAPTER 32

Beartrack knew that he could not depend on accidents of nature for sustenance. He had to provide himself with weapons. He walked back along the banks of the slough and cut several tall river canes. Even though they were dead, Beartrack knew that the seasoning only made them stronger. He could hear their strong hollow stalks pop as his knife cut into them. He carefully cut the largest, straightest one into a shoulder high length. Guiding the knife very carefully, he split another slightly longer cane into quarters. Sharpening the split cane then hardening the point in the fire, he started drilling and tapping out the thin walls that separated the joints of cane. Sighting down the bore of this newly made blowgun, he satisfied himself that it was perfectly straight. Since thistledown and milkweed seed pods would be impossible to find during the winter, he twirled the fine down from the duck between his palms to make an air tight seal at the rear of the needle-like darts. With a little practice, the old childhood skill came back. At the time, he had thought of the blow gun as a rare attempt by his grandfather to amuse him. With it, he was now able to feed himself on rabbits and quail, which he cooked on the coals or on a flat rock laid at an angle by the fire.

By carefully weaving some of this split cane into a large screen he was able to shut the winter wind out of the cavern. It would also serve to conceal himself and his fire from any casual passers-by. He shaved down a spear shaft from a tall, slim, dead cedar then hardened its point in the fire. Next came the throwing stick often called an atlatl. Its socket fit over the end of the short spear. By holding the spear in his left hand and keeping the throwing stick folded under the spear in his right hand, he could throw the spear and lever it forward at the same time, adding force and accuracy. He didn't take the time to make the front part of the small spear out of a separate piece of wood as his grandfather would have done. He did not add a flint point to it. That would come later when he had killed a deer. Without sinew to bind the point on securely, it would be useless. He was glad in his heart that his grandfather had taught him the old ways. The bow and arrow were good, but the spear would enable him to survive until he killed a deer for its meat, sinew, hide and bone. Beartrack survived on rabbits for a few days, making sure to eat plenty of water cress from the spring. He had heard of some of his people starving to death on rabbit meat during the time of the hungry moon. Early one morning he managed to kill a young buck that had come to drink at the warm spring. He allowed himself a slight smile as he stood over it. He talked to the spirit of the deer, making it understand that he must have the meat to survive.

Within a few days he had tanned the skin of the deer with its own brains, smoking it, then working it back and forth across a projecting knob of his rock shelter to soften it. Using an antler, he started carefully working down nodules of flint into arrowhead and spear points. He made a fine bow out of Bois d'Arc and with the sharp flakes of flint shaved down cedar into straight arrows. He preferred the cedar over river cane for arrow shafts because of their heavier weight.

Thus over the years did Beartrack feed and clothe himself. He tended the grave of Tranquilla, and over time his hatred for the whites started to fade. He periodically made long trips in a wide circle that often lasted up to a week. He often satisfied his longing for human companionship by sitting well-hidden outside the settler's clearings and watching their work and the play of their children. None of the settlers ever offered to shoot at him; nevertheless, he didn't get within range to tempt them. He watched the Williams boys grow up over the years. He spent hours at a time watching them at play and longed for his own sons. He knew that the settlers were aware of his presence, but since they themselves were so busy with trying to carve farms out of the wilderness, they pretty much ignored the strange Indian, though children were very curious about him. Thus Beartrack lived with his loss and sorrow for the next twenty years, keeping to himself, living by hunting and trapping. The white settlers knew where he lived and avoided the ridge in their own hunting.

Then came the morning that Sarah Casey, newly arrived in Arkansas, came down to her own spring to get water. There, unconscious, and burning up with fever, lay the Indian. There was no hysteria, Sarah was not the type for such foolishness. She ran and got her husband and together they carried him back to their cabin. Over the next few days, with willow bark tea and thin soup, they nursed him. One morning they came in from clearing land and he was gone! Thereafter they would often find a deer haunch or a wild turkey on the limestone ledge that formed their front door step. When the boy Sam was born, Beartrack started to drop by to sit on the porch. The Caseys, over a long period of time, bit by bit, were able to find out about his family.

Beartrack was very aware of the beginning of yet another white man's war. He had watched warily from his hiding place as armies marched west. Several nights he had crept close enough to the campfires to hear their talk. He learned that many of his people were fighting on the side of the ones he thought of as the Graycoats, because their chiefs wore them. Most of the white soldiers were dressed in homespun like the settlers he knew.

He heard Stand Watie's name mentioned. Beartrack had spent a lot of time talking to Watie on the long trip down the Tennessee. They had instinctively liked each other, and Beartrack was saddened by the thought of his people getting involved in yet another white man's war. A few days later, on one of his scouting trips, Beartrack ranged farther north to the path of the talking wires. There were many bluecoat soldiers moving along the road. Their smart uniforms were a sharp contrast to the plain clothing of the graycoats. They had stiff backpacks instead of the shabby blanket rolls of the Southern soldiers. He saw that some of his people had also joined themselves with the Bluecoats.

Ezekiel Proctor, a half blood, whom Beartrack remembered as a boy, stood in front of the campfire. He was shaking his fist and speaking passionately to his fellow soldiers while Beartrack lay in the tall grass a few yards away. Several times Beartrack almost stood up and made himself known to them, but something made him hesitate and they were gone the next day.

Two weeks later, the Indian watched as the Graycoats came marching back east. They were fewer now, their ranks filled with wounded. The wounds were covered with dirty ragged bandages and their shoulders were bowed with the weariness of the march.

Now the white soldiers were back, only this time they wore blue coats. He had watched several patrols of Bluecoats ride through, but this bunch was different. These bluecoats had killed the Casey's and for this they must die. According to the old ways of the Tsa'-ragi, their deaths must be as slow and painful as possible.

Beartrack watched, keeping out of sight. He knew of the one-legged man, the murder of Mrs. Williams, as well as the ambush of the three bushwhackers. Moreover he had watched Gatlin and the Sapps bury them in the corn patch. But these were affairs of the whites and Beartrack cared not if they killed each other off completely.

Then came the day that Beartrack, returning from one of his long hunting trips, came to the Casey's cabin. He had a deer quarter tied to his shoulder, knowing they could always use the meat.

Something was wrong, very wrong. Spending his life in the woods had honed his natural intuition to a fine edge. He pulled an arrow from the back of his deerskin frock and nocked it. Moving forward he smelled death hanging heavy in the late afternoon air. He knew it was not human, the smell of a dead person is very distinct and recognizable, as are most other species. No, it had to be a cow or horse. A few wisps of smoke still drifted up from the ruined cabin.

In a few minutes Beartrack read the whole story. It was as clear to him as a written history would have been to a professor. Soon Beartrack's long strides were taking him up the same two-track road toward the Williams cabin. He was but a few hours behind Gatlin.

After a few days of observation, Beartrack decided that Sarah Casey and Sam were relatively safe with the one-legged man, so he started ranging out again, checking on them but not showing himself to Gatlin. Not knowing Gatlin, he knew there was a chance of being shot by him, so he satisfied himself with watching from a distance.

Now Beartrack knew that there was a good chance that the band of killers would go by the cabin. As he ran he knew he had underestimated them, figuring that they thought all the Caseys were dead. He had to get there and warn the one-legged man, but he knew the odds of beating them were slim. He turned and started down toward the creek bottom in a long lope. His chest ached as his breath came faster, but he ran on.

CHAPTER 33
The Zulu

Cain listened to his men grumble for a moment, then spoke again. He knew that food always interested them. "There's probably some garden sass near that cabin we passed on our way up," he said. At this, the men settled down.

The Zulu sat slouched in the McClellan saddle, his body moving slightly with the horse's rhythmic gait. He seemed relaxed, but another look would show that his dark eyes, shaded by the blue kepi, swept the landscape, missing nothing. He still carried the slave catcher's shotgun, although now the weapon showed none of the neglect it had suffered at the hands of its former owner. He carried two 1860 calvary model Colts snugged down in their black issue holsters. The Zulu had purposely rubbed the holsters with sand rock to dull their finish. He took no chances on reflected sunlight giving away his position. He rarely spoke to any of Cain's command, and because of this, they disliked him, even hated him. He knew that Colonel Cain took it for granted that he was like the rest of them, that he would follow orders without question.

As he rode, the Zulu's mind drifted back to his homeland, the southern portion of what the whites called Africa. He thought of his people, the proud Zulu, with their kraals clustered along the broad Umfolozi River. He thought of the carefree days he had spent fishing and swimming in its cool waters with the other village children. Often as they played, they hid and watched the dugout canoes of the Arab traders loaded with goods go up the river. Weeks later, these same canoes drifted back down with the current, but now they were loaded with young men and women sitting with their heads down, chained together with iron collars around their necks. Maqubu, as he was called then, knew from listening to his parents that the elders of some lesser tribes up the river sold their own people, as well as any others they could capture, into slavery for a few of the Arab's baubles. The dugouts also carried elephant ivory, and the yellow metal, gold, that the Arabs seemed to crave so much. The Zulu were contemptuous of the traders and had very little contact with them. Besides the Arabs there were Dutch settlers who had founded a settlement they called Cape Colony. The next generation of Dutch called themselves Boers, or Afrikaners, but this had very little to do with the daily life of the Zulus.

Early one morning, Maqubu, then ten years old, went down to the river by himself. By the time the sun cleared the horizon he had managed to catch several fish. He knew his mother would be proud of him. It was best to do the fishing early in the morning before the rest of the village children started splashing around and made the fish wary. Maqubu was so busy stringing the fish on a limber tree branch he failed to see the single long dugout drifting silently down the river with its miserable human cargo, the fight long beaten out of them, also silent.

Upon sighting the boy fishing alone, the dugout drifted to the bank and the Arab in front stepped out. In a very few minutes the dugout was again on its way, Maqubu lying in the bottom of the boat, bound and gagged, a large knot forming on his head from the blow of the trader's club. As he started to slowly regain consciousness, they were already many miles down the river. It would be late afternoon before he was missed by his parents and the other villagers.

Because of his age, he was considered more valuable and was therefore accorded a little better treatment than the others. Upon arrival at the coast, the slaves were confined in a tall barracoon hidden back in the jungle to avoid detection by British warships that patrolled the coast in regular fashion to prevent the movement of slaves to Cuba, Brazil or on to the vast cotton fields of the southern United States. Soon other traders started arriving and within a few days the barracoon was fairly bulging with over two hundred people. Most of the newly captured slaves were too miserable to give the traders any trouble, and since they were chained together it was almost impossible to escape.

The slaves were fed a gruel made of maize and palm oil. The Arabs had learned from years of experience that this mixture would keep the human cargo healthy with a minimum of expense. Maqubu sat chained by himself. His parents had told him that those stolen as slaves were taken to a land far away and would never see their homeland again. As he lay there on the damp ground, Maqubu tried unsuccessfully to slip the chains off his wrists and thought of his father's kraal. He thought of the times he had sat on the polished floor made of dried cow dung with its earthy smell. Oh, how he wished he could hear his sister sing the Izibongo in praise of the Zulu kings. He sat silently and wouldn't allow himself the luxury of tears, although many adults in the barracoon wailed through the long nights.

Maqubu reached down and pulled the carving from the waistband of the cotton wrap that had been given to him. Glancing around to see if he was being watched, he turned it over in his hand. He looked down at it. The yellow ivory gleamed dully in the subdued sunlight. He turned it over in his hand. The detail work was still amazing to the boy, even after looking at it hundreds of times. He knew without looking that every tiny detail was visible on the carving, down to the tiny tic bird on its back. He ran his fingers down the cord of woven elephant hair that had always held it around his neck. He was thankful that he had recovered from the blow enough to hide it while the traders were still paddling frantically to get away. Looking around again, he studied the carved elephant, one leg raised, the other planted on a lion. The head and trunk were raised high and Maqubu could almost hear the triumphant roar of a bull elephant echo between the elegant tusks.

The Arab slave traders were afraid enough of the Zulu not to try to capture any of them, but the boy alone, out of sight of the village, had been too much of a temptation. Maqubu guessed that his parents would, after searching for days, finally conclude that the had drowned or been eaten by the plentiful crocodiles along the river, so there was no hope of either rescue or escape. On the fourth day, a darkened, low lying ship, flying no flag, slid into the bay. In the middle of the night the slaver loaded its cargo of human chattels and slipped out into the open ocean again. Maqubu was chained up on deck, while all the adults were put in two decks below, each about four feet high. The Zulu boy watched as the crew tended the guns, many times larger than the guns he had seen in the hands of the Arab traders. They had no sooner cleared the mouth of the bay than a British man-of-war was in pursuit.

CHAPTER 34

By straining upward against the rough chain around his neck, Maqubu could see the British ship as it cut across their wake. The white foam behind the sleek vessel was highlighted by the fluorescence of the countless tiny organisms disturbed by its passing. The slave runner's crew rushed about, putting on every inch of canvas. His mouth dry, Maqubu watched as the other ship slowly started to fall behind. Suddenly square holes appeared down the battleship's sides; seconds later they disappeared as a solid wall of orange flame belched out. It was followed by clouds of white smoke. The cannonballs made a peculiar whistling sound as they ripped through the air like raptors in search of prey. The boy watched, fascinated, as they started hitting around the ship, each one sending up a plume of white water. Each one getting closer as the limey gunners found the range. Maqubu felt a shudder run through the ship, then he was slammed against the deck. A cloud of wooden splinters blew out of an open hatch from the shot that had hit below decks. The screams of the wounded and dying were ignored by the survivors as they concentrated on putting distance between themselves and certain death. Moments later it became obvious that the heavier battleship was losing the race. It fired another broadside, but this time the plumes fell well behind the slaver. The Zulu had greeted the appearance of the Britisher with an uplifted spirit, hoping for rescue, but with the cannon shots realized they had no intention of rescuing anyone; they were only interested in stopping the slaver.

The crew of the slaver, their pock-marked faces covered by a variety of styles and colors of beards, moved with the ease of long practice.Their greasy, hairy bodies were clad only in drab, rough canvas breeches, and their wide leather belts were filled with weaponry. To Maqubu every man-jack of them appeared to take the attack in stride, part of a normal days work. They ran to their tasks throughout the rest of the night, putting as much distance between themselves and their pursuers as possible. Not one of them had a moment to pull up the hatch cover to check on their miserable cargo. Maqubu could not tell how many were wounded from the sounds drifting up from below. As the night dragged on, the screams and howls of the wounded started to subside, as they either accepted their condition or died. Maqubu finally fell into a fitful sleep, his body rolling with the movements of the ship.

With the cool, damp morning, he awoke to find the crew, their eyes luminous with exhaustion, pulling out the dead and wounded from the damaged area and after cutting them loose from the others with a chisel and large hammer, then quickly throwing them over the side. Maqubu watched, horrified, as each body rolled over in the frothy wake a few times, then disappeared into the depths. The crew then fell to repairing the damaged area while the slaver, with lookout aloft, plowed its way north. Once a day buckets of water and the maize mixture were lowered to the wretches below, the nearest one dipping the mixture out with earthen bowls and then passing it down the chain until those that wanted it had been taken care of. Many of them wouldn't, or because of seasickness couldn't, eat, and so grew steadily weaker. So by the third day, the steadily increasing smell of their misery floated out of the hatch in waves each time it was opened. The putrid smell assaulted Maqubu's nostrils with growing intensity until he had to concentrate to keep from retching.

By the eighth day, not a morning passed without at least one limp body being dragged up from the hold and unceremoniously tossed into the trackless Atlantic. Pushed along by the southeast trade winds, the slave ship moved swiftly up the western coast of Africa.

The Zulu boy intently watched the sailors as they went about their tasks. He constantly hatched and discarded plans to free those people below decks, take over the ship and sail it back to their homeland. He saw how hopeless this was when their leader whom they called Captain Trogar walked over to him on the morning of the tenth day and viciously kicked the boy awake.

"Cut him loose," he ordered harshly. "You feed them," he said, looking down at Maqubu. Seeing the boy's uncomprehending look, he shook his head in disgust. "Show him," he ordered, pointing at a ragged specimen who resembled the Arab slave dealers. The sailor moved forward, earrings dangling from both ears, and showed the Zulu by motions and a few Zulu words how to feed the chained slaves. While trying to feed them, Maqubu discovered that not one of the prisoners spoke anything resembling his language. He tried sign language, but the poor pitiful creatures merely stared at him without comprehension.

He felt himself starting to lose hope, for he knew now that he would never escape. Maqubu began to experience emotions new to him, among them hatred and despair. He constantly had to remind himself that he was a Zulu, one of the greatest warriors of all time. After all, wasn't he the grandson of the great warrior Dingane?

Maqubu did his work quickly and well, so, as a result, the captain stopped kicking him awake each morning. Changes were going on inside the boy as well. He felt the dispair turn to determination. He was regaining control of himself. He could feel his resolve stiffen. He would return to his homeland! He would fight the Arab traders and he would keep them from stealing any more people. After a few more days, he was allowed to sleep on deck unchained since there was no hope of escape.

The sixtieth day of the voyage, according to the marks Maqubu had made under the rail by his sleeping place, dawned still, muggy and unbearably hot. As the hatch was pulled back the Zulu noticed that the poor wretches below were more restless than usual. The sailors frequently glanced up at the sky as they went about their daily tasks. Several times the Zulu had seen bad storms in his native village and he knew one was brewing.

At first the spectre resembled fog that often rose from the river and blanketed his village. Then it became clear that what he was seeing was a solid wall of water, reaching high into the sky, and slowly moving toward the ship.

"Snap too, lads," Captain Trogar yelled, "Fetch me a line." Wrapping it tightly around his waist, he lashed himself tightly to the wheel housing, leaving the excess rope loosely coiled on the deck. "Furl those sails! Get the hatches battened!" His voice was carried away in the wind as he rechecked the square knots holding him.

Maqubu knew this meant the slaves would be locked below. There would be no air movement at all. If the ship should capsize or sink they would be drowned like the rats that evidently had free run of the ship. Being cramped below decks without fresh air would be the least of their problems.

The wall of water moved slowly up behind them, traveling slightly faster than the ship. When the water and savage wind finally overtook them, the Zulu boy grabbed for the chain which had formerly held him and wrapped it around his wrist. He held on so tight he could feel the flakes of rust bite into his fingers. Since there was no room below, the crew was forced to seek shelter where they could find it. Between the sheets of rain Maqubu saw the muscles of Trogar's back bulge as he fought the rudder. As a stronger gust hit, he could see that the captain was losing his grip. Turning toward the crew, Trogar shouted for help, but the sound was lost to the continous shriek of the wind. The boy knew instinctively that the wheel must be held steady or they would all perish. As the ship started to list he turned loose of the chain and started across the deck, half sliding, half crawling reaching around Trogar and grabbing hold of the wheel. The Zulu's additional strength and weight, although slight, allowed the captain a moment's respite and he regained control.

Throughout the rest of the day and into the night the storm continued. The two, the Zulu boy and the slave ship captain, should have been bitter enemies under any circumstances. Now they labored together as if they had done it for years, each knowing that their survival and that of the ship depended on them alone. They kept themselves braced against the housing and fought the rudder until the muscles of their arms and legs knotted from fatigue. Blisters formed and burst, then formed and burst again in their sodden skin, made rotten by soaking. Knuckles were bloodied, dark skin wrinkled and turned shades lighter. There was no difference between the waves that washed across the deck and the almost horizontal rain that fell in sheets. The ship drove into the heavy slow waves, then her bow would rise, shaking off water like a wet dog, only to repeat the process again moments later. They lived in a world of water and darkness. No words were exchanged, nor could there have been. There was no respite, not a moment, but they traded sides often as the night wore on, allowing their cramped muscles to change position, affording them some slight relief.

Sometime during the wee hours of the morning the wind and rain started to ease up, unnoticed by the two whose hands were so clamped to the wheel that the crewmen had to pry them loose. They collapsed and slept on the deck, rolling back and forth in response to the movements of the slowly calming sea.

The next day dawned clear and bright with the ever present trade winds moving them northward. Maqubu's own food improved noticably and the crew no longer paid attention to his wanderings around the ship when he was not feeding the slaves. He was careful to listen to the crew's talk, determined to try to learn this strange language they spoke.

CHAPTER 35

One hundred fifty-three days later the slave ship slipped into the mouth of the Pearl River in the dark of night. The survivors were dashed with buckets of salt water as they were marched off the ship, their chains rattling. There was no talk as they huddled together all night in a dark barn. In spite of his misery, Maqubu sat and listened to the night sounds of this strange land. It had been illegal to import slaves into the U.S. since the 1830's, but Trogar and his men had made many trips from Africa to Mississippi. Experienced smugglers, they had no fear of apprehension once they had landed on the Mississippi coast. Stopping the importation of slaves was obviously a matter of low priority to the authorities.

A little light filtered through the cracks between the boards. Maqubu could see the gleam of the crew's weapons as they shuffled around, talking in low whispers. Most of the captives sat, not looking up, seemingly unaware of the change in their surroundings.

"Cowards!" He thought as he saw some of the crew peering out through the cracks. "They're afraid of the dark." Listening carefully, he was able to pick out the sounds of some frogs that reminded him of the ones along the Umfolozi. For the most part the smells were strange, although he knew the fishy smells of the river mingled with rotting vegetation. Faintly in the distance, he heard a roar that he knew had to be a crocodile or one of its relatives.

The next morning the miserable, tired captives were paraded in front of buyers who closely examined each one. Maqubu submitted himself to being prodded, even having fingers run around his gums. Most of the prospective buyers were big rough-looking, loud-talking men. Many of them had light hair and red skin, something he had not seen among the Arabs. They laughed as they examined each slave, especially the women, who cowered before them. The white men all looked alike to him.

Finally he saw a stooped old man moving up the line, his linen suit wrinkled, both hands wrapped around a cane. A long black cigar, unlit, was clamped between his teeth. Beside him walked a huge black man. His biceps were as large as Maqubu's thigh. The iron bracelets on each wrist told of his status as a plantation black-smith. The old man stopped and looked each slave in the eyes as he moved along. Many of the prospective purchases kept their eyes down-cast, instinctively trying to keep from being noticed. Trogar, remind-ing Maqubu of a fawning puppy, moved alongside him, chattering about the merits of each slave as though he knew each one person-ally.

"This one's strong, good teeth, make a good field han'," he said as the old man moved along. Trogar grabbed the next captive in the line, a winsome young girl. He cupped his hand beneath her jaw and opened her mouth, exposing even, pearly teeth. "This'n's purty," he said with a knowing leer. "She'll do in case you need a young'un to warm your bed. I kept my men away from her a'purpose to save her for ye'."

The old man turned and looked at Trogar for a long moment, then slowly removed the sodden cigar from his mouth. "Shut your filthy mouth," he said. Trogar glanced from the old man to the black-smith beside him. The slave runner felt his skin go clammy as he looked into the face of a man whom Trogar knew could and would snap his neck like a cedar twig on a command from his master. The blacksmith looked back at him calmly, but there was something in his eyes that told Trogar that his intuition was right.

Maqubu had listened carefully to the speech of the pirates and now could understand most English, even though he still had some difficulty speaking it. He practiced it to himself at every opportunity, as well as some words he knew to be French.

The old man stopped in front of him, and gazed across, his watery blue eyes full of age and knowledge of life, meeting the steady gaze of dark brown unreadable ones. They stood this way for a long time. The old man and the boy each "sized" the other. The slave captain started up again with what he imagined to be his sales pitch. He kept on addressing the old man as Mista' Johnson.

Without moving his eyes, the old man snarled "Didn't I tell you to shut up?" Whereupon the slave ship's captain cut off his sentence in mid-syllable. The old man then turned to the captain, "I'll take him," he said, "take the chains off."

"Ain't you gonna ask the price of this slave your'a buyin'?" Trogar asked.

"If a man has to ask the price of something, he can't afford it," the old man said simply.

Maqubu stood off to one side with the old man and the blacksmith as the other slaves were sold. Then they walked back to the banks of the river. Most of the other slave buyers loaded their purchases into small boats and paddled out into the river. A few had brought light wagons even though visible roads were nonexistent in the piney woods.

By noon the trio were on a steamboat. They pulled in to the bank in response to the old man's wave. At night Maqubu and blacksmith slept on the deck outside Mista' Johnson's small room. By the actions of the other slaves and the white people on the boat, Maqubu knew it was pointless to try to escape. He had no idea where they were in relation to his homeland. He studied the people and the country they passed through, hoping for some opportunity to get away. He tried to ask the blacksmith, whom the old man called Ulysses, questions about the country. The blacksmith was friendly, but apparently had never traveled this far away from the plantation before.

Each night the two slaves were fed a chunk of cornbread and allowed water from a barrel to wash it down. Maqubu quickly adjusted to the sound of the steam engines, and getting well rested, he began to chafe at this enforced idleness, but Ulysses particularly enjoyed it. "Dey be plenty work, when we gets there," he said.

They arrived at the city called Jackson and got off the steamboat. They picked up the old man's hack at a livery stable and started up a road that Mista' Johnson called the "Trace".

Ulysses drove the horse and Maqubu rode with his legs hanging off the back. Mista' Johnson talked to him like an old friend, noting points of interest along the way. In spite of his depression and weariness, Maqubu became interested in this new land.

The second morning out, Maqubu watched as a man on horseback trotted past them. About an hour later they passed the horse tied to a tree beside the trace, the man was nowhere in sight. About another hour passed and Maqubu looked toward the front again, only to see the man trudging along beside the road. Mista' Johnson laughed as they caught up with the walker.

"Hop on the wagon and ride awhile there, stranger. We don't get to see many of you 'ride and tie' men up our way." Mista' Johnson said.

The man plopped down in the back of the wagon, beside Maqubu.

"Well, sir, it ain't as good as riding all the way, but it beats the heck out of walking all the way. Besides that, horses is mighty expensive in Natchez."

About that time the horse trotted past them again, this time with another rider. He slowed down and spoke, then went on out of sight. They lost their passenger when they again caught up with the horse tied beside the trace.

As they camped each night Mista' Johnson made no attempt to chain the Zulu, but allowed him to help cook their simple meals. On the third day out of Jackson the old man announced, "I believe I'll call you Jonas. Jonas was a man that was swallowed by a fish."

By the time they arrived at Sunflower Plantation, the new slave boy, now getting used to being called Jonas, knew all about the plantation and the small town of Iuka. He found that Mista' Johnson had about twenty slaves. The old man lived by himself in a huge white house with numerous smaller buildings around it. Just beyond them lay the fields of a crop the old man called cotton. Along a creek branch was a line of slave cabins where Jonas was assigned a small cabin of his own.

He quickly found out that there were two classes of slaves on the plantation. The field hands were the ones who plowed, cultivated and gathered the cotton, corn and beans. Then there were the "house nigras", who took care of cleaning, cooking and keeping the big house. They also tended to Mista' Johnson. Jonas, as he was already beginning to think of himself, soon knew that he had been bought to be a personal servant to the old man. He had no idea why, but most of the slaves seemed to be old, except for Ulysses and the one they called Big George. Jonas' english gradually became better and he was horrified to find himself thinking in this new language.

Every day he drove Mista' Johnson around on his inspections of his property. The old man had no white overseer, and from what Jonas could find out, the old man was the only white person on the place. Lonely and missing his own people and homeland, Jonas found himself liking the old man. Mista Johnson was kind and talked constantly, so much that soon Jonas knew all about the day-to-day operation of the plantation. Mista' Johnson hunted almost every day, with Jonas driving the hack past the field hands working in the cotton fields and on to the land along the creeks. Mista' Johnson told Jonas that it was against the law but he soon started letting Jonas shoot as well. "Don't ever let on like you know anything about guns around white people," he cautioned Jonas. He had an extensive collection of weapons and taught the slave boy to load, use and care for them; and after every day's hunting it was Jonas who cleaned and stored them.

The old man taught him about horses and harness and how to use and care for them. Almost every day Mista' Johnson spent some time teaching Jonas another aspect of the plantation. He learned how to raise corn for the mules and horses. Before long, he knew how to take care of the cattle kept for their beef and milk. He spent hours with Ulysses, the blacksmith. The old man and the boy were like grandfather and grandson.

The other slaves naturally resented Jonas' close association with the old massa, and therefore none of them offered to befriend him. He could feel their hostile stares boring into his back as he and the old man passed the fields on their morning rounds. One of them didn't bother to wait until they passed. Jonas had never, even among the Arabs, felt as much hatred and contempt as when they passed by Big George, the field hand overseer. Since none of them were Zulu, Jonas told himself he didn't care. Once in a while he had a bad dream, and in the dream he was always stumbling along in waist deep water with Big George gaining on him with every step, his double-bitted ax swinging both ways.

For six years this existence went on. As time passed, Jonas' memories of himself as the Zulu boy called Maqubu started to fade. The images of his beloved homeland dimmed, but he still thought of returning to his people. Many nights he could have cried for his family, but he didn't allow himself to mourn, remembering he was a Zulu.

"Boy," Mista Johnson said one morning as they were making their rounds, "You probably wonder just why I've gone to the trouble all these years to teach you, a coal black slave, an African, the ways of free white men."

"Yes, sir, I've wondered." Jonas replied. He was now tall, broad of shoulder, with smooth well-defined muscles, the finest example of his tribe. He bore little resemblance to the scared boy who had made the long journey from the land of the Zulu.

The old man raised his hand and Jonas stopped the horse and turned to listen. "Well, I went down that river to buy me a young slave and to see first hand what they looked like fresh out of Africa. I hoped to get me a fresh start. I planned on going back later to get a female. All of my nigras were getting old, and the few children that were born here never seemed to make it. Anyway, I never went back to get any more because there was no need.

"Unless things change boy, there's going to be war, a war in this country, a war between two ways of life." The old man stopped talking and sat for a while, silent, marshalling his thoughts. "There's two ways of life in this country. I've never been there, but they say that up north, there are no plantations and no slaves. Down here it's mostly plantations and farms, and most of them raise cotton. Them yankees up north, they ain't even of the same stock as the rest of us. Up there they say there's little towns full of different shops and if anyone needs help, they pay other people to work for them. I'm sure you've heard some of our talk."

Jonas was not surprised at the talk. He was not totally unaware of what had been going on in the country. He had driven Mista' Johnson into Iuka regularly and often went around to other plantations. Because most slaves had recognized him as "different," he was not often approached or befriended by the resident slaves as he drove the old man around. He often lounged in the hack or in a nearby shade as the white men talked on the porches. They paid no more attention to him than they did to the horse he drove, and so spoke freely. He had heard of states' rights, and of the talk of secession. He knew of the greatest fear of the southern planter, the spectre of a slave uprising. The subject came up every time plantation owners gathered. He had sat and listened by the hour as they talked of John Brown and Nat Turner and their failed attempts to spark a slave rebellion. "Yes, sir, I've listened when you white folk talked," he said.

At this the old man continued,"Well, I've studied about it for a good long while, and I'm sure that slavery has got to end. It has only worked this long because of the cotton. I ain't talking about the fact that slavery is wrong. I reckon any God-fearin' man with one eye and half sense knows that, although I'd venture to say that I'm the only white man south of the Mason-Dixon line that would say that out loud. The other reason slavery can't last is because it is a wasteful inefficient system. A slave simply won't work as hard for a master as he would if he stood some chance of getting ahead. Why should he work hard unless he's whipped to it? He can work hard all of his life and still he'll be a slave, year in and year out. He'll live a slave and he'll die a slave. What's worse is that his kids and his kids' kids will all be slaves, forever, with no chance to ever be free. My nigras think I don't know how much they slack off the work, even with Big George watching them. That's even with them them knowing that I treat them better than any plantation owner around. They slack off and after summer's over I still got to feed them the rest of the year. They's a lot of people 'round here don't like that. They think I've let them get out of hand. If they knew what I have taught you, they'd probably have this old man in jail, first thing. The next thing they'd do is sell you down the river. That's why I told you to act like you're kinda simple when they's other white folks around."

"Yessir, I's done that, jes' like you tole' me to," Jonas said affecting the act he used around other people, smiling at the old man. "I acts like I don't hear or see nothin'."

"You sure better be careful. I doubt that they would hang an old man like me, but nobody in the country would have anything to do with me and they really might put me in jail. Anyways, you are a very smart young man, and as I said before, slavery won't last. I have simply been preparing you for life as a free man when the time comes."

Tears started to flow down Jonas face. He had managed to keep his feelings of homesickness and loneliness under control by burying them under layers of gratitude because he held a privileged position. Jonas had wondered about a lot of things and Mista' Johnson had just answered most of his questions.

The old man looked away, so as not to embarrass the boy. "I ain't a young man, I ain't been a young man in a long time. I know I can't live too much longer. So I've made a paper that gives all of you your freedom after I die. I just hope you'll be able to make a good living with what you've been taught."

"Do you mean I could go back to my home, my real home?" Jonas asked, wiping his eyes with the back of his hand.

The old man smiled indulgently. "I suppose you could if you

worked hard enough after you're free."

The very word, freedom, occupied the biggest part of Jonas' mind for the next few days. It was something to look forward to-freedom. It might not be soon, but it was coming. Something to look forward to, something to live for. He would not be a slave 'til the day he died. He was going to be free. In a way his slavery had been worse than that of the field hands. He had once known freedom while they had not. He had also been off the plantation. He had seen an actual town, while most field hands had never been off the place where they were born. Even though he was as much a slave as they, Jonas had experienced a level of freedom none of them had ever known and he thirsted for more. He would never be happy until he was totally free. He had conceived hundreds of escape plans and discarded them all as unworkable. He had heard of what had happened to escaped slaves who had been recaptured. Every slave knew the horror stories. Their masters may have kept most news from their slaves, but they made absolutely sure that stories of escape and recapture were always told. Not only told, but exaggerated and embellished. Now Jonas' whole world had changed, he was going to be free, with a paper to prove it.

He thought on these things through the long winter nights. One March morning in the year the whites called 1860, Jonas rolled out of his sleeping pallet in the kitchen behind the big house. Rubbing his eyes, he walked the few limestone steps to the big house, remembering that Mista' Johnson had told him that today they would go to the slough to hunt ducks. Even after the winter, the ducks still carried enought fat to be a welcome addition to usual winter diet on the plantation. A diet which relied heavily on fat-back and several different kinds of beans. The few potatoes that were left were turning green and sprouting.

As he walked in eagerly, he saw that the old massa hadn't come down yet and Yelda, the cook, was looking anxiously up the stairs. As Joab started up the stairs she dropped her usual cheerful tone, "Yo betta not go up there, the massa be mad if you wakes him up."

Jonas looked around at her, "He may be sick," he replied. He eased around the corner of the upstairs hall. There was no movement from the tall old hand carved bed. He moved closer, and looked down. There was no rise and fall of the chest. Jonas moved closer, then stepped back. He finally reached out tenatively and poked at the Mista' Johnson's shoulder. There was only a slack movement. The old man had evidently died in his sleep. Yelda, walking up behind him, let out a wail, turned, and ran down the stairs. Dry-eyed, Jonas stood there looking down at him for a long time. He had not noticed how the old man had aged in the last six years. Now that he thought about it, he had assumed that the old man would always be there. Jonas should not have had any feeling for the old man, who, after all, owned him; but he had been the nearest thing to a friend the boy had known since leaving Africa.

Taking charge, Jonas sent word to the nearest plantation. From there the news spread rapidly. The white folks started gathering for the burying. They came from miles around, since the old man had been loved and well-respected, even if people thought him a little strange. Some of the plantation owners took over the arrangements, and the field hands set to digging the grave. The plantation wives came, bringing their house servants and soon the smell of frying food filled the big house. The morning after the old man died, Jonas was standing in the kitchen, when Yelda looked out the open door and exclaimed, "Dere's that shiftless boy done come back."

CHAPTER 36

Upon closer study, Jonas saw that the man did closely resemble Mista' Johnson, but there was an unpleasant expression about his narrow face. His eyes were small and set a little too close together on each side of a narrow nose. The wispy beard was an obvious vain attempt to hide a receding chin. All in all, his face lacked the force and strength of character the old man had possessed. Jonas wondered just where he had been for the last six years and how he found out about the old man's death so quickly.

He dismounted and yelled at Jonas in an overly loud, belligerent tone.

"Boy, put this horse up, get a move on. My old man always did keep a bunch of worthless slaves around. Slaves nobody else would have put up with."

Without looking at Jonas, he walked up the steps and started talking to the other plantation owners. Jonas instinctively knew to keep his mouth shut around this man, so, head down, he did as he was bid.

He noticed that the rest of the white folks didn't seem too happy to see the returning son, either. Hershel, he heard them call him. After greeting the guests, Hershel proceeded to take charge, ordering the slaves back to the fields. Traditionally, the field hands had always been allowed to attend any family funeral. They usually stood together, well behind the whites. Except for the household servants, the custom was for the slaves to be allowed the rest of the day off, provided they stayed near their tiny cabins. This was obviously not to be the case with this funeral.

Jonas went to the stables to clean the stalls. Ulysses merely looked up from his work as Jonas walked by. The big blacksmith went back to pounding on an almost white-hot bar of iron. Iron that would soon cool into a wagon rim. As he worked, Jonas could look out the stable window and see a small knot of people gathered on the hillside, the red dirt of the open grave contrasting with the green of the grass.

Jonas had, on many mornings, driven Mista' Johnson across that same hillside to visit his wife's grave. He wondered what would become of him and the rest of the slaves, and stood for a few moments looking out, tears rolling down his ebony cheeks, weeping as much for himself, perhaps, as for the deceased.

He didn't have to wonder for long. Early the next morning, the big cast iron bell started to ring vigorously. It was a signal for all the field slaves and house servants to gather on the spacious lawn in front of the big house.

Hershel Johnson did not mince any words.

"My father was much too easy on his slaves. He allowed himself to get soft, and he often bragged to other plantation owners about how good he treated his nigras. My father was a fool. He didn't know how to raise cotton, didn't know how to work slaves. I'm going to hire an overseer to straighten you niggers out, but for now, Big George will be in charge of the field hands, and I will personally oversee the house slaves. Now get to work."

Heads bowed, they all walked toward the fields. Unsure of his place in this new scheme of things, Jonas hesitated for a moment, drawing Hershel Johnson's full attention.

"Are you the boy they say was with the old man all the time?"

Jonas dropped his head and mumbled, "Yousa."

Johnson spoke again, "The old man won't be needing you, now that he's dead. Go work in the fields." Jonas turned and trudged away. He realized now that he really had loved the old man, and that his life would never be the same again. He brushed away the tears with the back of his hand. A Zulu warrior did not shed tears.

Mista' Johnson had taught Jonas how to use the broad-bladed hand-forged cotton hoes. He picked up a freshly sharpened one lying in the turn row. Its thick hickory handle was polished slick by years of use.

He walked to the field and started to work, chopping the weeds off beneath the surface of the soil, then pulling the fresh soil up high on the stem of each little mineral-hungry cotton plant. He heard the other slaves talking about him in low voices as they passed each other. He did the best he could, knowing that Big George was watching every move he made.

After sundown on the first day, he had started back to his pallet in the kitchen, when Big George stopped him, "You stay heah with us now, de massa he say you a field han' now," he said, an edge clipping his words more than usual.

Four days after the old man was buried, Mista' Hershel showed up in the late afternoon. The sun reflected off the ivory handle and shiny leather of the slim iron-cored riding crop in his hand. He sat in the horsehide seat that Jonas had often occupied.

He stopped the horse. "Come here, boy," he said pointing to Jonas with the crop. Jonas hesitantly stepped over to the hack. "They say you went with the old man everywhere," he said harshly. Jonas nodded. "You know what gold is boy?" Jonas nodded again. His people had sometimes used the heavy soft metal for decoration. Hershel Johnson continued, "The old man had some gold money. I want to know where he kept it hid."

"No sir, I don't know nuthin' 'bout no gold," Jonas replied, careful to keep his tone servile. Johnson must have expected this answer, because his reaction was instant. The riding crop caught Jonas in the side of the neck and laid a welt diagonally across to his hip. Jonas was totally unprepared for the blow, the surprise almost as intense as the pain.

The other slaves pretended to ignore the ruckus and continued with their work, all except for Big George, who looked on with obvious delight. As the next blow, backhanded, arched across his shoulder, Jonas tried to raise his arm to fend it off. This defensive action, feeble though it was, only served to further infuriate Hershel Johnson. He jumped from the hack, raining blows, each one raising an angry purple line across the unprotected skin of the youth. Jonas ran backward between the cotton rows keeping his face and eyes covered with his crossed arms. As he stumbled into the mass of slaves chopping cotton, they moved out of the way, and he fell to his knees, his hands clutching handfuls of the soft black delta soil. His chest heaved and his white cotton shirt soaked through with sweat from his exertion.

Hershel Johnson looked around. He realized that his lack of control would only foment unrest among the slaves. However, he wanted to have the last word. "You belong to me, boy, and don't you forget it." He let his eyes sweep across the rest of the slaves, "Don't any of you forget, all of you belong to me now. The old man was stupid and weak, and now he's dead."

Johnson looked over at Big George, "Bring this boy up to the big house." He said.

Big George walked over and kicked Jonas in the side with a thick skinned foot. "Come on boy. Ah knowed yo' uppity ways would ketch up with you."

The pain let up a little as Jonas walked behind the overseer to the big house. Hershel Johnson was sitting on a rough hewn seat in the shade, having changed to a fresh shirt.

"Now, boy," he said without preamble, "I've got to have the old man's money and you know where it is. You will tell me where it's hidden, or Big George here will get out the old blacksnake. Do you know 'bout the blacksnake, boy?"

Jonas looked up the steps. "Mista' Johnson, he never tol' me nuthin' 'bout no money." The urge to fall down and beg was almost overwhelming, but Jonas knew that the effort would be completely wasted.

"Well what did you and the old man talk about while you was

driving him around so high and mighty, like you was a human or something?"

Jonas didn't know why he said it, the words just seemed to come out by themselves. In an instant it was too late "All he talk 'bout was he'd write a paper to make all us free when he die."

Johnson's face was contorted in fury. Jonas dropped his head and when he looked up he saw a pecular expression in the massa's eyes. He dropped his head again, wishing he had kept quiet. Now he would pay, all of them would pay. In sweat and blood they would pay.

"I refuse to discuss such foolishness, you'll all stay here 'til the day you die." Johnson stood up, that look still fixed on his face. He motioned to Big George. "Take him to the stables," he said.

Jonas knew it was useless to resist. He was physically no match for the big field hand, whom he knew would not hesitate to maim or even kill him. He just had time to slip his carving into his mouth before Big George jerked his thin shirt off and slammed him against the stable door. Moving easily the field boss tied his arms and legs to each corner of the door with pieces of check line. Jonas, still in shock from the earlier beating, rested his cheek against the rough oak and wondered how he would survive.

244

CHAPTER 37

Jonas felt the vibration of the boots as they moved across the hard packed dirt floor. The vibrations traveled up the oak posts that held up the long low stables, then across through the unplaned stable door. Jonas could feel them, his eyes closed, as tiny splinters fuzzed off the oak into the sensitive skin of his cheek. He was scared, more scared than he had been after his kidnapping, more scared than he had been at any time during the ocean voyage. There had been a brief time after his capture when he didn't care if he lived or died, but now he wanted to live, wanted so desperately to live. The boots stopped and he heard a faint slithering sound as the heavy wooden handled bullwhip uncurled on the floor. He braced himself, but the blow didn't come.

"Boy, it don' have to be this way. You ain't got no use for gold money, being a slave and all. Tell me where it's at, and I'll see that you have an easy time of it from now on."

Hershel Johnson tried to make his voice sound friendly and concerned, but Jonas knew better. He didn't bother to reply, there was no use. He knew nothing of the yellow metal that this white man seemed to value so.

The shock of the first blow followed the whistle of the lash through the heavy stable air. The pain washed across his back like liquid fire, then again, and again. The worst part was the timing. It was knowing exactly the length of the pause between each heavy blow. It was knowing exactly how the blow would land, first the thicker part, followed a split second later by the rolling snap of the lash.

Jonas bit down on the carving in his mouth. Each time he was hit his teeth clamped tighter. He could feel his jaw muscles bulge from the hinge of his jaw to the top of his head. His cheekbones bulged from the internal pressure. He screwed his eyes down tight and pushed against the door with all of his might, but it did no good.

By concentrating every fiber of his being, Jonas revisited Maqubu, the happy Zulu boy he had been before the slavers came. As each blow tore into him, he visualized the faces of his parents, his aunts, and uncles and his friends. He remembered the slow lazy days spent fishing in the river. He remembered his father telling him about Shaka, the greatest Zulu chief of all time, who had succeeded in welding over two hundred of the small tribes together into one mighty conquering army.

"He trained his men, to run barefooted on thorns," his father had said, "I was only a little boy but I remember it well. He armed the Zulu with short stabbing assengais instead of the throwing spears used by their enemies. Their throwing spears had proven to be easily deflected and ineffective against the wall of Zulu shields. After each enemy warrior had thrown his customary three spears, The Zulu moved in to the killing ground, easily overcoming now unarmed warriors of the enemy tribes. As soon as the enemy leaders were killed, Shaka inducted the defeated warriors into his army. They were always willing, since any sign or mutiny or disloyalty was rewarded with death by impalement."

Maqubu had stood in wide-eyed wonder as his father discribed the white cowhide shield of Shaka with its one black dot in the center. He saw the sadness in his father's eyes as he told of how Shaka seemed to go crazy after the death of his mother. He had allowed the factions of his people to turn against each other. Thus began a great slaughter that swept the land and left untold thousands dead and the survivors starving, desolate, and leaderless. He told how his father, Maqubu's grandfather, had fled to the river with his family and managed to find peace and safety there after the bloodshed had abated. He constantly reminded Maqubu that he, Maqubu, was of the same warrior stock. Each time he heard the whistle of the lash, the Zulu focused the image of Shaka's shield in front of his eyes. As the black dot in the center of the shield floated in front of him, he softly moaned the Zulu war cry. He knew he was going to die and there was no sangoma to call his spirit home. Without the diviner's help, his spirit might become a umkhovu, one of the cursed unburied corpses.

After an eternity of pain he felt the strings that held him loosen. He fell to his all-fours on the straw of the stable floor. Raising his head he saw without too much surprise that is was Big George that held the whip loosely in his hamlike hand. Trying to catch his breath, Jonas let the carving slip out of his mouth, hanging down in plain sight.

"Well, well, what have we here?" Johnson's voice was suddenly light and cheerful. It changed instantly back to a menacing growl. "Hand it up here, boy."

Jonas held on to the carving for a moment. He had seen the pistol stuck in Johnson's waistband. Now was not the time to resist. There was no need to sacrifice his own life. The Zulu slipped the braided thong over his head and handed it up. He couldn't bring himself to look as it was jerked from his hand.

"What's a common nigra' slave like you doing with a carving like this? You must have stolen it from my father."

Jonas could tell that the man knew better. He was being baited.

"I brought it from my homeland, and it is sacred."

Jonas' last hope was that even an evil man such as this might have a soft spot for something that had been carried so far. He tried to make his voice sound even more humble. "It belonged to my ancestors." Surely Johnson would have respect for a man's ancestors.

"What kind of ancestors would a nigra' slave have? Monkeys? I thought all of you came from monkeys."

Jonas forced himself to remain calm. This was an obvious attempt by a stupid man to goad him into doing something foolish. He knew Johnson would not hesitate to use the pistol. He was probably even hoping for such a excuse.

"Answer me, boy, ain't you part monkey?" Johnson's voice held a kind of savage joy. For a instant, Jonas considered grabbing for the pistol. He knew he could shoot Johnson, but Big George was out of position behind him, and Jonas knew the field boss could tear the flesh right off of his bones with that lash. Smiling down as if reading his mind, Johnson said "You belong to me, boy, and anything you have is mine. You should have sense enought to know that it is illegal for slaves to own property. I'll keep this precious carving that belonged to your so-called ancestors. Now, you hear me, you hear me good, I own you boy, I could kill you right now and nothing would ever be said. You remember that."

Hershel Johnson turned and walked away, followed by the big field boss. After a time, Jonas felt arms slide under him. He was aware of a gentle lifting. He felt himself floating and then he passed out of consciousness. He awoke to the feel of strong hands spreading something very cool and greasy across his lacerated back.

Noticing his patient was awake, Ulysses spoke in a low growl, "He won' kill you boy, not right off. But he sho' nuff' gon' bust you up, it don' matter now whether you knows nuthin' or not, Big George gon' beat you 'cause he likes it! Mista' Johnson, he don' care whether you lives or dies, longs' he gits that money. I heered 'em talkin,' soon's you gets healed up they gon' do it again and again until you gets so stove up you can' work no mo' Den' dey will sell you down de' river, and nobody eva' comes back from down de' river.

"You gots to run, you gots to run nawth boy, dey say slaves is free in the Nawth, you gots to get acrost the O-hi-o river, boy, you gots to get away while you still can."

"Go with me, go with me, Ulysses," the boy asked, "go with me to the Nawth" He still couldn't fully comprehend how his situation could have gotten so desperate in just the last three days.

The big man merely shook his head, "I's done been here too long, boy. Ol' Ulysses is plumb afraid to run. You see, boy, a man ain' really no slave, 'til they makes him a slave in here." He held his clenched fist against his chest, "Ol' Ulysses reckons they done took his heart away. I'll never go, not now, not ever, but you gots to, befo' they does it to you." Ulysses turned his head to hide the tears that spilled down his cheeks. Jonas stood, his head down, not knowing what to say.

Jonas was back in the fields the next day under the hateful gaze of Big George. He knew he had better turn in a days work, so with every nerve in his back crying for relief, he started chopping the weeds again. Having to concentrate to keep from crying out, he didn't notice Big George behind him until he almost bumped into him.

"Evah seven days de' massa says, evah seven days I's gon' beat you, 'til you tells him what it is he wants to know. That'll learn you to think you's bett'ern us. Jus' 'cause the ol' massa liked you, you thinks you is white folks, well, you ain't nuthin' but a nigra slave just like me." The back of the thick hamlike hand drew flashes of light as it met Jonas' cheekbone. He hit the ground hard, and tried to rise. As he looked up he saw Big George walking away, totally contemptuous of any attempt the boy might make to fight back.

At mid-day when one of the house servants brought corn pone from the kitchens, Jonas found that by design, he was given none. Every night Yelda sneaked him down some food from the kitchen. Thus it went, every seven days he was dragged into the stable, beaten thoroughly, then fed and doctored by Ulysses, and sent back to the fields. By the third beating, he could feel his strength, although bolstered by his youth, start to leave him.

He reached the point that the soreness did not abate before the next beating, forcing such screams of agony that even the field hands, who had resented him so, tried to move out of earshot to avoid listening. He lost every vestige of dignity, crawling to Johnson, wrapping his arms around the white man's legs, begging him to quit. Johnson stood looking down at him, then deliberately raised a heavy boot. The kick sent the the Zulu into a half spin only to land face down and receive another kick in the ribs for daring to touch the massa'. As he rolled over, he opened his eyes only to see Johnson bending over him. The carving was hanging in plain sight around Johnson's neck . "The gold, where did the old man hide his gold?"

Johnson left him writhing there on the ground. Lying there, he knew Ulysses was right, the massa was having him beaten because he knew no other way, and Big George was beating him, not only because he was ordered to do so, but more because he enjoyed it.

Then with the fourth beating, the boy Maqubu died within him, and the boy Jonas, who had become his master's favorite slave, was no more. The humanity and kindness within him ceased to exist, and he became a mindless thing that only knew hurt, the pain filling every corner of his soul. As the whip devoured him, he could hear himself screaming, but the screaming was coming from somewhere else. The last vestige of his natural dignity had been jerked away by the leather lash, now stained black and stiffened by repeated application of his own blood. The dried hardened flakes caused the whip to bite even more deeply, thus drawing still more blood. He ceased to feel any gratitude toward Ulysses for doctoring him, for keeping him from dying, for keeping him alive for the next lashing. But as his body was suffering, something new and strong was born in the Zulu youth, something that started as a small white hot flame burning just behind his eyes. It made his head seem larger somehow as the flame started to grow, to fill his entire being. He fanned this tiny torch, revelling in it. It made him feel strong, this hate, so strong that it would enable him to survive. He knew now that he would survive, survive for the vengeance he knew would be his, some day, somehow.

That night he managed to drag himself off the floor of the stable and move over to the area where Ulysses did his blacksmith work. Twisting and bending he worked the soreness until it started to ease. Thanks to Ulysses' greasy medicine the scabs did not crack open. The movement nauseated him for a few moments, then let up. Casting about, he saw a hay knife leaning against the anvil, its freshly filed teeth gleaming dully in the moonlight. Picking it up, he turned it over in his hands, hefting it. It reminded him of the assengais carried by every Zulu warrior. Holding it by his side he moved carefully down the path leading to the slave cabins. Unsure of his exact course of action, he slipped into the doorway of the big field bosses's quarters. Big George was lying on his back, stretched out across the rude pallet that covered the floor, his deep, regular breathing told Jonas that he was sound asleep. Jonas moved forward, his bare feet making no noise on the packed earthen floor. Then something, perhaps a sense of being watched, had alerted the sleeping man. His deep breathing caught, then suddenly he sat up, reacting immediately to the intruder's presence. Recognizing Jonas, he started to rise, his short cotton britches appearing silver in the moonlight.

Panicked, Jonas tried to take a step backward. The huge overseer, seeing his hesitancy, smiled, "What was you doin' boy, comin' to kill ol' Big George?" He whispered, his voice carrying easily over the sound of the tree frogs and crickets. With one quick step he closed in, his huge right hand starting its swing. Jonas, realizing that this time the overseer would kill him with his bare hands, swung blindly with the long hay knife. The tempered steel made a curious liquid sound as it vibrated through the air. It narrowly missed Big George's jawbone, sinking to the depth of the teeth in Big George's neck. The youth, losing his balance, started to fall, and instinctively pulled on the saw, trying frantically to recover his balance. As Big George jerked backward against the irresistible pull, the saw, driven by two opposing forces, caught his jugular vein and windpipe, severing both completely. Big George lunged at the Zulu, spraying Jonas with hot metallic tasting blood. Taking a step forward, he grabbed the boy around the throat with both hands, and started to squeeze. The Zulu twisted and squirmed, trying to escape, then pushed at Big George's eyes with both thumbs, all the while almost drowning in the spray of blood produced by each beat of the mighty field boss's heart. Jonas' vision started to fade, turning brown around the edges until he could only see directly in front of him. As consciousness slipped away, he felt the hands start to slacken their grip. Now the wild look of rage in the eyes facing him was fading. It was replaced by a look of shock, of uncomprehending disbelief and horror. The eyes became blank, unseeing. The face started to go slack. Jonas, released at last, jumped back, gasping for air.

Now Big George gripped at his own throat with both hands in a futile effort to stanch the gush of blood. Failing this, he sank to his knees, then fell forward to the cabin floor. Seeing the big man lying at his feet, the life rapidly leaving the huge body, Jonas felt a sense of relief and the remnants of his fear rapidly fading away. He bent forward, palms on his knees. His chest heaved as he sucked in great gulps of air, the whistling sounds echoing in the small cabin. He had to move, he had to get away. Every muscle in his body locked as his empty stomach repeatedly heaved.

The door of the big house was open to take advantage of any stray breeze that might find its way through the summer night on the delta. In order for his vengeance to be complete and to slow down pursuit, The Zulu knew he must also now kill Hershel Johnson. The guns were in the same upstairs room, the old man's room. To try to get one would surely wake the sleeping man, and the discharge of a firearm would alert the entire plantation.

Jonas passed by the huge brown sandstone fireplace, picking up the poker as he started up the wide stairway. Consumed by hatred, and soaked with blood, Jonas moved into the room, only to find that Johnson was not asleep. He had been reading by the light of a small candle by the side of the bed. Johnson froze for a second as the bloody apparition stepped into the room. His eyes bulged as the mighty Zulu war cry that had bred terror into the hearts of transplanted European settlers a quarter century earlier echoed through the big house! Johnson grabbed for the Colt's revolver on his nightstand as the Zulu warrior charged with the poker held high over his head. Opting for the larger target, Jonas brought the poker down with the power of both arms. It hit squarely across the white man's shin bones. As the poker bounced up from its destructive work, he backhanded it into Johnson's face. Grabbing the pistol from where it had fallen on the floor, he was out the door and in a few moments and soon slipped into Ulysses tiny cabin.

The blacksmith, sound asleep on his pallet, turned over and groaned as the Zulu shook him awake.

"Ulysses, get up, you've gots to help me. I gots to get away, I done killed Big George and the massa!" Jonas said. His voice was hoarse.

. Ulysses was instantly awake as he sat up. The Zulu was covered with blood. The blacksmith could see it, black in the moonlight. His eyes almost glowed in contrast. As was his nature, the big man didn't waste time asking questions.

"You gots to run boy, they'll hang you fo' sho'. I can't light no light, somebody might see. You go on to the smoke house now. You cut you down a hunk of that ham meat. They's a butcher knife there, stick it in yo' belt. Git a big handful of red pepper. They'll be after you with they dogs and horses. When they turns they dogs loose after you, you wait 'til the dogs get real clost then you take out a'runnin' and string that red pepper along behind. Now you head nawth. In the mawnin' you keep the sun on your right. In the evenin' you keep it on your lef'. Of a night you can follow the Nawth Star. Don' cross the big river on your right, dat's the Tennessee. Try to stay fairly close to it. Don't cross the river on your left, dat's the Hatchee. Two big rivers meet at a place in Kentucky called Pa-duker or sumthin'. When de' meet, you cross de' one on yo' right. You den' be on the Ohi-o. Den' you stay clost' to the big river, you be real careful. They'll be patrollers watchin' for runaway slaves. You unnerstan' me boy?"

Ulysses wiped the sweat from his face, "Now listen boy, you stay clos't to that river to a place called Cincinnatti. Den' foller the river up de' river to a town called Ripley, dat's in O-hi-o and cross de' river. Don' you talk to no white folks, less'un they got on a flat brim' hat that got a round crown."

"Round crown?" asked the Zulu. "Who is they?"

"They is called Quakers and they'll he'p you, but don' you talk to no other white folk. You lets on like you is deef and dumb. You be mighty careful who you talk to. Some niggers turn a man in jes' to get they massa take it easy on them. You don' fo-get, you can' trust nobody."

"They say you can see the house that belong' to a white man name of John Rankin, his house is clos't to the river. They says there is always a light in the upper room at night. He is a preacha' man, and he'll hep' you, When you see the lights from a big town, you turn and go 'round it. Go way 'round it."

"How'd you know all this, Ulysses?" Jonas asked.

"Boy, don' you think ol' Ulysses wants to be free too? I's laid awake many a night, a hopin' and a'plannin'. I listen to everythin' I hears 'bout the nawth. I learn 'bout it all, but I ain' never goin.' I's done got too old, and I's too scared.

"Now you watch for them patrollers. They say them patrollers is thick as bees on nawth of here. They say dat on the other side of the river is the promised lan,' where a man can stan' up on his hin' lags and be a man, where they ain't no slaves allowed. Now git. They'd kill me shore if they knowed I helped you."

The big man turned over and slid something out from under his pallet, as he handed it to the Zulu it flashed in the moonlight. I found this," he said. "They calls it a lens. It'll start a fire if you hold it in de' sun and make it shine on dry leaves." He reached down again and pulled out a copper disk. It was tarnished, but Jonas could see that it had numbers stamped on it. "Dis' is a tag that says you is a servant. If you gets caught you can try to let on that you is a slave that has been hired out by yo' massa. Now git gone boy, time's a'wastin'"

Zulu ran to the smokehouse. His hands shaking, the Zulu cut off the butt half of a ham and stuffed it in a tow sack, dropping the butcher knife and the tin of red pepper. Throwing it over his shoulder, he started toward the North Star running. It was harder to run carrying the sack and the pistol, but he ran until his heart felt as if it would jump out of his chest. He imagined that he could hear the baying of the dogs getting closer behind him. From long habit he reached down to feel the carving around his neck, but all he could feel was that hateful copper slave disc. Then his hand dropped as he remembered. Johnson had taken it. He had been too scared and excited to get it back before he ran. It had probably been around Johnson's neck or in his room. But it was too late now. He couldn't go back. There was no doubt in his mind that he had killed Hershel Johnson. He felt no remorse, he felt nothing. Only a keen sense of disappointment over the loss of the carving, the only thing left of his other life in Africa. He had to forget about it. He had to go on.

As he ran he thought about Ulysses, and wondered why the blacksmith wouldn't run with him. Then he remembered what he had heard about some of the African tribes training elephants for work. They always tried to catch a baby elephant. They would then tie it to a stake by one front leg. No matter how the baby struggled it couldn't free itself from the strong rope. The handler also kept the baby elephant half-starved for food and water, so that the creature became totally dependent on the man. In time, the elephant gave up and accepted his lot in life. Jonas had heard that they could keep a huge bull elephant tethered with the same size rope they used on a calf. The animal had become defeated in mind and didn't believe it could escape. That was what Ulysses had been trying to tell him. Like the elephant, Ulysses had been bound too long. Well, the Zulu wouldn't be defeated, he wouldn't accept captivity, he had rather be dead.

Jonas tried to pace himself. He knew he was running too fast for the long haul, yet his body seemed intent on running. He hoped that, since the massa was the only white man on the place, there would be no pursuit, at least for a day or two.

* * *

The sorry-looking gray horse stood tied to the porch with its head down. Its owner paced back and forth as the assembled slaves stood. They all shifted around uncomfortably in the morning sunlight.

"All you niggers know who I am. I've lived neighbor to Mista' Johnson nearly my whole life. He thought of me jest like kin. I was hired on by your master after the old man died. So I come up here this mornin' to take over as overseer and what do I find out? I find out that you bunch of lazy-good-for-nothin' niggers done let that boy go crazy and cripple your master and kill a good fiel' hand."

Ulysses stood toward the back of the bunch. He had laid awake the rest of the night after the Zulu left. He knew that the attack on the masta' and the killing of Big George would only bring more suffering to the slaves of Greenwood Plantation.

Sure enough, Ransom Claus and his good-for-nothing son Jasper had come by that morning before Hershel Johnson regained consciousness. Claus sent Jasper to Iuka for the doctor, and had not wasted any time in finding out that the Zulu was missing. Ulysses stood with his head down, lest the white overseer somehow read in his expression the contempt he felt for him and his kind. Known by slaves and planters alike as "po' white trash," Claus had always eschewed any type of meaningful work. He had been employed by a couple of plantation owners over the years as an overseer, but had been discharged for thieving and unnecessary cruelty to the slaves. The last few years he had managed to exist by stealing and doing a bit of trapping. Ulysses had heard old Massa' Johnson say that Claus' wife had died from overwork and the desire to get away from him and his one blank-faced offspring. Knowing the dislike the old man felt for him, Claus always slunk past the plantation, sneaking down the road like an egg-sucking dog. He didn't show his face around Greenwood as long as the massa' was alive. Now that fool of a son had done gone and hired him for an overseer.

Claus turned around to see Jasper riding toward the house with Doctor Vester following along in his buggy. The old man climbed out with his bag and leaned back, groaning as his back muscles unknotted themselves. Still holding his hands to the small of his back, he turned to Ransom Claus.

"If I hadn't thought the world of that old man, I wouldn't have wasted my time coming out here to patch up his worthless son," he said. "By the way, Claus, you still owe me two dollars for digging that birdshot out of your hind end last year. Too bad they didn't use a rifle and aim a little higher." Not waiting for an answer, Vester turned and walked up the steps into the house where Yelda was keeping wet rags on Hershel Johnson's ruined face.

Anger flooded through Claus. He struggled for words to reply, then stood, glowering at the doctor's retreating back. There were always barns and houses to burn. Somehow, he would make Vester pay for belittling him in front of the assembled slaves. He turned toward them. The slaves had all looked up, interested in the exchange. Now they all quickly looked down at the ground, knowing he would transfer his rage to them, the ones who had no recourse but to suffer. He spoke, wrath obvious in his tone.

"Now you slaves git to the fields and git to work. Me and my boy, we'ins is gonna hunt down this murderer, then we're gonna bring him back here and we're gonna hang him. We're going to hang him right over there." He pointed at a large live oak in the corner of the yard. "If we find out that any of you worthless niggers helped him 'scape, you're going to hang right alongside him."

Claus had hoped that one of the slaves would be able to tell him which way the escaped slave had gone. Yet Claus was a man who had survived by animal cunning and he thought could tell by their expressions that none of them would talk.

Ulysses walked slowly back to his small shop and started fitting the hub bands to the wagon he was building, but his mind was racing. What if the Clauses brought in dogs? The dogs would follow the Zulu's trail right up to his cabin. There was no doubt in his mind that he would be hung in the same tree with the Zulu when they caught him, and there was no doubt they would catch him. They always caught them. In his younger days, Ulysses had watched the few that had tried to escape from area plantations being brought back. The slave owners made their slaves line up along the road to watch as an object lesson. He saw the hopelessness, the pain, the tired resignation. It was written all over their faces. But worst of all was the hopelessness. They wasn't ever the same. Getting caught broke something deep inside a man, something that wouldn't heal, something that couldn't be fixed. The ones who had run for the first time were generally beaten and put back to work. But what work? Work of the lowest meanest kind. Work of the kind meant to slowly weaken, degrade and kill. Work that slowly eroded away what was left of the spirit, until what was left welcomed death. Yes, he had seen the ones who had run. The ones who had run before were beaten and sold down the river, never to return. He had heard that they were worked to death in the sugar cane fields far to the south. By listening carefully to the escapee's stories, stories that were always whispered around the slave cabins, Ulysses had pieced together enough to give the Zulu his meager directions. However, Ulysses had never heard of an escaping slave killing anyone before. He had no idea what would happen now. He glanced up from his work to see the Clauses heading out. He relaxed. They didn't have any dogs with them. Ulysses knew that they expected to catch the runaway in a hurry from the way they were pushing their horses.

* * * TRACKER JACK. * * *

He was a small skinny man, five foot-seven or so. He was no longer young, this small skinny man. He had few earthly goods, yet there was a certain assurance, a cold confidence in his manner. His mother had been one of the last of the Natchez Indians, the tribe that fiercely defended the Mississippi River bluffs of their homeland against the French, until forced to make a temporary peace. Then in 1722 The Natchez had made total war against the French settlements and this time were almost annihilated by the muskets and cannon of the French army two years later. Jacks mother's family and a few other survivors fled to their kinsmen, the Chickasaws, who lived along the brakes of the Tennessee River. They remained there even when the Chickasaws were removed in the 1830's. Jack's father had been an escaped slave who had managed to elude the slave catchers.

Few had ever said a word about Jack, a half-black, living as a free man. Nobody had ever bothered him. One look at his black eyes was enough to tell that here was a man who was best left alone. He lived in the brakes, him and a skinny blue roan horse and a bunch of skinny brindle hounds. He lived by trapping and hunting. Occasionally he would be hired to hunt a runaway cow or bull that had gotten away along the river. Fact was, he made most folks mighty uncomfortable. There were stories circulated among the slave cabins, stories about runaway slaves run down by that same pack of hounds, runaways that never came back. The whites, to all appearances, found it useful to pretend that he didn't even exist. A few slaves claimed that they had been sent down to the river with a message, but they didn't talk about it much. They feared the cane brakes along the river, filled with wild boars and cottonmouth moccasins. Some people claimed that he could always catch whatever he started after; some claimed that he had second sight, that his father was of the JuJu people, skilled with spells and poisons. Others even said his mother was a Natchez medicine woman. Others said that he was born with a caul over his head. Tracker Jack gave no thought to what they said.

Tracker Jack moved along the pens, tossing each dog a chunk of cracklin' cornbread. He spoke kindly to each, he had painstakingly bred them up out of bulldog and bluetick hound stock with a sprinkling of slick- haired cur thrown every few generations. Fifteen minutes earlier he had spotted the three men trotting their horses down the crooked path that led to his cabin. He knew all of them: Childers, Montgomery and Fremont were all rich planters. Jack was surprised to see them, but it didn't show. He rarely got company, and when he did, it was most generally always one of the slaves sent with a message.

As they got close, Jack stepped over to the rail fence and

waited, his leg hiked up on the top rail.

"You the one they call Tracker Jack?"

Jack nodded, letting his hand drop to the well worn Whitneyville-Hartford revolver that never left his side. It was old and loose on the cylinder pin but it still shot well enough. The significance of the movement was not lost on the planters. This was not going as planned. They had expected the half-breed to be impressed by their appearance or at least show some amount of deference.

They decided to state their business immediately.

"That young slave that old man Johnson treated so good done killed one of the field hands and crippled Hershel Johnson." Fremont, the speaker, puffed up with his own self importance, waited for the tracker to react to this news, but the tracker didn't even change expression. The planter continued, trying to put a authoritative note in his voice. "After he done it he took off. Ransom Claus and his half-wit boy Jasper happened along the next morning, and they took off after him. When they got to Eastport they must've tied their horses and went down to the river afoot. One of the Avey boys, hunting a milch cow, seen the buzzards circling. It was the Clauses, both of them, graveyard dead. One shot each, right through the brisket."

"I seen a long time ago that the boy was a different breed of cat from most slaves. Besides that, the old man taught him everything from guns to business. I wouldn't be surprised if Johnson might've even taught him how to read and write."

"Old man Johnson was getting soft in the head, treatin' him that way. Everybody knows that you've got to keep them nigras in their place. I'll be the first to admit that young Johnson is as sorry as the old man was good, but we've got to get that boy back. He's got to be beat and then hung as an example. If he gets away, ever' slave in Mississippi will try to run. That's what's kept 'em under control so long, they know that there's no chance of escape. We've got to stick together on this," Fremont said.

Tracker Jack pulled the corncob pipe from his mouth with his left hand and studied the gray ash forming on top of the tobacco. So far he had given no indication that he had heard a word that had been spoken.

"We figgered we might get you to take your dogs and go over there and bring that boy back, alive, if possible. He's got to be made an example out of."

Tracker Jack took a long pull on the pipe, then looked over at them. He hated them all for their soft lives and superior ways. "You figgered wrong," he said, dropping his leg and turning around as if to go.

"What do you mean?" Fremont said, glaring at Jack, jamming the tip of his ivory-tipped cane into the ground. "You've got to go."

"I don't have to do anything. I've got nothin' agin' that boy," Jack said. "You people make me sick. You talk about how slavery is the natural order of things. You try to make yourselves believe that your slaves are better off and happier than they would be as free men. The truth is, all of you are scared to death. You're scared that you'll have to get out and work for a living like everybody else. You'all are afraid that you'll have to give up them big fine houses and them fancy carriages you parade 'round in. The Romans depended on slave labor and you can see where it got them. Now what if all your slaves rebell and start beating and hanging you high-up white folks?" He could see that he had hit a nerve. He stopped, a little surprised at himself, for it was the longest speech he had ever made in his life. "It will cost you three hundred dollars in gold or silver, your choice." He stood and looked at them for a long second. "In advance, and I don't guarantee nothing."

Fremont stepped back, stuttering as he tried to think of something that would put this uppity nigger in his place. Him standing there talking about Romans and such, like he was educated or something. "That's idiotic, we won't pay it!" He said. "The slave catchers will bring him back for one hundred dollars."

"Then send them out there after him, or go yourselves."

"We oughta' take you and give you a taste of the lash. Ain't nothin' I hate worse than a nigger breed, and I ain't puttin' up with you talkin' to me thataway," Fremont said. He reached toward the horse pistol hanging in a saddle holster.

"Suit yourself," Tracker Jack said, his right hand dropping to the pistol while the left knocked the dottle from his pipe on the top fence rail. He waited for a long moment to see if Fremont was really going to get the gun or if he was bluffing. Fremont froze with his hand on the butt of the pistol. He felt a sudden chill that didn't come from the air, he shuddered. Satisfied that Fremont was bluffing. Jack turned toward the cabin again.

"Wait," said Montgomery, ever practical. "We'll pay it. How soon can you start?"

"How soon can you pay?"

"One hundred now. If you like you can come by my place tomorrow morning for the rest. Now when can you start?"

"Then I'll start tomorrow morning, sunrise." Said the tracker.

He stood rolling the coins from one hand to the other as he watched them ride away. For some reason what little gold he had handled always felt warm in his hand. He wished he had asked for more money. He was almost disappointed that they had agreed so quickly. He knew he was playing a dangerous game and that if he pushed them too far, they would bring enough help and come after him.

* * *

The Zulu looked down at the bodies, the blood on their filthy shirts already starting to darken and dry. They had been poor trackers, but pure luck had caused them to nearly step on him as he lay hidden in a thick patch of bullrushes. They hadn't been carrying sidearms, only rusty old shotguns. He didn't bother to pick up the guns, with their extra weight and length, they would be useless to him. He left their bodies right where they had fallen. He didn't bother to hunt for their horses, it would take too much time. Besides that there may have been more than just the two of them, so he ran again.

Now there were only three loads left in the pistol. The hammer had been resting on an empty cylinder.

The Zulu headed north. It was now very seldom that he thought of himself as Jonas, Massa' Johnson's favorite slave. Now he was the Zulu, born to war. He traveled at night, hiding by day along small streams. He wished he had taken more of the ham meat. At the time he had thought it would be too much weight. He did manage to kill enough frogs and fish trapped in tiny backwater sloughs to insure his survival. Sometimes he managed to start a tiny fire with the lens. He hadn't been eating regularly and his strength was slowly fading, but his hatred, undiminished, drove him on.

The next morning the Zulu awoke to the familiar slicing sound of a cotton hoe as it bit into the bottom land soil. He slowly raised up from his hiding place to find a young black man working not twenty feet from him! He had thought he was getting close to the river, and now the long cotton rows were proof of it. The Zulu avoided staring at him. To stare might possibly cause an alarm sense to kick in. Jonas' mind started racing. Here was his chance. If he could get this young slave to to take him down to the slave cabins when dark came, he could talk to them, all of them. There might be a way to convince some of them to join him in his bid for freedom. A larger group might even be able to fight if they ran into the patrollers. He was sure that there were guns in the owner's house, armed and together they might have a chance.

Looking back, he could see about ten more slaves, both men and women hoeing their way toward him. This one was just a little faster and had gotten to the end of the row a ways ahead of the rest of them. He laid down his hoe and stepped into the weeds, obviously about to relieve himself.

The Zulu glanced back at the other workers, then slowly raised up from his hiding place. To his relief the slave didn't yell out, but just stopped dead in his tracks, staring at the Zulu, fear and apprehension plain on his face.

"Who is you hiding there in them bushes?" he asked.

"I'm Jonas," the Zulu said. "I's on an errand fo' my massa' and got lost last night."

"You a runaway! I knows you is a runaway! They'll ketch you fo' sho'! We heerd the slave catchers askin' the massa 'bout you. De' say you kilt yo' massa, and the whole country's huntin' fo' you! They'd use the hide on me fo' jus' talkin' to you! Now you get 'way from me!" The young black started to back away, his eyes wide, fearful. He thought of yelling, then looked down at the pistol in the Zulu's hand.

"Now you listen. I ain' no runaway. You gets yo' self back to work and don' you go tellin' nobody 'bout me. After dark, I'll come down to yo' cabin for some hoecake, 'den I be on my way."

The young slave bobbed his head and started hoeing again, stepped quickly off on another row and headed the other way. The Zulu sank back down into the weeds and lay very still. He could hear the talk of the other slaves as they got to the end of the row. He held his breath, hoping that none of them would step into the weeds.

As soon as they all turned back on the next row, the Zulu started north again, the morning sun warming his face. He moved quietly until he was a hundred yards away, then started to run. He had made a bad mistake. That slave was going to tell as soon as he could find his massa. The Zulu could see it in his eyes. Now he had to move in daylight, the very thing Ulysses had warned him about.

He started running into an area of thick stands of willow. His breath came faster as the rounded rocks twisted and turned beneath his bare feet. The backs of his legs began to feel rubbery. It was so tempting to throw down the sack containing the pistol and the red pepper. He had eaten the last bit of cured ham the day before. He hadn't dared to stop and shoot any game, afraid that the shot might be heard. The lack of food and rest was starting to tell on him now. The air turned to liquid fire as he sucked it deep into his aching lungs. He had to stop, but first he had to put some distance between himself and that cotton patch. By now he was sure that the young slave had started talking. Maybe they would wait until the next morning to pursue him. The Zulu judged he had run about seven miles toward the river. He staggered, then took a few more reeling steps and managed to get stopped without falling. He bent over, resting the palms of his hands on his knees, trying to keep from gagging. As painful as it was, he sucked in the warm humid air. He had done what Ulysses told him not to. He had assumed he could trust another human being because his color was the same.

The sound didn't register on him at first, for it was so soft, so distant and melodious as to almost fade into the background sounds. It was almost restful. He tried to slow down his breathing to hear it better. It took him a few moments to identify the sound. It was hounds all right, scattered and far away, but definitely coming closer. He couldn't pick out the baying of each individual in the pack yet. That meant he had a little time.

Jonas fought back panic, for panic meant death. He had to use the red pepper, and it was now or never. He pulled the box from the tow sack and pouring it into his palm, started spreading it with a sowing motion of his hand as he walked. As soon as the can was empty he threw it down. He started to throw the sack down as well, but continued to carry it with the pistol inside.

He allowed himself the luxury of walking for a little while, then pushing the pain down, he started to run again. He wondered about the men behind him. Were they professional slave hunters? Or were they just a bunch of farmers with their fox hounds? Either could be equally dangerous.

He scooped up a handful of water from a small branch and licked it out of his hand as he ran. The river had to be near. Ulysses had told him that he shouldn't cross it, that he should follow the river north to another river. Just how big was the big river? If he couldn't swim it, he was going to be trapped against its banks. As the sun got low in the sky, he stopped long enough to realize that he couldn't hear the dogs any more.

The Zulu picked up on a very fishy smell as he crossed a gulley, then followed it down to the river. He walked along the bank slowly, not wanting to disturb the cottonmouths basking in plain sight on the tree roots growing out of the river bank. He moved carefully, knowing that beavers often built their lodges back under the river banks. It would be a sure death trap if he fell through the top of one. Besides that, Ol' Massa Johnson had told him of patches of sand with no bottom, sand that could suck a man under, leaving him to slowly drown.

He could see the river through the trees. The river itself wasn't too wide, because just beyond it he could see a plowed field. As he got closer, he could see that there was a creek emptying into the river on the south side of the flat. That had to be Bear Creek. He stood on top of the bank and looked across. It was just getting dusky dark. The Zulu knew he didn't have the strength to swim the river. He listened for a minute, but couldn't hear the baying of the hounds. They had surely gotten to the red pepper by now. Maybe if he lay down just for a few minutes and rested, he could give swimming a try.

"Three shots left. It don' look to me like you looked too far ahead. You ain' even got no caps, powder or ball to reload with." The voice broke the soft sounds of the river country and caused some of the sounds to stop. The Zulu jerked wide awake, to find that the moon had risen, full. The man in front of him was holding his pistol, casually rolling the cylinder with the palm of his hand. It made an oily whirring noise, not unlike that of a cricket. Jonas could see the speaker's dark outline. There was none of the characteristic paleness of a white man and he tried unsuccessfully to place the accent. The Zulu considered making a lunge at him, but the distance was a little too far. He lay still and tried to make out the features of the man standing about eight feet away.

"They tell me you done killed Ol' Big George and smashed Hershel Johnson's face. That must have took some doing. Now, killing them worthless Clauses don't count for much, in my opinion. They tell me you put out Hershel Johnson's eye, and he'll be a cripple for the rest of his life." His voice was calm, his manner easy, almost friendly.

Jonas lay there waiting, his mind digesting the fact that Hershel Johnson was still alive. He supposed it could be true. The Zulu shifted position a little and the tracker brought the pistol to bear on him with the mere twitch of his hand.

"They paid me, Ol' Tracker Jack, fifteen gold double eagles jes' to mosey on over here with my hounds and bring you back to Iuka to be hung. Now ain't that something? They' scared to death of they' own slaves. They' scared they'll be killed in they' sleep some night, so they say you got to be hung, to scare the rest of them."

The Natchez Indian half of Tracker Jack repected raw courage and very little else. Before him lay an exhausted man, but one that watched for an opening or a chance to escape, the same as he himself would have done.

"I found the pepper can. I've seen it used before, but most always they throw it in the same spot and they' ain't all the dogs gets they' noses full. But you done good, won't be none of my dogs worth nothin' for two-three days."

The Zulu watched, realizing that here was a man who could handle him with no trouble. He waited silent, not wanting to give this man any way to take the measure of him.

The tracker spoke again. "Now, I ain' never had no use for Hershel Johnson. I never thought about the Clause's and Big George one way or the other. What you done took sand, no doubt about that. Now I reckon if I would've got here and found your tracks going down to the river, I'd jes' figger natural-like that you had tried to swim the river and drowned in the tryin'. Now if you was to get a'holt of that big ol' cottonwood log layin over there in the edge of the water, I 'spect that you could hold on to that sack and pistol and somehow make it acrost. Then if you was to make it, I 'spect you could go up on the other side of the river for a couple of weeks. You make shore you keep a'headin' north. Iff'n you get caught and ever mention my name, you'll rue the day you was borned. Now I'm goin' to lay this here sack down and head on back. I'll brang my dogs back soon's they're able to smell, it 'ort to be 'bout two-three days." With that Tracker Jack pushed the pistol down into the sack, dropped it on the ground and walked away, not looking back.

* * *

He moved along the worn path he had created. His tread was careful, measured, and he moved easily for a fat man. His job as day clerk at the Leatherwood Hotel afforded small physical exercise. The town people considered him a bit strange, but he didn't care what the residents of this backwater town thought. None of them knew anything of his past.

The Zulu sat in the brush as the fat man tied the horse to a tree and started toward the river. The escaped slave's curiosity was aroused in spite of the danger. What was this man doing? Should he just kill him and take the horse? It could be done easily. The Zulu wasted no time in debating the right or wrong of the murder. He couldn't let himself be taken alive.

The clerk glanced toward the sun. It would be sunset soon and then they would come. They always bathed here, where Bear Creek emptied into the river. He licked his lips in anticipation of seeing so many naked black bodies at once. Nobody knew. He always walked down among the trees to old man Andrews farm. Old Andrews was nearly blind and his wife was always busy taking care of him. The horse was always eager for the apple or other treat that was his pay for carrying this mound of flesh to the river.

The Zulu lay very still, puzzling over the white man's motive for hiding here. Soon he began to hear soft singing that steadily grew louder as the line of slave women, through for the day, came to take their baths.

* * *

It was three days later, with the town puzzling over the clerk's disappearance, that two boys going fishing were attracted by the soft rustling sounds and nearly stumbled over the naked body. It was almost black with legions of boat-tailed carrion beetles. The rustling sound of their folded wings got louder as the boy's presence disturbed them. The rag was still twisted around the neck, with a stick for leverage.

The Zulu crossed Tennessee and passed to the west of the Cumberlands and into Kentucky, having crossed back to the east side of the Tennessee River. He rode mostly at night, careful not to push the horse too hard. He ate whatever he could find. Hitting the expanse of the Ohio, he followed it. The fat man's clothes swallowed him but they were better than the rags he had worn before. There had been a few coins in the pockets and he used them to buy information and silence from slaves he passed along the way. As he moved along, the slave tag in plain sight, he ran into a few of the white people of the flat hats, and summoning up his courage, asked directions. Each time, he held the Colt underneath his shirt, hammer cocked.

He managed to elude band of slave catchers patrolling the south bank of the Ohio. Finally he pulled up and looked across at what had to be the town of Ripley, Ohio. At dawn he almost collapsed with relief when he saw a lantern. It was lit and hanging in the second story of the house on the hill just across the river. Turning the horse loose along the river, he swam the broad Ohio, holding on to a drift log as he kicked his way along. With each stroke he wondered what the land across the river held in store for him. Would there be freedom at last? Or would there be death?

* * *

Tap. Tap. Tap. He was awake. Rolling off the bed so as not to wake his wife, he straightened his nightshirt and padded across the floor to the back door. "Boys," he said quietly as he passed the open door to their room. In seconds he could sense rather than see them in the island of darkness. He smelled gun oil, and he knew that both of them were holding double-barrelled shotguns. Not for bird hunting, these weapons. The barrels had been sawed off at about sixteen inches. Both weapons were loaded with 110 grains of black powder per barrel and each tube held forty of the tiny, twenty-eight calibre round balls. He knew because he had watched the boys count them into each barrel, then tamp in pillow ticking for wadding, the latter to keep the shot from rolling out the end of the barrel. They never knew then they might open the door to a mob of slave catchers, so they slept prepared. "If a man stays ready he dont't have to get ready." Their pa had drilled this into them their whole lives.

"Who is it?" He asked, half in dread, half in anticipation.

"A friend, alone." The first thought that crossed Rankin's mind was that the law had finally caught up with him. He analyzed the voice carefully. The intonations of the southern slave were clearly present, but there was a difference there, too. He hesitated, was it a trap? Rankin didn't live in constant fear of his life but knew that some slave owners had offered $2,500 for the abduction or assassination of Rankin and some other conductors on the Underground Railroad. According to the Fugitive Slave Act he could be fined $1,000 and have to serve up to six months in jail if caught. Rankin could also have to pay an extra $1,000 to the owner of any slave he or his sons aided to escape.

He pulled the door open and stepped back to give the boys a clear field of fire in case they needed it.They didn't, but a man never knew from one time to the next. If it had been the slave catchers, they would have been showing a light. They didn't like ambushes either. If they had been out there, they would have walked into a hail of death. He relaxed a tiny bit.

"Are you Reveren' John Rankin?"

"That I am. Come on in." Rankin knew what type of person he was dealing with, always scared, wet, and hungry. Some of them had nearly frozen to death, the Ohio River ice already solid on them, weighing them down. This one was fortunate. It was still warm weather.

The Zulu gripped the Colt, concealed as it was beneath the baggy clothes. He had managed to keep it dry by pushing a log along as he crossed the river. It was almost more than he could stand to trust this white man, but he had to. There was no choice. "Will you hide me?" He asked. "Help me stay here in the promis' lan'?"

"That I will, son, that I will." Only when they had reached the long, low cellar and closed the door did one of John Rankin's boys light the lantern.

Rankin looked the fugitive over, he seemed to be all right, but there was something there, something definitely different about the way he met Rankin's gaze. Somehow Rankin felt that he was being measured, evaluated. Most of the escaping slaves he had helped wouldn't look up at his face. Yielding to a lifetime of servitude, most of them just stood with their heads down. This one carried himself with some indefinable quality, something Rankin couldn't quite put his finger on. Rankin noticed that his speech was a little different, but that wasn't it. He was a fine looking lad and carried himself well, as if he had been born to a leadership role. Perhaps he was a killer. Rankin knew that some of them were. In any case, Rankin knew he would rest easier when this one was gone.

The old horse, grazed peacefully along the lush grass close to the Ohio River fully forty miles downstream from Ripley. His bridle and saddle removed, he had traveled south toward his home, then stopped, and, is the way of horses, promptly forgot his original destination. The saddle and bridle rested on the bottom of the river about ten feet out from the shore directly across from John Rankin's house. The horse was found late that fall, and since the owner could not be found, the finder, a farmer, used him to plow his small acreage. During the drought of 1932, a child, swimming in the Ohio, stubbed his toe on something imbedded in the soft bottom and dragged up the saddle tree with a few rotten strips of leather clinging to it. Unimpressed, he let it fall back into the shallow water, and went back to swimming with his friends.

Two weeks later, the Zulu was living as a free man. Rankin arranged to place him into a job milking cows on a dairy farm. The owner, a fellow Presbyterian, had a farming operation up on White Oak Creek. The Colt, with three loads left in it, was safely wrapped in the fat clerk's clothing and hidden in the corner of the small shack that the Zulu had to himself. As the months passed he began to relax, and if not happy, at least he was satisfied for the time being to let his body heal.

The Zulu had no way of knowing about the Fugitive Slave Act. He didn't know that his employer could be forced to cooperate with the patrollers. He didn't see the slave catcher talking to the farmer, who had no time to warn him. The Zulu, contrary to his nature, had become complacent with his new freedom. Becoming accustomed to the regular hours and solid food, he had dropped his guard. He didn't see the slaver walk into the barn. In a moment it was over, and he was looking down the barrels of the shotgun, with no chance to fight or run. In a few minutes the slaver had him tied and they were on their way south. That was how he fell into the grasp of the slaver.

After Cain later freed him from the slaver, he found Cain to be of the same type of man as Hershel Johnson, whom he had believed dead, until his encounter with Tracker Jack. He felt no gratitude to the Colonel for giving him the opportunity to escape from the slaver. He knew that the act of freeing him had nothing to do with human kindness. He rode with Cain, not because of any sense of loyalty, for the need of human contact was no longer a part of him, but merely because it suited his purposes of the moment.

CHAPTER 38

Gatlin was restless. He had started out early working in the garden, but he finished there, he went with Sam and the dog to check the snares, and they were empty. They usually always caught something along the creek, but not today. The sky had been an ugly color for the past few hours, and his sweat seemed to cling to him instead of evaporating, as if he was covered with a greasy film. Sam and the dog, Tige, had gone off over the bluff again, and would probably return with a rabbit or two.

He wandered back to the cabin, where he found Sarah busy with cleaning. She smiled with warmth, but it was a flat type of smile. He wondered how she had resolved his sudden appearance into her and the boy's shattered lives. She had started to talk to Sam during the last day or two, but, of course, could not hear his replies. It gave the boy some comfort. Sam began to act more like normal boys his age. Sarah seemed to remember that Sam was her son, but sometimes when he was in the house, she stared at him with a puzzled frown.

It was strange that, Rit Gatlin, who hadn't known love since he was a child, and who had only known a mother's love through Mrs. Williams, found himself loving this woman. This woman, who although she hadn't died of her head injuries, might never recover. She might, for the rest of her life, remain unaware of the raid, the death of her husband and the loss of her home. He had been aware of her attractiveness from the very start, and had gotten used to the fact that if she didn't recover from her injuries, he would care for her and raise her son. But loving her? He hadn't really thought about. Was what he felt for her just pity? No, he had felt pity before and this feeling wasn't pity. Yes, he definitely loved her, but that in itself would bring on more problems. Another thought came. He wanted to marry her. But how could he ask her to marry him when she wasn't aware of who he was? It was this war, this miserable war. He had not seen another living soul except Sarah and Sam since he had returned to the cabin. He supposed that the settlers who were still alive had packed up and moved off to safer areas. It might be months or even years before a preacher came through to marry them. Supposing that he did marry her in this impaired condition? Then suppose one day that she regained all of her memory. She would remember her husband and her own near-death. She naturally wouldn't want to be married to a man who had only one leg and who had married her without her full consent. Yet, Gatlin knew it wasn't fitting and proper for an un-married man and woman to be living under the same roof, even if they didn't sleep within twenty feet of each other.

Back outside, Gatlin was aware of a distinct difference. Everything seemed oddly different. An almost transparent aqua-green had replaced the normal blue of the afternoon sky. A reflected light changed the entire spectrum of colors around him. He felt like an outsider, a spectator, as if his eyes weren't focusing properly. He turned and looked to the southwest and the brilliant white clouds were outlined in black. They were being pushed upward by the boiling clouds below and behind them. By watching for a few minutes he could see that they were moving to the northeast. Gatlin had seen these same types of clouds before in Little Rock and they had always presaged a severe storm. Once he had even seen a cyclone in the far distance as it did its deadly dance across the flat country along the Arkansas River. He had better get the boy and his mother to a safer place. But where? The Williams' cabin lay right along the top of a ridge and would be hit for sure if it came a cyclone.

As Gatlin started around the corner of the cabin he saw a knot of blue-clad riders moving at a fast walk around the curve. In a few minutes they would be there. It must be Captain Hughes out on another scout. Maybe the Union troops had news of the war and Captain Hughes might have some idea of when it all might end. Gatlin's eyes narrowed. The rider in front did not slouch over in his saddle as Captain Hughes had. This soldier rode very erect, and it appeared that at least one of his men was black, or was it possible that the soldier was just riding under the shadow of a tree?

CHAPTER 39

Cain was very irritable, perhaps because his skin was chapped and his eyes felt gritty. He was tired of sleeping on the ground, and tired of eating tasteless half-cooked food and tired of having to associate himself with a bunch of robbers and deserters. He thought he deserved better than this. The only one of them that possessed any intelligence was the Zulu, and he seemed to hold all of them, including Cain, in cold contempt. Cain knew that they shouldn't have come back this way. He was almost positive that the boy was dead. He had likely been wounded in the attack or died of exposure afterward, making the whole trip pointless. Yet, he couldn't afford to take that chance. If the boy should survive, Cain's chance to build an empire in the hills could be finished.

He heard the men grumbling predictably as they rode along. He knew that his hold on them was tenuous at best, and that sooner or later they would figure out that they were being used. His plans, slowly shaping up in his head, made no allowances for any of these human scum living long enough to figure out anything. Cain heard a loud clink and turned in his saddle, irritated, knowing that another small rock had popped out from under on the the mountain howitzer's wheels only to bounce off the gleaming bronze barrel.

"Private Abbott, can't you keep that blasted thing quiet?" he snapped. "I don't know why on earth I let you bring it along."

The lanky private looked up from his self-appointed task of leading the big sorrel mule. The mule's ears were laid back. She was obviously not happy about being harnessed to the gun carriage. The gunner leaned forward in his saddle and spat an amber stream of tobacco juice across the neck of his horse. "It'll be all right, Kunnel," he said in a slow Georgia drawl. The accent by itself told that the blue uniform was not the one he was wearing when the war started. "I'll take care of her."

Turning back around, Colonel Cain had to admit that Abbott, who had obviously been an artilleryman before he deserted, had done a good job of taking care of the small cannon ever since they had taken it in the raid on the Union supply wagon. He just hoped that they would find a use for it sometime.

* * *

Gatlin started back toward the front door, feeling the sudden slackening of taut muscles that only relief brings. Finally, here was a Union patrol. He would probably have to show his discharge papers again, but that would be a small inconvenience. He wondered if they would check out the area for the band of bushwhackers that had raided the Casey homestead. He hoped the Federal patrol would either chase out the marauders or ascertain whether they had left the area. Gatlin hoped for the latter. He had been afraid to leave the woman and kid unprotected while he scouted around. He hoped this officer was indeed Captain Hughes, because Hughes was a man of purpose. He seemed to be fair, and underneath it all, not unkind. Nevertheless, Gatlin felt his hand drop down to the LeMat as it lay heavy against his hip, as if seeking some assurance. He could hear Sarah. He thought of her as Sarah, his Sarah, busy behind him in the house somewhere. He looked to the west, wondering if the calvarymen would arrive before the storm hit. The boiling clouds could be seen at three different levels now, the high wispy ones seemingly oblivious to the disturbances going on beneath them. He could see a solid sheet of dark gray moving across the hills to the west. Lightning shot its lacy bolts between the dark rows of thunderheads, first one way, then the other, without pattern or sequence. The air began to feel heavy and still, and he heard the metallic sounds of the horses hooves as they struck the ledges of sedimentary limestone that cut the road into shallow irregular steps. Now that they were closer, he could see that the man in front was not Captain Hughes. Captain Hughes had been a farmer before the war, and it showed in his bearing. This was a different breed of cat entirely. This man's bearing carried with it an air of haughtiness and cruelty. Gatlin was vaguely disturbed.

As the troop of cavalry drew rein in front of him, Gatlin was surprised to see that the commander wore the gold eagles of a full Colonel! It struck him as strange that an officer of such rank would be in command of such a small unit. His training almost prompted him to salute. Yet, when the Colonel tilted back his hat preparatory to speaking, Gatlin was oddly struck by his gray eyes. They had a flat look to them. Gatlin shuddered inwardly. The other times he had seen that expressionless stare were in the eyes of men already dead. There was a craziness in the dull eyes. Gatlin knew instinctively that here was a man who was not quite sane.

In sharp contrast to the eyes of the Colonel was the unfathomable darkness in the eyes that set deep and close together in the face of the black man riding beside him. Gatlin noticed he was wearing sergeant's stripes. The sergeant slouched in his McClellan saddle slightly to the right and behind the Colonel. Gatlin had heard that there were Union army units made up of former slaves, but he was surprised to see a lone black soldier attached to a unit of regular cavalry. Gatlin, who had survived by his wits all his life, felt his muscles tighten as alarm crept through him. As he opened his mouth to speak, he was interrupted by the Colonel's direct question.

"Do you live here alone?" The tone was arrogant, rimmed with contempt.

Gatlin instantly felt a sense of impending conflict.

This man invited trouble. Gatlin's scalp tightened and the hairs on the back of his neck began to tingle. Gatlin calmed himself. There was no need to pick up the glove, especially outnumbered as he was. As Gatlin started to frame his reply, Sam and his dog, intent on some errand known only to themselves, skipped around the corner of the cabin, almost running into the group of soldiers. The boy skidded to a halt, his happy expression turned to shocked surprise, then to stark fear, contorting his face.

"Kunnel, it's the kid!" came a shout from one of the soldiers.

There was a flash of movement as Colonel Cain's hand dropped to his pistol.

In a split-second Gatlin realized that these were the bush-whackers, even as his right hand started pulling the LeMat from its cut-down holster. The big brindle dog, its reflexes faster than either of the two men, took two running leaps and launched into the air, his teeth sinking clean to the gums into Colonel Cain's left shoulder. The impact knocked Cain sideways. Cain's horse, overbalanced by loss of the rider and the impact of the dog, stumbled sideways into the black sergeant's mount. The Zulu was on the ground before his lightning-fast reflexes could come into play.

The mule, not used to gunfire, set her legs and reared, jerking Abbott backward. The cannoneer's horse, spurred by his riders re-flex action, jumped smack-dab into the middle of the already whirl-ing mass of men and animals.

Gatlin, quickly recovering from the mind-numbing turn of events, fired into the melee. Through the white cloud of gunsmoke he saw Sam start to run. He triggered the LeMat, his thumb hauling the heavy crooked hammer back to full cock each time. He began firing at Cain. Gatlin saw the soldier behind him go down. Cain and the black man hit the ground at the same time. First one, then the other, were being wooled viciously by the dog.

His eyes watering from the powder flashes and the gritty gunsmoke, Cain was only vaguely aware that two of the men in the rear ranks were on the ground. One had died instantly, gray striped turkey feathers protruding from where he had exposed his arm pit as he tried in vain to maintain his balance. The other bushwhacker was sitting flat on the ground, trying without success to pull the red cedar arrow from his side.

Return fire, although inaccurate, started to pour into the cabin from the remaining bushwhackers. Gatlin heard a scream. It started low and hoarse, then started to rise very rapidly in both pitch and volume until it made his teeth vibrate. Punctuated by gunfire, the scream filled the house. Gatlin turned and there stood Sarah, the scream still coming from her open mouth.

Her eyes were full of the bleak horror of a lost soul staring down into the depths of some unspeakable hell. Gatlin grabbed Sarah's arm and shoved the squirrel rifle into her left hand. He knew that somehow down deep inside where she still lived, Sarah had recognized some of her assailants. That scream had been the first sign that she remembered it all, but there was no time to think of that now.

Jerking Sarah along by the arm, Gatlin took off through the cabin and out the back door, pausing only to grab the leather bag containing powder and ball. Pushing her ahead, he could see Sam and a buckskin-clad figure just disappearing into the woods. He stepped ahead and grabbed her outstretched hand. As they reached the tangle of oak trees, interspersed with green briars and grapevines, he looked back. None of the bushwhackers had rounded the cabin as yet, but he knew it was but a matter of seconds until the bushwhackers recovered from their surprise and organized a pursuit. As Gatlin started to turn into the woods, he saw old Tige bounding toward them, unhurt, with what seemed to be a big doggy grin across his hairy face.

CHAPTER 40

The big dog looked up at Gatlin and Sarah as he trotted past. Glancing at Sarah, Gatlin saw a look of recognition cross her face as she spotted the dog. Gatlin knew that with the afternoon passing so quickly he had better find Sam and whoever had shot the arrows. The arrows? He hadn't been consciously aware of the arrows before. The thought hit him with a start as he stepped into the edge of the brush. In his mind, he replayed the gunfight, if it could be called such. Yes, there had been arrows, and yes, he had seen Sam rush into the brush behind someone wearing buckskins. The Indian. It had to be the Indian. Sam's friend. Sam had called him Beartrack.

"We've got to run some more, Sarah," he said, grabbing her hand again. He was already starting to lose his wind. In the excitement, he had forgotten she couldn't hear. After the minute or so of silence following the gunfight, a single shot from the Sharp's carbine sounded loud even over their heavy breathing. Gatlin slammed to the ground, a heavy burning sensation in his side. His momentary hesitation had cost them dearly! He felt sick, and his vision turned black for a moment. He was doubled up, threshing on the ground. He saw Sarah staring down at him, hands clasped to the sides of her head. He had to get up, he had to! Allowing himself the luxury of pain would be to sacrifice Sarah to the killers.

Gatlin heaved himself up, and started to run again, pulling Sarah with him. Looking back over his shoulder for a second, he could see the black man, rifle in hand, turn back into the cabin. As he turned, the black man raised his hand for an instant, as if to salute. It must be my imagination, Gatlin thought as he ran. His stump started to hurt again from the pounding, but he knew that to hesitate again was to die. He could feel the warm blood as it started to run down his faded gray uniform shirt. He knew that if they could stay ahead of the bushwhackers until the storm hit, or night came, they would have a chance, not a good chance, but a chance nevertheless. He didn't know how bad he was hurt, but he knew instinctively that these people took no prisoners.

Then an, Indian stepped out of the thick brush, Sam and the dog close behind him. The boy ran to his mother and clung to her. She looked down and smiled, but it was no longer the vacant smile Gatlin had gotten used to.

"You come with me," the Indian said in a thick voice that sounded as if he hadn't spoken in a long time. His english was slow and precise as if it was late learned and long unused. Gatlin eyes met the measured gaze of the Indian. He knew that somehow he was being evaluated, rated. Gritting his teeth in pain, Gatlin, in turn, looked the Indian over. It was obvious that he was a fairly old man, his long, gray-streaked hair bound back with rawhide, his clothing roughly made, his dark eyes timeless. The Indian turned and set a rapid pace down over the steep hillside into a grove of tall red oaks. Gatlin and Sarah followed Sam and Beartrack, who had vanished into the forest.

* * *

The Zulu lowered the Sharps, a grim smile on his face, and turned back into the cabin. He had seen the man fall, then get up and disappear into the woods. He knew he had wounded him, perhaps mortally. It would be an interesting game now, and he would get a chance to use his tracking skills. The outcome was a foregone conclusion now. It seemed strange that he felt a little twinge of sadness.

The Zulu stepped out the front door. Colonel Cain was just getting up off the ground, yelling incoherent orders to the men, his face contorted with pain and crazed rage. The blue ringed puncture wounds in his shoulder were slowly oozing blood, clearly visible through the tears in the blue uniform. Colonel Cain saw that he had three men down wounded, one seriously. Behind them were the two men shot with arrows, one dead, the other would die in a few minutes.

Robertson, who claimed to have deserted from both armies, was down on the ground with the wounded. He looked up, his face pale. "Colonel, I don't rightly know what you're trying to pull, but we've lost too many men." His voice was tight and strained.

Cain, his rage out of control again, bent and grabbed his pistol off the ground where it had fallen. Face expressionless, he carefully and slowly wiped it off on his uniform blouse, and without preamble, shot Robertson in the face. He turned to the other men and gestured at the body, "Anybody else want to question my orders?" he screamed. They dropped their eyes, refusing to meet his murderous glare. "Now," he said, "We've got to go after them."

The Zulu, his carbine turned casually so that it was pointed at the Colonel's belly, spoke. "Colonel, there's a bad storm coming, we've got wounded, and there's only that man, a woman and the kid. They won't get far."

Reason slowly returned to Cain's eyes, "You're right," he replied. "You men, get the wounded inside."

* * *

Beartrack stepped to the side of the dim game trail, as Sarah and Sam hurried past. He dropped back beside Gatlin, "How bad are you?" he asked in a low voice glancing over his shoulder at their back trail.

"I don't think it hit a bone, but I'm bleedin' bad." Gatlin replied. Beartrack jerked up the left side of Gatlin's shirt, and pulling a piece of doeskin out from under his leggings, crammed it into the wound. Then he pulled Gatlin's belt up over it, tightening it down to stop the bleeding. As they caught up with the woman and her son, they began to hear a distinct rumbling, almost imperceptible at first.

It was low in pitch, more pronounced as a vibration than a sound. It seemed to move deep within the Earth.

"The storm, it is here," Beartrack said as he hurriedly pushed them down under the hollow of a low limestone ledge, "Cover your heads."

The Zulu heard the sound and knew it for what it was. It was not unlike the storms that had struck the rolling hills of his native land. He hoped the man survived the storm. The man was a brave warrior. The man had drawn his gun on them without hesitation, even though outnumbered and outgunned. In the land of the Zulus, there were many such brave men. He had allowed himself to think that all men in this beautiful land were jackals like Cain and his followers.

CHAPTER 41

It had started a few days before, with no concern for the puny humans and their petty problems. This great upsweep of warm moisture-laden air originated in the yet uncharted and unsettled regions of the Gulf of Mexico. Roaring northeastward, a summer hurricane that through some accident of nature had slid around Florida's west coast far enough away to barely ripple the waters of Tampa Bay, had come ashore a little west of Port Arthur, Texas. Then it started to slow down. Because of the friction between the air which was saturated with water vapor and the rugged land below it, the big storm started to disintegrate. In so doing, it spawned many smaller disturbances. These storms worked their way into Indian Territory. Some of them were then pushed east by cooler air spilling across the great plains from the north. These storms were made more intense by the natural tendency of the warm, moist, less dense air near the Earth's surface to rise. In contrast, the heavier cooler air higher up began to sink. As the warm air started to rise, it began to spin slowly, then with increasing velocity spiraled upward in towering, stately, invisible columns. All this rubbing of air together produced static charges which built up until they could no longer be sustained. These charges then struck the Earth's surface, which had been building up shadow charges along its surface. These shadow charges were correspondingly opposite to the ones above. It was one of these storms, small and insignificant by global standards, that moved across the face of the ancient eroded plateau that had become the Ozark mountains. Once there, it moved swiftly into the lives of the mortals below.

Two opposing groups, one the ruthless hunters, and the other the victims. The victims, the eternal prey, the rabbits, as it were, locked into a life and death struggle which they did not understand. Yet, like the rabbit, they understood that they must survive at all costs. Only one group would emerge victorious, and not all of them would live. Yet, out of all this, only one man, the one named after the ancient murderer Cain, knew the real reason for the conflict.

One of the static discharges lit up the darkened sky with a jagged flash as it instantly vaporized the water in a tall red oak about thirty yards above the limestone ledge where the victims huddled together. They were on their knees, arms around each other, the lower edge of the limestone their only protection. The water, now turned to steam, exploded the fibrous oak into long murderous daggers that whirred overhead, some burying themselves like giant jagged arrows into the bark of neighboring trees. Gatlin's eyes flew open involuntarily as the lightning bolt hit the ground, causing balls of blue fire to roll in all directions from the base of the tree. They resembled titanic cosmic cockleburs as the static charges played across their surfaces! The shock wave that shook the ground an instant
later almost vibrated their teeth from their skulls. Gatlin felt fear close its iron grip on his throat; it made a hateful metallic taste, gluing his tongue to the roof of his mouth. He started to pray, with some embarrassment. It crossed his mind that it was very likely that God never heard from anyone who wasn't in dire straits. His experience had been that people became solid converts only when the chips were down and there was nowhere else to turn. He felt Sam's muscles tightening, he was going to run! In anticipation, Gatlin tightened his grip on the little boy's shoulders. It was all Gatlin could do to keep from running himself.

Then came another sound, almost lost in the sound of the storm. It was recognizable at first as a mere vibration. It started to rumble, then rose in both pitch and volume, until it became a roar, then a scream. It rose until it seemed the gates of Hell had been thrown wide open and the moans of ten thousand tormented demons came drifting out. The mortals began to feel the force pulling at them. It was almost irresistible, this force! It was steadily pulling them away from their meager windbreak, sucking them into its black towering maw. The cyclone occupied their world until there was nothing else but the sound and that dragging force. They held on to each other still tighter. It seemed that there was a flowing between them, some sort of communication. Should they survive, they would always feel a solid bond, something that others would never understand. The big dog wormed his way into the middle of them. Gatlin opened his eyes again. Through the blowing grit and fine gravel that threatened to scour the skin from their bodies, he could see that Sarah was screaming, with no chance of being heard. Wiping his eyes he could see it between them and the cabin. It was a huge black column that had no definable edges. Huge oaks and cedars whirled around in it, the giant spidery bare roots swinging around their crowns.

As Gatlin strained to see through the fog of grit, the great whirling mass slowly disappeared from view. It left behind it a path of total destruction. Most of the trees had been uprooted; many of the others had been twisted off above ground level. The twister was followed closely by a few large, cold, stinging drops of rain, which turned swiftly into small chunks of ice. The chunks rapidly increased in size, until they were hailstones the size of grapes, rapidly turning the ground white and pounding the refugee's exposed backs into aching numbness. Finally, when it stopped, the silence was thick, broken only by the roar of the storm as it faded off to the northeast. Gatlin and Beartrack both stood up slowly, painfully, very aware that they were all lucky to be alive. A loud hiss of rain falling onto the stump of the lightning struck tree caused a billowing gray cloud of smoke and steam to rise in the stillness.

Gatlin felt of his side, and his hand came away sticky. The wound was oozing blood again. As nearly as he could tell, a bullet had gone completely through between his hipbone and short ribs. He knew that if it had hit his innards, he would be in much worse shape now. The wound might not be too serious if he could just be still and keep it from bleeding.

Beartrack looked back toward the cabin, "We will go now, the storm will not stop them" he said. Gatlin realized that if the storm hadn't blown the cabin away the bushwhackers would be after them immediately. And the bushwhackers would be in better shape, not having been exposed to the elements.

CHAPTER 42

"Halt, who goes there? Advance and be recognized."

"I is Aaron, this is Burrill. We done swum that big river, we wants to jine up with the blue soldiers, we wants to be free.

"You're already free. This post is U.S. territory "

"You won' send us back?"

The sentry gave his fellow soldier a knowing smile. They were all alike. They knew nothing of what had been going on. They were almost pitiful, all determined to gain something of which they seemed to know only the word, and nothing of what it really meant. Well, they all caught on quickly. He turned over his shoulder and gave the all clear signal. "No, we won't send you back. Walk right down that road between the tents, and they'll feed you."

"See, Burrill, see, I tole' you it'd be all right. We free now."

* * *

"We've got to do something with them, sir, and there's a whole bunch and more come in every day. I would have thought that them Secesh would have had at least a few outposts out there just to make it hard for them to get in here."

"Why would they, Captain? They had their chance and messed it up. Besides that, they've lost Vicksburg, and now we control the entire Mississippi River from one end to the other. There's no way they can hold out without control of at least part of the river."

"I wouldn't count them out yet, sir. There's still a lot of fight left in them."

"I'm getting tired of this foolishness. Captain, swear these men into the army. We've got three regiments of them already. We'll just form a fourth. I don't see that it's a big problem. We've got enough uniforms and weapons. Fall them out there and drill them. We've got enough non-coms around here to train them. We're going to need every man Jack that can carry a gun when we start the push toward Little Rock. By the way, captain, make sure all of them have a last name. If they can't come up with one, have their sergeants assign them one."

* * *

"What's yourn?"

"The sergeant said it was Hurvey. Now on I is to be called Aaron Hurvey. What's yourn?"

Burrill stood up proudly, " Sergeant, he say my name is Eastman, count of we come 'crost the river from the east. Now I is Burrill Eastman, free man!"

CHAPTER 43

The Zulu stood and impassively watched the approaching storm through the open window while the men, including Colonel Cain, had all piled into the corner of the cabin. The fear was plain on each peaked face. The Zulu gave them a look of contempt. He rubbed his right cheek bone where one of Gatlin's bullets had passed close enough to cut a deep groove in the skin. He flexed his muscles and they were sore from the fall. He would kill the crippled white man and gain a certain amount of satisfaction from doing so, but he still would have respect for him. He had no respect for the scum with which he had associated himself. Like the American Indian, his people respected courage. These people had no courage, and for a moment he was ashamed to be here.

Most of Cain's men knew the scream of the tornado for what it was, for if they had never experienced such a storm, they knew someone who had. The Zulu felt no real fear of the storm, knowing fear was a waste of energy in the face of something he had no power over.

The Zulu knew now that both the woman and boy were alive and represented a threat to Cain's plans. Cain had not confided in him, but he felt that only two things could prompt the Colonel's determination to destroy the little family. He believed that Cain had wanted the woman, but that had been only a thought of the moment. Cain seemed to want this part of the country empty; therefore, it could only be wealth, power or, more likely both, that motivated him.

The Zulu examined his own motives. He wanted to, no, he had to get back to his homeland. The only way to accomplish that was to get some of the golden metal that both Arabs and whites seemed to value so much. With gold, enough gold, he could buy passage back to his homeland, or perhaps get a boat and sail back himself, although he didn't think that was possible. He had joined up with Cain, hoping to achieve this end, but now he could see that he had allied himself with a man who was thoroughly insane.

The Zulu had learned to trust no man, and while he categorically hated all whites, he did not allow himself to be consumed by this hatred. He was beginning to see that Cain and his men would never succeed at anything. It seemed that they wasted their time robbing and murdering people who had nothing to begin with. All the deserters were interested in was loot and whiskey, along with any of the settler women they might come across in the process of pillaging the country. They were little more than animals, with intelligence to match. By listening to Cain, they were risking their lives, hunting down the woman and boy, both of whom the Zulu could have easily shot during the raid on their homestead.

Turning his back on the men, the Zulu leisurely closed the heavy split board shutter, then, through a small crack in its corner, watched the destruction wrought by the storm as it passed. He thought at first that it was going to hit the cabin, when the cyclone appeared to stand still for a long moment, and headed directly for them. Then the dark shape suddenly turned and passed a few hundred yards to their south. He felt the impact of debris being absorbed by the thick oak walls. He walked to the front porch and watched the dark mass as it passed out of sight, much slower than he would have supposed. He ignored the rest of Cain's men as he walked out on the porch.

Robertson's body lay off to one side of the other two in the muddy yard. The arrows, their soggy feathers plainly visible, made the Zulu curious. There had been someone else in the fight, and that someone could only be one of the Indians that he had heard the men talking about. He walked over to one of the dead man, and placing his foot against his chest, pulled out the arrow. As he examined the flint tip curiously, he noticed that the horses had run off a little way, and stood, heads down against the wind. The mule, still hooked to the cannon, its ammunition pack askew, stood with them. The Zulu found himself looking forward to the coming fight. It should be interesting to see if the Indians lived up to their reputation as brave warriors. He wondered how they compared to his own tribe.

Colonel Cain stirred in the corner. He stared at the men, the taunt plain on his face, daring any of them to mention his fear of the storm. None of them met his cold gaze. The Colonel walked outside and looked at his dead soldiers without emotion. "We'll spend the night here," he said. "In the morning we may find that the storm has done our work for us."

* * *

Gatlin gazed at Sarah, her eyes and expression now fully alert. He hadn't observed her long enough to see if she had recovered her mental faculties.

"Sarah, are you all right"? She read his lips, nodding her head. The boy, without being told, leaned under the ledge and recovered the weaponry.

"The storm is not over yet," Beartrack said as he turned and started down the dim game trail. They had to hurry, it would be dark soon. Following along, Gatlin realized he had no idea where they were headed and he well knew that if it hadn't been for the Indian's interference in the gunfight, the bushwhackers would have settled their hash for good. Sam handed up the LeMat and Gatlin let him carry the squirrel rifle. He regretted having to leave the shotgun behind, but he knew that it's extra cumbrousness would have slowed them down.

They came out into a creek bottom grown high with the same narrow- bladed native buffalo grass that Gatlin had weeded out of the corn patch. Along the bends of the creek the switch canes grew to better than ten feet high. Within a few steps Gatlin looked down and saw that his arms were bleeding from dozens of tiny cuts inflicted by the thin blades of the switch canes. He looked back. Sarah was managing to keep up. Sam was trying to carry the long squirrel rifle held across his chest exactly as he had seen Gatlin do. True to what Beartrack had said, the sky started darkening again as they waded across the already swollen stream.

"Hold the rifle high over your head, Sam" Gatlin called out.

"Yessir," Sam said, as he tried to keep his balance while dodging floating logs as they whirled past.

Gatlin held his powder horn high over his head. Several times he felt his foot start to slip on the patches of blue clay scattered along the gravel bottom. Gatlin hoped he could avoid falling into one of the deep washed-out pools hidden by the muddy water. Those small packages of powder and percussion caps were all that stood between them and certain death if the bushwhackers caught up with them. That the bushwhackers would catch up with them was almost a certainty, since they would undoubtably be mounted. He hoped the tornado had totally blown them away, but he knew that the chances were slim to none at all.

Beartrack looked around anxiously. He could see that another storm was almost upon them. He had experienced the storms that always followed a tor-na-do. They seemed to rush in and fill the void left by the first storm. If he only had time he could construct some trip snares to slow their pursuers. He could hide their tracks, but there was no time to hide four sets of tracks in the mud. He was sure that at least some of the evil ones had survived. He had to get the woman and kid to his cave, hoping that, once there, they would be difficult to dislodge.

Gatlin's stump ached much worse and blood starting to trickle down his side. He knew that he would weaken if he had to walk much farther. They had walked about half a mile across the creek bottom, and it now looked as if they were coming to a hill so steep as to be almost a bluff. He didn't know if he could make it or not. He just had to rest for a moment. Then he looked up toward the end of the little valley and saw what he knew had to be Beartrack's shelter.

CHAPTER 44

The old man pulled the loupe away from his watering eye. He dabbed at it with a faded red bandana.

"It's not a design around the edge at all, Willie" he said. "It's definitely tooth marks. You can see that the marks are only around about three fourths of it." The old man smiled, " I would even speculate that the person who bit down on it was younger than 20. You see there are only two molars on each side. He or she hadn't cut their wisdom teeth yet." He lovingly turned it over in the strong light. "It must have taken an unbelievable amount of pressure to make them marks. Whoever made them was either very mad or in a lot of pain, that's all I can say." The yellowed ivory looked warm. The raised carving of the elephant dominated the flat disk, which was a little smaller than a silver dollar. The elephant's trunk was raised in triumph, one forefoot raised, the other resting on the body of a male lion. It was amazing that every detail was visible. The lion's face was contorted into a roar as his raised paws futilely struck at his tormentor. "I'm not any world class African expert, but the carving looks to be South African. I would have thought that it would have been in some rich dude's private collection or maybe in a museum by now."

Willie could tell that the crafty old pawnbroker was fishing for information, so he obliged. "It was left to me by my Great Aunt Catherine, she died last week of cancer." Willie Johnson shifted uncomfortably as he spoke. He glanced out through the heavily-barred grime incrusted window that faced the street. The 2600 block of Franklin was definitely not the best spot to park his truck full of tools this late in the day. St. Louis had changed so much. He had been scared to death each time he went to check on the old lady, who had lived her whole life in the Walnut Park area with its tall brick buildings. He had been tempted to carry his pistol but was afraid of the police. A black man, even a middle-aged one, was immediately suspect if armed. So instead he kept his rigging ax close by, on the seat. After all, who would question a roofer with a rigging ax?

"Sorry to hear about her passing away. I wonder where she got it?" The old man was nothing if not persistent. Knowing other people's business had kept him out of trouble on many different occasions.

"My aunt said that my great-grandfather, Ulysses Johnson, took it off a dead white man. But my Great-Grandfather told her that it had belonged to one he called the Zulu. I don't know which story is right, she was old and her mind may have been starting to go. Tell me, Mr. Rosenburger, how much is it worth?"

"Finally," thought the old man, "she's not even cold in the ground and here he is trying to sell it." Well, he couldn't really blame Willie. Financial handships had forced the roofer to the pawn shop many times over the years. The pawnbroker had probably kept the Johnson's wedding rings more than they had. "I'll give you nine thousand dollars for it," he said flatly. "Cash, whether you report it as income or not, is your business."

Willie stood there for a moment, thinking about how much nine thousand dollars would mean to his daughter Kesha, who was struggling to get through Forest Park Community College. He was so proud of her. She would be the first of his family to ever attend college. He thought of all the nice things he could buy for his wife and the boys. Nine thousand dollars was a lot of money. There might even be enough to buy him a pretty good old used truck, maybe one with a heater that half way worked.

"No, thank you, Mr Rosenburger, I promised my aunt I'd keep it in the family," he replied. Still, it gave him a pleasant glow to think about owning something so valuable.

The old man gruffly clapped him on the back. "Then what are you doing in here wasting my time? It's late and I should have been closed an hour ago. Get out of here and go home to that wife and houseful of young'uns." The old man, long past greed and envy, chuckled as he idly watched Johnson head out the door toward his beat-up truck.

Suddenly the old man straightened up, his attention focused. Something had moved from the shadows into the periphery of his vision.

302

CHAPTER 45

He felt another bite. "Dang graybacks," he thought as he scratched some more. They were in the blankets, in the uniforms, and worst of all, they were in the few beds to be found at Camp Adams, his included. He shifted his weight on the puncheon bench, thinking of the corn shucks they used down at the latrines and how sore he was. He wondered what they would do when the corn shucks ran out. He reached under his clothing and grabbed one of the offending body lice. Dropping it on his report, he studied it for a moment, watching it's slow sluggish movements, bloated as it was with his blood. He felt a surge of grim satisfaction as he smashed it with a rolling motion of his thumbnail. At first just a few men had them, then they spread like wildfire through the entire camp. Now he was going to have to order out a detail to dig poke salat roots. Boiling the roots, then taking a bath in the water, would kill the lice in a hurry. Naturally, all the clothes and bedding would have to be boiled in the same smelly solution. It wasn't going to be pleasant, but it was necessary.

He stood up, stretched and started to walk to the door to call his aide. Colonel Shaler was still irritated with himself over the mistake he had almost made with Private Silas Turnbo. He had been so tired and on edge that he had nearly had Turnbo court martialed for merely following orders on sentry duty. If Lieutenants Rea and Woods hadn't come and talked some sense into him, he would have done something he regretted the rest of his life.

He looked out of the second story window of the hewn-log

hotel and saw them. There was an older man and woman, the woman riding. Riding beside them was a younger woman with two kids behind her. A man, her husband, no doubt, walked alongside, leading the horse. But the two things that drew the Colonel's attention were the horses and their weaponry. The horses were long-legged and deep barreled. They were of much better quality than he was used to seeing, and of riding stock. These people were obviously settlers, since they were dressed in various combinations of buckskins and lindsey-woolsey. They should have been riding mules or rarely, heavy draft horses. The older man carried a rabbit-eared shotgun, the younger one a squirrel rifle, as he would have expected, but both of them were wearing Colt's revolvers belted on. This he would not have expected. Colonel Shaler was always interested in talking to the dozens of civilians that passed through the camp every week. Refugees from the war, or more correctly, from the murderous raids of the bushwhackers, they were moving south if they were of the Secesh persuasion. Union sympathizers, on the other hand, usually fled north toward Rolla or Springfield. More often than not they brought him valuable information about the Union Patrols that had begun to be seen more and more frequently in the area.

"Sergeant," he yelled out the door. His aide bounded up the narrow stairs with the same energy he himself had possessed before the war had begun. Now he could never be young again, the burden of command riding too heavily on his thin shoulders. "Sergeant, bring those two men up to my office," he said as he pointed down to the yard below. In a few minutes they were standing before him, obviously made nervous by being summoned to the camp commander's office almost upon arrival. Colonel Shaler stood up and shook hands with each man, obviously a
father and son. "I'm Colonel Shaler" he said.

The older man, his ragged hat held against his chest, replied "We're the Sapp's. I'm Thomas and this here is my boy, William."

"Please sit down," the Colonel indicated a split plank bench. He continued, "Would you like some boiled acorn and chicory? That's what passes for coffee around here, although sometimes we get some Sassafras roots dug and make some tea." He sat down heavily behind his desk.

Thomas Sapp shook his head, and continued speaking. "We're from Bennett's Bayou over north of New Atherns," he said, putting the "r" in "Athens" as all hill people did. "In case you are wonderin' how we got them fancy horses and these here new revolvers, I'll jes' tell you. We got into a shooting scrape with some bushwhackers, us and a one legged neighbor of our'n named Rit Gatlin."

The Colonel interrupted, "The same Gatlin that delivered the courier's horse to us, I'm sure."

Thomas Sapp continued, "Yep, it's the same man, he's got sand, that one has." Colonel Shaler then sat, his hands making a steeple on the desk in front of him as the Sapps told essentially the same story that Rit Gatlin had told him a few weeks earlier. "We was scared to death that somehow some of them bushwhackers would find out that we had kilt them three and come after us, not that they need any excuse to kill folks. Then when we saw that bunch of Union Cavalry come through and then seen the smoke from the burning houses, we gathered up what little stuff we could and took off. We've got some kinfolk down at Onset* so we stopped off there for a few weeks and visited. But they're having sech a hard time their ownselves that we decided we'd best light a shuck out of there before we all starved out."

William Sapp said, "They say some kid killed a Union deserter over near Rapp's Barren** the other day. Our uncle said that the varmint broke into their house in the middle of the night and attacked the kid's mama. They said the kid put three slugs right through through his gizzard. It's time some of them border scum got their just deserts."

"You saw Union cavalry, you say?" Colonel Shaler asked.

"Yessir, they must have been ten or twelve in the bunch we seen, blue uniforms and all. You know, it's kindly funny. They was a good ways off, but I could've almost swore that one of them was black." Young William Sapp was getting his chance to talk to someone important and he was making the most of it.

"I hear tell that the yanks are putting freed slaves in the field against our troops all right, but I hear tell that they fight in their own units, commanded by regular Union officers." The Colonel said.

"Well, we couldn't be too sure, the man could have been one of them Dutchmans they talk about. I don't know, I ain't never seen a Dutchman myself, I hear they got lop-ears, so I'm a' guessin' they could be awful dark, too.

"Could you see how many officers were with them?" Colonel Shaler asked. He could see that further discussion about the dark Union soldier was leading nowhere.

Thomas Sapp answered, "Nawsah, we stayed hid out and hoped they didn't notice us. You never know what them Yankees have got in their heads."

Colonel Shaler, assured that they had told him all they knew, yelled at the red-headed sergeant again, " Sergeant, get these people some grub, and try to find them a dry place to sleep tonight. Then find Lieutenant Davenport. We might just have to find out what's going on up there on the Bayou."

---

* Onset is now called Rea Valley, it is located near the White River in Baxter County, Arkansas, between Mountain Home and Flippin.

** Rapps Barren is now called Mountain Home, the county seat of Baxter County.

CHAPTER 46

The afternoon faded as they started to climb the steep slope below the Cherokee's shelter. Gatlin looked nervously over his shoulder. If they happened to be spotted by the bushwhackers, they were exposed enough to be picked off like squirrels on a tree limb. The front of the shelter was covered by a screen made by splitting switch canes and then basket weaving them tightly together. The canes had long ago turned brown, but still blended into the greens, browns and grays of the boulder- strewn hillside. The Indian took a moment to glance at Sarah and Sam, making sure they were all right. He bent down, and with flint and steel soon had a small fire going. Gatlin, who was all in after the fast walk down the bluff and across the creek, gratefully flopped down in the cave and leaned against the back wall. He felt of his side and was pleased there hadn't been any new bleeding in the last little while. He decided to leave the belt pulled over it for now.

After Gatlin had rested for a few minutes he started to look around. He could see the black smudge from countless fires on the ceiling. and to his left he could see faded paintings on the wall. They all appeared to be of some type of pale red color. He squinted, studying them as the fire started to burn brightly enough to reveal details. There were pictures that were obviously buffalo, along with hand prints of several different sizes. There were markings that may have indicated the passage of time and other figures that were obviously human. As he studied them he began to notice that some of them did not resemble any animals he had ever seen before. A few of them were much larger than the other animals. Gatlin knew about Elephants, but they were all supposed to come from Africa or India. The elephants in these drawings, if they were elephants, appeared to have long hair and great curving tusks. His curiosity overcame his tiredness and pain, so he pulled himself up to get closer to them. The shelter was fairly small and he had to squeeze past Beartrack. The Indian was draping strips of some kind of dried meat across a flat rock that leaned at an angle near the fire. Sarah and Sam sat in the corner, the mother's arm around her son. It was getting dark and the driving rain had started again. Beartrack left the meat warming and stepped up next to Gatlin, his buckskins giving off a wet dog smell.

"Did you do the paintings"? Gatlin asked.

"They were done by the ones who came before, the old ones," said the deep-voiced Indian. "They were gone many white man years before my people hunted here, longer than the oldest Tsa' ragi can remember. The old cane cover over the front fell down, but me, Beartrack, made a new one many seasons back." His english was good, Gatlin noted, but had long been unused. "Many people come and go, some leave marks, some leave no marks. Every people think they are the only ones, but there were always others who came before. Sometimes they die out, sometimes they are killed in battle. But new ones always come."

The Indian handed Gatlin a piece of deer antler. It had been drilled for a leather thong. There was a perfect likeness of one of the elephant-like creatures carved on it. "It was back there," Beartrack pointed back toward the back of the cave.

Gatlin turned it over in his hand. "I've never seen anything like it," he said.

"There is one thing more," the Indian said as he pulled a metal object from the front of his hunting shirt. "Look at this, white man." He said as he handed it over.

Gatlin turned it over in his hand. It resembled a thick bronze needle. It was about four inches long. As he turned it he saw that it had been beaten flat on all four sides, tapering to a sharp point. The other end had intricate circles around it. The end with the circles ended in a ring, attached to a leather thong similar to the one on the deer antler. "Did you find this here in the cave?" Gatlin asked.

"No, it belonged to my grandfather this many times, or more," the Indian held up all ten fingers. "His people fought with the men of the North. This was long ago, before we were the Tsa'ragi, before we came south to what you whites call the Carolinas. The Northmen had war dogs this big." Beartrack measured up nearly to his straddle. "Our people had more than one battle with the Northmen. My grandfather, he fight with one of them. They fight for a long, long time. The Northman was very tall, very big with hair like corn silk. He wore a cap of the white man's iron with horns of the white man's cattle on it. My grandfather did kill him. He took a very long knife, what you white men call a sword from the Northman. He took this and the head of one of the great dogs. My people say that the Northmen use this pin to hold their robes together. The skull of the dog and the long knife is gone many years. I have only this. It has the strong medicine of the Northman in it. It will last forever. Some of the Tsa'ragi say that the metal fell from the stars, that the Northmen gather it and make their weapons." Beartrack sat for a moment, "I do not believe it fell from the stars," he said.

The Cherokee turned back to the fire, lost in his memories, oblivious that Gatlin was even there. Moving the meat away from the fire, he deftly slid it over unto a large flat cedar slab then carefully pulled the sticks back from the fire and ground them into the dirt until they were dead.

Gatlin knew that the bushwhackers could find them if they tried, and there was no doubt they would try. Gatlin also knew that neither himself or the woman could travel very fast, so it was here that they would make their stand. The Indian's cave would be almost impossible to attack successfully as long as the inhabitants had food and water. Gatlin had noticed that there was a small tunnel that appeared to run at an angle up out of the South side of the cave. It was up near the roof and most of the smoke eventually found its way out of the shelter that way. It was here in this tunnel that Gatlin could see Beartrack had stored plenty of dried food. There was jerked meat, ears of corn and skins filled with dried wild fruits. Gatlin could see bowls made of turtle shells, with mussel-shell spoons. Just to the outside of the shelter to the north a wet weather spring ran a stream as big as his flat palm. This stream ran out and down the hillside. Gatlin tried to believe that they were safe. Instead he found himself carefully calculating the odds. He had given up thinking that the bushwhackers would just go away and let them be. There was something much bigger at work here.

Gatlin wasn't sure how many men the Union Colonel had left, but he estimated between 8 and 10. In the excitement of the gunfight he had seen two of the troopers go down, but he doubted if his own hurried shots had done much damage.

Beartrack retrieved another slab of cedar from the mouth of the tunnel which was just about eye level. As he watched him, Gatlin wondered if it offered a way out in case they were cornered, and right now that looked very likely. It was possible that the boy could get out through it, maybe. Beartrack slid half of the slices of warm meat over on the slab and handed it down to Sarah and the boy, she smiled gratefully and without further ado they both began to eat. The dog had followed them into the shelter and now lay near the boy with his head resting on his extended paws. Beartrack, with one motion, reached up and got a dried bone with his other hand and the dog easily caught it as it sailed across the cave, and immediately started cracking it to get at the marrow.

Beartrack walked over holding the other slab, "You want your side fixed now or you eat first?" he asked bluntly.

Gatlin knew it was likely that he would get sick when the belt was removed, so he said, "Doctor me up first."

The old Indian set the meat aside and motioned for Gatlin to lie down. Without ceremony Beartrack pulled the belt down and jerked the soft doeskin away from the wound, tearing it open again.

Sharp pain shot up Gatlin's side. It must have been temporarily numbed by the chill rain and the shock of the bullet, for now he felt as if he was going to pass out. Reaching up in the tunnel again, the Cherokee pulled out a handful of something very sticky and slapped it on both the entrance and the exit wound.

"Spider web, it will stop bleeding good." He then pulled out a gourd of smelly , greasy salve and smeared it liberally to the wounds. He reached up and got another piece of clean doeskin and placed it over the wound. "It will get plenty sore, but you will live unless bad mans shoot you more," he said smiling at his own gallows humor. Gatlin saw that Sarah, Sam and Tige had all piled together in the back corner of the cave, sound asleep.

Beartrack looked at them, then down at Gatlin. His smile was gone and there was a worried expression on his face. "They got cannon, a cannon is worth many guns." Gatlin had a fleeting memory of the mule-pulled cannon carriage.

"Then we got no chance if they find us," Gatlin said, thinking out loud.

Beartrack anwered, "My grandfather teach me how to stop this cannon, but I can go only at night, and get close."

Gatlin knew that although the stronghold could be successfully defended against any small arms attack, a few good loads of canister richocheting around those rocks would quickly make it a death trap for those inside. He would need Beartrack.

312

CHAPTER 47

As the rat moved toward the front of the cave, its heart rate accelerated. The white patch at her throat was moving up and down rapidly. Now was the most dangerous time for her brood. There were so many of them, seven in this litter. Already weaned, they were old enough to start foraging on their own. It was at this point in their lives that they knew enough to get food for themselves, but had not faced the dangers of their world enough to be cautious. They were brash, overconfident, each one having in his pea-sized brain the certain knowledge that he and he alone held the key to the survival and prosperity of the entire genera of Rattus. These overconfident ones were different in many ways, but in one way they were alike. They were always the first to perish. They had such confidence, not knowing that a least one time each day they would be given a final exam, a very practical exam in which failure was certain, instant and unpleasant death. Success only meant survival for another block of time. The time might be an hour or it might be a full day. The rats faced numerous predators, some their mother tried to teach them to beware of, and others which she, herself, had never seen.

She moved forward. There seemed to be an unusual amount of activity. She had always managed to creep forward and fill her cheek pouches, then ease back into the recesses of the cave to eat and feed her young undisturbed. She moved her head back and forth, catching scent particles. Some of the smells were new and strange, so she froze in place, waiting. Her oversized, bulbous eyes sought for some movement, some intimation of the danger. She decided that there was no immediate danger, and partially motivated by the fear that some of her offspring, either curious or hungry, might be following along behind her, she moved toward the store of nuts, carefully leaving a dull gray rock lying on the ledge. The rock was soft, and still held the impression of her chisel-shaped incisors.

CHAPTER 48

He shifted his weight in the saddle, gaining only a momentary respite. His butt was so incredibly numb. It shouldn't hurt so bad, but it did, and the skin on his ankles was starting to blister from rubbing against the stirrup leathers. It was hotter than the pitchforks of hell, but then, some of the men said that September was always hot in Mississippi. He jerked off his blue kepi and wiped his face with the back of his sleeve. What kind of buck-eyed fool had Colonel Murphey been to pull out and leave the town and its supplies to the Confederates?

"That pompous idiot!" he said, then realized that he had spoken out loud. He looked around. The Sergeant was looking over at him expectantly. He felt himself flush red under his tanned skin. It was hard to give orders to a man who was old enough to be his father. He deliberately made his voice stern as he asked. "Sergeant, how much further to Iuka?"

The sergeant leaned over and spat a long stream of amber, grunting as it splattered against the ground. "It's about one more of your miles," he said his voice thick with German inflections.

Lieutenant Kytle had heard that the Confederates always referred to the Germans as the "Lop-eared Dutch" ever since Segel's army of immigrants had fought at Wilson's Creek. There was even some resentment towards the recent immigrants among the regular Union troops. The sergeant had handled himself and his men very well and the Lieutenant relied heavily on them.

The Lieutenant could see his scouts coming in. Sergeant

McGahan rode up with his three men and gave his report to the Dutchman, who then rode back to Lieutenant Kytle.

"They've located a big plantation house, sir. It sits on a hill with a good view of Iuka. The Confederates evidently have not moved this far," the Sergeant said.

"Very well, Sergeant, you know Colonel Holman's orders, to find a large house and establish a forward headquarters. We're to occupy and hold it until the main army arrives. Have the occupants of the house fled?"

"I think so, sir. We couldn't see much activity."

As the troop of cavalry rode up the shaded buggy drive, Jackson could see that the house had once been beautiful and the grounds well maintained. Now it was run down and shabby.

"Sir, there's someone in that front porch swing," the sergeant said.

"I'm not blind, Sergeant. I thought you told me that the house was abandoned." The irritation was plain in the Lieutenant's voice.

"It'll be no problem, sir. I'm sure these folks have some relatives around they can go visit for a few days. It's not like the battle is going to take place right here. General Rosecrans and his staff won't hurt anything. These people might even be Union supporters," the sergeant said.

As their horses pulled up to the porch, the huddled figure straightened up and looked down at the soldiers.

"What do you bluebellies want?" The speaker turned his head in order to focus his one bleary alcoholic eye. There was no matching orb, just a sunk-in scar set out of kilter with the rest of the ruined face. His voice was hoarse, dead in tone, but held an edge of hatred and contempt.

The Lieutenant looked at the blanket covering the man's lap. The legs under it were bent and useless, the outline of the bones plain through their covering "We're sorry, but we have to commandeer your house, sir." The Lieutenant was determined to treat civilians with respect if at all possible.

"You can go to Hell, you and the rest of your kind!" With that the man's left hand reached down and grasped the edge of the blanket, throwing it back. His right hand was already bringing up the Colt Dragoon before the blanket slid to the floor.

The Sergeant, his reflexes honed by the long campaign, reacted, twisting his right arm as he grabbed at his pistol, cursing, already knowing he would be too late. The shot, aimed at the lieutenant, passed beside his neck, hitting one of the soldiers behind him in the stomach. A split second later the thumb-sized bullet from the newly-issued Spencer .56 in the hands of an alert trooper beside the sergeant slammed the crippled man back against the shattered swing.

The long silence that followed was broken only by the creaking of the rusty chains holding the swing to the porch beams. The white powder smoke whirled around their heads for a moment and was gone.

The Lieutenant, tasting his first battle, fought back the gorge rising in his throat. He dropped off his horse, motioning at two troopers to dismount and help him tend to his wounded cavalryman. The Sergeant, embarrassed at being caught off guard, slid his pistol back into its holster and snapped it, the click of the snap clearly audible above the grunts of the wounded man.

A black man, hurrying toward the ruckus, pushed out through the front door only to find every gun in the troop trained on him.

"Where are the rest of the slaves?" The Lieutenant, recovered now, made sure his voice sounded crisp and authoritative

"They done took off, suh," the huge black man said, unintimidated by the soldiers, who were now lowering their weapons slowly.

"Then what are you doing still here?" the Lieutenant asked.

"Well, suh, somebody had to take care of Masta' Johnson, and I's the only one left."

Lieutenant Kytle realized that this man wasn't going to volunteer any information. His entire life had been spent speaking only when he was spoken to.

"What do they call you?" the Lieutenant asked.

The big man's face settled into a proud, almost haughty look. "My name is Ulysses, the old massa said he name me afta' another big stout man."

"Well, Ulysses, you're free now. You don't have to stay here anymore." The Lieutenant said, "You can go anywhere you want. Do you understand what free means?"

Ulysses looked down off the porch at his questioner, his face tightening with anger. "Yes, suh, I understands. You don' have to talk to me like I's dumb. I've been a slave on this plantation all my life, but that don' make me dumb. They ain' none of us as dumb as we been made out to be. I knowed I was free, but I still stayed. They was nobody else to do it, so I stayed."

"Did you work in the field, Ulysses?" the Lieutenant asked. He was somewhat embarrassed, for the man was right, he had been condescending. He resolved to make up for it.

"No, suh, I was the blacksmith. The ol' massa, he even hired me out to other plantations to shoe horses and make fancy iron purties for their big houses," Ulysses said.

The Lieutenant couldn't help smiling. Here was exactly what his men needed, a blacksmith and tinkerer. His orders were to send any slaves he found back to the rear, there they would be fed and put to work digging fortifications and such like. He knew there had to be some way to keep this man along with his troop.

"Well, Ulysses, I'd like to hire you on as a free man to be a blacksmith for the Union Army," the Lieutenant said. He pulled a silver dollar out of his pocket and flipped it to Ulysses, who looked at it in wonder. "Now we need you to bury that man. By the way, Ulysses, what is your last name?"

Ulysses, dropped his head and stared for a long time at the silver dollar gleaming in his rough palm. He felt vaguely ashamed to admit that he only had one name, like a horse or a dog. He had never given it a thought before, but now it seemed important. He looked back up at the Lieutenant, who was watching him expectantly.

"My last name is Johnson." He hesitated a second. "Ulysses Johnson, my name is Ulysses Johnson." He said it with new-found confidence. After all, the ol' massa had treated him well. With the evil thing lying there in the porch swing dead, there would be nobody left to carry on ol' Massa Johnson's good name.

If the Lieutenant was aware of Ulysses' struggle, he concealed it. He said, "Well Mister Ulysses Johnson, we were going to use this house as headquarters for the Union Army. Now, I believe we'll try to find another one. General Rosecrans wouldn't like this business, wouldn't like it at all. If you'll bury that man, then you can catch up with us." The lieutenant jerked out a piece of paper. He wrote on it, then handed it to Ulysses. "You show it to any soldier and tell them to send you to Lieutenant Kytle in Lieutenant Colonel John H. Holman's command. When you catch up, we'll get you fed and outfitted then. We'll get you started shoeing horses and fixing things that need fixing."

After digging the hole, Ulysses bent over to pick up the body of the slave owner. The man who had inspired so much fear and hatred in the slaves now seemed light and somehow inconsequential. Ulysses noticed that the heavy bullet had just barely missed the ivory carving that hung around Hershel Johnson's neck.

"He would've been the bes' help you ever had. You orten' to have beat him, he didn't know nothin' 'bout no gold. You was a fool, and you died like a fool." With that, Ulysses pulled the carving off and slipped it around his own neck. It laid heavy against his skin. He liked it. Wrapping the blanket around the body, he held it away from himself as he walked. He dumped it into the grave. Looking down, he saw that he had blood on himself. He shoveled the hole full of dirt, the clods falling soundlessly, building up until the blanket was covered. Then until the hole was filled. Throwing the shovel on top of the grave, he walked up the steps past the swing without glancing at it.

Ulysses Johnson reached inside his shirt and felt the warm ivory. It was the only thing left of the young man he had considered a friend. He was free, for the blue soldier man had told him so. He started down the road whistling, and within an hour he was shoeing horses in the yard of Rosecrans' headquarters. Lieutenant Kytle had moved the McDonald family out and his men were stacking furniture into one of the back rooms. They were hurrying, getting the house ready for the arrival of the general. Ulysses somehow felt different. This freedom made him feel light. He felt as if he could fly if he just had wings.

* * *

SARAH'S STORY

At first there had only been the pain, it was in her head, it traveled down the right side of her neck and out to the point of her shoulder. Every breath caused sharp pain to shoot deep between her ribs, her right hip and leg sore all the way to the bottom of her foot. She was thirsty, so thirsty. Then there were gentle, sure hands giving her water. She must have slept then. Later the same hands were pushing warm food into her mouth, then there was no awareness for a while. Then there was the motion that she knew was that of a horse. The pain was worse with every step the horse took, fiery bolts of pain cutting courses up and down her right side. The ache in her head, the slow pound with each heartbeat never varied. Then she slept again. She didn't know how long she slept. Then there was a period of time that she was fed, and slept, time meaning nothing.

When Sarah awoke, there was food beside the bed; she sat up painfully and fed herself. She looked around, and the cabin wasn't her cabin and even though it seemed familiar, the bed wasn't her bed. She glanced around the room. This was not her home. A man came in and smiled at her, kindness in his face. The man sat down. She wondered who was he? He wasn't her husband Levi. Who was he then? Had Levi gone off and left this man here? A boy came in. He was her son, she knew that. Sam, Samuel Timothy. The big dog was Tige, Sam's dog. Sam and the dog seemed to accept the man, so he must belong here. All this thinking made her so tired. Later when she awoke, this man, this kind man with his quiet face, was putting food into her mouth again. She took the spoon and started to feed herself. Poor man, he couldn't talk, his lips moved, but no sound came out. She had to finish eating and get to work, there was always so much work to do. She slept again, a dreamless sleep. The dreams would come later.

After days of almost uninterrupted sleep, she started to move around the house. She had to get to work; there was so much to do. She started to clean the place up, but everything was out of place. She seemed to remember some things, and was able to do things instinctively, without conscious thought. But her head didn't work right. A thought would pop into her mind, but then before she could focus on it, it would be gone, leaving no trace. Had she gone crazy? Had Levi left while she was crazy? She should ask this man about Levi, where he had gone? When would he be back? But the man couldn't talk, so he couldn't tell her, could he? She started to busy herself around the cabin. The man came in, bringing a brace of rabbits. He started to cut them up. Somehow she knew that cooking was her job. She moved over and took them out of his hands. She started to say something, but she was embarrassed to talk to the strange man, since he couldn't talk, it might be ill-mannered to try to talk to him.

How could she remember how to cook the rabbits, when she couldn't remember anything else but her son? But she did cook them and they turned out quite well. She noticed that Sam acted very strange. He stared at her a lot and didn't come close for the hugs that he always pretended not to like. While they were eating, she realized that Sam couldn't talk either. His lips moved but there was silence. The silence! There was no sound anywhere! There was only the emptiness, the same empty silence she heard in the winter, the silence that seemed to roar, when there were no crickets, jar flies or grasshoppers. As she looked out the window, she saw a flight of crows go over the cabin. Shouldn't she be able to hear them cawing? Crows were never silent. Then she realized that although she could feel the breeze on her face, there was no faint hiss as it moved past her ears.

There was no moan of the wind through the cedars. She moved to the fireplace, pulling the dutch oven off its claw, and taken by a sudden impulse, she slammed it to the hearth. The cast iron vibrated against the solid sandstone, but there was no familiar ring! She dropped it and clapped her hands to the sides of her head. Was she deaf? There was no sound!

The headache, had it caused her to be deaf? Had the headache caused Levi to leave? Had he really ever existed at all? Yes, Sam was here, so Levi must have gone off hunting. She had to think about this, so she sat down hard on the hand-split bench, bent over, her hands covering her face. She sat for a long time, the tears puddling on the floor, searching for answers.

After a few days of keeping herself busy cleaning and cooking, the headache pain slowly, almost imperceptibly, started to fade. It didn't occupy her being as it had before. Her whole right side turned black, then gradually faded to blue, then finally started to show various greens and yellows. She had no trouble knowing what the colors were. However, she still found herself moving in an unfamiliar world. Some things her hands seemed to remember, even if her mind didn't. There were other things that she knew should be familiar, but they were strange. The man sometimes came in from working outside, sat down and drank acorn coffee. He seemed to enjoy watching her work, and his eyes possessed a deep abiding loneliness. Somehow she knew about loneliness, but how?

Things then settled into some sort of routine. The man didn't try to talk to her, and seemed to be aware that she couldn't hear. He smiled encouragingly at her at every opportunity. But when would her husband return? What would Levi think when he found out that she couldn't hear? Sometimes when the man and boy were outside, she practiced talking out loud. But how could she be sure the words were right? She could feel the vibration of her voice, but the words might be all wrong. Suddenly, Sarah Casey was frightened, frightened as she had never been before. She might never be able to communicate with another human being again. She might stay in a confused silent state forever.

It was hard to keep up with the passage of days. Some days she couldn't remember the day before, but Sam had started to come near her again. She got comfort from the animation of his face as he talked.

Then one morning after a breakfast of fried squirrel, Sam and the dog had gone off to play and Gatlin had come in with the garden sass. Suddenly she became aware of vibration. She didn't know how long she had been feeling it, but it was definitely a vibration. It became more intense. She could feel it as it passed along the puncheon floor, and she turned curiously from doing her housework. She had been nervously watching the clouds boil in from the west through the open window as she worked. She had seen dark clouds like this before, and she knew that somehow they were no good. As she saw the man get up and open the front door, she moved up behind him and peeked around his left shoulder, grasping his arm as she did so. The yard was full of horses and blue-clad riders!

CHAPTER 49

Sarah's vision turned brown around the edges and she felt herself start to sway. Trying to keep from falling, she leaned against the man. He felt solid and strong, like Levi! Then in one flash everything became clear. They were the ones! These same men, all shooting! Levi falling! The black man taking aim at her, she was trying to get away, but the horse seemed to be running in molasses, she couldn't make it! The horse was falling, falling into the black bottomless pit.

She screamed then, the scream of a primeval animal! A scream that came from the depths of her tortured soul, a scream of shattered hopes and dreams that would never be, of a formless pain that would never, could never, be put into words. The scream echoed through the small cabin, a scream that embodied her lost world, all of the agony of a tortured mind as it tried to make sense out of what had happened. Goose bumps raced across Gatlin's skin as the realization that the men were the murderers, hit him. Moving away from Sarah, he instinctively grabbed for the LeMat. The pistol came easily into his hand as he had practiced so often.

She watched, transfixed, as the flame leapt from the muzzle of the pistol and the white powder smoke billowed into the room. As Gatlin turned and fled, Sarah allowed him to drag her out the back door. She started to run, her survival instincts surfacing as she ran with this man, this man about whom she knew nothing but somehow trusted. She ran, fearing that any moment they could both be cut down by a hail of bullets. She felt as if she had awakened from a long sleep. Her body in slow motion from the unaccustomed running and the control her brain was now exercising over it. She saw the slow orange burst of flame from the black man's rifle and felt the kind man tense as the bullet entered his side. Her own side hurt from the exertion, and the heavy hot air started to burn down her throat. She saw a flash of movement ahead. It was Beartrack, Sam and the dog. Beartrack turned away with the affectionate look in his eyes indicating that he was glad to see her and somehow knew she was all right.

As the storm hit and they huddled under the ledge, she concentrated on keeping her terror under control and refusing to give place to the mental pictures that kept pushing themselves into her consciousness. She knew that such storms produced thunderous noises, but she could only feel the vibrations of the thunder resulting from the broad bolts of lightning as they danced between the tall oaks. The lack of noise made her feel like a bystander in the storm, even though she was soaked by the rain and hail.

She was exhausted by the time they reached Beartrack's shelter, and as it got dark, she sprawled on the ground near the fire. She looked around curiously. She remembered wondering just where the Indian lived, but she had never thought of it as being a cave. She became conscious of her appearance for the first time in a long while. Her soaking wet clothing clung with her every movement. She longed for a comb, but that would have to wait, right now she was so tired.

Accepting the hot strips of dried meat from Beartrack, she slowly chewed them as she silently sat beside her son and the ever present dog. She lay back and, with her son beside her, waited for sleep; but instead, long buried memories crept out from the dark corners of her mind.

* * *

CROSSVILLE, TENNESSEE, JULY 24, 1857

They hadn't been rich by any means, her family. Sarah's family had been storekeepers in the little town of Crossville in the part of Tennessee that lay in the western foothills of the Great Smoky Mountains. They sold goods to the farmers and stockmen who settled along Sequatchie Creek. Sarah Reeves, as she was named then, had at the age of 18, blossomed from an slightly overweight bookish girl into a very fetching young lady. Having decided that there would be no sons, her father set about to teach her about running a business, and from the time she was six, she worked in the store after school hours. The store was something which her mother had absolutely no interest in, preferring to stay at home to cook and sew for her husband and Sarah. Oh, her mother did have interest in church affairs and such, as long as it didn't involve the business of storekeeping.

Sarah had caught on rapidly and was quite content to tend store now that she had finished school. As she tended store, there was a constant stream of young men, who found excuses to come by regularly and somehow linger around the huge potbellied stove, each of them seeking to catch her attention. Sarah, although she was polite and friendly to each of them, gave none of them too much encouragement. She didn't know any of them well, except the ones she had gone to school with. Her mother doggedly urged Sarah to get serious about finding a husband. It was almost a standing joke between them, but one which had a brittle edge.

"You'll end up being an old maid, if you're not careful."

If Sarah had heard it once, she had heard it a thousand times. Although she never took time to think about it, there were several of the young men who would, judging from their backgrounds, make good husbands should she find herself in the market for a good husband sometime in the future, the distant future.

One night her father had gone home early, and as he often did, left Sarah to close up the store. At six o'clock she had closed the door, stepped into the street, and fumbling with the lock, her eyes averted, bumped into a man! Even before she could look up to tell who he was, she could smell the raw smell of corn liquor mixed with the rancid smell of a body long left unwashed. As she looked up, startled, a shiver of fear ran through her. The man called Clebourne was a sometime fur trapper and seemed to always be around the little settlement. She had often been made uneasy by his leering eyes as they followed her every move. Clebourne always seemed to have friends hanging about, but on this particular night he was alone, and as she stepped back, her hand flew to her face in shock. She immediately saw that he was drunker than usual.

"Evenin' lass," he spoke in a slur, "Are ye wishful of company?"

Before she could reply, he grabbed her by both arms just above the elbows. Sarah instinctively drew back, but she was held in his viselike grip, his long dirty fingernails digging into her flesh.

"Let go of me," she demanded. She knew screaming was useless, since there was no one on the street, and, anyway, she had never been the screaming type. "Let go of me," she repeated, twisting, trying to free herself. As they struggled, Clebourne started to laugh, clearly enjoying himself. As she succeeded in momentarily jerking one arm loose, the bag containing the day's receipts fell from her dress pocket, but Clebourne paid scant attention to it. As he pulled her closer to him, she could see the glow of his yellow teeth in the swirling mass of black beard. She swung her fist at his face but he, laughing still louder, caught her small fist in one of his massive paws. He grabbed her throat with the other hand and started to squeeze. She knew that unless she could get loose in the next minute or so, he would be able to do anything he wished with her!

She saw Clebourne's eyes go wide as he blearily tried to focus on something behind her. With one hand he jerked her out of his way and went into the characteristic crouch of the experienced street fighter. Drunk he may have been, but he sobered himself for a crazy instant. Sarah turned and recognized a young farmer she knew as Levi Casey. Casey sprang off the wagon seat and in one motion felled the drunken trapper with a roundhouse right to the side of the jaw.

Clebourne hit the ground, rolled and came up swinging with both fists. He was clearly an accomplished fighter, and outweighed Casey by a good thirty pounds. He doesn't have a chance! Sarah thought as she moved back out of the way. She had seen fights all of her life in Tennessee where the time-honored method of settling neighborhood disputes was a fist fight on Saturday morning, when everyone came to town. Her earlier fear subdued, she could only watch as these two powerful men tore at each other like angry bulls. Casey waited until Clebourne made his move, then stepped easily inside the two swinging fists and hit Clebourne one, two, three times in the solar plexus with short left jabs. Casey then stepped back and delivered a roundhouse right to Clebourne's mouth. Clebourne turned his head and spat out two teeth on the ground. With a snarl he attacked Casey with a series of blows so furious that the lighter man had to fall back. As Casey was forced back, Clebourne backheeled him, dropping him into the dusty street, shoulders first. As Clebourne moved in and tried to kick Levi in the face, Casey rolled over, and moving with the blow, he grabbed the bigger man's heavy boot, levering himself to his feet. As Casey straightened up, the trapper caught him with an uppercut that glanced off his right cheekbone, making his head ring. Sensing victory, Clebourne moved in for the kill. However, Casey, hardened by a lifetime of hard work, recovered almost instantly. He moved in close, and landed several trip hammer blows to Clebourne's drink-softened belly. As he staggered under the fierce attack, Casey grabbed his bulging red nose between the first two fingers of his left hand, and swinging his right hand into a high arc, he brought it down on the junction of his hand and Clebourne's nose. Clebourne fell like a pole-axed steer.

As Casey started to turn toward Sarah, Clebourne came off the ground with a roar, the short, broad, double-edged blade of the Scottish Dirk almost hidden in his hairy ham of a fist. Sarah saw a flicker of fear cross the young farmer's face as he turned to face this new threat. Clebourne held the blade low as he circled, watching for an opening. Levi, realizing that to be defensive was to die, moved in toward the knife wielder. As they closed, Clebourne made a vicious upward slash with the dirk, and Casey shifted his weigh, leaning back from the waist just enough to allow the blade to pass his stomach. As Clebourne's hand shot upward, Casey grabbed the wrist and gave it a mighty shove. The knife hand, with the full strength of both men behind it, moved in a short arc, and and the short blade buried itself to the hilt just below the hinge of Clebourne's jaw. The handle was half hidden in his bushy beard. Casey stepped away from him. Surprise and shock crossed Clebourne's face. Mortally wounded, he started grabbing frantically at the knife. His hand failed to get a grip on the handle, already slick with blood. His mouth flew open and blood started spilling down the front of his dirty shirt. Then his hand dropped to his side. He took two short steps forward, fell on his face, and lay kicking on the ground. In a few seconds his struggles ceased and his body seemed to settle in the dust.

CHAPTER 50

Sarah stepped back, both hands clutched tightly to her throat, her eyes glued in horrified fascination on her fallen assailant. It had all happened so quickly. The blood, turning black in the fading light, was slowly pooling in the dust beneath Clebourne's head. For a long moment, the only sound was the ragged noise of Levi Casey catching his breath. Then there was a crowd gathering around them, everyone talking at once. Only the appearance of Jenkins, the town constable, caused silence to fall on the group. Jenkins listened to Casey's story, then the testimony of two or three in the crowd who had witnessed the last part of the incident.

Casually Jenkins rolled the body over with his foot, "Killed with his own knife. If ever a feller had it comin', he did," was his slow comment. Jenkins reached down, plucked the dirk from Clebourne's throat, wiped it on the dead man' dirty collarless cotton shirt, then stood there and studied it for a while in silence. The crowd was still quiet when he finally spoke again. "Casey," he said, "Clebourne needed killing and if you hadn't done it, likely somebody else would have had to, but he's got a lot of kin back there in the Clinch Mountains. Likely they didn't have much use for him neither, but they're a bunch of radical high strung Bible-toters and ever' one of 'em is gun handy. They'll feel duty bound to avenge his death. Myself, I don't want no more killin's, so I'd advise you to give Miss Sarah here a ride on home and then take off for parts unknown. Miss Sarah, I wisht you had a place to go. I'm afraid that they may try to blame part of this on you. After Casey leaves, I don't reckon it'll be necessary to be in an all-fired hurry to notify them kinfolks of his death."

Casey looked the constable straight in the eye. "I don't reckon I'll run" he said grimly, "I had no intention of killing him, but he brung it to me. If that bunch comes looking for trouble, I reckon they'll find it. I ain't gon' never have it said that Levi Casey took water off of no man." He turned to Sarah, "Miss Reeves," he said, "May I escort you home?"

Jenkins stood silently for a moment, then as he turned away, he said, "Casey, you'd better stop to consider that even if you kill one of them, more will come, and they'll keep coming. You can't watch your back 24 hours a day. Sooner or later they'll get you."

Sarah allowed herself to be assisted up onto the seat of the weatherbeaten farm wagon. She noticed that although the wagon was old, it had been expertly repaired, and that the horses, although not of the best quality, appeared to be well cared for.

They sat in silence during the short drive. Sarah thought about trying to make small talk, but there seemed to be nothing to say. When Casey offered her a hand down, she could see concern, but there was no fear in his eyes. He held onto her hand for a moment, then took a deep breath and spoke, "I've been thinking on the way out here, I'm not afraid of them, but I don't want to have to spend the rest of my life fighting them either. I've heard tell there's land to be had in Arkansas." He stopped, took a deep breath, then blurted out, "Miss Sarah, would you marry a pore farmer and move West?"

She looked at him for a long shocked moment. She never thought of this young man as a potential suitor, although he always seemed to be polite and well mannered. She considered for a moment whether she would be acting out of gratitude, made her decision, and heard her voice say "yes." He leaned over and hugged her briefly, then drew back, shyly.

* * *

At first, worried by what the townspeople might think, then deciding she didn't really care, Sarah's mother was overjoyed by the news. She rose to the occasion and promptly took charge. She was adamant that no daughter of hers was leaving without being properly wed. So in due course, by the next afternoon, they were man and wife, these two nearly strangers.

The morning after the wedding found them headed west toward Nashville, the wagon loaded with what farming tools Levi deemed essential in this new land. He had sold the rest to his neighbors, said goodbye to his parents and left the farm to his brothers. After a tearful leave-taking of her folks, Sarah sat on the wagon seat in silent reflection as the wagon pulled out toward Murfeesboro. Sarah was very happy, but somehow uneasy. She was suddenly afraid, afraid that her silly romantic notions had got in the way of her usual good sense. When she was younger, she had spent a lot of time reading the novels of Sir Walter Scott and poring over a volume of Tennyson's poetry. Her favorite reading, however, had been Shakespeare's *Romeo and Juliet*. She had read it so often she almost had it memorized. Had she made her choice on a silly impulse, or was there more? Was there such a thing as love at first sight, or had her vision of Levi Casey as her savior been the only reason for her doing such an impulsive thing? He might be lazy, or worse yet, he could be a crook or a thief. Laziness was the one thing that Sarah's father would never tolerate. He often said that men could overcome the worst parts of their own nature in many ways. He had often told her that he had seen drunks become sober, rough men become gentle, and thieves become honest, but he had never, ever, seen a lazy man become industrious. Disease rots the body, but laziness rots the soul, he liked to say. Sarah thought that from the looks of his wagon and farming tools that her new husband was certainly not lazy. She sat and resolved that whatever the outcome, she was going to see it through. She would not admit defeat. To go back now would be to endure the gossip of the townspeople for the rest of her life. She was determined that she was going to love this man and make a home for them in Arkansas.

After stopping to buy food and getting the horses and themselves used to travel, it was the twelfth day after their hasty marriage before they pulled into Murfeesboro. They made camp on the wagon grounds on the edge of town, and since it was late afternoon, they decided to walk along Main Street. They turned into a huge store that, to Sarah, accustomed as she was to their small store in Crossville, looked like all the merchandise in the world was stacked in it. There was even a covered wagon inside! Levi meandered away as she looked at the ready-made dresses.

In a few minutes he was back holding a rifle, "Look at this rifle, Sarah," he said excitedly. "It's a double rifle." He held it up. It had two barrels, each one with its own nipple and set of sights. He grasped the barrels, and turned each one to align with the back action lock. "She's a .40 calibre, just right for squirrels, and deer and the man said there's plenty of both in Arkansas." She hadn't seen Levi like this before. He was acting just like the children that came into her parents' store. "It was made by Melchoir Fordney, of Lancaster town in Pennsylvania. The store man said he was killed by a crazy man with an ax. Fordney had tried to keep the maniac from shooting his own horse."

Sarah smiled, "How much is it Levi?" she asked.

"It's only nine dollars," he replied excitedly.

Sarah mentally counted their money and nodded her head. Listening to his enthusiastic talk as they walked back to the wagon, she knew that she was genuinely falling in love with this young farmer, her husband.

The days stretched into weeks as they camped on the Duck River, near Columbia. Turning south, they stayed on the well-beaten wagon road. They crossed the swift Tennessee River on a ferry at Clifton, then found themselves traveling in the middle of an oxbow with the river on both sides. Once across the Tennessee, they headed out toward Memphis. Growing accustomed to traveling, they talked for hours and it seemed at times that they were the only people in the world.

Now, an eternity later, lying there in Beartrack's cave, tears spilled down Sarah's face as she remembered those distant carefree days. The rain pouring down, her world now silent, those days, even though just six years ago, seemed part of someone else's life. That happy carefree Sarah was no more, and Levi was gone. She reached over and squeezed Sam's arm, reassuring herself that at least her son was still there. Her mind fled back to the memories.

About six miles east of Memphis, the young couple had found themselves bouncing along on what had been an obvious attempt to improve the roadway by covering it with planks. The rolling motion of untold numbers of iron-tired wagons had separated the planks, pushing them to the outside, leaving deep ruts in the gaps. Some of the planks had snapped under the heavy loads and broken ends were sticking up everywhere, ready to snag the axle of any unwary travelers vehicle. At the end of the day they were camped just inside the city, sore and stiff from the unaccustomed pounding.

The next morning the Caseys' wound through the sprawling city and found their way to the water front by the simple expedient of following the sound of the shrieking steamboat whistles. When they arrived, Levi and Sarah stood in open-mouthed wonder at the more than fifty flatboats pulled up at the docks. Shouting and cursing, the rivermen, clad in homespun and leather, labored alongside chanting slaves. They were unloading produce – cotton, hides, lumber and cured pork – from the handmade flatboats. Some of the goods were loaded into wagons that were aimed toward town. As each wagon was loaded, it moved away and another quickly took its place. Most of the goods appeared to be moving toward a row of two story warehouses.

Grabbing his arm and pointing, Sarah said, "Look at those huge buildings, Levi." The businesswoman in her was showing through. "They're designed to load at ground level at both the top and bottom of the bluff." Levi stopped the team in front of an open shed and watched as a team of huge sorrel mules stepped out from behind the largest warehouse. Sarah could see that they were hitched to a complex system of pulleys. As the mules moved forward, an elevator platform inside the warehouse moved slowly upward. At the shouted command "Whoa," the team stopped and waited patiently while the platform was unloaded on the third story. When the command "back" came, the mules backed up smartly, lowering the elevator to ground level again, where it was promptly reloaded.

"The biggest warehouse and the mules both belong to Mr. Immanuel Young. He's got a pair of matched blacks that are every bit as good as the sorrels. The two smaller warehouses belong to Patrick Meager and Mr. Thomas D. Carr." The young people were both visibly startled at the sound of the voice, since they had been engrossed in watching the work. The speaker, unsmiling, was leaning against one of the sheds support posts. His posture was drooped, but Sarah could detect a certain tension about him. She couldn't help but look up at the sign hanging under the ridgepole. N.B. FORREST- LIVESTOCK AND SLAVE MARKET. Sarah's sharp intake of breath caused Forrest to stand up straight, slinging the wheat straw on which he had been chewing to the ground.

"Now, don't you start getting uppety on me, missy." he said, his tone harsh. "I treat my slaves good. People are going to own slaves and somebody is going to make a living buying and selling them, so it may as well be me. I'll bet you people are some of that Irish trash from down in the pinch."

Sarah's eyes flashed as she formed her reply, "Mr. Forrest, if that is your name, I'll have you know that I'm part Irish and proud of it! Furthermore I don't believe in slavery in any way, form or fashion! We'll go now, Levi." Surprised by his bride's outburst of temper, Levi slapped the check lines across the horse's backs and they moved out into the street.

They rode in silence for a few moments, then Levi laughed out loud. "So my new wife has a temper. I just wish you would have just given me time to ask where the wagon grounds are."

"We'll find the place," said Sarah. She sat in silence as they passed long stacks of wood ricked along the street. Finally, she had to ask why there was so much of it.

"They've got the wood there to sell to the steamboat captains," was Levi's explanation as he stopped and stepped off the wagon. They tied the team and walked toward the dock. As they walked a young well-dressed man fell in step be beside them.

"Where ya' headed?" He asked, an ingratiating smile pasted across his face.

Levi looked around, surprised, then studying the speaker for a moment, knew he was not going to like this man. There was something a little too quick about him. Not wishing to appear impolite, he replied, "We're on our way to Arkansas. We plan on settling there. I don't guess you would know of any steamships going that way, would you?"

The man's face broke into a broad grin, "It just so happens that the KATE KIRKWOOD, there, is leaving for Arkansas in just a few hours."

"Is it too late to book passage on her?" Sarah asked as she thought of the endless miles they had traveled and how much further they had to go.

"Not at all, my good lady. You just happen to be talking to the booking agent for the KIRKWOOD. Yes ma'am, I'll have you on board in no time at all, is there just the two of you?"

"Just us and our rig," Levi turned and pointed at the team, standing hipshot in front of the wagon.

"I'm Nat Thorne, booking agent. I'm glad to meet you folks." The man smiled and stuck out his hand.

"How much will passage cost us?" Sarah asked anxiously.

"It'll be a twenty dollar gold piece for each of you and forty extry dollars for your team and wagon. That's good passage to Jacksonport, up on the White River."

Levi fretted. The passage was going to take a large bite out of their cash money.

Thorne spoke again, sensing Casey's hesitation. "Tell you

what I'll do, I'll knock ten dollars off the deal if you'll pay gold in advance."

Levi stepped back, his hand moving to his money pouch. He hesitated. Something was wrong here, he could sense it. He looked down at Sarah, wanting her opinion. This man who had just come into their lives was just a little too forward, even pushy. As Levi stood there, indecisive, Thorne, sensing that he was losing control, reached inside his coat and pulled out a short pocket pistol. "All right," he hissed, "I tried to be nice. Now I want it all."

Levi, caught unarmed and unprepared, stared at the huge muzzle tilted up at him. The first thing he thought of was Sarah. She could be killed! Trying desperately to think of a way out of the situation, he slowly started to pull out his money. What were his chances of tackling the thief and wrestling the gun away? Reluctantly, he decided they were slim to none. The gun could go off and shoot Sarah. He didn't worry about his own safety, for he was too angry at his own stupidity to be scared. Suddenly, the con man looked behind them, his eyes opening wide, he started to raise the pistol, then whirled and started to run!

"Hit the ground!" came a ringing command. Without hesitation, Levi pushed Sarah to the ground and sprawled beside her. He heard three pistol balls drone over their heads even as he rolled over to see their origin. A tall, thin, old man, the wind unfurling the tails of his clawhammer coat, stopped his stiff-legged, awkward run, and raised his revolver to shoulder level. He sent two more shots after the fleeing felon. Casey saw the man stagger and a spot of red start to spread on his upper arm as he rounded one of the waterfront warehouses and disappeared. Their rescuer stopped beside the young couple lying on the ground, his eyes still fixed on the warehouse. When he had satisfied himself that the malefactor was indeed gone, he transferred the pistol to his left hand and extended his right down to Levi. The frosty beard parted into a smile below the pale blue eyes. "Well, young man, I'm glad you had enough sense to drop when I yelled!"

Levi grasped the old man's hand and stood up, then lifted Sarah to her feet. "We thank you. That man was shore 'nuff gonna rob us right here in broad open daylight. We are much obliged," Levi hesitated, realizing that he was talking too fast, sounding foolish. He took a deep breath, then continued, "We are headed for Arkansas, and that man told us he could get us passage on that steamboat there." He pointed at the KIRKWOOD. "But I'm sure she's booked up." The old man straightened up and pointed to the brim of his cap, "I'm Cap'n Thomas Tunstall, owner and Captain of the KATE KIRKWOOD, and we are indeed booked with passengers, although we could carry your team and wagon."

Levi shook his head, "No," he said, disappointment evident in his voice, "We'll just stay here, and wait for the next ship."

Just then a somewhat foppishly dressed young man, who, along with a small crowd of bystanders, had evidently been attracted by the uproar, stepped up. "Captain Tunstall, I would be glad to give my cabin to the lady. That would give me an excuse to stay here in Memphis for a few more days and try to recoup a some bad investments I've made in colored pasteboards. But there wouldn't be room for both of them, her husband would have to sleep on the deck."

Captain Tunstall turned back to Levi and Sarah. Then pointing to the young man, he spoke. "Folks this is Lucian Cotesworth Gause. He's a law student, as if the world needs more lawyers."

Gause stepped up and shook their hands, smiling. "My friends call me L.C. and it's plain that Cap'n Tunstall has no use at all for lawyers, so we always have an interesting discussion on their attributes every time I go back home to Jacksonport for a visit."

"Where do you attend?" Levi asked politely.

"Cumberland University."

Both Levi and Sarah's interest quickened, "We used to live fairly close to there," Sarah said, delighted to meet someone who at least knew their part of Tennessee.

They would have continued their small talk but Captain Tunstall, holstering his pistol, looked over at Levi and asked, "You ever work on a river boat, boy?"

Levi, not liking the reference to his youth, replied a little stiffly, "No sir. But I've done a fair amount of 'most any outside work you could name, including sawmilling."

The Captain had seen many young men like him, full of pride and sure of themselves. He didn't laugh. In fact, he could remember being the same way in his day. "I could use another deck hand, if you're willing to work for passage and sleep on the quarterdeck. Your wife can take Gause's cabin, and I've got room for your horses and wagon."

Levi, surprised and pleased at the offer, stood for a moment, making a transparent effort not to seem too eager. "That would be fine, sir, real fine."

"L.C. you be careful now and don't let one of them river rats slip a knife between your ribs, you hear?" Tunstall said.

"Don't you worry, Capt'n I carry the difference right here." Gause pulled his coat open.

"Nice," The Captain appreciatively eyed the pair of .31 calibre Colt pocket pistols stuck down in the wide sash around young Gause's waist. "But you be careful just the same."

The old man then turned around and started to walk down to his ship, the young couple following behind. They all turned back and waved at the young lawyer as he headed back toward the gambling district.

* * *

The gold Double Eagle caught the light each time it was flipped, throwing a soft yellow spot on the wall as it turned over and faintly slapped into the waiting palm. The man awakened with a start. His shoulder throbbed with each beat of his heart. As awareness crept over him he raised his head and looked around, the mists of laudenum still lingering in his brain. He jumped again as he caught a glimpse of the man. It had to be a man, leaning against the wall in the shadow thrown by the coal oil lamp. He had a vague impression of homespun clothes, colored butternut with walnut stain. The rankness of home-grown tobacco blended its smell with that of the cheap perfume already in the room. The man sometimes known as Thorne roused himself enough to ask,"Who are you, and what do you want?" He hoped he sounded tough.

The reply came in a voice that was deep and slow. The voice of someone who wasted no time on small talk. "I believe you are in a bit of difficulty, my friend. You see, the waterfront is too vital to the city of Memphis to allow robbery in broad open daylight. Do you really believe this bunch of whores will hide you if the law really comes looking? No, they'll look after their own hides. Besides that, you're liable to get blood poisoning in that arm."

Thorne, was awake now, fully conscious of his own rapid heartbeat and the sweat already starting to drip down his face, waited, watching the gold piece making it's circuit, hand to air, air to hand.

"Could you describe the young couple you tried to rob?" Thorne twisted painfully in the bed and started talking. He tried to hide the fear that was making his voice quiver. This man was not one of the scared travelers he was used to bullying. This man would kill, and not only kill, but enjoy it in the process. Thorne felt a sudden sickness that loosened his bowels as he felt his legs go cold. As the man shifted position in the cane bottomed chair, Thorne could see the mountain pistol hanging on a belt hook. On the opposite side was a D-handled Bowie-style knife in a cowhide scabbard. The fear loosened his mouth. Thorne went into more detail. Involuntarily, he glanced over at his pistol lying beneath his clothes. His adversary noticed the look and his teeth became visible in the shadows as he allowed himself a wolfish smile. The waterfront con man and thief, who often called himself Thorne, knew then that he was going to be lucky to leave this little room in the waterfront bordello alive. When the man finally stood up, still keeping his face out of the light, Thorne had told all he knew about the Caseys, Captain Tunstall, and the White River country. Finally the visitor held the gold piece out in the lamplight. "Surely you don't expect to be paid for this bit of information, do you"?

"Nossir, I surely don't. I was glad to help, yessir, glad to help," His guts ached, and he closed his eyes as he waited helplessly for the shot that would end his miserable existence. He heard a click. It could only be the gun hammer coming back. He started to plead, to beg, but his throat was paralyzed, he couldn't speak. He lay there, waiting, half-holding his breath, spots dancing in front of his tightly-shut eyes. He started to pray, his eyes closed, mumbling the words of some long half-remembered prayer from his childhood. He prayed to a God that he hadn't thought of since his mama had read to him from the Bible, as she had tried to make up for the bad influence of his father who was later hanged. He had been hanged mainly for his ineptitude as a cutpurse and petty con man. His son was destined to die the same way, but not this day, and not by the hand of the visitor. Perhaps it was difficult to kill a man who was praying so fervently. He lay there for an hour or more, muscles locked, waiting to hear the explosion of black powder that never came. Then the man called Thorne gathered the small amount of courage he possessed, and slipped off the bed and out the door. He sneaked off into the darkness, peeping around every corner. A few minutes later a woman stood over the soiled bed. She reached over on the table, and pulled the cork on the bottle of Laudenum with her teeth. She drank deeply, then held it up and read the label DR. TISHNER'S TONIC, as her face tightened into a grimace at the taste. Cursing to herself and vowing to never take pity on another man as long as she lived, she walked out and closed the door.

* * *

The muddy water drained from the stern wheel of the KATE KIRKWOOD in thin sheets as she slowly passed Montgomery's Point and churned her way out of the broad Mississippi and into the snake-like White River. Captain Tunstall leaned forward out of the wheel-house, and yelled "Casey, get Mrs. Casey and yourself up here." Levi carefully coiled the rope he had been repairing and walked up the steep narrow stairs to the small wheelhouse. Sarah was already sitting on a small swivel stool bolted to the deck. "You Caseys seem to be real fine people, so I'll tell you a little history of this area we're traveling through if you're interested. It gets pretty lonesome up here sometimes. It's just about ten miles down to the mouth of the Arkansas River from here. Up here just a little ways there's a small creek they call the Cutoff Bayou connecting the White and the Arkansas. I've seen the time when the banks along here were lined with Quapaw Indian huts."

"What happened to them?" Levi asked.

"Well, the government moved most of them out back in '18. Many of those that were left started catching the white man's diseases such as the smallpox. I've seen them standing along these banks right here, sick and starving. It was a sad thing, I can tell you. 'Course all our government ever cared about was getting them out so they could move in gobs of settlers. Actually, about the only people that will live on this swampy land is thieves and murderers, like that Merrill bunch that used to operate up north of here, around Forrest City. As for this land, it ain't good for nothin' that I know of. It's too thick to drink and too wet to plow. If you turn up the Arkansas about thirty mile you get to where a sawyer got my first boat back in '35." The old man's eyes watered just a little and both of the Caseys looked off for a moment to spare him embarrassment. He looked off up the river for a long moment, and turned the wheel slightly. "The boat was called the WILLIAM PARSONS, and I knowed in my own mind that it was bad luck to name a boat anything but a woman's name.

"You had a boat sink from under you?" Sarah asked.

Captain Tunstall looked down at her, a trace of a sad smile on his weatherbeaten face. "No, child, I've had two boats sink out from under me. I had a new one called the HARP, that was also gutted by a sawyer down by Frog Bayou in Louisiana in '38. Not to mention the WABASH VALLEY that was struck below Memphis by the BULLETIN in '46. The BULLETIN'S captain didn't even stop to see if we was still alive. I hope I've used up my life's share of bad luck."

He turned and looked back upstream, "Course, I've never had a boiler blow, and I'm still alive. As far as the money goes, a man can make it all back again if he's alive and kickin'. But then I would never again name a boat anything but a lady's name. Now for the history and geography lesson" he continued. "As I said, the Arkansas empties into the Mississippi downstream about ten miles. There's the remains of an old Spanish fort there. They've found some pieces of old armor there, some say that the garrison was wiped out by Indians. But it's been so long nobody knows for sure. By the way, Casey, you and your wife had both better get started on quinine for the malaria."

Levi looked up at the captain, surprised. "Quinine?" he asked.

"Yep," the captain said, taking his pipe from his mouth. "If you don't take it, you're almost sure to get the seasoning as some people call it. Did you have it in Tennessee?"

"No, "Levi replied, "They didn't have much of it on the Tennessee River. You see, there ain't no swamps to speak of on the Tennessee. It's got hills all around it."

"Anyway," Captain Tunstall glanced up the river and turned the wheel slightly to the right, "if you don't take the quinine regular, you're almost sure to get the malaria. You'll have to start taking it right away and don't stop until you've at least reached Major Wolf's place. I hear tell that there's even a few cases farther north than Wolf's. Casey took the envelope Tunstall offered and started to stick it down inside his pants, when the captain smiled. "Go ahead, take a pinch of it on your tongue." Levi took a pinch and put it on his tongue. He could feel his jaw muscles lock and the glands under his tongue contract. The bitterness flooded his whole mouth. He spat, but it was already dissolved and only the lingering aftertaste remained for the next couple of hours.

CHAPTER 51

Sarah Casey thoroughly enjoyed Captain Tunstall's company and while Levi was working she spent almost all of her time in the wheelhouse. The river narrowed imperceptably as it rolled between eroded dirt banks. The loops of the meandering river were so wide that some of them almost made a complete O. "Sometimes, the bend cuts off and makes a slough," Captain Tunstall said, pronouncing it as "slew." "When we get further up the river there's some danger from river pirates."

Sarah felt invincible. She just laughed. "We'll make it," she said.

As they chugged their way up the river, they often stopped by the neatly ricked wood stacked along the shore to replenish their fuel. The captain always left payment in gold stuck down in a stump. "They'll have some more cut, ricked and ready for the next boat," he said.

With each day's sunset Sarah had thrilled at watching the female mallards with their dull plumage come out from beneath the banks and play with their little ones in the shallows. The baby ducks reminded her of miniature steamboats as they planed across the river surface. There were always deer standing knee-deep, water dripping from their muzzles, as their large ears waved, obviously unafraid of the hiss and thump of the steamboat. Waiting for Levi to quit working each night, Sarah enjoyed standing at the rail and watching the fog as it lay along the water like a wool blanket in the moonlight. As night fell, it rose until it enveloped the boat. "You've got to watch out for flatboats, missy," the old captain had said, pulling his pipe from his mouth. "Those flatboat boys take it mighty unkindly if we run them down in the dark. Besides, it messes up the paddle wheel somethin' awful." The twinkle in his eye told her he was just joking.

On the sunset of the fourth day on the steamboat, they passed a small island, more of a sand bar actually, barely fifty feet long and not more than ten feet wide. A man in a fancy broadcloth suit was standing on it. When he spotted the steamboat, he started jumping up and down, waving his arms. Sarah knew he was yelling, although he couldn't be heard above the sounds of the steamboat.

"Captain," she said, "why is that man out on the small island?"

Captain Tunstall, his face set in stern lines, watched without comment as the steamboat passed the would-be passenger. The man turned away, but not before raising his hand in an obscene gesture.

"Captain Tunstall, you passed up that stranded man," she said, uncertain. "What if he drowns or something else awful happens to him? Then you'll be to blame!"

"I can live with that blame, missy, but us picking up that crooked gambler would be like Cleopatra holding the asp to her breast. He was put off of some steamboat or other for cheating at cards. He'll give it up and swim to shore, or he'll stay there and starve. It makes no nevermind to me, but I'll be danged if I let him on my boat to cause trouble and maybe get somebody shot." said Tunstall.

Sarah didn't know what to say. "I'm sorry Captain Tunstall," she said, "I didn't know. I'll try to keep quiet from now on."

"Oh, don't do that lassie. You've served to brighten up an old man's lonely job."

After that, Sarah felt better and started asking questions again. "How far is it up to Jacksonport?" She asked.

"Well, they say it's about 265 miles and most of the time we can make the run in about 12 days if the river's not up".

The next morning, Sarah watched as Captain Tunstall sounded one long blast, then a short one, waited a moment and gave another very long one. She watched two trappers come out of the woods as the crew of the KIRKWOOD pulled in to take on more wood. After watching the two load their furs on the steamer she walked across the Texas to the port side and watched a small boat slow in the current and the two men in it lift a long pole out of the water. It was bending in the middle from the weight of the mussels hanging from short staging lines attached to it. She had seen mussels before, but the contraption was new to her. She walked to the rail for a closer look.

"Strange looking thing, isn't it?" Sarah nearly jumped out of her skin

"I've seen them before. They're called crowfoot bars."

"Why, Levi, I didn't know you knew anything about rivers and mussel fishing," she smiled to let him know she was only teasing. "I thought all you knew about was hill country farming."

Levi felt suddenly shy in front of his new wife. "Truth is, Sarah, I ain't never really seen them before. I just heard the darkies talking about them. Them mussels, they're just layin' there straining their food out of the water. They drag the poles along close to the bottom, and the line passes between the halves of the mussel shell. The mussels clamp down on the line and all the men have got to do is haul them up."

"What do they do with them? It looks like too many to eat."

Levi laughed, "Oh, no, they wouldn't eat 'em a'tall, they bile 'em out in big kettles and use them for catfish bait. First they look through them for pearls. They say they're starting to sell the shells for buttons. I read one time that some German feller by the name of Boepple come over here and figured a way to stamp out perfect buttons out of them mussel shells." The mere mention of pearls caught Sarah's attention and she jumped again when she heard the captain yell from the pilot house. "Levi, I'm not paying you passage to stand there and flirt with your wife. That's my job. Now sound depth as we pull away."

With a big smile, Levi waved up at the captain and took off. He soon had the weighted line hanging over the bow. "Maaark" he yelled, signalling six feet of depth as the plank was drawn in and the bell rang for full speed ahead. The captain steered into the river until he heard the yell "Maaark Twain" then gave the huge spoked wheel a spin and the boat slowly straightened up and they were on their way upstream again.

"They're starting a rail road that will connect Little Rock and DeVall's Bluff. Eventually it's supposed to reach to the Mississippi. Some say the rail road will put the steam boats out of business, but I don't believe it, for shipping by rail would be way too expensive."

Sarah was half-listening to the captain as they made the deep curve of the river at DeVall's Bluff. She knew it would just be a few days until they got off the boat at Jacksonport. She almost regretted it. During the enforced rest aboard the steamboat she had recuperated from the long wagon ride, and had begun to enjoy life on the river. The captain said they would pass Des Arc and Augusta on the way. She always watched for the small current driven ferries that marked the location of the settlements scattered up the river every ten miles or so. The captain seemed to know every one of the ferrymen by name and could recite the history of each one and his family back two or three generations.

On the morning of the twelfth day, as Sarah walked around the deck, she looked down at the water in surprise. They were floating along in clear water, yet just a few feet over, the river was muddy!

"Levi", he looked up from his labors and waved at her. The slaves all looked up and smiled. Everyone on the boat had come to like this hard-working young man and his wife.

"Levi, look at the water," she pointed down.

"I know, capt'n said the water from the White and the Black flow side by side for a good ways before they start to mix, ain't that somethin'? Capt'n said when we seen that mixed water we'd be real close to Jacksonport."

An hour later the KATE KIRKWOOD nosed into Jack's Creek and the eager hands tied her fast to the dock. "Come on, kids," Captain Tunstall said as he stepped off the boat, "I'll give you the ten cent tour." Sarah and Levi tried to keep up with the captain as he strode through his town. He had somehow neglected to tell them that he had founded the town of Jacksonport, as well as a hotel there. "Got my son-in-law George Caldwell running the hotel. It keeps him out of trouble." The Caseys were impressed by the fact that he seemed to know everyone in town. They walked past the stores owned by L.L. Moore and Company, which were across from the store of James Paine and catty-cornered from the one belonging to Pool, Pulliam and Company, and, on the advice of the captain, they bought more quinine at Dr. Jones drug store.

"It's too bad I've got to get back to Memphis. If you'd waited a month I would have took you right to the dock at Liberty. That's right close to where I think you'll want to settle. By the time you get your team and wagon off the boat they'll be ready to load the timber and my hired hand is bringing forty or fifty head of hogs off my farm."

"You've got a farm, too?" Levi asked, obviously surprised.

The captain smiled tolerantly, "Yep, I bought the old John Merrill place. Nobody else wanted it, and they claimed it was haunted by the ghosts of the people him and his gang murdered. I'm sure you've heard of Merrill."

Both of the Caseys had heard of Merrill, and they would have both liked to ask more questions, but Captain Tunstall was already talking again.

"Last of all, they'll load the deer meat and and a few bear hams. The flies will try to blow the meat, even though it's been salt cured." Tunstall looked anxiously back down toward the river. "We don't ship the bear lard from here. That bunch up at Oil Trough renders it out and then they let it harden in hollered-out logs and float it down the river to try to save shipping costs. They still have to ship the bear bacon, but they usually send it down to Montgomery's point on flat boats. The whole things going to be over before too many years anyways."

"Why is that?" Levi asked.

350

"Well, they've nearly killed out all the bears." the captain said. "I kinda hate to see them all go, but they're sure death on young pigs and just the slightest smell of bear will stampede every cow brute in the country."

Soon they were back at the boat. The young couple hooked up the team, frisky now after their enforced inactivity, and prepared to pull out. Captain Tunstall had shaken hands with Levi, "Now you fight shy of that bunch up at Oil Trough. They lean heavy toward knife fightin' and whiskey drinkin', and they smell worse than a boar bear. If you need any supplies you just fetch yourselves on up to Batesville. Another thing, just a couple of miles up here is Tidwell's Ferry. I think Tidwell's trying to get people to start calling it Newport nowadays. Anyways, don't let Tidwell talk you into shooting dice with him. You can drop one pair of his dice into a glass of water and they'll fall snake-eyes every time. He's got another pair that'll fall sevens every time."

Sarah looked up at the captain, "Levi doesn't gamble." Levi winked at Captain Tunstall, who touched his hat as they pulled out.

They had started up the dim trail that more or less paralleled the river. They were fortunate in that it was the dry time of the year and they did not have to navigate the endless swamp that, unbeknownst to them, the White River was capable of becoming during the late fall and again during the spring floods. They camped at night, eating of the plentiful small game and fish that abounded in the bottom lands. They occasionally had to skirt around large wet areas covered with cypress that were better than five feet through, and the burr oaks that lived in the slightly drier areas around them.

They could smell Oil Trough at least an hour before they passed down the narrow trail that wound between the rows of smoking kettles. There were a few ramshackle shacks and a low log structure that had to be a saloon. After the captain's warning Sarah was nervous and anxious to get on through it. Suddenly the plank door to the saloon was jerked open and a man fell out and stumbled to his knees, right in front of the Casey's team. As Levi jerked the nervous team to a halt, his hand instinctively fell to the Fordney rifle.

It didn't matter. The drunk didn't appear to have taken any notice of them at all. He was a wild-looking uncurried speciman clothed in filthy buckskins. He rolled over once in the dirt and stumbled to his feet. Jerking his hat down low over his eyes with both hands and leaning forward from the waist, he stomped toward the door. As Levi started to cluck the team forward, the man staggered out again, his right hand grasped tightly in his left. Dark blood was pouring out from between his fingers in thin streams. He made it into the path of their wagon once more, falling forward and twisting in pain. The whole thing had occurred without a sound.

"What are you two staring at?"

The thick Irish brogue caught Sarah completely by surprise. Her head jerked around toward the door of the saloon, her mouth flying open. Levi looked just as shocked.

The speaker reached down, found her grease-encrusted apron and wiped the meat cleaver across it. "Serves him right for starting a fight in my saloon." She stood there looking at the Caseys, obvious challenge in her stance.

"Who is he?" Levi asked, hoping his voice wouldn't reveal his nervousness in front of his new wife.

Meanwhile, his new wife was trying not to stare at what was probably the meanest looking woman she had ever laid eyes on. She was huge, this woman, red of hair and skin. She was intimidating and obviously proud of being so. The woman looked down at the fallen man as if she was surprised to see him still lying there, writhing in pain. "Him? That'd be Lon, my hired man. Now mister who ever you are, I'll be looking for somebody to stir them kettles and cure the bear meat that the hunters bring in while Lon's laid up, are you needin' a job?"

Levi pulled the team hard left around the man. "No, ma'am, it seems to me you're a little hard on your help."

"Suit yourself," she said as she turned away, and the couple resumed their long journey.

Finally, after eight days, they arrived at Batesville as Bates Town was now beginning to be called, having sprung up along the banks of the White River. There were three churches and a bank.

"I guess it's pretty much civilized here," Levi said. "There's two lawyers offices. It seems like a country can't hardly get settled until folks start lawin' at each other."

They camped in the wagon yard down by the river. There were two other wagons there, obviously belonging to people who were also headed west, seeking land. They didn't seem friendly, so Sarah and Levi just nodded greeting at them and let it go at that. The next morning Levi bought a gallon of coal oil for medicinal purposes and they turned north. They pretty well had the country to themselves. At least once a day they would pass some type of farm, usually with a milch cow and a passel of kids. They camped close to the river, and often Levi caught lineside and brown bass for their supper from under the ledges lining the clear river.

They stopped and admired the beautiful Calico Rocks. They could see a few rough houses build right on the edge of the bluff. They were so worn out that they didn't approach any of them, but camped on a small creek just above them over night, then headed upriver to Liberty.

CHAPTER 52

"Its beautiful, I've never seen a place with such a view. Are you sure your parents don't mind if we build a house here?" she asked.

"No, I think they'd be tickled to death, although dad did say that the wind coming up across that hill would freeze us to death in the winter time," he replied, hugging her to him as they sat close against each other in the ragged front seat of the old green farm truck.

"Can we get out and walk around?" she asked, anxious to please her soon-to-be husband.

"Sure, hop right out," he said as he pushed the squealing door open and stepped down. "Look at them tall Cedars. You can bet they're over a hundred years old."

They walked through the cedars. The monsterous evergreens had grown tall, then sunk their heavy roots into the thick layers of limestone,their roots pushing some ledges aside, and breaking some. The young couple were walking shoulder to shoulder when she moved away and leaned back against the bole of one of the cedars, holding out her arms to be held and kissed.

He jerked her away, "Don't lean on them. You'll get that sticky sap all over your clothes."

"You just don't want to kiss me," she said, giving him a hard shove. She covered her mouth in mock horror as he tripped on a root and fell backwards, sitting down hard on a limestone shelf.

Irritated at having shown what he percieved as a weakness, he reached up, holding out his hand. She made a elaborate show of offering her hand to help pull him up. As both knew would happen, he pulled her down beside him. She caught herself with her palm against the ground. There, beneath the grass, was something hard. It wasn't a rock, it was too round. She leaned over and parted the grass, digging it out of the dirt with her fingers.

"Look what I've found!" She rubbed off some of the dirt, holding it up to the light, trying to figure out what it was.

When he first saw it, it looked like an Indian corn grinder. "Let me see it!" he said. She reluctantly handed it over.

He jumped up and jerked out his shirt tail. Holding it in the cloth he rubbed off the accumulated dirt. "I'll be danged, it's a pocket watch!" He carefully pried open the cover and looked at the crystal. It was clouded after years of contact with soil acids, but remarkably, was still intact. He knew enough about pocket watches to know that this one was old. It even had a place for a winding key. He rubbed the case some more, "I believe it's real gold!" he said excitedly. "It's stamped Waltham on the case, it may be worth something." He stuck it in his pocket.

"Hey, I'm the one that found it,"she said, pretending to be angry. Looking down, she had already seen something that looked more valuable to her than an old tarnished pocket watch. "Honey," she said. "You're going to have to dig out this piece of rock and make me a rock picnic table out of it. It looks just like a table top."

He stood, still rubbing the watch. "Yeah," he said, still carried away with the discovery of the watch. If she wanted a rock picnic table, a rock picnic table she would have. "I could jack it up with that big hydraulic jack and slide two of these other blocks of limestone under it. That would work perfect."

CHAPTER 53

As Sarah sat in the wagon trying to take in the beehive of activity around the place, the largest black woman she had ever laid eyes on stepped out of what must have been the log kitchen next to the house. She had a large wooden spoon in her left hand. She immediately spied the young couple with their rounded up wagon and let out a loud whoop!

"Lawsey me, we done got us some more shore 'nuff settlers. Y'all come on up heah to de' big house. De Maja' shore gon' wan' to talk to you folks." She stopped for a breath. "I'm Mammy Julie. Come on up."

Soon Levi and Sarah found themselves sitting on a split-oak bench outside the kitchen enthusiastically eating warm slabs of honey-sweetened gingerbread with the first fresh-from-the-spring-house buttermilk they had tasted since leaving Tennessee. They watched two men sawing boards with a pit saw and listened to Mammy Julie's chatter with the rasp of the saw in the background. After they had frogged their sides on the sweets, Mammy Julie took them up to meet Major Wolf.

"Heavens to Betsey! Is that a real buffalo?" Sarah asked, as she noticed the huge beast calmly grazing in the yard. When it spotted the strangers, it walked over and stood, obviously waiting to be petted. Sarah and Levi started rubbing its wooly head as Mammy Julie stood by proudly.

"I see you've met my yard cutter." They both turned and saw a man who could only be Major Wolf, leaning against a porch post.

356

"We've seen drawings and heard of them, but buffalo are long gone from our part of the country," Levi said.

"And where would that be?" asked the Major.

"Oh, we're from Tennessee, from the Cumberlands." Levi said.

"I know them well," the Major said. "Well, what do you think of my pet?"

"He's a monster," Sarah said. "Did you raise him from a calf?"

"No, as a matter of fact, I traded Paten Keesee an old muley cow for him. This buffalo's no young'un. He's near fourteen years old, he was ten when I got him."

"How old do buffalo live to be, Major?" Levi asked.

"I really don't know. Into their twenties, I would imagine," the Major said.

The major ushered them into a large room. There was a big ledger lying on the table. It was obvious that Mammy Julie held a special place in the old Major's heart from the respectful way he spoke to her.

After the young couple were seated, the Major sat down, then leaned back and stretched. "I'm proud to have an excuse to quit the accounts books. Welcome to Izard County. Have you come to take up land?"

As Levi told the story of their marriage and leaving Tennessee, he left out nothing, figuring that the old man would, at some point find out anyway. Since they were going to live nearby he wanted to establish a solid relationship with the wily old Indian Agent. As Levi talked, Sarah studied the man that Mammy Julie had unashamedly described as "the most 'portant man in these parts." He was tall, and sat proudly erect in the way of his German forebears, his thin aristocratic face with its piercing blue eyes framed by full side whiskers that came down even with his thin lips. Here was a man that would be a force to reckon with, even at his age, if angered.

"Step over here young man," the major got up from his beaver-lined chair and walked over to a map drawn on the flesh side of what Levi knew had to be a tanned Buffalo hide that was tacked to the log wall with rough hand beaten iron nails. The nails had doubtlessly been forged in Liberty's own blacksmith shop. Major Wolf pointed to the White River on the map. He drew a line with his finger up to where the Norfork forked off to the north.

"We are here," he said. "Now my advice to you, young feller, is to go up the river to where these creeks take off from it. There's Bennett's River and Bennett's Bayou. There's a lot of good land up there that hasn't been taken up. You can homestead 160 acres of it, but be sure someone else isn't already building on it. Then you get you a cabin built as quickly as possible. Now, you be sure and build on a hill above one of the little branches or creeks. Don't build on the bottom land, no matter how pretty it is, and be sure you find a good spring close by." He turned to Sarah, "Now you, young lady, don't you try to talk him into building next to a creek. This country is terrible bad to flood. It may not happen the first year, and maybe not for twenty years, but it will happen, and when it does you'd be lucky to escape with your lives."

Sarah was irritated that he had thought she lacked judgment. "Major, I'll have you know I was raised in the hills of Tennessee and I know all about floods." He looked at her, his eyes twinkling, and smiled. Sarah knew then that he had baited her just enough to take a measure of her spirit, and she smiled back to let him know that she knew.

The Major turned back to Levi and spoke again."You'll get acquainted with the Sapps, the Talburts, the Wells, the Stinnetts, and the Shrables. They are all good people, mostly from Tennessee and Kentucky, so you should get along with them just fine."

The smile suddenly disappeared from the old man's face. "Now, young Casey," he said. "There's going to be serious trouble in these United States within the next few years if I'm not badly mistaken. First it was the Indian trouble. There is no need to beat around the bush about it, our government just flat-out stole the eastern lands from the Indians. I'm afraid that we haven't heard the last of those

Indians. Of course some officials of our government managed to get a lot of their chiefs killed during the time they were being moved West. But you mind what I tell you, they'll raise up new leaders that will hate all white men for what Ol' Hickory did to them." With that the Major walked back over and plopped back down into his chair, but he hardly interrupted the flow of his talk.

"Now, it's plain to see that I own slaves and I treat them like family. If you get right down to it, it's downright wrong for one man to own another, but that's the way it is right now. My slaves are happy and I'm happy. There's a certain group of people that would free the slaves, but they never think beyond that. I don't know what they plan to do with them once they're free. I guess they mean to let them starve, since there's nobody to help them get used to freedom. Any fool can see that slavery has to go, even aside from the rightness and wrongness of it. Slavery is not, and never has been, an economical system. It worked back in Roman days only because the Romans had a source of cheap slaves in the prisoners of war they took. In this country slaves are no longer cheap. Therefore it won't work for long. I hear tell that them Yankees up north mistreat their free white factory workers like dogs, so what's the difference? There's got to be something done to help both."

The old man was in fine form now that he had an interested audience, so he continued, his hands moving as he talked. He continued, "The same bunch of politicians up at the capitol would take all the state's rights away and have everything run from Washington City. There's been many a great man set his boots under my table, and every man-jack of them believed that each state had the right to determine its own destiny. Why, old Davy Crockett himself felt strongly enough about it that he went down to Texas to fight along with Sam Houston when our own government wouldn't raise a hand to help Texas fight the Mexicans." He stopped for breath, "That's not entirely true. The government did send a few men and some arms and ammunition to help out, but it was too late to help old Davy, rest his soul. Me and him spent many a night talking politics and bear hunting right here in front of this old fireplace. Sam Houston stayed here for a while, too. He was kinda hard to keep away from the medicine liquor, but his wife Tiana settled him down a whole lot. She's mostly Cherokee, you know".

Levi and Sarah sat in wonderment listening to the oratory. These men he described had only been known to them through newspaper accounts. Levi and Sarah were amazed that they had actually been here under this very roof. Major Wolf stood up again and poured all of them another steaming cup of coffee. He poured a short dollop of whiskey in his cup, then held the bottle out to Levi, who shook his head. Sipping at the coffee, the old man started talking again. "Anyway, to make a long story short, I keep hearing of big trouble up in Missouri. That Lane feller and his bunch of redlegs are making raids down into Missouri from Kansas. They're killing a bunch of people and carrying slaves and everything of value they can steal back up the road into Kansas. Some of the Missouri boys have started raiding back into Kansas. I'm afraid the whole thing is going to erupt into a war, and when it does it'll be Katy-bar-the-door. That would be the worst thing that could happen to this country right now. Now, the whole thing might settle down yet, but that's a long shot with a limb in the way. So if I was you young people, I would stay away from Missouri. I know the land looks good and the Missouri border is only a few miles from where you are headed, but I'd make sure that I was staying on the Arkansas side of the border if I were you." He stopped and his eyes calmed down. Then he continued speaking.

"You must be exhausted from your trip. Of course you'll take supper with me and my family and spend a few days here. You've been so long getting here that a few more nights isn't going to make much difference. Besides that, we can have another discussion. My own wife gets tired of me always talking politics."

Sarah and Levi pulled themselves wearily up the long stairs and fell gratefully into a giant feather bed.

CHAPTER 54

Turning over on the floor of the cave, Sarah raised up, and in the glow of the dying coals looked over at the two men. One, the old Indian who had been such a friend to her family, and the other, the kind-faced man with the crippled leg. She wondered what all had happened while she had been hurt. She now knew for a certainty that Levi was dead. Dead. The word had finally come into her consciousness. Not gone, not passed away, not anything but dead. She had been vaguely aware of that fact for a while. It had been lying there in the back of her mind, and now it forced itself into full awareness. Levi was dead, and those men had killed him, and now they were trying to kill her and Sam. Somehow Beartrack and the young man had fought them off long enough to escape. The tears came then, as Sarah sat there in her silent world, the tears that carried away with them the remnants of the dreams that she and Levi had shared, the plans of more children, of more property, of building on to the cabin to produce a large house of hewed logs, similar to the Wolf house. They had made such grandiose plans while lying together in Major Wolf's guest bed so long ago. Now, it would never happen. She wasn't old now, but she had been so young then, so young and innocent of the evil that would be visited on her family.

Gatlin, sitting there in the cave, was watching in the darkness. He became aware of the roar of the flooded creek, and happened to glance over at Sarah. He could see her tears in the glow of the dying fire. He wanted to move over and put his arms around her, to somehow let her know that he, too, felt her pain. To have her understand that he loved her, that if they lived...he sat bolt upright! What was he thinking? If they lived? They were going to live! They were going to somehow defeat the bushwhackers, for they had no choice. It was win or die!

Sarah sat there, her arms wrapped around her bent knees. She was starting to get cold, but she knew that to build up the fire was to invite the bushwhackers. They were out there, she knew that. They may have been caught on the other side of the flood-swollen creek, but as soon as the creek went down, they would come. Why? Why did these people want to kill them? All she and Levi had wanted was to be left alone to raise their family, to accumulate something, to have a part in building something great, a country in which the common people could have a say. This country was so big, and there were so many people wanting a place, a place of their own, a place to belong.

Her mind drifted back to the few days they had spent with Major Wolf and his family. It had been such a happy carefree time. The Major had a houseful of kids and grandkids, and she admired the way they all apparently worked and played together in such harmony. Every night the long hand-hewn walnut table fairly groaned with food, all the dishes showing the rare talent of Mammy Julie. There was music and singing around a real piano, and there were fiddlers playing some of the tunes she had grown up with, such as *Turkey In The Straw* and the unforgettable *Sally Good'un*. Every night she and Levi slept upstairs in an oak four poster bed which had been made by Liberty's own carpenters, or so the Major had proudly told them. The mattress was filled with duck and goose down from the wild birds that crowded the shallows of the Norfork every fall.

For the next few days they had felt like real honeymooners, forgetting all of the troubles they had left behind them in Tennessee. At least once each day the Major summoned them to his office and asked them question after question about the way things were going in Tennessee and the rest of the nation. He was especially interested in what they had read about the troubles on the Missouri-Kansas border.

When he heard the stories, his sad comment was, "It is as I told you, I'm afraid there is war on the way."

Both Levi and Sarah had been avid readers, but because Sarah had been daily in the store, she had been exposed to much more information, and the major was interested in hearing every detail. Sarah knew from watching the old man's eyes that every scrap of information was being mentally filed away, ready to be used in business or politics.

On the fourth morning after their arrival, the Caseys hitched up their now rested team and turned north along the banks of the North Fork of the White River. It was even more beautiful than the land of the Calico Rocks. For a good while they had to stay well back from the river because of the bluffs, but they could see the broad river bottoms, some of them already under cultivation. The river twisted and turned back on itself, reminding Sarah of a miniature version of the serpentine Tennessee. They found crossings along the small creeks that ran into the North Fork, and after three days, came to a small cluster of cabins sitting on the southwest side of a rounded bald, as Major Wolf had told them the treeless grass-covered hill tops were called. Two men, obviously a father and son, were busy digging out a huge red oak stump from a garden spot near the house. They stopped and were wiping the sweat from their faces when the visitors drove up.

By the time they got the team stopped, the Sapp family had gathered around and were all eager to meet the new neighbors and make friends. Sarah wondered where they were now. Had the bushwhackers killed them? She sat and thought for a while about her deafness. She had always been a scrapper, so she wasted little time in feeling sorry for herself. She might get better, and she might not, but for now she had to assume that she would be this way for the rest of her life. She had to figure out a way to communicate with Beartrack and the other man. She had to find out how long it had been since she had been hurt and what had happened to the neighbors. Sam didn't look much older, so it had probably only been a few weeks, but she wasn't really sure.

"My husband?" She asked, wanting to try to communicate as much as anything else. She had to see if she could communicate.

Gatlin had heard. Her voice sounded like a normal voice, a rather nice voice. He looked at her for a moment, then shook his head, "He's gone."

Sarah watched his lips move. Now she knew she could do it. She could tell what he said by watching his lips move. She could learn to do this. As long as a person was looking directly at her, she could talk to them. She had known for a while that it was so. She was sad, but couldn't help feel a childish excitement at the prospect of being able to communicate.

CHAPTER 55

The night passed slowly, the inhabitants of the cave shelter sleeping fitfully, the fire gradually fading to a few glowing coals masked by a film of gray ash. The roaring of the flooded creek below them provided a pleasant background sound. Rit Gatlin was thankful to be in the dry, as he watched a thin sheet of water slide off the dark green moss, and, cutting a pockmarked ditch, start to work its way down the hill into the creek. Ultimately the water would find its way to the sea. It would fall again as rain. Perhaps it would fall in some peaceful happy place, perhaps in some Eden, such an Eden as the Ozarks would be without the war. It seemed that it had always been here, the endless war, the war that spared nothing, not life, not property, not even simple human dignity. Perhaps even human dignity was an illusion. Gatlin had always been a man of few illusions. He was sure that tomorrow or perhaps the day after, people would die, perhaps he would be one of them. It was strange, he thought, that when he first drifted into this Ozark country he was, looking back at it now, merely looking for a place to die. He had been much like an old wounded animal, who knew that its time had come, and only wanted to be by itself.

Now everything had changed, now there were people who depended on him. Mrs. Williams had depended on him and he wasn't there when she needed him. Gatlin didn't try to fool himself. He wouldn't have had a chance against those three bushwhackers. It wasn't until he was consumed by a desire for vengeance that he became capable of defeating them. Now he was motivated by his love for this woman and her son. Now he was not the old wounded animal searching for a place to die, but a savage beast backed into a corner, wounded all right, but now desperate enough to risk everything to win.

His thoughts were interrupted by the old Indian. "White man?" the deep voice asked, "What are you called?"

"I am called Gatlin, Rit Gatlin," was the reply. "The boy, Sam, called you Beartrack, he said you were his friend."

Gatlin heard a soft rustle as the Indian shifted his position. "They saved my life, they were very good people, they are all I've got left. Me, the Chickamauga, who hated the whites most of my life. I call these two," Beartrack's gesture was almost invisible in the darkness, "I call them my family now." There was a long silence, then the old man spoke again, "I think many will die. I think maybe I die, too. It would be so easy to die. Are you ready to die, Gat-lin?"

Gatlin was a little surprised that the old Indian was thinking along the same lines as himself. On the other hand, he supposed that roughly these same thoughts had passed through the minds of many men who knew that they would be going into battle soon. It was strange that he hadn't had any of these thoughts as he walked toward the battlefield in Kentucky. He realized now that in spite of his having to rustle for himself most of his life, he had no real conception of the harsh realities of war. He had heard that fully one fourth of the men in the Battle of Oak Hills* had become casualties. At the time, they were just numbers that meant nothing to him. He had heard minor battles referred to as "skirmishes," and if they were all killed by the bushwhackers, there wouldn't be anyone left to report it. But they would be dead just the same. So, if it was a battle or a skirmish, it really didn't matter to the dead and wounded. Gatlin realized he had sat for several minutes without answering Beartrack's question.

"I will destroy them or be destroyed."

"You feel much anger, Gat-lin, and much hatred. Only the young feel anger. Anger causes a man to act foolishly, and many of the young die because of the anger."

"What about hatred.?" Gatlin asked.

"Hatred destroys the hater. Once I felt much hatred in my heart for the whites, but now it is gone away. Time took it away. The Tsa-ragi' is tired. In my heart I know we will die, fighting against so many. But we must make death pay a high price. We will die, but they," the old Indian pointed up the valley in the darkness "they must die. The evil must stop, we cannot stop all evil, but we must stop this evil.

"I wonder why these Union men shot a civilian like Casey?" Gatlin said, half asking, half thinking out loud. Although he had spent a lot of time thinking about death and dying, he was still uncomfortable talking about it.

"They wear blue but they are not blue soldiers," the Indian said. "They are the same kind of men who took the Indian's land in what you whites call Carolina and Tennessee, they are the eaters of the dead, the bush buzzards. They have killed Casey. They will now kill the woman and boy. Sleep now, white man, the day comes, and I will keep watch."

The day dawned with the rain still falling. Gatlin awoke with a start, realizing that he had slept too long. The Indian was still sitting on his hunkers, staring up the long low valley as the wisps of fog moved like thin white ribbons below them. "Anything out there?" he asked, a little embarrassed at not relieving the old man. There was no reply. Gatlin sat up, and feeling lightheaded for a moment from the loss of blood, started to ease the dressing back from his wound. It felt a little hot and he wondered if it was going to set up blood poisoning.

"Leave it alone," the Indian spoke quietly without looking around. "It will heal. Do not touch it. The atsi'ra, the fire, it will not get in the wound if you do not touch it. I think the killing and the dying will not begin today. The awa', the water in the creek is still too deep, but when the rain stops, then they will come.

"You know, Gat-lin, you would have made a good Tsa'ragi,' what you white men call the Cherokee. For years we have known what it is to fight. We fought, knowing we would lose, but still the Tsa'ragi' fought. In the beginning we used the bow, the spear, and the atlatl. Then the Eng-lish give us weapons to keep out the whites. It was no good. They are too many. They are always too many. Then we go to the white man's court, we win, but white man say it is no good, so we fight some more. Andrew Jackson, our friend, turned into the enemy of all Indians. That is the way it is now, Gat-lin, it is you and me, we cannot win against so many, but we fight, we die, because we must."

Gatlin sat there a moment, glad that the old Indian did not know just how scared he really was. He spoke then, "We can at least give the woman and boy a chance to get away, to live. The cannon, that's the key. If they didn't have the cannon, we could hold out here for a long time." Gatlin continued to think out loud, "Maybe they won't be able to cross the creek with it."

"They will get it across. They will use it." the Cherokee replied.

Gatlin could see his face tighten into what could have been called a smile. Perhaps the old man was looking forward to this fight. This would be his chance to strike back at a race whose members had done his people so much wrong.

Gatlin, noticing that Sarah was awake, reached over and touched her shoulder. "Do you want something to eat?" He asked, making an eating motion with his hand.

"No," she replied in a clear vibrant low pitched voice, "But Sam may."

Gatlin suddenly realized he was smiling foolishly at her, so happy was he to hear her speaking logically. He had been so afraid that she would never recover. She seemed to be totally deaf, but it didn't matter, they could communicate. As the boy stirred from his sleep, Gatlin looked over at Beartrack. "Her spirit has returned from the other world," the old man said.

---

* The Battle of Oak Hills is also known as the Battle of Wilson's Creek, fought near what is now the Battlefield Mall in Springfield, Missouri.

CHAPTER 56

"Aaron, why you rushin' along so? We gots all day!"

"I tells you why. 'De sergeant said fo' us get down there 'den watch de river. Jes' cause we whupped them boys don' mean they won' come back."

"Well 'der is 'de river, now you happy?"

Aaron Hurvey stood and looked out at the river. The dock where he had unloaded the boats was only recognizable by the stone quay leading up from the water. The dock was gone, and he could count at least six steamers burnt and partially sunk out in the river. The little shed where he had been kept after his first escape was still standing. It all seemed like a lifetime ago. He looked over at Burrill. They always ended up being paired for assignments, it seemed. He thought of how dirty, scared and hungry the both of them had been just a few months ago. Neither of them could swim and the Mississippi looked a mile across. There had been no way of knowing if there was pursuit or how close it was. Aaron had looked down and seen the big Chinquapin log thrown up against the shore. "Burrill, we'll ketch a'holt on 'dat log and kick with our feet. We'll be across in two shakes 'ob a dead sheep's tail."

"I ain' a goin'." Burrill had said, panic raising his voice an octave.

"You gots to, Mista' Dickenson. He'll ketch you fo' sho if you stays here." Somehow Aaron had to talk Burrill into going on.

"Aaron, 'dat rivers bank-full of snakes 'n 'gators. I's scared of snakes 'n 'gators. 'Sides I can' swim." He stood for a moment, embarrassed. "I's afeared of water."

Aaron had turned and looked back over Burrill's shoulder, "I hear 'dem dogs a'comin.' They'll chaw us to bits! We gots to go now!" He shoved Burrill out into to deep water, and in a moment they were in over their heads. Burrill wasn't much help, but he had held on for dear life and they made it across in spite of his fears.

"Jes' look at us, Burrill, we sho' looks fine in 'des blue uniforms. Even 'de white folk don' look 'dis good."

The memory of their escape faded as Aaron heard someone call his name.

"Aaron, is that you Aaron?" Aaron turned, startled and could see someone in the little shed. He moved closer trying to see in the dim light.

"Is 'dat you, Mista' Ashley?"

"Aaron, why you wearin' that Yankee uniform? You surely didn't join up with them Yankees. Look what they went and done." The sweep of the old man's arm encompassed the entire waterfront. "The Yankees done sunk all the boats, then the rest of my slaves all run off. Aaron, I ain' got nobody to unload the boats, even if they was here to unload. My wife died, and she wasn't even cold in the ground before a bunch of Yankee soldiers took over our house."

Aaron stood for a long moment trying to take all of this in. It was unbelievable, Mista' Ashley was rich, rich beyond belief. Even the white help, like Gatlin, had always talked about what a big fine house he lived in.

Ever since Aaron had found out about the expedition to Little Rock he wondered how he would feel when he finally visited the area where he had worked so hard day in and day out. Now he found himself feeling a deep sense of loss. It was hard to believe the difference, in such a short time, the whole waterfront area was almost unrecognizable. Mista' Ashley looked so old and worn out. He still kept himself clean, but his ragged clothes hung on his gaunt frame. What struck Aaron most was the look in his eyes, it was the same tired defeated look he had seen in the eyes of some of his own people.

Aaron would have guessed that he himself would feel hatred, maybe a seeking for revenge; but he felt neither, only a sorrowful kind of pity. Things had been the way they had been, and now all that was gone, and things were the way they were.

"Lucas, who are you talking to?" The voice came from inside the shed. Aaron turned his head and tried to see back into the tiny building. "Lucas, who is it? Is it Isaac? Is he come home? Is my boy finally come home?

"It's Mrs. McCollum, Isaac's mother. You remember her, don't you Aaron? She used to do laundry down here on the riverfront." Ashley looked furtively back in the shed, then turned back and whispered. "They sent her a letter, you know, saying he was killed up in Kentucky somewhere, but when I read it to her, she just didn't seem to hear me. She ain't right in the head somehow. All she talks about is when he's coming home, so I built a fire with the letter. Me and her, we've been a comfort to each other."

Aaron reached down in his pocket, for the still five dollars left from his last pay. He grabbed Mista' Ashley's hand and pressed the money into it, then turned and walked away quickly, and he didn't look back.

Burrill hurried to catch up with him, "Aaron, who was 'dem white folks, anyway?"

Aaron walked faster, "Burrill, 'dem was jes' some folks I used to know back befo' 'de war, that's all." His tone told Burrill that the subject was closed. Suddenly it dawned on him that the way Mista' Ashley had treated was different. Ashley had spoken to him as an equal, another man, not as a piece of property. He raised his head up, and straightened his shoulders as he walked. He suddenly felt better, a lot better.

"Aaron, why you hurry so, I tole' you we gots all day," Burrill grumbled as he tried to match Aaron's long strides.

CHAPTER 57

Gatlin had heard that, before the white man, war was a way of life deeply ingrained into the culture, even the genetics of the Indian. To the Indian, war was the only way he could amass wealth and prestige. Their raids often involved stealing of women, which prevented inbreeding. After the Spanish came to the new world, raids against them also served to spread the horse and its related skills. Gatlin had also heard that there were relatively few injuries and deaths from the wars among the Indians. To an Indian, touching a living enemy was of far more importance than killing him. Before the arrival of the white man, the concept of wars of attrition was totally foreign to the Indian.

"Beartrack," Gatlin paused. "Beartrack, are you afraid of dying?"

The old man sat for a long time staring at the creek still rolling out of its banks in the low spots. Gatlin wasn't sure the old man had heard him.

He finally spoke, "Beartrack has lived many years alone. The Tsa'ragi` has no family except these." He gestured toward the woman and her son. "Beartrack has made his peace with the God of the white man and also with the gods of the old ones, the gods that the Tsa'ragi` worshiped before. I do not fear death, neither do I welcome death, although I should. But I will fight, I will fight until the evil whites are all dead or I am dead. You, the white man, and Beartrack the Tsa'ragi`, we will fight well, but it will not be on this day, this day it will rain."

The old Indian was wrong, for a little past mid-day the rain stopped. They had spent the time watching Sam, who was delightedly talking to his mother, and Sarah, in turn, was trying to learn to read lips. They could see that the level of the creek was slowly dropping, until it was no longer visible above its banks. As the sun started to drop in the West, Gatlin, looking up, saw the glint of metal at the head of the valley. He started to say something, but saw that Beartrack's eyes were already fixed on the small cannon and the nine men who rode in a watchful circle around it. They moved with a caution that bespoke more than a passing acquaintance with the techniques of ambush. Gatlin watched as a bunch of crows dive bombed a red-tailed hawk sitting calmly on a dead limb in the top of a big red oak. Each crow by turn climbed high, then wings folded, banked to within inches of the big bird of prey. Each sortie was accompanied by harsh calls of encouragement from its dark brethren. The hawk occasionally shifted his weight from one foot to the other, but, otherwise, gave no indication that he was aware of their presence. All of the birds were totally oblivious to the violence about to unfold in the valley below them.

Gatlin reached over and pulled the old squirrel rifle over to him. He screwed the ball puller onto the ramrod and removed the ball and powder. He very carefully measured the powder and rolled the .36 calibre ball up and down his britches leg until it was smooth as glass. Placing the greased muslin patch squarely over the barrel, he set the ball down on it and pushed it down even with the muzzle. Cutting off the excess patching he seated the ball, pushing the ramrod down in one easy motion. Next, he poured the fine priming powder into the pan and brushed the frizzen off with his thumb. He licked his forefinger then wiped it across the edge of the flint to ensure a good hot spark. Gatlin was now ready for one long shot, but he didn't want to take it now, there was always a possibility that the bushwhackers wouldn't see them. He was still restless, so he pulled the loads out of the LeMat, and reloaded it, putting a little extra powder and shot in the shotgun barrel. As he worked, he noticed that Beartrack was studying the movement of the bushwhackers intently.

Gatlin glanced back to the red oak. The crows had disappeared, and the red-tail was calmly using his beak to pull ebony feathers from the object held in his claws. "Patience wins," Gatlin thought. "Sometimes."

* * *

Colonel Cain looked up from watching the men struggle with the cannon. He had wanted to leave it at the cabin, but feeling that his men were close to mutiny, didn't want to make an issue of it.

He looked over at the Zulu. "Jonas," he said, calling the Zulu by name for the first time, "You scout on ahead and see if you can locate them." The Zulu gave him a hard look, then dismounted, handed the reins over, and disappeared into the brush. By the time they arrived at the creek bank, he was back.

He spoke in his own odd English, "They are in a cave at the far end of the valley, there." He pointed to the bluff a little less than five hundred yards away. "It is up high," he gestured with his hand.

"It will be hard," Cain looked back at Abbott, tightening his face into what would have passed for a smile. "Well, it looks like this popgun is finally going to be useful for something besides wearing out a good mule."

The eight men who were left, wishing for the whole business to be over, fell to work with a vengeance and soon had the cannon across to the other side. By then the sun was starting to go down and Cain knew better than to try to send his men into a fight so near to darkness. But they could set up the cannon and get the range. He turned to the Zulu. "Point out the exact location of the cave," he directed.

After locating the cave, Abbott, an experienced cannon gunner before his desertion, went to work. He was glad for a chance to at last prove he could do something worthwhile. He had endured the jibes of the other men and the cold contempt of Colonel Cain. It wasn't that the cannon wasn't useful in war. It was just that it had slowed them down and caused a lot of extra work. If it had been broken down into its components and packed by the usual three mules, the Colonel would never have put up with it. It was much easier to deal with when pulled by a single mule, although it's narrow- tracked carriage did have a tendency to tip over.

Abbott obviously enjoyed his sudden importance. He knew the rest of the deserters had been infantry and calvarymen and knew next to nothing about the serving of the mountain howitzer. Capital- izing on the attention, he talked as he worked. After pointing the cannon at the cave, he unhooked the light oak shafts from the mule. Handing the reins to Delaney, Abbott adjusted the windage on the piece with one of the poles stuck in the lunette ring. He leaned over and sighted along the barrel and spun the elevation screw to raise the muzzle slightly.

He glanced up to see if he was the center of attention. Satis- fied that he was, he said, "First you got's to swab out the bore." The gunner then passed the sponge-tipped rod the full length of the can- non barrel. "Then you push down the powder." He took a saltpetre- soaked cotton sack of black powder from the ammunition chest, tossed it into the muzzle and shoved it down with the rammer. "Reckon we'll give 'em a load of canster to chew on." He held up the 12 pound load of canster with its attached wooden sabot. The sabot, along with the smaller chamber, allowed a larger load to be fired with a relatively light powder charge. "There's 33 cast iron balls in there, every one of them an inch acros't." Abbott glanced around, proud that he was probably the only one who knew exactly how many of the lethal pellets the giant shotgun could throw. "Then you slap her down the bore."

Colonel Cain's cold voice cut across the lecture, "Abbott, if you're going to get off even one shot before dark, you'd better quit jawing and get it done."

Abbott, his pride stung, angrily slammed the metal shot case home. He stomped back to the breech of the Howitzer and ran a pick down the vent hole, punching a hole in the powder sack. Evidently the big gun had not been fired much, because there was still an ample supply of friction primers. He pushed one of them deep into the powder and snapped on the lanyard ring. He glanced over at his commander, "She's ready," he said, his resentment already fading into his childlike enthusiasm over finally getting to use the cannon.

* * *

Gatlin had sat on the cave floor, almost motionless, his eyes squinted to slits as he intently watched the cannon being loaded. He had dug the heel of his wooden leg into the loose dirt of the cave floor and waited, the old squirrel rifle resting across his raised knees. He glanced over at Sarah and as their eyes met, he realized that she had been studying his face. He smiled what he hoped was a confident smile at her and was rewarded by seeing her whole face light up. He turned away, embarrassed. She believed in him. She too, had sat and watched the cannon being loaded, but she honestly believed that he and the old Indian could actually win against such overwhelming odds. He had to believe it, too, he had to. He saw that the gunner had finished and was about to fire. He made a flat motion with his hand and Beartrack, Sarah and the boy all fell flat against the floor, as if they had practiced the maneuver for years. Gatlin raised the rifle, bracing his elbows against his good knee, effectively locking it into place. He peered across the sights and followed the gunner with the muzzle. If only the man would stand still, there was a chance of at least scaring him. He knew that if he hoped to score a hit he would have to hold the sights about six feet above his target. He hoped that it would take at least one shot for the cannoneer to get the range, giving him a little time.

Abbott stood, lanyard in hand, looking at the black hole that was the cave in the bluff. He knew the Colonel wanted these people dead and he really hadn't thought about why. Abbott had fired a cannon in several battles before, killing and wounding numerous men. Not being a man given to introspection, he jerked the lanyard, and was as always, a little surprised by the magnitude of the power he had unleashed as nearly four feet of orange flame leapt from the end of the bronze barrel. The cannon jumped backward about two feet, the wheels lifting and its trail digging a groove in the ground as it spent it's reactive force. His ears rang from the explosion. Abbott stood, his hand visoring his face from the sun, and tried to peer through the billowing cloud of white gunsmoke that surrounded him. Colonel Cain, standing off to one side, watched intently as the hail of iron hurled itself into the trees and tall grass growing on the overhanging lip of rock that formed the covering of the cave. The vegetation was there one moment; the next there was a long strip of ground that looked as if it had been plowed, the narrow furrows extending up the hillside. A shower of leaves, severed by the blast, slowly drifted down past the cave mouth. They were barely visible in the rapidly failing light.

Five seconds of dead silence passed, as Cain started to open his mouth to berate Abbott for missing, he heard a high pitched whistle, reminding him of the sound of wind through the pines. The faint sodden thud that followed was no louder than the snap of of a man's fingers. He saw the puff of smoke from the cave mouth, then the report of the rifle nearly a full second later.

Cain turned, "Abbott, you idiot," he began disgustedly, then saw the surprised look on Abbott's face and the patch of blood no bigger than the palm of his hand on the front of the blue uniform shirt. Abbott wiped the palm of his hand across the shirt, then stood and intently studied the resulting crimson smear. He was still staring at his hand as he sat down abruptly. The patch spread rapidly, darkening the cloth in a ragged pattern. Abbott turned toward the colonel, opened his mouth to speak, then pitched over on his side, his eyes wide and staring.

Cain's men all hit the ground on their bellies as he started to scream at them. "Get 'em, return fire! What's the matter with you?" They scrambled to obey his orders, jerking out their weapons and firing rapidly. None of them wanted to be the one to tell the Colonel that it was useless, the range was too long for their short repeaters.

Cain was crazy with anger. He screamed and cursed at his men as they emptied their guns. He had let his guard down, had made the common error of underestimating his enemy. He had been a fool, setting up the cannon in the open with no cover. The Zulu contemptuously turned his back on them and started to walk back toward the creek.

As Cain's men started to fire at the cave, he quickly became certain of two things; the range was beyond that of the short barreled carbines, and the light was fading too fast for accurate shooting.

"Cease fire!" he ordered as the men stopped to reload. He must not let his anger goad him into rushing the cave. His victims were trapped, and in the morning one of the other men could fire the cannon. For now Cain had to be content to let them sit and worry, knowing that in the morning the air would be full of whistling death.

CHAPTER 58

Willie Johnson walked out and let the pawnshop door close behind him. The tiny bell hanging above the door jingled slightly. Who would ever have thought that something like the carving would stay in such a poor family for so many years. It was a legacy, that's what it was. Before this, all his family had was just stories passed down from generation to generation. Now the old stories, stories that had so often been told around the old heating stove, had real substance. He glanced down again at it as he walked.

He had tried to talk about his feelings concerning his peoples' past to several of his friends over the years. He had tried hard, but without success. Most of them looked back on the days before the Civil War as ancient history, not worth mentioning. He knew some people that carried a barely concealed resentment for all whites because of the slavery issue. Cerebrally they all knew that none of the white people alive in the Twentieth Century had anything to do with slavery. They knew there was only the tiniest percentage of white people who had even the remotist connection to the relatively few plantation owners who had owned slaves. Still, in their guts, many black people felt that the accumulated wealth of white society was largely built on the forced labor of blacks.

Willie had watched several nights in a row as the nightly news cameras focused on the bodies of murdered Africans of some unpronounceable tribe or other as they spilled over a waterfall and floated in the backwaters. For his part of it, he was proud that his ancestors had been kidnapped and brought to the young United States of America. Although he knew he didn't dare express this opinion to his friends, he felt far less kinship to the feuding Africans than he did to the whites of the United States, even those who were members of the hate groups. At least he understood both white and black Americans. He understood nothing about Africa, except that the people of the whole continent seemed to be both starving and at war constantly. He knew that he would never bother to do enough research to understand the African situation, for he was always too tired and didn't care enough. Those happenings were far, far away from his everyday world and he was so glad of it. It almost amused Willie that when he was a young man his people were still commonly being called the "N" word that no one wanted to say nowadays. Later, he had become "colored," then "negro," then "black," and lately the politically correct news media had started referring to his race as "African-Americans." No, it didn't amuse him, now that he thought about it. It was an irritation, he hated to be humored. Being humored was far worse than out-and-out discrimination. He didn't care if people liked him or not, but he wished they would be honest about it. He felt no identification with the people of the Dark Continent. He had never heard whites referred to as English-Americans, Dutch-Americans, or French-Americans. Now the same almighty "THEM" was starting to refer to Indians as "Native-Americans."

Willie had watched many young people of his race as they travelled the streets in groups. Even the ones who weren't associated with gangs revelled in the discomfort they caused the white people they met on the sidewalk and in elevators. Willie had explained all this to his own children. He had tried so hard to teach them to regard people as individuals and not as a member of a group or race. He explained that while prejudices do exist, they cannot be used as a rationalization for every failure experienced by every black American. He hoped that he had taught them some amount of tolerance if nothing else. He had at least taught them the value of hard honest work. He knew for a fact he had taught them that much.

Everything about the kid was thin and wasted looking but the heavy automatic in his hand. "Hand it over mister!" Just for an instant an almost comic thought flashed across his brain. Here was one the movies had never shown, a white juvenile robbing a black man. "Take it easy with that gun, son."

"Give it to me. I know you've got some money. I saw you stick it in yo' pocket. Give it to me or I'll blow you away!" Excitement was making his voice rise in pitch, verging on hysteria.

Student of the human condition that he was, Willie couldn't help looking the kid over. The 5:30 news would probably call him Irish-American, about thirteen, looking ten, with an air of starvation about him. His face had a feral look to it, teeth unbraced with noticible cavities. His straight reddish hair had been burr-cut. "Probably cut at home with a pair of triple-aught shears," was the odd thought that ran throught Willie's head, but at the moment the boy was in need of a haircut. His jeans were slick with accumulated grime, and he was scared. Willie has heard all his life that amateur criminals were the most dangerous kind. Then Willie looked at the gun.

Willie felt a strange calm settle over him as he studied the boy. "What will you do with the money, son?"

"I'm not your son. Now give-it-to-me! I'm telling you, give it here or I'll shoot." The heavy pistol was starting to move around as the boy's forearm muscles tired.

The Winchester '97 pump gun had sat behind the counter of the pawn shop for years. Mr. Rosenburger had kept it cleaned and its magazine always held five fresh loads of 00-buckshot. Originally it was advertised in the Sears and Roebuck catalog as the goose-hunting model with the 32 inch barrel. It had, by virtue of contact with a hacksaw, been shortened to about twenty inches. This had been verified by several overzealous B.A.T.F. agents over the years, all of them commenting on the fact that the magazine plug had been removed.

The old man moved fast for his years, and had a load chambered as he cleared the door. With the noise of the bell, the boy started to swing around, the pistol moving in an arc with him. One long step and Willie had snatched it from his hand, at the same time pinning the boy to him with his arm around his shoulders. He hoped the old man wasn't so excited that he would shoot both of them.

"It's OK, Mr. Rosenburger, he wasn't going to hurt me."

"What do you mean? He would've shot you deader'n hell if I hadn't happened to have been watching you out the window!" The old man was puffing from the excitement that made his chest hurt.

Willie held up the pistol, "It's an old Daisy B.B. gun. Some of the old ones look like .45 automatics if you don't look too close. This thing must be thirty or forty years old."

"I'll go call the police," the old man started to turn back to the door.

"No, Mr. Rosenburger, don't call the police. I'll take the boy home. His mother will be worried about him."

The boy looked up at Willie, trying to hide his surprise and failing. "Do you know my mother?" He asked.

"No, but I know a lot of her sisters in a manner of speaking," the black man replied.

The boy, knowing that there was no chance to escape this iron-like grip, had ceased to struggle. Then he seemed to wilt into himself, becoming even smaller and more vulnerable looking. He stood silently with his head down when Willie released him to open the truck door. Willie glanced over at him, pleased to see that the boy was puzzling over his remark. He knew the boy wouldn't ask what he had meant.

The old man stood and watched them drive away, then realized he was standing out in the open street holding a shotgun. He shrugged his shoulders and walked back into the shop. The older he got, the stranger his fellow human beings became. Sometimes he felt as if he were the last sane person left on Earth, and he was becoming less sure of himself every day.

CHAPTER 59

After seeing that his shot had dropped the gunner in his tracks, Gatlin flung himself flat on the floor of the cave with the others. The return shots ricocheted off the walls and roof of the cave sounding like a swarm of angry hornets. Fortunately, in their haste for vengeance, the bushwhackers were all neglecting to allow for the fact that in shooting uphill there is a tendency to shoot high. For this Gatlin was very thankful. As it started to get fully dark he could barely make out, in the graying light, blue-clad figures reloading the cannon. He had been surprised to see that his first shot had taken effect. He took another rest off his knees, sighting along the long barrel, then stopped. He hesitated to fire again, wanting them to think that he was capable of such shots consistently, maybe it would serve to make them more cautious.

The firing stopped and they all sat up. Sarah found herself desperately wishing for a fire and some warm food. Beartrack rose cautiously, even though it was now fully dark and handed around chunks of dried meat. Then Gatlin could see that he was fiddling with the dying embers of the fire.

He sat down beside Gatlin, chewed for a while, then spoke. "The thunder of the big gun must be stopped. I will go, you will stay." When Gatlin started to protest, the old Indian gripped his arm in the darkness and was gone.

Sam, who had remained silent for a long time, spoke up. "Why are they trying to kill us, Mister Rit?

"I don't know, son, but don't worry. We'll be all right." He wished he felt as confident as he sounded.

**

Cain sat by the small fire which the Zulu had built on the backside of a large drift log, shielding it from the cave. He was still as mad as a sore-tailed tom cat. He kept glancing toward the cave. Even in the darkness he had a crawly feeling in his groin. There had been something uncanny about the shot that got Abbott. He had heard of the judgment of God. Maybe there was something supernatural about that shot. He wondered if that man in the cave was at this moment drawing a bead on his back. It took every ounce of his will power not to jump up and run back into the darkness, but there might be something out there as well. He could still remember the arrows. He thought about the kind of hole a thing like that would tear in a man's belly. So he sat there alone, eating some of the last rations taken from the supply wagon. The rest of the men sat in a huddle, casting glances of hatred toward him. The Zulu sat by himself, keeping his own counsel. Cain knew there was coming a time when he would probably have to kill the Zulu. He would never be a man who would obey orders, and Cain couldn't forget how easily the black man had outmaneuvered him back there on the banks of the Mississippi.

Cain forced himself to stay awake, knowing that to sleep might mean death at the hands of his own men. They would never forgive him for shooting Robertson. Cain thought he understood these men. They were cowardly scum, banding together because of mutual greed and, perhaps deep down, mutual fear. Most of them had no liking for each other, but they still had a certain amount of pack instinct and loyalty, and by shooting one of them, he had violated that loyalty. The war had to be all over with soon, and he wouldn't need any of them. In fact, with what they knew about him, they would be in the way of his ambitions.

One more well-aimed cannon shot in the morning and they would be rid of the ones in the cave. At one time he had wanted the woman, but now, she was nothing but an obstacle. He knew very little about her, except for her beauty. He had seen her, wanted her, and decided to take her, but no more. To have survived, she had to be strong-willed. Strong-willed women did not fit into his plans. There would be other women. Women who could be easily manipulated. Those who would do what they were told. He really didn't like women. They always asked too many questions, yet he realized that he had to have a woman for window dressing, to assure the people he wanted to impress that he was really on the up and up.

Cain sat for a while visualizing the position he would hold as owner of this area. When people moved back here, he would be in control. First, he had to build a house, a house such as had never been seen in the hills. Then he would hire timber cutters, miners and herders. Next would come the politics. He had enough stolen gold to start. He had observed that once a man had obtained money, enough money, few people questioned how he had gotten it. Cain was an expert on human nature, having used it to his advantage many times. He knew that it was the nature of most people to want to ingratiate themselves with those in power. Doubtlessly they hoped some success would rub off on them. Others hoped to pounce on money, crumbs that fell from the rich man's table, as it were.

The bushwhackers started to nod off to sleep, their stolen Union blankets spread on the still wet ground near the fire. Cain's head started to nod. Only the Zulu remained alert. He squatted in the darkness with the fire slightly behind him. He avoided looking into the fire, for to do so was to lose night vision, at least temporarily.

The dark orb of the moon rose over the low hills, its crescent edge ablaze with silver, but it lent very little light to the globe below. There was no discernible movement, but something glided by the still body of the gunner. Not one of the bushwhackers had even glanced at Abbott. They knew that sooner or later Cain would order one of them to move him. The effect of Abbott's death was to remind each of them that whatever Cain had in mind, it wasn't worth getting what Abbott got. Had any of Cain's men been listening, they would have heard the ever so faint slop of the handful of grayish-blue clay mud as it was dumped into the bore of the cannon. A buckskin clad arm wiped the residue from the muzzle. The Zulu heard a sound but reckoned it to be some small animal moving along the creek bank. Emboldened by success, the shadow moved to the ammunition chests, which Abbott had removed from the mule and carefully set them the prescribed 15 yards from the cannon. The lid was raised on one of them and the Zulu, who happened to glance in that direction, thought he saw a momentary glow. Any other man would have looked hard then decided it was some trick of his imagination, but not the Zulu. The Zulu had learned at a very early age to trust his own finely honed senses. His reaction was instantaneous. He was on his feet, pistol in hand.

He stood, searching for a target. "Cain," the Zulu spoke the word, and Cain, his nerves already on edge, jumped to his feet. The Zulu started firing into the darkness past the ammunition chests. The rest of the men, following his lead, kept up a steady fire with the Sharps carbines, then with their revolvers. Emptying their weapons, they stopped firing, realizing that their quarry had to be out of range by now.

"Check the ammunition boxes men," Cain commanded, wondering why someone would try to steal the cannon powder.

Eager to do something, anything, to appease the anger of their commander, the anger which they knew would now turn on them, they rushed to the ammunition boxes. Bending over one of them, Corporal Nathan Greenwood, lately of the 14th Missouri Volunteers, lifted the lid. The glowing coal, carried in its nest of cedar bark inside a dried gourd, now getting a whiff of oxygen, had chosen that final, thundrous moment to burn through to the ignition primers inside the chest.

CHAPTER 60

Gatlin sat, sweeping his gaze back and forth. He knew from long nights on the river that movement is more easily picked up along the edges of a man's vision. There was only the dim light from the crescent moon, and he found that it was hard to separate the little imaginary scatterings of light from any real ones he might have seen. Then he saw them, orange tongues of flame, and knew, even before he heard the reports, they had to be gunfire! His heart started to pound.The flashes were all pointed in the same direction. Beartrack had been discovered! He jumped up and watched intently, hoping to see some movement, something, anything. His eyes started to ache from the strain, but the darkness revealed nothing. It seemed impossible that any living thing could have survived such a firestorm.

The firing slacked off after a few seconds and he could see the the shower of sparks fly upward as they threw more wood on the fire. He swung the squirrel rifle up, wondering if one of them might move between him and the fire, offering the chance for another lucky shot.

Since Gatlin had encountered the first bushwhackers, his sense of fair play had been abandoned in favor of the law of tooth and claw, of survival. The men he faced would stop at nothing and had given none of their victims a fair chance. Gatlin had bothered no one, had started no trouble. As a result, he felt very little compunction about shooting them where they stood. He knew instinctively that if he and his were to survive, there could be no fair chances given. With him, the woman, (his woman – it was strange that he had started to think of her as his woman – and her son) stood a slight chance of survival. Without him, there was no chance for them whatsoever. The men he faced were better armed, faster and probably smarter than he, but Gatlin's survival instincts had been honed to a fine edge. To him, the stakes were higher. He simply could not lose and would use every possible means at his disposal to win.

As with the gunshots, Gatlin saw the brilliant flash of the explosion first, then the fiery trails left by the burning chunks as they were hurled into the air and fell in the tall buffalo grass. A second later, he heard the dull boom echo up and down the long valley, followed shortly by the screams that could only have come from someone in mortal agony. Probably blinded, Gatlin thought. Then there was another flash, downward this time, and the screaming stopped. No doubt he had just witnessed a mercy shot. Gatlin eased his rifle down, peering into the darkness around the distant fire. Every muscle in his frame shook from the tension. Was it Beartrack? Had he succeeded in causing the explosion? Was it the cannon? What had happened to him? Gatlin was sure that Beartrack was lying out in the valley. It was almost certain that the Indian had been a victim of the curtain of lead that Gatlin was sure had accompanied the first flashes he had seen.

He was also sure that it was not the nature of the men who stalked them to have given the Indian the mercy of a quick death had he been captured. He glanced toward Sarah and the boy, they were invisible in the darkness. He wanted to say something, to reassure them, at least to reassure Sam. He needed to communicate somehow to Sarah that everything was going to be all right. He hated to give them false hope, but what would it hurt? Hope was all they had at this point.

***

The Zulu threw another chunk of drift wood on the fire then looked around him in complete disgust. Three men, all dead, two with chunks of the ammunition box blown completely through their bodies, and one blinded and maimed beyond repair. He himself had put a bullet through the poor wretch's head.

The Zulu was tempted to shoot Cain and the other three, take their horses to sell and ride out. He had hoped to make enough gold to get back to his homeland, but now that possibility seemed to be getting farther and farther away. Cain seemed to be coming apart at the seams, for the Zulu could see the madness in his eyes. He remembered a few people like that from his childhood in what the whites called Africa. They wandered around the outside of villages, often feeding on scraps or by some pitying family member. The Zulu stood and stared into the darkness for several long minutes, then decided to stay. After all, they still had one more shot in the loaded cannon. The whites in the cave had to die. The Zulu had hoped for single combat with the white man or the dark old man. The old man must be one of the people who lived here before the whites came. The ones who had been driven out, the whites called them the Indians. The Zulu could understand the Indians, for they, like his people, had been true warriors, not weak like many of the whites. He had hoped to fight one of them to see if they were truly brave. Strange, he wouldn't have had such a thought when he was a boy in Africa.

***

Gatlin realized that he had been hearing the low sound for several seconds before it registered on his conscious mind. It was the shuffling sound a snake or small animal makes as it moves through leaves. Gatlin turned loose of the rifle with his right hand and reached for his pistol. The cool metal of the LeMat reassured him as he waited. Gatlin had learned that often the first to move is the first to die, so he sat unmoving. There it was again, the shuffling sound, then heavy breathing with a low gurgling whistle. He eased the hammer back on the pistol, but the hammer still made a loud click when it locked back at full cock.

"You would shoot an old Indian, white man"? The voice was almost inaudible. Gatlin almost went limp with relief. Then he realized that something was wrong, very wrong. Glimpsing movement, he holstered the pistol, stood up and reached down, and misjudging the distance, almost fell. Flattening his palm he felt warm, sticky, slippery buckskin. Instantly he was down beside the old man.

"Be still", Gatlin said, as he rolled the old man over and grabbing him by the shoulders, unceremoniously dragged him into the cave, up next to the dying fire. Sarah and Sam, percieving something was wrong, moved over next to him as Gatlin eased several small seasoned red oak sticks into the fire. Gatlin hurriedly glanced up the valley, hoping that the bushwhackers were too busy with their own troubles to notice the light. It was risky, but he had to have light. He made sure that he didn't outline himself as he fed the fire.

As soon as he could see, Gatlin pulled the knife from the Indian's waist and sliced the shirt up the front. He heard the sodden buckskin hiss as the knife moved through it. The wounds were bad, there was no doubt about it. Both bullets had gone completely through the Cherokee. One, a rifle bullet from the size of the hole, had just missed the ribs on his right side. Gatlin could see that the blood was almost black. It had hit the liver, no doubt. The other smaller wound, which had gone in under the left shoulder blade, had angled out the front. The blood was bubbling bright, glistening, and showing almost crimson in the firelight. Lung shot. Gatlin looked down at the lined, weathered face, "We'll wrap you up. You'll be all right".

The reply came through clenched teeth, "You are bad liar, white man. Now you listen. The thunder of the cannon will not be heard when they fire it. You get the woman and boy out. Then you hide and shoot them when they come."

Beartrack arched his back, and turning his head, looked back. "Boy", he said, "boy, you come here." Sam, his eyes round in the firelight, moved closer, "Boy, remember the old ways Beartrack has taught you. Now you are the Tsa'ragi.' You will make the Indian proud. Where's your mother?" Gatlin motioned to Sarah, then gently pushed her into the old man's range of vision. Sarah looked down at the old Indian, her eyes bright with tears. Beartrack started coughing, as thin streams of blood ran out each side of his mouth.

The old man reached up and got Sarah's hand and joined it with Gatlin's, clasping them together to his ruined chest. He looked up at both of them in the dim light and nodded, smiling peacefully. Gatlin felt the tension leave the Indian's muscles and he was gone.

CHAPTER 61

Gatlin sat, his throat tight with grief, staring down at the old man who had so willingly sacrificed his life to try and save theirs. Gatlin had not had the opportunity to know him long, but he knew that the Tsa'ragi's kind were as old as time. They were the dependable ones, the ones who would always do the right thing, giving everything they had, even their lives if necessary. They would die for whatever lost cause they happened to believe in. They were the last ones to leave, the ones to sling the last rock or hurl the last spear before retreating over the hill in the face of an advancing foe. They were the ones who paid the ultimate sacrifice, used themselves up to make things easier for those who followed. They were the ones whose bleached bones marked a thousand forgotten battlefields. The ones whose names would never be written in the history books, because nobody remembered them for greatness, only that they had made things a little better, a little smoother, a little easier for the ones who came after them. Beartrack had done that for the Caseys, even though the white race had done nothing but wrong to him and his people.

Gatlin looked into Sarah's eyes, then down to where their hands were still joined across the old man's chest. Her touch seemed somehow familiar, as if he had known her before, had always known her. Maybe this was the way such things were supposed to be. Conscious of the boy's quiet sobbing, he finally nodded his head toward him. Sarah, coming to herself, withdrew her hand and wrapped both arms around her son. Gatlin couldn't help wondering how the sight of so much death would affect one so young. Knowing his own resilience, he could only hope... He had forgotten for a moment that the enemy was still out there.

They would come, he knew they would. He hoped that Beartrack had done enough damage to keep them occupied until daylight. The old man had distinctly said that the cannon would not work. With it out of the way, they had a better chance. How much better he didn't know. The Indian's wife had to be buried nearby. Naturally, he would want to be buried near her. It seemed odd to be thinking about a burial. Yet Gatlin had to face the fact that someone, or more likely several someones, would die tomorrow. He had seen too much death to be anything but a realist about it. Tomorrow, death would come to the the slowest, the unwariest, the unwittingest, or perhaps even the unluckiest, maybe especially the unluckiest. He knew that if he died, the woman and boy would be killed, so he mustn't allow himself to think of failure. The fire started to die down again, and he eased the LeMat out of the holster again, and rolling the cylinder with his hand, made sure that the percussion caps were still in place. Leaning down, he pulled the worn old trade tomahawk from Beartrack's belt and handed it and the knife over to Sam.

"Boy," he said, "you take care of yourself and your mama. When the fight starts, I want you to grab your mama by the hand and run. No matter what happens, don't look back. Go to the Sapp's house or try to find another one of the other neighbors. Don't go back to the cabin. Do you understand?" The boy straightened himself up, wiped the tears with his grimy little fist and taking the weapons, nodded solemnly. Gatlin looked at Sarah again. She understood; he could see it in her eyes. She knew that there would be no compromise, that to lose was to die. He wanted to tell her it would be all right, that he loved her, instead he said "Let's get some sleep." She looked into his eyes for a long moment, then nodded and laid down beside Sam. Gatlin rubbed his thumb across the bottom of the flint, wiping off the powder residue, and reloaded the squirrel rifle, then laid it beside him and realizing he was very tired, closed his eyes.

***

Cain sat staring into the fire. He felt as if every nerve in his body was on fire, and his belly was as sore as a boil. Then there was the constant itching of the mosquito bites. What could have gone wrong? He had a good plan, and now these idiots that he had associated himself with had wrecked it. His hand strayed to the pistol at his belt. He could shoot the Zulu and the others, then just ride away. He could sell their horses and start fresh somewhere else. He glanced across at the Zulu, whose dark eyes with their contemptuous expression were watching him. The black man seemed to always know what he was thinking. He straightened up. What was he thinking? His mission had not ended in failure. All was not lost! All that remained to be done was to use the one shot left in the cannon to blast them out of the cave in the morning. There for a moment he had found himself thinking of defeat. Even if the cannon failed, the five of them could surely storm the cave, even as steep as the approaches were. Then he would control the whole area. Of course, and he was almost afraid to give place to the thought; the Zulu could not be allowed to live. He was too smart, and if he wasn't killed in the fighting, it would be a simple matter to get behind him and put a pistol ball in the broad back. Cain turned his head, afraid that somehow the Zulu would divine his very thoughts, and looked at the other three men. They weren't any prizes, any of them. The biggest trouble with being a criminal was the class of people one had to associate oneself with.

Hulse and Barnhill, both deserters from the Confederate Army, were chronic complainers, as well as known sneak thieves, and, so far, had not distinquished themselves in any way. Now they were sitting across the fire from Cain, holding their heads in their hands, doubtlessly suffering headaches from the concussion produced by the exploding ammunition box.

Ross, the one with the coal-black beard, sat by himself. He seemed capable enough, and would probably be the one to fire the cannon. Abbott had it pretty well aimed before he was shot, so it would be a simple matter of touching it off. After the cannon shot, Cain would send the three up to the cave to finish off any survivors, then he would move in behind them.

* * *

Gatlin lay there as the night crawled past. The sky was clear now and the great white arc of the Milky Way spread itself in front of the cave. As the fire died down again he watched the slow progression of the brightest stars across the heavens. He glanced over at the woman and boy. They were asleep. Only the eyes of the big dog glowed in the dim light of the coals. How many other lonely men had spent their last night on Earth gazing up at the same stars? How many thousands of years had the nightly progression taken place? Gatlin had never traveled, but he had read everything he could get his hands on. He had read of people of other lands, and some of their ways. He had spent many nights reading discarded newspapers and the few books he could find, moving himself around in the hogshead to get the benefit of the lights of the waterfront. The ragged Bible the old wheelwright had given him had taught him much of the thoughts of men, for they were all represented in its pages. There were the cowards such as Baalam. Then there were the brave, the often-time reluctant fighters, such as Gideon. Gatlin could relate to Gideon, who had not wanted to fight, but fought because it was the right thing to do. Now that he thought about it, he was sure that there was really no such thing as a hero. The heroes were just ordinary men in circumstances not of their own making. They were men who were forced into a fight, but once into it, they gave it all they had. Throughout history, they had fought, tooth and nail, because they had no choice. It was a fight for survival, and, oftentimes, they were considered heroes by historians only if their side happened to win.

CHAPTER 62

Gatlin sat up in the glow of the dying fire and tried to imagine himself in his enemy's place. Gatlin knew Cain must be as cunning as a wolf. He had to be cunning, as well as intelligent, in order to command a band of outlaws and killers such as these. Arkansas had always been well supplied with brigands, as had the other border states. The waterfront in Little Rock was always alive with rumors of John Merrill, the Arkansas River outlaw chief of whom there were thousands of tales told but very few facts known. Gatlin wondered if the leader was really a Union Colonel. He had heard that 'Bloody' Bill Anderson and his men always wore Federal uniforms. It had been said that Anderson and his men were all armed with at least two and sometimes as many as eight of the Colt's revolvers. Once the guerrillas had gotten close using the uniform guise, a wild horse-back charge usually carried the day against their poorly-mounted enemy. In addition, most Federal troops still used muzzle-loading rifles, limiting them to only one shot each before reloading. Gatlin had not had the time to think about the possible motives of their attackers, but now, as the night dragged on, he thought about them.

Gatlin seriously doubted if the bushwhackers belonged to either Anderson's or Quantrill's guerrillas. First of all, both leaders were dead. Gatlin figured what was left of either bunch wouldn't have any reason to waste their time hunting two men, a woman and a kid. He had also heard that the guerrillas went out of their way to be kind to women, even though they might shoot their men down in front of their eyes. Without a doubt these men down below intended to murder all of them, Sarah and Sam included. There had to be more to the story than met the eye. He pulled his mind back from its wool-gathering and tried to concentrate on the coming attack.

Gatlin felt something warm slowly moving down his side. He touched it, knowing he had torn his wound open again when he pulled Beartrack into the cave. Maybe if he sat very still it would stop bleeding again.

Gatlin doubted that they would try a frontal assault, for the bluff was too steep. It would slow them down and since there was so little cover, the bushwhackers would be exposed almost all the way. No, they would fire the cannon first, and then they would try to get above the cave and move in from the sides. Probably both sides at once, forcing him to try to twist his body to cover two fronts. Now, because he was alone, the seemingly impregnable cave had become a trap. Yet, Gatlin knew it was too late to move. This was the place, the place where they would live or die. Gatlin realized that he had been preparing himself mentally to die. His fervent hope was that somehow he could use his death to buy at least a chance for the woman and boy. He knew he had to sell his life dearly, to fight until there was not a speck of life left in him, to take as many of them with him as possible.

Sarah lay toward the back of the cave, her eyes wide open. Sam, exhausted, had drifted off to sleep, his mother's arms wrapped around him. The dog lay silently, head on paws, missing nothing.

Sarah slowly raised herself up on one elbow, then sat up, watching the silhouette of the man, her man. She almost jumped at the unbidden thought. Now she dropped her eyes, ashamed of herself. She had loved Levi, had loved him with all her heart and soul. He had been a good man, her best friend as well as her husband. It seemed as if she had known Levi was the one as soon as she saw him, but now Levi was gone. Gone were all their hopes and dreams, all the things they had talked about during the long nights in the little log cabin. Now she had to think of the future, if there was a future, and somehow she had to make sure that Sam, at least, survived. She had accepted that fact that Levi was gone, and yet here was a man who, like Levi, seemed to be kind, yet strong. Maybe it was just the fact that she had been dependent on him, but there was the same breathless feeling she had experienced when she first met Levi. The very fact that she was thinking about him would have scandalized the women she had known back in Crossville. The women, her mother included, would have considered it lewd for a widow to even notice a man for at least two years after her husband's death. But this was a different place and everything had changed, and she had the feeling that it would never change back. The Old South, with its way of life, would never survive this war. Of course, they would likely all be killed in the attack that was sure to come in the morning, yet Sarah couldn't help but believe that somehow, this one-legged man would manage to save them. She knew in her heart that she would fight to the death. Even though there were only the two guns, they still had the knife and the tomahawk. She grew drowsy in spite of her resolve to stay awake.

The night cat-footed slowly by, the roar of the creek gradually starting to fade to a murmur. Gatlin dozed, as scenes from the past paraded themselves back and forth in his mind, few of them pleasant. The pain in his side gradually faded to a slow throb which only occasionally awakened him. He knew that to sleep soundly was to die, but the loss of blood had weakened both his body and his resolution. He awoke suddenly, the first rays of the sun hitting him in the face. He moved around slowly, his muscles sore and cramped from his sitting position. He looked back at Sarah. She and the boy were still sound asleep. Since they were lying down, he decided not to wake them. He sincerely hoped the Indian had been right about the cannon. It may have blown up in the explosion last night, but he couldn't depend on it.

Then came the explosion! It sounded more like the ripping of a giant piece of fabric than the boom of any cannon Gatlin had ever heard. There was no whistling of shot overhead, no tearing of the trees and ground; there was only that peculiar sound, then the multiple echoes fading off into the distance. Gatlin sat, shading his eyes with his hand. There had been a flash and a cloud of smoke. He could make out the cannon lying on its side! He smiled to himself. The old Indian had done it! He had wrecked the cannon! Gatlin almost laughed out loud. Now, Gatlin could see what could be the bodies of two men lying motionless near the blown-off wheel of the cannon. Two others lay closer to the fire. Beartrack had been successful beyond Gatlin's wildest hopes. He tried to count the dead, but the debris obscured his view. Then he realized that he didn't really know how many there had been in the bunch to begin with. There had to be some of them left alive, but where were they now? He concentrated on his hearing. His ears were honed to every sound, as he tried to separate out the background noise. He hoped he could recognize the sounds of the impending rush. He knew they would come, for after all this they wouldn't give up. He waited.

Ross eased through the switch canes along the creek, his knuckles white around the 1860 Army Colt gripped in his right hand. The long jagged oak splinter torn from the cannon carriage was still embedded deep between the bones of his left forearm. It was deep, only visible as a pale blue streak beneath the skin. It had to be gotten out quick or else it would set up blood poisoning. Hulse and Barnhill had been so eager to fire the cannon that he had stood back, slightly amused, and let them have at it. From more than ten feet away, their bodies would have looked like bundles of old rags, still lying where they had been flung by the tremendous force of the disintegrating howitzer.

Colonel Cain and the Zulu, standing farther away, had both suffered several slight wounds from the screaming chunks of bronze shrapnel created by the explosion. When Ross got up from where he had been blown by the concussion, his ears were ringing. Shaking his head to get oriented, he found himself staring into the menacing black muzzle of Cain's pistol. "You go down the creek and sneak up on the right side of the cave," Cain ordered. "Me and the Zulu will circle around to the left."

Ross wasn't stupid. He knew he was being used as bait. He

had seen the flat look in both their eyes. It was as if he was already dead. He, just for one second, wondered if he could possibly get both of them before they shot him. No, he had no chance that way. Ross hated them, hated them all. He had deserted the Union Militia looking for something easier, and now it had come to this. Ross had always considered himself a brave man, but he had never faced death alone before. He moved carefully through the switch canes. He was certain that the man in the cave would kill him before he had a chance to get in a good shot. Ross knew that if he waded the creek and walked up the hill, he would hit the road. So what if he was afoot and wounded? With the gun he could steal a horse, then get his arm doctored and leave this forsaken country, maybe go back to Missouri. He stood for a moment and looked up at the sky. So blue, he didn't remember it ever being such a clear blue. He realized then how badly he wanted to live. He felt goose bumps race across his skin as a flock of six crows flew over. According to the old-timers, six crows always meant death.

The long barrel of the old squirrel rifle slowly followed the careless movement of the switch canes. Gatlin didn't want the ball deflected, so he waited, his cheek firmly pressed to the stock, the pleasant, oily smell of the whiskey ash in his nostrils. His right forefinger reached up and pulled the hammer back, the same finger then slowly, deliberately, moved down to the trigger.

CHAPTER 63

In spite of the fact that the bushwhackers were thieving murderers and would stop at nothing to kill him and his, a part of Gatlin
still recoiled at shooting one of them from ambush. He hesitated for
a moment. Aiming at the flashes of blue uniform now visible through
the tall green canes, and leading his target a little, he squeezed the
trigger. There was a slight hesitation as the tiny spark leapt from
frizzen to priming powder to main charge. Then the pea-sized round
ball was away. Gatlin knew instantly that he had missed, as the man
ducked and started an awkward run. The morning was still and Gatlin
could plainly hear the cane stalks rattle as the bushwhacker ran.

* * *

The rat was young, barely two months old. He had always
been the risk taker of the litter. He was the one whose back and neck
were often sore from warning bites. The mother rat had finally accepted the fact that he wouldn't survive and concentrated her teaching on the others He had dropped his little chunk of shiny rock. His
mother had always taught them to get a nut and move back into the
recesses of the cave to eat. Instead, he filled his belly as he sat next to
Beartrack's store of nuts. He was very thirsty. His mother had always
trained them to drink what little water they needed from a slow drip
back in the depths of the cave. His bulging eyes were unaccustomed
to daylight, but he could see that it was only a few feet across the
cave floor to a nice little pool of fresh rainwater. He sniffed, the long
bristles around his nostrils twitching. His eyes bugged out a little

more as he made his move. There was a noise, a slight rustle, as the rat saw the movement of a shadow. He hesitated, his tiny heart racing, then turned to run for the safety of his nest.

* * *

Cain was moving forward in a crouch, the pistol extended in front of him. The toe of his boot came down on the rat's left hind foot, crushing it. Immediately squeaks of pain filled the cave. Cain jerked his foot back reflexively, throwing himself off balance for a critical three seconds.

The dog slept soundly, lying on his side. With the first squeak, the mistakable distress signal of prey, he was wide awake. One fluid muscle contraction rolled him onto his belly and without preamble he launched himself at the intruders. His canine brain instantly sensed his old enemies, the men who had hurt him before, but he was a gnat's eyelash too slow, for two soft lead slugs from the Zulu's Colt dropped him in mid-bound.

Gatlin had been watching the canes for another glimpse of the running man. But for the enraged roar of the dog and the sound of the shots he would have been caught totally unawares. The distraction gave him a second of warning. Shaking his head, the dog had rolled back on his belly and started to crawl toward his assailants, his eyes glowing with blood lust.

Sarah's screamed warning seemed to fill the entirety of the closed space. As Gatlin twisted, grabbed for the LeMat. Cain's face was glowing with hate and the lust for blood. His lips were drawn back in an evil leer of triumph. Now he would win, he would kill them, kill them all.

Sam was just a kid, but he remembered every word that Beartrack had told him. He believed them with all his heart. Now the bushwhackers had shot his dog, his soul mate, the one thing he owned in the whole world. With a shrill childish version of the war cry of the Chickamauga Cherokee, he attacked the Zulu, swinging Beartrack's knife in front of him like a broadsword. The Zulu danced backward, the gun in his hand temporarily forgotten, trying to ward off this small maelstrom of fury. A backhand blow succeeded in slapping the boy almost senseless, but not before Zulu suffered a deep slash across the ribs: Cain gave barely a glance to the struggle behind him. The Zulu would have to fend for himself. An orange flame leapt from Cain's Colt even as Gatlin started triggering his weapon. As the LeMat bucked against his palm, Gatlin felt a sharp sickening pain as a .44 bullet slammed him backward, almost knocking him down. The thunder of gunfire in the small space vibrated billowing clouds of white powder smoke, dimming the bright orange gun flashes. Gatlin knew he was hit but there was no stopping; he had to get both of them. Sarah and the boy had to have a chance. He started to stumble toward them, still firing into the smoke until the pistol clicked, empty, its nine shots gone. For an instant the smoke cleared and he got a frozen picture of Sam trying to crawl toward his fallen dog.

Gatlin moved the striker to fire the shotgun barrel, and started to raise it again. Suddenly he felt his strength run out of him like water. His arm was not working, his hand was not coming up! Now he was on his knees, falling into a roaring black pit. He fought it, trying to aim at the two shadowy figures! He could no longer see out to the sides. He was looking down two long tunnels, the tunnels became pinholes, then blinked closed. He felt his head hit the floor of the cave. He raised up, then sank back, helpless.

With the enraged scream of a hunting hawk defending her mate, Sarah ran and fell on her knees beside him. With a herculean effort, she jerked the pistol from Gatlin's clutching fingers. Raising the unwieldy weapon with both hands, she eared the hammer back with both thumbs, feeling its sharp serrations biting into her flesh. Cain, mad with pain and murder, started to raise his pistol again. Sarah closed her eyes and yanked the trigger! The teaspoon of peppercorn size shot spread into a pie pan sized pattern as it left the .63 calibre smoothbore barrel which also served as the LeMat's cylinder pin. As it tore into Cain's left shoulder and neck, he spun and fell to his knees, the front of the blue Colonel's uniform hanging in bloody shreds. The pistol was torn from Sarah's hand by the recoil, and now empty, fell to the floor of the cave. From four feet away, his shirt soaked with the blood from four body wounds, Cain started to raise the Colt again. He concentrated with every fiber of his being. He knew his hatred would keep him alive; he would make it as long as he had his hatred. All of the malice Cain had built up in his life was now focused on this woman, this woman he had first desired, then despised. Now he was dying, and he knew he was dying, but she would die first, she had to die. He had to win. He would not be defeated.

A solid kick to the middle of Cain's back drove him face first into the dirt. He spat, and tried feebly to grasp the gun, to raise his head, to shoot; but the Zulu stepped forward and delivered another kick, this one knocking the pistol from Cain's clawing fingers. The Zulu stepped forward, placing his foot in the middle of the bushwhacker's back, the force of the heavy boot holding him against the ground.

Cain's right eye focused on a rock about six inches from his face. It was a curious rock. It looked like it was mostly metal, with a faint gleam to it. He wanted to reach out and touch it. It was the silver! It had to be the silver! This was the Taylor Cave! He had to get a pocketful of it! He had to tell his men! They would follow him anywhere if he paid them in silver. Then he remembered they were gone, all gone. But the Zulu was there, he would listen. Cain opened his mouth, but his efforts at speech were only gurgling, gagging noises.

The Zulu stood silently, blood dripping from the knife slash across his ribs and watched impassively as Cain's struggles gradually grew feebler, then stopped. He looked down and was surprised to see that another bullet had hit him in the fleshy part of the upper leg. He looked down at the woman, "You are a brave woman." Then he looked over at Sam. "You would make a great Zulu warrior." He paused, "It is over. I will go." He stood for a moment. Sarah watched, fascinated, as his mouth quivered, trying to shape the words. "I was not always evil, once I was like him," he said as he raised a shaking hand and pointed at Sam. As they watched, incredulous, he turned around and limped slowly, painfully away and down the steep bluff. He caught up his horse, swung into the McClellan saddle, then rode off to the west without a backward glance, head held high, his back straight as a ramrod.

* * *

The scout was bent over a body. He reacted as the troop of men rode up. "Federal uniform, sir. He was hurt bad, had a huge chunk of wood in his arm. Dang fool started shooting when I yelled at him to surrender. Don't know what he was trying to prove. I also heard a lot of shooting up ahead."

Weapons drawn, the patrol moved up the path to the cave. That night, working by the light of Beartrack's fire, the doctor finished digging two bullets from Gatlin's thigh and managed to get the bleeding stopped from the one that passed completely through the lower lobe of his right lung. The big dog lay calm as the surgeon carefully wrapped a ragged gray blanket tightly around his chest.

The boy stood, silently and anxiously watching. The boy's eye had turned black, and the side of his face was still swelling.

"Will he be all right, mister? Will Ol' Tige make it? Please don't let him die mister. My daddy got shot and he died. You can't let Ol' Tige die. You've got to help him and mister Rit, you can't let them die." He sobbed softly, gazing at his dog and Rit.

The doctor put the palm of his hand across the back of his neck and leaned back, giving a grunt of satisfaction as his tired neck popped.

"Son," he said, "I only wish we were all as healthy as that old cur dog."

The boy blustered, "That ain't no cur dog, mister. He's a regular bulldog."

The patrol stayed in the area for ten days, searching the area for more bushwhackers. As they rode out, they left the barrel of the ruined cannon laid across a common grave.

High on the bluff, there were two graves in the cracks in the ledge. One was old; one was new. As the patrol rode away, they could see the man, his woman and the boy, their arms around each other, waving.

Much later, on June 2, 1865, Gatlin looked down the road, beneath the oaks, and saw a mounted man sitting and looking down at the graves in the family cemetery. Mrs. Williams' long lost son, John B, had returned home.

EPILOGUE

"Ritchard," she yelled, louder than necessary, "I don't know why you insisted on taking us down this gosh-forsaken old dusty dirt road. It seems like you would get enough of that old boring Civil War history. After all, you teach it for nine months a year. Now, let's get on up to Branson. You've been promising the kids this trip all winter. After all, this is the craft festival at Silver Dollar City."

He glanced down to where she was standing, by the truck parked on the low concrete bridge, her arms placed angrily on her hips. She was chunky. He tried to avoid thinking of her as fat, or that her flowered halter top was obscene, rather than revealing. Her pink lyra cotton shorts were pulled high. She wore matching pink flip-flops offset by hot-pink toe nails. He felt a sudden urge to turn and climb the ridge. Maybe there was a fresh start on the other side. Surely there had to be some place where he could just disappear. He pushed the thought aside because, down deep, he knew he would never have the nerve.

He raised up from his bent position in the cave. He had earlier scraped away the white lead oxide on the bullets that had splattered like bird droppings on the gray limestone. Now he was turning the green tarnished brass button, the US barely visible, over in his hand. The button appeared to have a small round dent in it. He slipped it into his pocket as he yelled to calm her down, as he had a hundred times before. Hearing a slight rustling sound he turned and caught a glimpse of gray fur as something disappeared into a tunnel near the roof. It was strange how that streak on the back wall glittered so in the morning sun. Taking a step toward it, he was interrupted by the excited squeals of the boys from up above the cave. Bored with watching their dad, they had followed a fleeing ground squirrel up the bluff.

"Dad, Dad, come here quick," they yelled, their words echoing up and down the little valley. Long steps carried his lean body uphill. As he walked, he resolved for the thousandth time to give up smoking. Moving closer, he could see the black-streaked rusty knife and hatchet, side by side, driven deep into the trunk of the gnarled paw-paw tree. He stood for a moment, examining them. "What are they, dad? What are they? Can we take them?"

He turned to them, looked wistfully across the open oak-covered valleys, then down at his wife standing, her anger, disgust and impatience rolling off of her like heat waves. "Boys," he said, "if I'm not badly mistaken, what we have here is a Green River Skinning Knife and a Hudson's Bay Trade Tomahawk. See their black coloring? There's something in these oak leaves that combines with the steel, preventing it from rusting away. Also, the paw-paws grow very slowly; otherwise the tree would have grown around them by now. They probably belonged to an old Indian, and his spirit wouldn't want them moved." The boys listened wide-eyed. Maybe for once they were impressed with his knowledge, but he doubted it would last very long.

Picking up the iron hub band and jagged chunk of bronze he found in the valley below, he reluctantly walked back down. He climbed into his old truck ignoring the glares from his wife. He picked up the photocopies. He could barely make out the words PATROL TO BENNETT'S BAYOU, scrawled across the first page. He stuffed them back in a 10" by 12" manila envelope addressed to Dr. Ritchard Gatlin IV, Professor of History, Arkansas State University, State University, Arkansas 72467. Starting the truck, he turned his head once and looked back, telling himself that someday he would return and really look. He revved up the engine a few times, knowing how much the noise irritated her, then with the boy's rap music blasting his ears, and his wife still whining, he slowly drove toward the highway.

FACT OR FICTION?

Anytime a historical novel is published, people always want to know just how much is actual fact and how much is fiction. Usually writers put a disclaimer in the front of their novel saying that all the characters are fictional and bear no resemblance to actual persons, living or dead. This I cannot do, but I will try as best I can to separate the two.

1. According to a local Civil War legend, told by the late Clarence Talburt of the historical community of Pickren-Hall, Arkansas, the man Rit Gatlin was real; however, there is no evidence of his origins or early history. He and the neighbors actually did ambush the three bushwhackers, although their names and characterizations are fictional. There is no evidence of Rit Gatlin's being handicapped, neither is there any record of his later life. According to the story, the wounded bushwhacker fell dead off his horse in what is now my front yard. When my wife reads this she will probably insist that we move.

2. All of the major battles such as Gettysburg, Iuka, and Pea Ridge are as described.

3. The following people are still alive or were until recently. Knowing their characters personally I felt that they merited fictionalization and moving back in time some 133 years. All of them, given a choice, would have chosen to have lived in the 1800's.

Sloan Lessley, rifle maker living in Calico Rock, AR. passed away on May 27, 1998. He had friends everywhere, and they all miss him. He was such a character that no fictionalization was necessary.

Shorty Smith, retired river rat, lives along with his wife and sons in the historical town of Powhatan, AR. His story is based on a story about one of his great-great uncles. The Ficklin Ferry is historical.

Tracker Jack, as described, used to go into the swamps around Bossier City, Louisiana to hunt wild cattle and hogs that had escaped their owners. Sometimes he would be gone for two or three days, back there with his blue roan horse among the snakes and 'gators. I saw him once in the early eighties, it is my understanding that he has since passed away. I never knew his last name, and neither did anyone I asked. It was a short step to turn him into the slave hunter in my story. I would have liked to have gotten to know him. This country will miss him and others like him. In my opinion one of the greatest things wrong with this country is that we have let all the characters die out. We have become a nation of mealy-mouthed, lawsuit-loving, mall-shopping, interdependent, T.V. watch-ing, politically correct mini-van driving, excuse making, housing development living, complacent, whining small-minded cretins who are missing the most important things in life.

4. The battlefield hospital and the level of medical practice at the time were as described, including the methods of amputation and surgery.

5. Descriptions of acts of nature such as tornadoes and plant and animal lore are all true. The winter storm and earthquakes happened as described.

6. The house of Major Wolf is still standing at what is now called Norfork, Arkansas. It is the oldest house in Arkansas. All the people, descriptions and events surrounding the settlement of Liberty, also called Izard County Courthouse, were as described. The Major did actually buy a buffalo from Pater Keesee and kept him for a pet. Major Wolf tried to resist the takeover of his house by the Federal troops. In so doing, he pistol-whipped a Union soldier, for which he was imprisoned at Batesville for a year. He died soon after his release in 1863, his health broken by the imprisonment. He was

75 years old.

7. Phanta Williams, along with Levi, Sarah and Samuel Timothy Casey were shown on the 1860 census of Big Spring Township, Fulton County Arkansas. The William and Thomas Sapp families also were listed. None of them show up on the 1870 census. The actual historical people may have moved or they may have been killed by bushwhackers. The auditory and mental effects of Sarah Casey's closed head brain injuries are not atypical of that type of injury. All the rest of the events concerning them are fictional, including Mrs. Williams' sons. Although a Thomas Williams did serve in the 7th Arkansas. All descriptions of the 7th Arkansas are historical.

8. The men and events described are a historical part of the 2nd Arkansas Mounted Rifles, including: Jim and Newton Park, and Sergeant Atkins. The railroad to DuValls Bluff was historical as were the troop movements.

9. James Butler "Wild Bill" Hickok acted as a Union spy and scout through the Ozarks during the Civil War. The Shooting of Dave McCanles at Rock Creek Station was historical. On July 21, 1865, on the main street of Springfield, Missouri Hickok shot Dave Tutt one time through the heart in a fair fight. There is historical evidence that they were old enemies from the war. Tutt was from Yellville, Arkansas. It was only later that Hickok moved to Kansas and went on to become a wild west legend.

10. Nathan Bedford Forrest was a very successful slave dealer in Memphis before the Civil War. All descriptions of the Memphis area in the 1850's are historical. Forrest later made his own place in history.

11. All weaponry, methods of loading, etc. are historical.

12. Charles Cain was the actual leader of a band of bushwhackers, there actually was a skirmish between his band of bushwhackers and the Union militia cavalry as described. In this set-to, the bushwhacker Frank Russell and the Howard boy were killed and one bushwhacker was captured. Captain Hughes captured 16 horses from the bushwhackers. The dates of Captain Hughes' patrol into the

Ozarks was February 23 to March 8, 1864. All other events surrounding Charles Cain are fictional, as were the members of his gang.

13. Camp Adams at Yellville was as described. The officers and men of the camp are historical, including Colonel Shaler, Lieutenant Davenport and Silas Turnbo.

14. The Zulu and his story are fictional. Not many Zulu were captured and made slaves. Their homeland was on the wrong side of the African Continent. The story of the Zulu leader Shaka and his leadership role is historical.

However, the Zulu's life and escape were typical of that of many slaves. The slave ship and the chase by the British man-of-war are typical of historical battles.

15. The Indian, Dan Beartrack is fictional; however, the account of the Trail of Tears route and the hardships suffered is historical. When I was writing about this Indian, I was in desperate need of a name for him. I happened to pick up a newspaper one day and read an account of how an Oklahoma Indian boy, walking home from high school basketball practice, was shot and killed from a car, without apparent reason, by three white boys. He was able to write the license number of the killer's car on his arm, which led to the apprehension of the murderers. I would have liked to have had more information on the murder, but I was unable to secure the cooperation of the county sheriff's office or any of the local newspapers. The story touched my heart, and the name fit my character. The boys' name was Don Beartrack, so since the name Dan was far more common among the Cherokee, I changed one letter in the name and used it.

16. The settlement of Rapp's Barren is now known as Mountain Home, and is a popular north Arkansas vacation area. Onset is now known as Rea Valley and lies near the White River east of Flippin, Arkansas.

17. All of the information about Captain Tunstall, his steamboats and the town of Jacksonport are historical. Jacksonport was bypassed when the railroad was routed through Newport, a few miles away. In recent years Jacksonport has been restored with a museum

and an authentic river boat. However, Jacksonport, including the historical area, was devastated in 1996 by a tornado. My apologies to the residents of the town of Oil Trough, the town and the bear fat rendering is historical. The rest of the story is fictional.

18. All of the information about General Jeff Thompson, the Swamp Fox of the Confederacy, and his Indian scout, Ajax, is historical.

19. Bill Dark, the bushwhacker, is historical, as is his shooting by the teen-ager, Jim Berry. Quantrill and "Bloody" Bill Anderson are historical.

20. Big George the overseer, Ulysses Johnson, Mista' Johnson and his son Hershel, Greenwood plantation, the story of the carving and the pawnshop along with Mr. Rosenburg are all fictional, However, the discription of St.Louis is true.

21. The little people are part of the Cherokee legends.

22. The Indians who lived in caves and bluffs along the rivers and creeks of Arkansas were called Bluff Dwellers. Ozark caves contained many of their artifacts until they were stripped by relic hunters in the early 1900's. The mammoths did exist in the Ozarks, although fossil evidence of them is scarce. Baxter County also contains evidence of the Mound Builders who built many of their dirt mounds on both sides of the Mississippi.

23. Cain's raid on the Union supply wagon is fictional. The Irish Wilderness exists near Van Buren, Missouri. The Catholic settlement there was hard hit by bushwhackers during the war. There is no evidence that the settlement survived the war.

24. Professor Ritchard Gatlin IV is fictional, as are his wife and kids. Arkansas State University, my Alma Mater, is still alive and well.

25. The slave ship and its crew are fictional, but the slave pens, and conditions aboard the slave ship are typical of those of the period.

26. The slave, Aaron Hurvey, is historical, although there is no record of the details of his escape. Mista' Ashley and Mrs.

418

McCollums are fictional. Hurvey's grand nephew, Ronnie Nichols of Little Rock, AR, gave me permission to use Hurvey's life story.

27. According to local legend, the Taylor Cave silver mine exists and is still waiting to be found somewhere out there in the watershed of Lake Norfork in the Arkansas Ozarks.

28. Moses Pringle was a black Confederate soldier, as were thousands of others. Some started the war as bodyguards for their masters, others were free men of color and enlisted and fought on their own.

29. According to Ozarks folklore the madstone was a porous hard calcium deposit taken from the stomach of a white deer,(the deer presumably having been killed). In other words madstones were very rare. The madstone resembled a hard sponge but were usually only three inches or so across. When somebody in the area got mad dog bit, (for you outlanders, I'll translate: when a person in the locality had come in contact with the extended canine dentation of a rabid Canis familiaris)....anyway, when somebody got mad dog bit, they sent someone for the madstone if there happened to be one in the area. Before use, the madstone was boiled in sweet milk (as opposed to buttermilk) and became somewhat spongy. When the madstone was pressed to the dog bite it stuck to the wound and started drawing the pizen (poison) out. If the madstone didn't stick, then it was presumed that the dog hadn't been rabid in the first place and the bitten person went merrily on their way, greatly relieved. Since scientists now say that only about 50% of the people bitten and left untreated will develop rabies, the madstone probably worked just often enough to give it credibility. It is possible that some native Ozark families may still have a madstone and may not even know what it is!

30. All of the details of the Underground Railroad are true, including the facts surrounding the home and family of John Rankin.

BIBLIOGRAPHY

Davis, William C., *Fighting men of the Civil War*. New York: Smithmark Publishers Inc., 1991. ISBN 0-8317-3264-4

Messick, Mary Ann, *History of Baxter County (Arkansas)* Mountain Home, Arkansas: Mountain Home Chamber of Commerce, 1973. Library of Congress No. 78-82235

Ferguson, John L., *(editor) Arkansas and the Civil War*. Little Rock, AR. 1965. Library of Congress No. 64-25874

Lottubville, Savoie, (editor) *Travels into the Arkansas Territory during the year 1819*, by Thomas Nuttall. Norman, Oklahoma, University of Oklahoma Press.

Johnson, Boyd W., *The Arkansas Frontier.* 1957

Luker, Lady Elizabeth, *Fight and Survive, history of Jackson County Arkansas)* and Jacksonport.

O'Flaherty, Daniel, *General Jo Shelby, Undefeated Rebel.* Wilmington (N.C) 1987 Broadfoot Publishing Company

Randolph, Vance, *Ozark Magic and Folklore* New York 1964. Dover Publications. Library of Congress No. 64-18649 9.James, Garry (editor) *Guns and Ammo's Guide to Guns of the Gunfighters.* Los Angeles. 1975, Peterson Publishing Co. ISBN 0-8227-0095-6

Allsopp, Fred William, *Folklore of Romantic Arkansas, Volume 1.* 1931 The Grolier Society.

Blockson, Charles L. "Escape from Slavery, The Underground Railroad." *Washington D.C. July, 1984 National Geographic.* The National Geographic Society.

Judge, Joseph, "The Zulus: Black Nation in a land of Apart-

420

heid." *Washington D.C. National Geographic.* The National Geographic Society.

Crawford, Charles W., Yesterday's Memphis. 1976. Miami. E.A. Seemann Publishing, Inc. ISBN 0-912458-69-0

Randolph, Vance and Wilson, George P.,*Down In The Holler, a gallery of Ozark Folk speech,* Norman (OK) 1953 University of Oklahoma Press ISBN 0-8061-1535-1

Hubbell, Donald S. Jr. *Bennett's Bayou-Bennett's River 1830-1900:* 1981 Bull Shoals (AR.) The Enterprise Printing.

Ingenthron, Elmo, *Indians of the Ozark Plateau,* Point Lookout, (MO) The School Of The Ozarks Press

McGinnis, A.C. *A History of Independence County, Arkansas.* 1986 Batesville, AR. Independence County Historical Society.

Garrison, Webb, *Civil War Curiosities* 1994, Nashville, Rutledge Hill Press ISBN1-55853-315-x

Sayger, Bill, *History of DuVall's Bluff, unpublished manuscript.*

Palmer, Colon, "African Slave Trade;" Washington, D.C. *National Geographic* , The National Geographic Society

McLeod, Walter E. *Centennial Memorial History of Lawrence County ;(AR)* 1936, Russellville, (Ar.) Lawrence County Historical Society.

Kennedy, James Ronald and Walter Donald. *The South Was Right!* 1994 Gretna, LA. Pelican Publishing Company.

The Old Time Hill People, Various Ozark verbal legends passed down by family members through the years. They include:

A. The Legend of the Taylor Cave

B. The Legend of Rit Gatlin and the bushwhacker ambush.

To order additional copies of
BLESSED ARE THE PEACEMAKERS
please complete the following.

$19.95 EACH
*(plus $3.95 shipping & handling for first book,
add $2.00 for each additional book ordered.*

*Shipping and Handling costs for larger quantites
available upon request.*

Please send me _____ additional books at $19.95 + shipping & handling

Bill my: ❑ VISA   ❑ MasterCard   Expires _____

Card # _____

Signature _____

Daytime Phone Number _____

For credit card orders call 1-888-568-6329
TO ORDER ON-LINE VISIT: www.jmcompanies.com
OR SEND THIS ORDER FORM TO:
McCleery & Sons Publishing
PO Box 248
Gwinner, ND 58040-0248

I am enclosing $_____   ❑ Check   ❑ Money Order
Payable in US funds. No cash accepted.

SHIP TO:
Name _____
Mailing Address _____
City _____
State/Zip _____

Orders by check allow longer delivery time.
Money order and credit card orders will be shipped within 48 hours.
This offer is subject to change without notice.

Home In One Piece
While working alone on his parent's farm one January morning in 1992, eighteen year old John Thompson became entangled in a piece of machinery. Both barms were ripped from his body and he was knocked unconscious. He was awakened by his dog, got off the ground, and staggered to the house. John opened a door with his mouth and grasped a pen in his teeth to call for help on the phone. A truthful journey with themes of survival, recovery and enduring hope.
By John Thompson as told to Paula Crain Grosinger, RN. (162 pgs.)
$16.95 each in a 6 x 9 paperback.

Remembering Louis L'Amour
Reese Hawkins was a close friend of Louis L'Amour, one of the fastest selling writers of all time. Now Hawkins shares this friendship with L'Amour's legion of fans. Sit with Reese in L'Amour's study where characters were born and stories came to life. Travel with Louis and Reese in the 16 photo pages in this memoir. Learn about L'Amour's lifelong quest for knowledge and his philosophy of life. Written by Reese Hawkins and his daughter Meredith Hawkins Wallin.
(178 pgs.)
$16.95 each in a 5-1/2x8" paperback.

Whispers in the Darkness
In this fast paced, well thought out mystery with a twist of romance, Betty Pearson comes to a slow paced, small town. Little did she know she was following a missing link - what the dilapidated former Beardsley Manor she was drawn to, held for her. With twists and turns, the Manor's secrets are unraveled.
Written by Shirlee Taylor. (88 pgs.)
$14.95 each in a 6x9" paperback.

The Long, Blonde Pigtails with Big Red Bows
Teaching Children Not to Talk to Strangers
The story of three little mice who learn a heart-breaking lesson from a casual encounter with a "stranger" in their neighborhood. This is an integral message that appears throughout the book, to teach and protect our children.
Written by Mary Magill. Illustrated by Barbara Scheibling. (24 pgs.)
$14.95 each in a 8-1/2x8-1/2" paperback.

Charlie's Gold and Other Frontier Tales
Kamron's first collection of short stories gives you adventure tales about men and women of the west, made up of cowboys, Indians, and settlers.
Written by Kent Kamron. (174 pgs.)
$15.95 each in a 6x9" paperback.

A Time For Justice
This second collection of Kamron's short stories takes off where the first volume left off, satisfying the reader's hunger for more tales of the wide prairie.
Written by Kent Kamron. (182 pgs.)
$16.95 each in a 6x9" paperback.

Dr. Val Farmer's
Honey, I Shrunk The Farm
The first volume in a three part series of Rural Stress Survival Guides discusses the following in seven chapters: Farm Economics; Understanding The Farm Crisis; How To Cope With Hard Times; Families Going Through It Together; Dealing With Debt; Going For Help, Helping Others and Transitions Out of Farming.
Written by Val Farmer. (208 pgs.)
$16.95 each in a 6x9" paperback.

Pay Dirt
An absorbing story reveals how a man with the courage to follow his dream found both gold and unexpected adventure and adversity in Interior Alaska, while learning that human nature can be the most unpredictable of all.
Written by Otis Hahn & Alice Vollmar. (168 pgs.)
$15.95 each in a 6x9" paperback.

Pete's New Family
Pete's New Family is a tale for children (ages 4-8) lovingly written to help youngsters understand events of divorce that they are powerless to change.
Written by Brenda Jacobson.
$9.95 each in a 5-1/2x8-1/2" spiral bound book.

Bonanza Belle
In 1908, Carrie Amundson left her home to become employed on a bonanza farm. One tragedy after the other befell her and altered her life considerably and she found herself back on the farm.
Written by Elaine Ulness Swenson. (344 pgs.)
$15.95 each in a 6x8-1/4" paperback.

First The Dream
This story spans ninety years of Anna's life. She finds love, loses it, and finds in once again. A secret that Anna has kept is fully revealed at the end of her life.
Written by Elaine Ulness Swenson. (326 pgs.)
$15.95 each in a 6x8-1/4" paperback

Country-fied
Stories with a sense of humor and love for country and small town people who, like the author, grew up country-fied . . . Country-fied people grow up with a unique awareness of their dependence on the land. They live their lives with dignity, hard work, determination and the ability to laugh at themselves.
Written by Elaine Babcock. (184 pgs.)
$14.95 each in a 6x9" paperback.

It Really Happened Here!
Relive the days of farm-to-farm salesmen and hucksters, of ghost ships and locust plagues when you read Ethelyn Pearson's collection of strange but true tales. It captures the spirit of our ancestors in short, easy to read, colorful accounts that will have you yearning for more.
Written by Ethelyn Pearson. (168 pgs.)
$24.95 each in an 8-1/2x11" paperback.

(Add $3.95 shipping & handling for first book, add $2.00 for each additional book ordered.)

Prayers For Parker Cookbook
Parker Sebens is a 3 year old boy from Milnor, ND, who lost both of his arms in a tragic farm accident on September 18, 2000. He has undergone many surgeries to reattach his arms, but because his arms were damaged so extensively and the infection so fierce, they were unable to save his hands. Parker will face many more surgeries in his future, plus be fitted for protheses.

This 112 pg. cookbook is a project of the Country Friends Homemakers Club from Parker's community. All profits from the sale of this book will go to the Parker Sebens' Benefit Fund, a fund set up to help with medical-related expenses due to Parker's accident.
$8.00 ea. in a 5-1/4"x8-1'4" spiral bound book.